The Real Majority

RICHARD M. SCAMMON

AND

BEN J. WATTENBERG

Coward, McCann & Geoghegan, Inc.

NEW YORK

Distributed by Capricorn Books

To Mary and Marna

Library of Congress Catalog Card Number: 73–81024

PRINTED IN THE UNITED STATES OF AMERICA

Capricorn Edition, 1971

Fourth Impression

SBN 698-10308-4

Books by Richard M. Scammon and Ben J. Wattenberg

THIS U.S.A.

THE REAL MAJORITY

A Riddle as Preface

Here is a riddle for our time:

In a big industrial city in the United States there will be an election for mayor. It is a nonpartisan election, and there are two candidates.

One candidate is a black policeman. The local papers say he is a tough cop. He holds a master's degree in police administration from a large Eastern university. He has been accused of "taking a hard line" with students who took over a college dean's offices; he has been accused of brutality in arresting a local narcotics peddler.

This candidate says, "I've been a cop for twenty years, and by God, if I'm elected mayor, we're going to clean up this city, even if we have to put a lot of people in jail."

The second candidate is a white, bright, telegenic, energetic, charismatic lawyer. In his spare time he has devoted his legal talents to helping the underprivileged get fair representation and to taking some cases for the American Civil Liberties Union. One noteworthy case had the lawyer defending a newsdealer charged with selling pornographic literature. The defense was based on the unconstitutionality of the state's censorship statutes.

This candidate says that he will solve the grave urban crisis by getting better teachers in slum schools, by promoting a higher scale of welfare payments, by establishing health care facilities in the slums, and by fully integrating housing and schools throughout the city. "If we can attack the underlying causes of crime," he says, "we will lick crime. There are no bad boys, only bad environments."

The city population is 20 percent black.

The riddle comes in four parts:

1. Who will be elected—the tough black cop or the charismatic white lawyer?
2. Which is the more potent political issue in America: race or crime?
3. How will these issues affect the politics of the 1970's in the United States?
4. How will these issues affect the Presidential elections of 1972 and 1976?

The riddle of our time is: Why are the four questions so deeply related?

Acknowledgments

Anyone who writes in some depth about politics—or psephology, if you will—has big problems. One finds that irksome Law of Simultaneous but Contrary Truths cropping up everywhere: This is true, but so is that, and the two truths somehow don't always mesh.

In the attempt to track down where most of the truth lies, the authors have spoken to scores of helpful people. Not all these necessarily knew that they were being talked to for the purposes of this book; indeed at times neither did the authors. Certainly none of the names listed below should be associated with any opinions expressed herein; those, alas, must rest with the authors alone.

In the polling profession: Robert Coursen, Archibald Crossley, Frederick Currier, Mervin Field, George Gallup, Lou Harris, John Kraft, Warren Miller, Don Muchmore, Paul Perry, Oliver Quayle, Burns Roper, Arthur White, Daniel Yankelovich.

At the U.S. Bureau of the Census: Jerry T. Jennings, Charles E. Johnson, Jr., Herman Miller, Conrad Taeuber.

At the Elections Research Center: Mrs. Alice V. McGillivray and Miss Linda P. Sutherland, without whose joint labors this volume never would have made it.

From the press, the political community and friends: Joseph and Stewart Alsop, Sherry Arnstein, Al Barkan, Louis Bean, David Broder, Douglass Cater, Moe Coleman, William Connell, Tom Cronin, Fred Dutton, Dan Fenn, Wyche Fowler, Dun Gifford, David Gutman, Judy Hade, Phillip Hallen, Gerard Hegstrom, Roger Hennings, Seymour Hersh, Donald Herzberg, Donald J. Irwin, Evron Kirkpatrick, Joseph Kraft, Erwin Knoll, Peter Lisagor, Stuart Loorie, Richard Maguire, Louis Martin, Harry McPherson, Dr. Herbert Moskovitz, Don Nicoll, Robert Novak, Allen Otten, Fred Panzer, Neal Peirce, Howard Penniman, P. K. Peterson, Kevin Phillips, John Roche, William Safire, Richard Schifter, Jonathan, Gene and Rebecca Schull, Norman Sherman, Hugh Sidey, Alvin Spivak, William Steiff, Gerald Stern, Philip Stern, John Stewart, Robert Trautman, Ted Van Dyk, Milton Viorst, Mike Waldman, Jules Witcover.

Ervin S. Duggan suggested the title.

Jeffrey D. Stansbury was of invaluable editorial assistance.

May, 1970   RICHARD M. SCAMMON
Washington, D.C.   BEN J. WATTENBERG

Contents

PART FOUR: *The Ideas Confirmed:*
The Elections of 1969

PART FIVE: *The Fourth Idea*

Appendix

PART ONE

About Psephology

1

Pebble Watching

This is a book about certain elections in America, but not primarily about politicians or the anecdotage of political life.

And so, although this volume in some measure deals with the Presidential election of 1968, it deals neither with the alleged overhaul of Richard Nixon's personality nor with the agonizing at Hickory Hill about when and whether Robert F. Kennedy should become a candidate for the Presidency. The reader will not find here an account of what Stephen Smith said to Eugene McCarthy in Chicago, what reporters ate at Key Biscayne, what Hubert Humphrey's advance men failed to do, not even what Spiro Agnew had to say concerning the corpulence of a Japanese-American journalist.

If this volume does not focus on the interest many Americans have about political luminaries and their spear carriers, it may redeem itself by concentrating on what the political luminaries and their spear carriers are most interested in: the voters.

For the voters are very important people. Among other things, and despite what one may read about back-room political machinations, it is the voters who choose Presidents and lesser political leaders. It is the voters who in large measure shape the men they elect and, in shaping the men, shape ultimately the policies of the nation. Political leaders are leaders only insofar as they can lead voters. The leaders are in office only insofar as they can win elections. These are elementary truths, but frequently forgotten when the political shoptalk gets particularly precious and inbred.

This book, then, is an exercise in psephology, a word more familiar in British political parlance than in American. The word is defined as "the study of elections," and it derives from the Greek word *psēphos* which means "pebble." The derivation comes from the custom of ancient Greece for citizens to vote by dropping colored pebbles into the Greek equivalent of our ballot box.

More specifically, this book deals mostly with contemporary American psephology—that is, with the behavior of American voters at the polls in the recent past and the short-term future, let us say from the mid-1960's and on well into the 1970's. While this compass is wide, there is a narrower focus here as well: an effort to examine a fascinating political moment in America, a political moment framed in time by two Presidential elections— the last one and the next one.

Putting things back in their Greek context, one might say this volume asks three questions about the American voter:

—For whom did he cast his pebble?
—Why did he cast his pebble as he did?
—How will he cast his pebble in the years to come?

If we are to engage in pebble watching, it will be useful to mention briefly the working tools of the psephologist.

First, of course, are election results themselves. They are precise, they are definitive, and there is obviously nothing better for telling how voters actually voted than election returns. As director of the Elections Research Center in Washington for the last fifteen years and as an avocational election watcher for twenty years before that, Mr. Scammon has long been a student of elections in America by precinct, ward, city, and state.

While secrecy of the ballot guarantees an American voter that no one will know how he actually voted, a sophisticated view of precinct or ward returns can yield up important information about how *groups* vote. Essentially, this psephological maneuver is accomplished by matching up voting results to certain demographic characteristics such as race, income, and national origin—information usually derived from U.S. Census reports.

The Third Ward of Petersburg, Virginia, for example, is almost entirely black; its vote for President in 1968 was 1,092 for Humphrey, 17 for Nixon, and 3 for Wallace. When such patterns are repeated in thousands of black precincts across the nation, there is a clear message about black voting trends in 1968.

Similarly, there is a clear message available when one examines the voting returns of another minority group in the United States: wealthy whites. In 1968, for example, in the posh Third Precinct of Palos Verdes Estates in California, the vote tally was 355 for Nixon, 62 for Humphrey, and 16 for Wallace.

Finally, to see a third side of the prism, observe the not-untypical Southern voting tally in Beat 2 of Calhoun County, Alabama, in 1968. Mr. Nixon received 48 votes. Humphrey got 41 votes. George Wallace received 404 votes.

In addition to actual election returns coupled with demographic indices, the psephologist today can tap the work of public opinion pollsters. These surveys are of immense value in that they reveal not only voter preference for party and candidate over a period of time, but an entire range of attitudes as well. When the Gallup Poll reported in the spring of 1968 that, for the first time since Gallup started polling, the issue of "crime" was ranked as "the most important domestic problem" by the American people, still another message became available. It was not directly psephological, but as it turned out, it was directly translatable into votes when exploited by certain candidates.

There are three sorts of public opinion surveys: the published polls, private polls usually commissioned by parties or candidates, and academic surveys. For the most part (although not totally), the major attention here is paid to the published polls, the best known of which are the national surveys of the Gallup and Louis Harris organizations.

There are several reasons for our selectivity. First is credibility. Privately commissioned polls paid for by politicians or parties are always somewhat suspect in the public mind, although in fact no reputable pollster would provide a candidate with less than the unvarnished facts. Unfortunately, the campaign staffs of candidates sometimes release only those parts of polls that show their horses in a favorable way—and credibility is sacrificed in the process.

The academic polling operations, while credible and extremely valuable for certain purposes, have another handicap. Much of their information is available to scholars in the form of computer punch cards or tapes, but it may sometimes be years until results are published—too long a time lag for the sort of contemporaneous work this book hopes to be. When academic results have been available, they have been used here, to good effect we hope. Particularly noteworthy in this respect are the excellent survey data collected by the University of Michigan's Survey Research Center.

A final reason for our basic reliance on the published polls is the view of the authors that psephology—or, if you prefer, voting behavior, or political science, or politics—has been sold too long as an arcane field of knowledge in which special information is provided only to "experts," be they political, journalistic, or academic. But the regularly published public opinion polls, like election results, are available to all who read newspapers. Between these two sources and with some common sense, a man can know a good deal about elections. It is one intent, then, of this book to help Americans use the tools that are *available,* in order that they may best see and understand the political landscape.

Both authors have had face-to-face contact with many of the elections discussed here and with many of the candidates and their staffs. As an elections consultant for the National Broadcasting Company, Mr. Scammon visited each of the major primary states during the 1968 Presidential campaigns, as well as most of the major 1969 mayoralty sites. Mr. Wattenberg was a member of President Johnson's White House staff for several years and managed some moonlighting work for Vice President

Humphrey during the 1968 campaign. (Mr. Wattenberg has also been a dramatically unsuccessful local politician, running twice for office in Stamford, Connecticut, with a batting average of zero.)

Yet both authors feel that personal contacts are of limited value—and so are the "there-I-was-when-the-candidate-made-up-his-mind" types of election memoirs and campaign reportage. Perhaps the worst place in the nation to cover an election is at the elbow of a candidate, counting crowds, worrying about motorcade transportation, and watching to see which local politicians are how friendly to whom. Such reporting yields only a small part of the story. It is just as important—maybe more important—to watch television and read newspapers and magazines, thereby getting the same story that the voters are getting, able then to judge the campaign with a voter's eye rather than from an "insider's" view. And let us recall again: It is voters, not insiders, who elect candidates.

A clear example of these two distinctly separate perspectives was provided during the first few weeks of the late Robert Kennedy's campaign. The candidate drew ecstatic, screaming, jumping crowds of students, ghetto blacks, Mexican-Americans, and poverty-stricken Indians. The press and television covered the frenetic crowds on hand—and rhapsodized. At first, the Kennedy campaign staff was pleased, but they soon discovered something else: Millions of Americans watching television were appalled at what seemed to be the radical and frenetic nature of Senator Kennedy's campaign. His ratings in the polls fell, and soon the nature of Kennedy's campaign changed. The spot from which to properly observe and understand these crucial psephological events was not with the enthusiastic Kennedy campaign tour—but seated solidly in front of a television set, seeing no more and no less than the other tens of millions of potential voters.

Accordingly, one of the important tools of the contemporary psephologist is the humble television set. Psephology involves the study of masses of people. The political motorcade, or the prop-stop, or the auditorium speech deals with only relative handfuls compared to the tens of millions who watch television. The real action is where the real action isn't—where a man just home from work watches the two-minute film clip of Hubert Humphrey being baited by student militants.

These, then, are the basic tools of the trade: election returns; demographic indices; public opinion polls; press and video reports. On the surface they are mostly simple and easily available tools; using them enables an intelligent citizen to sound off with vigor about the ever-changing politics of a bumptious era. Such a citizen need not be intimidated by any who see elections as great cabals among power brokers, understandable only to those who sit at the right hand of the famous.

On the first level, then, this volume is intended to set forth appropriate data so that the reader can think through for himself the politics of our time. It is for this purpose, too, that a nonpartisan, nonideological appendix is included. Readers are invited to browse therein, perhaps to emerge with theories of their own.

Using the same public psephological tools, but hopefully digging somewhat deeper with them, the authors have come up with some opinions to set forth along with the data.

Our investigations lead us first to the three main notions that are discussed in the early parts of this book: a substantive notion, a structural notion, and a strategic notion.

The substantive idea is that many Americans have begun casting their ballots along the lines of issues relatively new to the American scene. For several decades Americans have voted basically along the lines of bread-and-butter economic issues. Now, in addition to the older, still potent economic concerns, Americans are apparently beginning to array themselves politically along the axes of certain social situations as well. These situations have been described variously as law and order, backlash, antiyouth, malaise, change, or alienation. These situations, we believe, constitute a new and potent political issue. We call it the Social Issue, and in our definition, it includes all these facets—and much more. It is an issue that has scared many, and yet, in our judgment, it is an issue that holds potential for good as well as for ill, for success or for defeat—for Democrats, for Republicans, for Wallaceites.

The structural idea concerns the makeup of the American electorate. The great majority of the voters in America are unyoung, unpoor, and unblack; they are middle-aged, middle-class, middle-minded. Understanding these simple demographics of the electorate is vital to any real psephological view of politics. For example, while the advocates of the New Politics in 1968 were reminding one another that half of all Americans were under twenty-five (which is roughly true), the canny psephologist was carefully noting that the average age of all *voters* was forty-seven (which is also true, and far more relevant).

The strategic idea deals with the manner in which candidates for office try to make hay with both the *substance* of an election and the *structure* of the electorate. In American political life this has almost invariably manifested itself as an attempt to capture the center ground of an electoral battlefield. The reason for this tropism toward the center is simple: That is where victory lies. A classic case in point was demonstrated in New York City in the 1969 mayoralty campaign when "law-and-order" candidate Mario Procaccino proclaimed himself liberal, while "liberal" candidate John V. Lindsay reminded one and all how tough he was on law and order. It can safely be said that the only extreme that is attractive to the large majority of American voters is the extreme center.

These are three relatively simple ideas, but who is to say that psephology is so terribly complicated after all? It is terribly easy to be complicated in the field of politics. Electoral votes can be put through tortuous combinations and permutations; majorities can be conjured up by adding the votes of second-generation Americans of Latvian descent with the votes of new Southern suburbanites and the support of union chieftains; personal political charisma can be analyzed till the cows come home; political swings can be charted on the basis of which bosses and which machines are actively "delivering" which votes to whom.

But when all is said and done, the complicated and conspira-
torial theories are usually too cute—cute enough sometimes for
the beleaguered columnists who must file three stories a week,
but frequently of little value in assessing what actually happens
in the voting booth on the first Tuesday after the first Monday
in November.

It is our contention that the simple ideas are of more importance. The tide is more important than the ripples or the waves.
Understanding the tide, when there is a tide, can explain what
happened recently and what is likely to happen.

With this understanding, a fourth major notion begins to
emerge, more directly relevant to who may be elected to what
in the years to come. When coupled with the three earlier ideas,
it provides, we believe, the beginning of a general theory of
contemporary elections.

This fourth notion is discussed at some length at the end of
this book. Simply put, it says that those politicians who ignore
the first three ideas do so at their electoral peril and that there
are forces at work within both major parties that seem bent on
such peril. It is our view that this hazard will more likely be
apparent within the Democratic Party, largely because it is
easier for an out party to succumb to a move away from the
center and toward an extreme, as the out-party Republicans did
in 1964 with their nomination of Senator Barry Goldwater. If
this happens, if Republicans capture the center as Democrats go
to the extreme, we may well see Republican Presidents in the
White House for a generation.

But a further thought must be immediately noted: Unless the
Democrats actively commit ritual suicide off in left field, there
is no reason to expect that they will die a sudden death. To the
contrary, a Democratic Party willing to recognize the reality of
the current political landscape, willing to recognize the inherent
wisdom in the voice of the people, can be a potent and beneficial
political force in America, potent enough to elect a President if
things go well. The struggle to capture the center in the 1970's,
both to listen to and to lead the real majority in America, will
determine who will be the next Presidents.

PART TWO

The Ideas Propounded

2

Tide Watching

Attempting to describe a series of elections in America—attempting to see tides, not waves—is a difficult chore.

To see how confusing everything is, we may pause for a moment to observe the muddled fate of other recent electoral theorizing.

On the afternoon of November 5, 1968, as the American people went to the polls, the agglomerated political wisdom of our time was attuned to the notion that America had been living through what was called a Democratic era. This era, as conventionally viewed, began with the election of Franklin Roosevelt in 1932 and continued through Lyndon Johnson's 1964 landslide. This Democratic era was broken only by the two Eisenhower victories. These were usually described as "personal victories" by a remarkably popular war hero with a wonderful grin.

Certainly a plausible view, considering recent political history up until that evening. Democrats *had* won the Presidency six of the last eight times, and Eisenhower *was* a remarkably popular war hero with a wonderful grin.

Yet, as the results came in on the evening of November 5, 1968, a man with a sharp pencil could start making some other calculations that would show rather drastically different conclusions. By the next morning these facts were true:

—Three of the last five Presidential elections were won by Republicans: Eisenhower twice and Nixon once.

—A Democratic Presidential candidate for President had received a *majority* of the popular vote only *once* in the last six elections (LBJ in 1964) .

—If one added up all the Democratic and all the Republican votes for President since World War II, they would be about dead even: 185,000,000 for Republicans and 186,-000,000 for Democrats. Some Democratic era!

So there is the hazard. It is easy, but often misleading, to declare the existence of grand political movements, potent political coalitions, well-oiled political machinery, and, yea, political tides. Unfortunately, not only do these theories have a way of falling of their own weight like Jello nailed to a wall, but there is always the further danger of encountering a man in the corner of the room who takes his cigar from his mouth and presents you with what may be called the personalistic view of recent Presidential elections. As follows:

—Nixon won in 1968 because Daley's cops hit kids on the head.

—Johnson won because Goldwater was a terrible candidate.

—Kennedy won because he was good-looking, a Catholic, and won the debates because of Nixon's bad television makeup.

—Eisenhower won because he reminded everyone of his father.

—Truman won because Dewey was overconfident and looked like the little man on the wedding cake.

This, too, is a limited way of looking at things.

It is tempting to say that American politics and elections are at once so inexact and so complex that they are perhaps the only field of human activity in which all the stated opinions are correct and so are their opposites. One observer has described this as the Political Law of Simultaneous but Contrary Truths. That is not quite right, or not always right. But it is at least generally so that for each stated correct opinion there is someone who is supposed to know what he is talking about and who is saying exactly the opposite.

For example, look at the middle sixties. Were one to rely on most media accounts of the 1964–68 period, the diagnosis might go something like this: Following the elections of 1964, the Republican Party was in a state of something called "disarray" because its "machinery" had failed, and there were grave doubts about whether it could survive as a "serious force" in American political life. Two years later, in 1966, following the restoration of normal Republican levels in the Congress, suddenly it was the Democratic Party that was in disarray because *its* machinery was creaky.

In late 1966, Nelson Rockefeller announced "unequivocally" that he was not a candidate for the Presidency, and his announcement was duly reported in the press. As the Presidential season wore on, as 1966 became 1967, we were told unequivocally that an incumbent President could not be denied his party's nomination. A leading columnist for the New York *Times* asked himself in print, "Isn't it possible that Johnson will withdraw?" and answered himself in the conventional Washington wisdom: "This wistful proposition can be demolished with some confidence. It is about as likely that Lyndon Johnson will quit the White House and go back to Texas as it is that Dean Rusk will turn dove, Dick Nixon will stop running, or J. Edgar Hoover will retire."

When Nixon began to surface, he was labeled "a loser." When Senator Eugene McCarthy started out in New Hampshire, he was dismissed as a quaint Don Quixote. After months of vigorous campaigning in New Hampshire, McCarthy *lost* to a write-in candidate who did not set foot in the state—and was hailed for his victory.

When 1968's primary battles between McCarthy and Robert Kennedy heated up, a new cliché came into popular currency

based on the simple arithmetic of adding together the Mc-
Carthy and Kennedy votes and calling them dove votes. "Eighty
percent of the American people have voted against the administration on Vietnam," we read in the wisest journals. Yet the
Gallup Polls in the early spring of 1968 showed that doves and
hawks ran about even, and by 51% to 40% Americans did *not*
want to "stop the bombing," which was then the dove rallying
cry. Harris showed at about the same time that 54% of the
public supported the war policy, that by 44% to 36%, Americans
favored an *invasion* of North Vietnam.

Finally came the August convention nominations of Humphrey and Nixon, and we were told that the conventions were
"rigged" and "undemocratic" because Rockefeller and Mc-
Carthy were clearly more appealing and "charismatic" candidates than Humphrey and Nixon. Yet in early August the
Gallup and Harris polls showed that among registered Democrats and registered Republicans across the country it was
Nixon and Humphrey leading their competitors by rather
large majorities. The only "democratic" choices for the conventions to make were the ones that were actually made.

So much for the day-to-day coverage of an election. Suffice it
to say that between the politicians who fulminate and the media
that sanctify and exaggerate the fulminations, it is very difficult
to get a true fix on what is happening. If political theoreticians
sometimes concentrate overly on tide watching, the press is
addicted to ripple watching. It is tempting to say that the first
rule of contemporary psephology is that the press is always
wrong. But, alas, even that is not so, for the contemporary press
is very good when it is read for the ripple-watching activity it
usually represents.

The elections game is triply mystifying for those who seek to
understand the ebb and flow of American political tides. Not
only are the numbers too easily viewed through different political prisms (have the last twenty years been a Republican era or
a Democratic era?), not only is each election too easily seen as a
highly personal affair (war hero, big grin, little man on wedding cake), but the contemporary reportage has at best a modest
batting average when viewed retrospectively.

So how is one to know? How does one gauge political tides?

It is the contention of the authors that it is difficult but not impossible. The first requisite is to acknowledge that there are not only tides, but waves and ripples also, and that there are times when only ripples and perhaps a few waves are visible on the horizon. There *are* political tides, but they are sometimes not discernible for years. It is the authors' view that there have been some big new-style waves in recent years, and it is conceivable, although by no means definite, that we are in for a tidal political era. This we hope to demonstrate.

To begin, let it be noted clearly that voters will at least make big waves when stimulated on specific occasions.

Observe:

In 1964 the virtually all-black Ward 17 in Baltimore voted for Lyndon B. Johnson for President by 95%.

Two years later a gentleman named George P. Mahoney won the Democratic nomination for governor of Maryland. Now Mr. Mahoney had a unique campaign slogan—"Your home is your castle—protect it"—and his campaign was keyed to opposition to a proposed open housing law in Maryland. The blacks in Ward 17 did not like Mr. Mahoney, even though he was a Democrat and even though everyone knows that "Negroes vote Democratic." The Ward 17 blacks, who gave 95% of their vote to the Democratic Mr. Johnson, gave exactly 7% to the Democratic Mr. Mahoney. This sort of tidal response helped elect a moderate, Rockefeller-type as Governor. His name: Spiro T. Agnew.

Or take the community of Stratham, New Hampshire: rock-ribbed, Republican New Englanders. In 1960 the voters of Stratham cast 80% of their ballots for Mr. Nixon over Mr. Kennedy, just as good Republicans might be expected to act. Yet in 1964 there was Mr. Goldwater, perceived as a rattler of nuclear weapons, perceived as threatening the aged by tampering with the Social Security system. Stratham voters—rock-ribbed, Protestant, Republican New Englanders—responded to Mr. Goldwater by voting 52% for Lyndon Johnson. When Republicanism went back to normality in 1968, the voters of

Stratham went back to normal, too, with 70% of the two-party vote going for Richard Nixon.

So, then, voters *will* move massively when confronted with a major issue or a personality that represents a specific stand on an emotional issue. Voters may behave dully and habitually for years or for decades until aroused. Then they will respond with vigor.

In a normal election there may be several separate issues at work at the same time and the same issues may be acting in different ways on different groups. But frequently, in tidal times, one big issue is motivating millions of voters. For lack of a better name, we call such an issue the Voting Issue. The Voting Issue becomes of surpassing political interest not only when it moves a single state or a single national election, but when it continues to hold sway over the electorate for many consecutive years or even consecutive decades. When the Voting Issue becomes a trend, when the big waves are thrashed into a tide, then psephologists have something real to work with, and their hearts are gladdened.

Looking back over the past three-quarters of a century of American life, two clear examples of a continuing, tidal-scale Voting Issue come to mind. We may now be living through the advent of a third such issue.

A depression (the Panic of 1893) and extremely turbulent times had poisoned the latter years of Grover Cleveland's second term as President—1893–97. As the historian Edward Stanwood describes it: ". . . commercial disaster and private distress, manifesting itself in demonstrations that always excited apprehension, and in some cases lapsed into lawlessness which the local authorities could not or would not suppress—such, in brief, were the evil conditions that prevailed during that eventful period."

Grover Cleveland was a Democrat, and the word about town was that Republicans "could nominate a rag baby and elect it President." Accordingly, it was obvious that the Republican candidate, William McKinley, would choose the standard theme of throwing the rascals out, simultaneously embracing the middle-class demand of the time: prosperity and social tranquillity, via the totem of the gold standard.

But William Jennings Bryan, the Democratic nominee, refused to be saddled with Cleveland's record and the country's hard times. He repudiated Cleveland. In his "Cross of Gold" convention speech Bryan made bimetallism the gut issue of a crucial election and "16 to 1" (silver to gold conversion ratio) the rallying cry for sharp social and economic change.

As the campaign developed, it looked this way:

To the silver supporters, bimetallism would mean lower interest rates and prosperity. Most important, it meant a shift of control from the Eastern Establishment to the plain people of the South and Midwest. (Bryan had also received the Populist Party nomination in 1896.)

To the gold supporters, bimetallism meant shaking up the established order. It meant continuing chaos. Because Bryan was supported by the Socialist Eugene V. Debs, the gold supporters indicated that Bryan and silver meant Socialism. Because Bryan was supported by Governor John P. Altgeld of Illinois, who had pardoned the anarchists of the Haymarket bombing, gold supporters indicated that Bryan and silver meant anarchism. In short, to many Americans, the thirty-six-year-old charismatic Bryan was seen as a radical.

What was most interesting was that both parties and both candidates were campaigning *against* things as they were. The electoral nerve had been rubbed raw by the depression and social upheaval, and it was clear that the voters wanted change. This is symptomatic of tidal movements in American political history; the Voting Issue is so pervasive, so deep, that all serious candidates will attempt to trim their sails to the clear will of public demands.

McKinley (gold) beat Bryan (silver). But far more important were the issues that were raised and the establishment of party images that were to last for a long time. McKinley and the Republican Party were perceived by a majority of Americans as the party that was against both economic depression and against social upheaval. McKinley ran on the slogan "The advance agent of prosperity," and prosperity did indeed return to America. Soon the Republicans would call themselves the party of the "full dinner pail." Republicans were also for social stability, and social stability did return to America.

On this Voting Issue—the issue of prosperity with order—Republicans rode a voting tide to unprecedented success. This was the so-called Golden Age of Republicanism, and it lasted, except for one largely self-inflicted interruption, for more than a third of a century.

Woodrow Wilson was the only Democratic President elected in thirty-six years. He won his first term with only 42% of the vote when William Howard Taft and Theodore Roosevelt split the Republican vote and won his second with 49%. Other than the minority Wilson years, the Republicans gained healthy Presidential majorities every four years. (See Appendix for data.)

Suddenly, in late 1929, a new depression came, and the Voting Issue changed. While the Republican issue had been somewhat a combination of social and economic factors, the new issue that put Democrats over the top was a straight economic issue. There had always been poor people who were poor. But in the Depression many middle-class people became poor, and those who didn't become poor became frightened.

Again, the new Voting Issue cut so deeply that *both* sides agreed that the Depression was heinous. Mr. Hoover, being an incumbent, could not very well repudiate the incumbent, as did Bryan. But Herbert Hoover did the next best thing: He declared that the Depression was almost over, and that, anyway, he could cure it more wisely and more quickly than Franklin Roosevelt.

But America wasn't buying that. The electoral nerve had been rubbed raw. Republican stability was fine if accompanied by middle-class prosperity, but *middle-class poverty* was a disaster, and the 4% unemployment of 1928 had become the 24% unemployment rate in 1932.

And so Democrats grabbed the new economic Voting Issue,

and Franklin Roosevelt in 1932 received more than 57% of the vote. In 1936 he raised that to a massive 61% of the vote.

By tracking the next three elections, one can observe that the Democratic majority began to dwindle as the core issue—the poverty of the middle class—began to lose relevance. In 1940, when unemployment was "down" to 15%, Roosevelt's majority was still a healthy 55%, but, nonetheless, a 6% drop. In 1944, when times were flush, when unemployment was less than 2%, his majority sank to 53%, even though Roosevelt was then heroic Commander in Chief of a nation at war. With the election of 1948, America entered what might be described as a tideless era or, if not that, an era when crosstides tended to neutralize one another. Harry Truman's vote in 1948 was 49.6% (when times were flush), and some of that vote, as discussed earlier, may well have been due to the fact that Mr. Dewey looked like the top of a wedding cake. From 1948 to 1964 there were ripples, there were some waves, but any tides were largely in the eye of the beholder.

The rubbed raw nerve of the Depression was apparently being salved by prosperity, and we can see the emergence of one of the central ironies of recent political life. It is summed up by the traditional Democratic slogan, "If you want to live like a Republican, vote Democratic." As Democrats see it, Democratic prosperity tends to be counterproductive to what had become the Democratic Issue: middle-class poverty. As middle-class poverty disappeared, so did some of the Democratic appeal.

To be sure, General Eisenhower's victories in the 1950's by percentages of 55 and 57 were partly due to his personal magnetism and his war-hero status. But equally certainly, his victories were due to general prosperity within the continually enlarging American middle class. The Democratic Issue had lost some potency as the memory of the Depression faded, and with the lack of a gut issue, voters could easily swing to the war hero and the man with the wonderful grin. Herein, a rule: Charisma counts, but *after* gut issues.

The 1960 election was essentially a dead heat, and it can be used to prove almost anything, especially that there was no tide.

The nation was in a recession of sorts, and Nixon did not have the grin, nor was he a war hero. Kennedy was an extremely attractive candidate, he beat Nixon in the first debate, and the Catholic issue cut both ways. That the Democrats no longer had a stranglehold on a clear-cut Voting Issue was true, for middle-class poverty had pretty well disappeared. On the other hand, neither was the Democratic Party of John Kennedy in 1960 the apparently radical party of William Jennings Bryan in 1896. It was a time between Voting Issues, and in such a time full weight can be awarded to the three C's of conventional politics—charisma, campaign, and circumstance, and all of these played a role in JFK's victory, in a time of political ebb tide.

‹ 3 ›

A New Tide Observed:

The Social Issue

In 1964 the first unpleasant political rumblings were heard from what may be a new Voting Issue. Early in the year, Governor George C. Wallace of Alabama challenged President Lyndon Johnson in a series of Democratic state primaries. Wallace, who had made his national reputation as a "segregation now; segregation forever" politician, did surprisingly well against the stand-ins who nominally represented President Lyndon Johnson. In Wisconsin—a state with a long liberal tradition—George Wallace received 34% of the Democratic primary vote against Governor John Reynolds. In Indiana, Wallace received 30% of the party primary vote against Governor Matthew Welsh. In Maryland, Wallace got 43% of the Democratic vote against Senator Daniel Brewster.

In 1964 Wallace was regarded primarily as an antiblack candidate, and the term "backlash" came into the political lexicon, describing a white response to what some whites perceived as "Negroes getting too much, too fast, with too much turmoil."

Lyndon Johnson, of course, didn't see it that way. In fact, in a speech to Congress he later picked up the rallying cry of young blacks seeking equity in America and announced to America and the world that "we shall overcome." Lyndon Johnson did overcome in 1964. When the Wallace candidacy dropped away, the backlash vote found a haven with Barry Goldwater, and Mr. Johnson noted one day that there were many Americans who believed in "frontlash" and a fair deal for blacks. Indeed there were, as the election returns showed.

By any purely statistical standard, the election of 1964 was "tidal." Lyndon Johnson—a then popular, activist President in a prosperous, peaceful time—won with 61% of the vote.

But the main reason behind the vote was a strange, onetime wave in the political ocean: Barry Goldwater. One of the precepts of this book is that American politicians normally drive toward the center of the political spectrum. But Senator Goldwater chose instead to head for the right flank. In so doing, Senator Goldwater showed what happens when a candidate moves away from the center: A political stick of dynamite is lit. As perceived by tens of millions of Americans, Senator Goldwater was that worst of all political types: an extremist. As so perceived, he sought to wreck Social Security, to sell TVA, and to put the decision to use nuclear weapons in the hands of field commanders in Vietnam. Voters were apparently voting neither on "backlash" nor on "frontlash," but on what might be called "otherlash"—*i.e.* Goldwater himself. When the electoral dynamite blew up, Goldwater was still holding the charge, still explaining that what America really wanted was a choice, not an echo.

The Goldwater defeat, however, was a one-shot loss owing mostly to the voters' perception of the candidate as an anti-centrist and radical. It was a big electoral wave, but not the sort of continuing tidal phenomenon that we have been chronicling here, such as the tides started by McKinley in 1896 and Franklin Roosevelt in 1932. As evidence, by 1968 no one was talking about junking Social Security, selling TVA, or putting nuclear weapons in the control of field commanders.

But perhaps ironically, perhaps coincidentally, and perhaps neither, it was the perception of Goldwater as an extreme candidate that masked the fact that among national major-party

Presidential candidates, he was the first to touch the raw nerve ending of the Social Issue. And as he was losing votes on TVA, "nukes," and Social Security, he was in some places gaining votes on race and crime. In Leake County, Mississippi, Barry Goldwater got 96% of the vote whereas Richard Nixon had received only 9% of the vote four years earlier. Farther north, in the largely "ethnic" Ward 2 of Baltimore, Goldwater got 24% of the vote whereas Nixon had received 15%.

Listen to Barry Goldwater phrase the Social Issue as he addresses the 1964 Republican Convention in San Francisco:

> . . . Tonight there is violence in our street, corruption in our highest offices, aimlessness among our youth, anxiety among our elderly, and there's a virtual despair among the many who look beyond material success toward the inner meaning of their lives. . . .
>
> The growing menace in our country tonight, to personal safety, to life, to limb and property, in homes, in churches, on the playgrounds and places of business, particularly in our great cities, is the mounting concern of every thoughtful citizen in the United States. Security from domestic violence, no less than from foreign aggression, is the most elementary and fundamental purpose of any government, and a government that cannot fulfill this purpose is one that cannot long command the loyalty of its citizens.

That Goldwater was speaking to a real issue that rather suddenly was concerning tens of millions of Americans is demonstrated from the following list published by the Gallup organization. It concerns what the American public perceives as "the most important problem" facing the nation, and it covers a full decade. The italics are ours.

1958

Feb. 2	Keeping out of war
Mar. 23	Unemployment
Nov. 16	Keeping out of war

1959

| Feb. 27 | Keeping world peace, high cost of living, *integration struggle* |
| Oct. 16 | Keeping out of war, high cost of living |

1960

| Mar. 2 | Defense "lag" |
| July 8 | Relations with Russia |

1961

| Mar. 15 | Keeping out of war |

1962

| Apr. 29 | International tensions, high cost of living, unemployment |

1963

| July 21 | *Racial problems,* Russia |
| Oct. 2 | *Racial problems* |

1964

Mar. 1	Keeping out of war
May 20	*Racial problems,* foreign affairs
June 3	*Integration,* unemployment
July 29	*Racial problems*
Aug. 21	International problems
Oct. 11	International problems
Nov. 18	Vietnam war, medical care for the aged

1965

Apr. 16	*Civil rights*
May 9	Education, *crime*
June 11	International problems
Aug. 11	Vietnam war, *civil rights*
Oct. 13	*Civil rights,* Vietnam war
Dec. 1	Vietnam war, *civil rights*

1966

| May 27 | Vietnam crisis, threat of war |
| Sept. 11 | Vietnam war, *racial problems,* cost of living |

1967

Oct. 18   High cost of living, taxes, health problems, cost of education, Vietnam war

1968

Feb. 28   *Crime, civil rights,* high cost of living

May 26   Vietnam war, *crime and lawlessness, race relations,* high cost of living

Aug. 4   Vietnam war, *crime and lawlessness, race relations,* high cost of living

Sept. 8   Vietnam war, *crime, civil rights* and high cost of living

Oct. 30   Vietnam war, *crime, race relations,* high cost of living

1969

March   Vietnam war, *crime and lawlessness, race relations,* high cost of living

1970

February   Vietnam war, high cost of living, *race relations, crime*

Suddenly, some time in the 1960's, "crime" and "race" and "lawlessness" and "civil rights" became the most important domestic issues in America.

The nondomestic issue of Vietnam was "more important" but as will be shown later in detail, Americans were not voting primarily on a pro-Vietnam or anti-Vietnam basis despite its "importance." An examination of public opinion polls over recent years shows an extremely ambivalent set of feelings about the Vietnam War, circling around the desire to "get out without bugging out." Insofar as both Presidents Johnson and Nixon stayed roughly close to this position, neither man was gaining or losing massive numbers of votes on the substantive hawk versus dove positions on Vietnam. This will be demonstrated. Some votes in 1968 did swing on a tangential feeling of malaise and nonaccomplishment in the field of foreign affairs generally and Vietnam specifically, but the numbers were not large. Many votes, however, did swing on the domestic side effects of the Vietnam War: disruption, dissention, demonstrations.

Generally speaking, it is the feeling of the authors that Americans vote for candidates largely on the basis of domestic issues, not international issues. The ever-potent Economic Issue always holds a high priority, and in a time of economic crisis—great inflation, depression, deep and lengthy recession—the Economic Issue will likely be the crucial Voting Issue in a national election. This is as it has been, as it is, and as it will likely continue to be.

But now a new element has been added. To the authors, the italicized words above seem to herald the clear emergence of a new and major Voting Issue in America, an issue so powerful that it may rival bimetallism and depression in American political history, an issue powerful enough that under certain circumstances it can compete in political potency with the older economic issues. We call this force the Social Issue, and, as shall now be noted, it is complex, and it deals with more than just race and crime as listed above.

We can begin by recounting some of the events and circumstances of recent years that swept the Social Issue to the forefront of the American political scene. They constitute a unique set of converging factors that acted one upon the other, beating ripples into waves and perhaps moving waves into a tide that will be politically observable for decades to come.

There was, first, the "crime wave." From a professional data-gathering point of view, the FBI statistics on crime are probably the worst collection of numbers regularly put between federal covers. Still, in recent years, there can be no doubt that there *has* been a sharp increase in crime, no matter how the statistics are tended. The data concerning "offenses against persons" show a 106% increase from 1960 to 1968. These crimes include the ones that frighten the public the most: murder; rape; robbery; aggravated assault. It is of interest to note that a great deal of the "crime wave" can be attributed to a sharp increase in the numbers of young people in recent years. There were more than half again as many Americans aged fifteen to nineteen in 1968 as there were fifteen years earlier, and these crimes that frighten are precisely the crimes that are disproportionately committed by young people.

But citizens afraid of being mugged weren't buying statistical explanations; they were buying guns for protection. Tens of millions of Americans felt unsafe as they walked the streets of their city neighborhoods at night. That the political jugular ran through these same attitudinal neighborhoods could have been gleaned from the results of the special election in New York City in 1966 concerning the setting up of a civilian review board as a check on alleged police brutality. Almost every major politician and Establishment leader endorsed the plan. Yet the voters turned it down 2 to 1. By August, 1968, when Mr. Nixon delivered his acceptance speech in Miami, he knew full well the potency of the crime issue. He spoke of "cities enveloped in smoke and flame" and of "sirens in the night." And then he said: "Time is running out for the merchants of crime and corruption in American society. The wave of crime is not going to be the wave of the future in the United States of America. We shall reestablish freedom from fear in America. . . ."

Race is certainly a second key element of the Social Issue, and of course, the racial question has always been with America. But in the last decade there has been a sharp, yet apparently paradoxical change in the perceptions that white Americans have of black Americans.

This can perhaps best be seen as a series of three fleeting video scenes flashed upon a television screen.

The first picture shows a young, clean-cut black man seated at a lunch counter in a Southern state. In the already archaic language of the late 1950's the young black is known as a New Negro—college-educated, articulate, neat. As he is seated at the lunch counter, a wiry, slack-jawed white man comes up behind him and pours ketchup on his head. Quietly, and with great dignity, the black man remains in his seat, determined to gain for himself and his people the elementary civil rights so long denied.

The second video scene shows buildings aflame, sirens wailing, and mobs of young black youths racing across a city street. We see next a jagged plate-glass window. Through the window comes a grinning young black, excited as at a carnival. He is carrying a television set.

The third scene is at Cornell University. A group of black students emerge from a campus building they have recently "taken over." They are carrying rifles.

It would be wrong to say that these three scenes represent the facts of the recent racial situation in America, but they do represent the perceptions that many Americans had and have, and these perceptions lay at the root of changing white attitudes as the Social Issue emerged. And yet, at the same time that white fear and resentment were growing, white attitudes toward civil rights for blacks were probably *liberalizing*. This paradox is explored later in this book.

In any event, in 1964 Harlem had a riot. In 1965 Watts had a riot. By 1966 every major city in America was asking itself, "Would it happen here?"—and major riots did erupt in Hough and Chicago. The apparent peak of a series of long hot summers was reached in 1967, when first Newark and then Detroit exploded in an orgy of violence, disorder, and looting. In April, 1968, on the night of Martin Luther King's assassination, outbreaks were reported in more than 100 cities, with Washington, Chicago, and Baltimore taking particularly heavy damage. The summers of 1968 and 1969 were quieter, but the electoral damage had been done. The electoral nerve had been rubbed raw. Voters were frightened and angry.

And then there was "kidlash." Among a highly publicized segment of young America, hair got long, skirts got short, foul language became ordinary, drugs became common, respect for elders became limited, the invasion and sacking of offices of college administrators became the initiation rite—and adults became fearful and upset. Again.

A fourth element of the Social Issue might simply be called values. Pornography blossomed with legal sanction; sexual codes became more permissive; priests were getting married; sex education was taught in the schools.

Further, the man who works hard, pays his taxes, rears his children—the man who has always been the hero of the American folk mythology—now found himself living in an era where the glorified man is the antihero: morose, introspective, unconcerned with God, country, family, or tax bill.

Finally, to this already combustible mixture, a new highly flammable element was added: the Vietnam protest movement. Suddenly American boys and girls were seen burning American flags on television; clergymen were pouring containers of blood on draft records; the President was jeered.

All these elements acted on one another and on the American voter. The Social Issue was in full flower. It may be defined as a set of public attitudes concerning the more personally frightening aspects of disruptive social change. Crime frightens. Young people, when they invade the dean's office, or destroy themselves with drugs, or destroy a corporate office with a bomb, frighten. Pornography, nudity, promiscuity are perceived to tear away the underpinnings of a moral code, and this, too, is frightening. Dissent that involves street riots frightens.

Put together, it spelled out great change. It was change that some few Americans perceived as beneficial, but measurably larger numbers did not. Most voters felt they gained little from crime, or integration, or wild kids, or new values, or dissent. Of many of the new facets of American life they were downright fearful. These voters became the core of an antidissent dissent, feeling the breath of the Social Issue hot and uncomfortable on their necks. When these voters had a chance to vote against it—in 1968 and again in 1969—they did. Other voters, approving of some of the changes but profoundly disturbed by others, felt only confusion.

Many of the political left, misreading both the issue and the popular reaction to it, feared an era of repression. Many of the political right chortled, sensing a clear turn of affairs their way. But both groups were probably premature in their judgments and very probably wrong.

As it stands now, at the beginning of the 1970's, the Social Issue appears up for grabs in the decade to come, an issue honestly and legitimately troubling tens of millions of Americans. As we shall examine it subsequently, the Social Issue is not a straight right/left or liberal/conservative issue. While the economic issues of the past will continue to shape much of our politics in whatever form they may appear, the Social Issue is a new factor in the political equation—or at least it is new in terms of its present massive impact. While we know less about it than we do of its economic counterpart, it seems clear that it will have great political effect in the years to come. When voters are afraid, they will vote their fears. Accordingly, it may well be that the party and the candidates that can best and most intelligently respond to the social turbulence that is presently perceived by American voters will be known by the simple word: winners.

4

Demography Is Destiny:

Unyoung, Unpoor, Unblack

Who are the men and women who will be choosing the next Presidents in the decade of the 1970's?

Quite a bit is known about these voters of the future. They are already born, so barring a catastrophe or an important geriatric breakthrough, we know their age distribution. Racially, those who are white are already white; those who are black are already black. The women are already female; the men, male. The great majority of the Americans who will be voting in the seventies have already finished their education, and by observing trends for the rest, we can adequately judge educational levels. We don't know *for sure* how many people will be living in the South or in New Jersey, how much they will be earning, or what kind of jobs they will be working in, but, again, a trend projected from current data will serve as a reliable guide.

This sort of demographic information is of the utmost importance to the psephologist. While it may overstate the case to paraphrase Heraclitus by saying, "Demography is destiny," in an electoral sense there is a good measure of truth in the phrase. For young people and old people may have different views on racial issues; rich and poor may disagree about welfare; farmers may have different views on urban problems from those of city dwellers. Liberals on the race issue are hard to find in white working-class neighborhoods that border on black neighborhoods, while they are not nearly so hard to find in the more affluent suburbs, far from where push meets shove. Furthermore, more than one of every three adults don't vote, and young people, poor people, and blacks are less likely to vote than the middle-aged, the wealthy, or whites.

If a typical voter in America turns out to be a forty-seven-year-old wife of a machinist living in suburban Dayton, Ohio, we will likely have a different brand of politics from that if the typical voter is a twenty-four-year-old instructor of political science at Yale University.

If it is too strong to say, "Demography is destiny" or even "Demography is ideology," it is certainly not too strong to say, "Demographic circumstances influence attitudes, which in turn influence elections." And accordingly, if we are further to examine attitudes—particularly attitudes that make up the Social Issue—we must first examine the demographic circumstances of American voters.

In a review of the data, it is clear the psephological power in America is held by the lady in suburban Dayton, not by the young instructor at Yale.

To sketch in this demographic portrait, we can begin by noting that American voters are mostly *unyoung*. They are also mostly *unold*.

PERCENT OF TOTAL VOTE, BY AGE, 1968

Age	Percent of Total Vote
Under 30	17%
30–64	68%
65 and over	15%

(*U.S. Census Bureau*)

If one reads "under 30" as young and "65 and over" as old, then the term "middle-aged" describes almost seven of every ten voters in America. In point of fact, the median voter—the fabled

Middle Voter—was forty-seven years old at the time of the 1968 election. Nor will this age structure change very much in the years to come. It has been argued that a vast new lot of voters— the baby crop of the 1950's—will soon reach voting age and that this will drop the average age of the American voter as the decade moves along. Indeed, the baby-boom babies are reaching maturity, but this will lower the median voting age by only a year or two. In fact, even if the voting age in every state of the Union were to be reduced to eighteen at some time in the 1970's, present estimates are that the average voter would still be well over forty.

But numbers in age groups are not everything. Political activism can often substitute for lack of numbers, and many a political movement has won success through the hard work of a limited number of people. Further, a small group, if it votes monolithically, can be a potent force in an election.

What about young people and the impact of their political work?

Obviously the "Be Clean for Gene" college students did much for Senator McCarthy in his 1968 primary campaigns. They demonstrated anew that a massive door-to-door canvass can be a major vote-winning technique. The young people who flocked to Robert Kennedy's banner were also effective, primarily in the amount of press attention they were able to draw to Senator Kennedy's campaign. When sixty-year-old Nelson Rockefeller made his stretch run prior to the Republican Convention, he valiantly attempted to prove that he too was in tune with America's youth and was entitled to don the mantle of New Politics. After the nominees were chosen, Vice President Humphrey vigorously sought the support of the activist student movement and to some extent was successful in gaining it.

Candidate Nixon also vowed, in the argot of a man who forgot the argot, that he would "sock it to them." Yet, Nixon ended up as the man who allegedly appealed least to the young, turned-on college generation. He won the election.

Still, one cannot assume that Messrs. McCarthy, Kennedy, Rockefeller, Humphrey, and Nixon were mistaken in seeking that youth support. For there are, in fact, two critical questions to ask about young voters when we think about their electoral impact. First: Can they by their votes actually elect anyone? Second: Can young people by their influence or activity get others to help elect a candidate?

To the first question we may answer: Few groups are as electorally weak as are young people.

An examination of the data on page 46 reminds us of certain obvious political and human truths: First, children don't vote, and, second, there are many, many more people over thirty than there are between twenty-one and thirty.*

Furthermore, although the rhetoric of the "kids" in 1968 dealt heavily with "participatory democracy," the cold fact is that young people eligible to vote are far less likely to participate than their elders.

ESTIMATED PERCENT OF ELIGIBLE POPULATION WHO VOTED,
BY AGE, 1968

Age	Percent Voted
18–20	33%
21–24	51%
25–29	60%
30–64	72%
65 and over	66%

(*U.S. Census Bureau*)

In part, this lack of participation is accounted for by the difficulties encountered by first-time registration and absentee ballot voting for students and military personnel. But regardless of reason, they simply take less part in elections than do their elders.

Still, one of every six voters is under thirty. This, of course, could be vitally important in a Presidential contest *if* young people voted monolithically. Some groups in American political life do. Young people don't.

---

* As of early 1970 only four states permit persons under twenty-one to vote: the voting age is eighteen in Georgia and Kentucky; nineteen in Alaska; twenty in Hawaii. Both former President Johnson and President Nixon have spoken in favor of a constitutional amendment to lower the voting age to eighteen throughout the nation.

On the eve of the Presidential election, at a time when young people were pictured in the press as liberal, college-educated, dovish on Vietnam, pro-Kennedy, pro-McCarthy intellectuals:

VIETNAM—HAWKS AND DOVES (Self-identified)

	Under 30	30–49	50 and over
Hawk	45%	48%	40%
Dove	43%	40%	42%
No Opinion	12%	12%	18%

(*Gallup, October, 1968*)

Young people were *more* hawkish than the over-fifty generation.

Surveys of 1968 voting tell us that young people were also slightly more likely to vote for *Wallace* than older voters, although they were also more pro-Humphrey. Obscured during the dramatic primary campaigns that pitted Senator McCarthy against Senator Kennedy was the fact that many young Americans were not for either one of them. It is too easy to forget that the hands which held the tire chains threatening Martin Luther King, Jr., when he marched to Cicero, Illinois, were young white hands. Being a young American apparently connotes nothing more than a chronological fact: Some are liberal, some conservative; some are of the right, some of the left; many are in the center. As a Daniel Yankelovich survey for the Columbia Broadcasting System showed in 1969, there is a much greater class gap between the attitudes of those young people in college and those not in college than there is a generation gap between young people generally and their parents.

The second question is harder to answer: Can young people, particularly the activist college youth, influence other voters? Are they a key electoral target for this reason?

That is certainly so, but it is a two-way street. When the McCarthy kids assembled thousands strong in New Hampshire and Wisconsin and rang every doorbell in sight, they showed that an ancient tactic of the Old Politics could be refitted and made to work on a grander scale. Door-to-door campaigning had been usually effective in the United States only when the candidate himself did it, typically in a local election. The idea of mounting a troop of 5,000 clear-eyed, articulate, appealing campaign workers in a state the size of New Hampshire would normally have been unthinkable. Had such a political troop been raised in more normal times it would likely have consisted of middle-aged women beginning to sag and middle-aged men smoking cigars—and there would always have been the question of whether they would gain votes for their candidates or repel them. There was little question of the effectiveness of the "Be Clean for Gene" kids. They were effective campaigners.

Yet consider the two-edged sword of strong identification with activist youth. In the spring of 1968 the students of Columbia took over the campus; in April, 1968, on the night of Martin Luther King's death, there was looting and burning in 100 cities, and Americans watched as (mostly young) black militants proclaimed their televised incantations about burning down a corrupt white society; in August, 1968, young peace demonstrators shouting obscenities clashed with Mayor Daley's police.* Rather suddenly, there was a legitimate question about "kidlash": Might not youth support be the kiss of death for any candidate who sought to appeal to the broad middle class of America?

In 1966, it may be argued, Ronald Reagan's stand against the Berkeley demonstrators won him the governorship of California. Suppose Eugene McCarthy had been nominated in 1968; suppose Robert Kennedy had not been murdered and had been nominated in 1968. Would they have been held indirectly accountable for any unruliness of their supporters— and, more critically, for *any* unruliness by *any* youth? What would have happened if the Weathermen and the Mad Dogs had gone wild as they did a year later in Chicago and Washington? Would a youth candidate have been vulnerable to a slashing attack precisely on the grounds of the Social Issue? It is not hard to imagine Richard Nixon and Spiro Agnew making political hay with any opponents identified with disruptive young activists.

---

* See page 162 for public reaction to the cops versus kids confrontation in Chicago.

There is a final thought about the so-called youth vote. Peter Pan is make-believe. People do get older. Advocates of the New Politics have used this fact to support the contention that in the years to come their influence and numbers will swell. This will happen as the young, highly educated activists of the 1960's mature to take on leadership positions and simultaneously become a larger fragment of the electorate due to reach voting age and to the increased voting participation that comes with age. Further, there will be newer youth cohorts, presumably equally radical, adding to the numbers of the New Left or the New Politics, or whatever the phrase may be next year.

There is probably some truth to this notion. When Socialist leader Michael Harrington writes of the large enthusiastic college audiences he speaks to around America, no one disputes him. A generation ago the late Norman Thomas spoke to similar enthusiastic audiences, and it may well be that some of his auditors are the parents of Harrington's listeners today. Surely, then, many of the articulate, politicized students of the 1960's will emerge as leadership cadre in the years to come. Surely, the current youth cohort will mature and vote in higher percentages. And there will no doubt be radicals in the new youth cohorts.

However, four thoughts partially mitigate this theory. First, it is not only the radical or activist youth who will be aging. The pro-Wallace youth, the Nixon youth, and the pro-Humphrey youth will be aging, too. The teen-age hands that held the tire chains in Cicero will soon be hands that are pushing baby carriages, lawn mowers, and the starter button on the engines of powerboats. The young people that were hawks will be getting older at the same rate as the youth who were doves.

Second, the fact that youths today are more likely to be college-educated would not normally correlate to a more *Democratic* or more *liberal* electorate in the future. In the past, the more educated a voter, the more likely he has been to be affluent, and the more educated *and* affluent the voter, the more likely he has been to vote *Republican* and think *conservatively*. This happened even though the 1930's equivalent of the "kids" were radicals, agitators, Communists, or what have you. There would not seem to be any good reason for this pattern to change. Only a small percentage of the current college youth are categorized as "revolutionaries," 3.5% in the Yankelovich/CBS survey. Another 9.5% are categorized as "radical reformers." The balance, about 87%, are "moderate reformers," "middle of the road," or "conservatives," and there are, incidentally, slightly more "conservatives" than "radical reformers." In short, the college experience may be regarded as liberalizing, but not revolting. And doctors who will be making $60,000 a year in the 1970's or 1980's would not seem to be good bets to be throwing rocks through hospital windows.

Third, even though the number of young Americans in college is greater today than it was in the past, in the decade of the seventies students will still have limited numerical power. These numbers will be explored at greater length in the education section that follows on pages 59–60. But by the decade's end a projection based on Census data reveals that only 10% of the electorate will be "young college graduates" (*i.e.*, under age forty in 1980). Later on in the century, in the elections of 1984, 1988, 1992, 1996, the percentage of college-educated in the electorate will be rising substantially. But an interesting question arises: In the land of the one-eyed is the one-eyed king? When most people are college-educated, will the fact of college education mean much politically? Isn't it likely then that the elitist will not be the "college graduate," but perhaps the PhD, while the mere college graduates are relegated to the ranks of the unwashed?

Fourth, something funny happens to people as they get a little older—and it even happens to the avant-garde. From only a slightly earlier era here is poetic evidence from the pen of Judith Viorst, reporting on life-styles in Greenwich Village:

> Alvin and Barbara are real Village people
> They lived together before they were married,
> And her father came to dinner.

She is a vegetarian and an ethical nihilist
He sings Gregorian chants.
They sleep on a mattress on the floor.

He would have loved her even if she were Negro.
She would have loved him even if he weren't Jewish.
They were made for each other.

Alvin and Barbara decided to marry
They said,
Because living together is square.

They have decided to have a baby,
They said,
Because being irresponsible is square.

They may even leave the Village,
They said,
Because the Village is getting square.

I hope they don't move to New Jersey.

There is demographic evidence that when the babies come, Alvin and Barbara do indeed move to suburban New Jersey. Once there, they do not turn conservative, but neither are they quite as ready to tear down the "corrupt middle-class society" that they have become a part of. The onset of orthodontistry for their children usually coincides with the making of two more deradicalized reformers. Beware, New Left; beware, New Politics—you'll become Old Liberals before you know it!

Summing up: Six of every seven Americans are over thirty, and the average voter is closer to fifty than he is to forty. Peter Pan rarely registers; people get older every four years; as they get older, they change.

If our electorate of the 1970's is to be unyoung, it will also be basically unpoor . . . and unrich, too.

It can be seen clearly that "poor people" as a group do not make up a major segment of the electorate, if one uses a line of $3,000 as "poor." And they are becoming an even smaller minority. In 1964 the percentage of under-$3,000 families was

VOTER PARTICIPATION, BY INCOME, 1968

Family Income Per Year	% of Total Vote	% of Eligibles Who Voted
Under $3,000	9%	54%
$3,000–$5,000	13%	58%
$5,000–$15,000	66%	72%
$15,000 and over	12%	84%

(U.S. Census Bureau)

much greater: 13 compared to the 1968 figure of 9. Even if one draws the poverty line at $5,000, the projection for 1972 reveals that only no more than 15% of the voters will be "poor." This is compared to the 22% in 1968.

Even that is a considerable number, to be sure. But again, as with youth, poor Americans show only small tendencies toward bloc voting as a "poor bloc." In the big cities of the North most poor are Democrats, but actually, the "poor" may be best seen as *many* blocs, each going its own way. When one thinks of who "poor people" are in America, this lack of bloc voting becomes almost self-evident. Poor people are blacks in big-city slums, who tended to vote for Humphrey. Poor people are rural whites in the Midwest, who tended to vote for Nixon. Poor people are rural whites who live in the South, who voted for Wallace. Disproportionately, poor people are aged, with their own political interests that may cross partisan lines.

Clearly, an aged white New Hampshire farm couple of limited income will have a different political background and a different political attitude from, say, a poor young black man living in East St. Louis. Yet both are "poor." Accordingly, except during depression times, a cohesive poor people's bloc has never really emerged in America. And like the "formerly young," there is no real evidence that the "formerly poor" continue to vote on the basis of previous poverty. In fact, a common remark one hears from those who weathered the Depression or who got out of a ghetto is: "I made it on my own, I worked my way up, why can't they?"

Although the "poor" are properly considered Democratic on balance, it is interesting to note that of the poorest dozen states in the nation, six went for Nixon, five went for Wallace, and only one for Humphrey. The richest state, Connecticut, went Democratic.*

Summing up: Depending on where one draws the poverty line, either four in five or nine of ten voters are *not* poor. Those that are poor do not vote similarly. The emergence of a "poor people's bloc" at a time when there are and will be fewer poor people than ever is unrealistic.

Unyoung, unpoor, the American electorate can also be viewed as unblack. (As will be noted later, the electorate is also un-Jewish, un-Catholic, un-Eastern, un-Western, un-Southern, and sometimes unnerving.) Blacks constitute only about 11% of the American population—about one in every nine.

Moreover, as in the case of young and poor, blacks in America are disproportionately less likely to vote.

PERCENTAGE AND NUMBER OF ELIGIBLE VOTERS
WHO VOTED, BY RACE, 1968

	Percent	Percent of Total Vote
White	69%	91%
Non-white	56%	9%

(*U.S. Census Bureau*)

Thus, while nonwhites are 11% of the population, they cast only about 9% of the vote.

But in one very crucial way, black voting behavior differs quite sharply from the behavior of the "young" and "poor" groups mentioned earlier. Blacks, having a more cohesive community of interest, *have* voted as a bloc:

NON-WHITE† VOTE 1964 AND 1968

	Republican	Democratic	A.I.P.
1968	12%	85%	3%
1964	6%	94%	—

(*Gallup*)

---

* The poorest dozen, ranked poorest first, by per capita income: Mississippi, Alabama, Arkansas, South Carolina, West Virginia, Tennessee, Kentucky, North Carolina, Louisiana, New Mexico, Idaho, Georgia.

† The data here are for "nonwhites," of whom roughly 90% are "Negro." Other sample data for purely black precincts show even higher percentages Democratic.

Because the blacks who do not vote are largely potential Democratic voters, it is apparent why the leaders of all the "Get Out the Vote" drives and "Be a Good Citizen" drives are so frequently Democrats. The pool of nonvoting blacks constitutes an important potential plus for Democrats.

Just how important can be seen from a breakdown of the Presidential vote in 1964 and 1968:

VOTER PARTICIPATION RATES BY RACE AND REGION,
1964 AND 1968

	1964	*1968*	*Difference 1964–1968*
In the South			
White	60%	62%	+2%
Non-White	44%	51%	+7% (!)
Outside the South			
White	75%	72%	−3%
Non-White	72%	61%	−11% (!)

(U.S. Census Bureau)

Blacks in the South voted in far greater numbers than ever before in American history. This increase can be largely attributed to the implementation of the Voting Rights Act of 1965 and the energetic work of organizing and registering blacks in Southern states. This work paid off, even though in the Presidential race Democrats carried only Texas and Maryland of all states south of the Mason-Dixon Line. However, the number of *local* black officeholders in the South increased dramatically. By early 1970 there were 565 black officeholders. In 1960 there had been fewer than 200.

At the same time, however, blacks outside the South were far *less* likely to vote: a decrease from 72% in 1964 to 61% in 1968.

How important was this on a national canvas? Very, because the election was so close. Had nonwhites outside the South come to the polls in 1968 as they had in 1964, *Hubert Humphrey would have received a greater popular vote than Nixon.* In short, while the black vote did turn out solidly Democratic, it did not solidly turn out.

What happened to the non-Southern black nonvote? Several reasons can be put forth explaining the poor showing.

There are those who say the heart went out of the black electorate when Robert Kennedy was killed. To be sure, Senator Kennedy had immense popularity among the black electorate, and it is interesting to ponder two points: Had he lived and *won* the nomination from Humphrey, could he have brought out those extra black votes needed for a Democratic victory without alienating white votes? Had he lived and *lost* the nomination and then campaigned for Hubert Humphrey, could he have brought out the additional black votes?

Another reason for the low black participation is that the effective choice in 1968 was Humphrey or Nixon, not, as in 1964, Johnson or Goldwater. While Humphrey was clearly superior from the point of view of most blacks, Mr. Nixon did not represent the sort of disaster that Mr. Goldwater represented. In 1968, it can be argued, Mr. Wallace represented the Goldwater position, and he never had a serious chance of winning. Therefore, blacks felt less threatened and felt less need to go to the polls.

Finally, in 1968, the voter turnout was somewhat lower all across the board. The Census Bureau in 1964 reported a voter turnout of 69.3%. In 1968 the Census figure was 67.8%.*

Summing up: Blacks constitute a small segment of the national vote. In recent times they have voted largely Democratic. In a close election, this can help. In a close election, anything helps.

In all: unyoung, unpoor, unblack. Furthermore, the young and the poor are unmonolithic in their Presidential voting behavior. Six in seven voters are over thirty. Nine out of ten are unpoor. Nine out of ten are white. Because there is some duplication—a young poor black man, for example—a fair guess is to say that seven of ten American voters are neither young, nor poor, nor black.

---

* Both these figures are a few percentage points too high. As the Census Bureau reports in its publication *Voting and Registration in the Election of November 1968*, "estimates of voter participation that are higher than the official counts have been the common experience of other survey organizations which have studied voting behavior."

Lesson: Talk about building a powerful "new political coalition" whose major components are all the young, all the poor, and all the blacks doesn't make much electoral sense.

Reprieve: That the electorate is unyoung, unpoor, and unblack does *not* mean they are antiyoung, antipoor, or antiblack. Remember that woman's suffrage was voted on by men. The electorate was unfemale. Not antifemale.

5

Demography Is Destiny:

Middle-Aged, Middle-Class Whites

If young, poor, and black are what most voters aren't, let us consider the electorate for what it largely is: white; median family income of $8,622; median age of about forty-seven. In short: middle-aged, middle-class whites.

This middle constituency can also be described as middle-educated. Typically, the middleman in America is a high school graduate, no more, no less:

VOTERS, BY YEARS OF SCHOOL COMPLETED, 1968	
Years of School Completed	*% of Electorate*
Elementary School or less	22%
High School:	
1–3 years	16%
4 years	36%
College:	
1–3 years	13%
4 years or more	13%
	(U.S. Census Bureau)

In other words:

—Almost three in four voters have never set foot in a college classroom (74%).

—Only one in eight voters has been graduated from college—any college—with major fields of study including animal husbandry and physical education (13%) .

Looking into the future, these figures will change, because larger proportions of young Americans are now going on to college. Yet because most of the electorate is middle-aged, the percentage of once-went-to-college among the electorate in the 1970's will not rise sharply. In 1968 about a quarter, 26%, had *some* college education. By 1972 this will have climbed to about 29%, and in 1976 to 31%. This will mean, still, that the greatest number of the electorate will have, at most, only the "middle" high school diploma. Accordingly, if we are to add to our categories of unyoung, unpoor, and unblack, we may say that the typical voter is, and will be through the seventies, "uncollege."

The typical voter is no "intellectual," if we assume that an intellectual has at least a college degree, but that not all college graduates are necessarily intellectual. If we move up the qualification a bit and apply the term only to those with *advanced* college degrees (MA, PhD, and the like) the weight of the oft-discussed "intellectual vote" is ridiculously minuscule.

But if the electorate is not "intellectual," it is most certainly not composed of ignoramuses. For a candidate to treat the voters largely as jerks (62% are at least high school graduates) would be as disastrous as considering them largely as intellectuals. Indeed, it might be impressionistically noted here that it is the authors' opinion that the inherent wisdom of the American voter is substantial. This point will be elaborated upon later. For now, let us observe rashly that the corporate wisdom of voters is often greater than that of politicians. For a truly shocking statement, it can be said that voters are even wiser than political theorists. Others have shared this view of voter wisdom. It was the distinguished political scientist V. O. Key in his esteemed work *The Responsible Electorate* who said:

> The perverse and unorthodox argument of this little book is that voters are not fools. To be sure, many individual voters act

in odd ways indeed; yet in the large the electorate behaves about as rationally and responsibly as we should expect, given the clarity of the alternatives presented to it and the character of the information available to it. In American presidential campaigns of recent decades the portrait of the American electorate that develops from the data is not one of an electorate straitjacketed by social determinants or moved by subconscious urges triggered by devilishly skillful propagandists. It is rather one of an electorate moved by concern about central and relevant questions of public policy, of governmental performance, and of executive personality.

Middle-income, middle-aged, middle-educated, and white, the voters in the middle can also be viewed vocationally as men and women primarily "at work with their hands, and not exclusively their minds."

VOTERS BY OCCUPATIONAL STATUS, 1968

	% of Total Electorate
High Level White Collar Workers*	19
Manual, Service, Clerical & Sales Workers	42
Farm Workers	3
Unemployed	1
Not in Labor Force	
Women (mostly housewives)	28
Men over 65 (mostly retired)	5
Other men	2
	(U.S. Census Bureau)

* Professional, technical, managerial, officials and proprietors.

Some of the numbers need further explanations:

The number of high-level white-collar workers is climbing. In the 1964 election the percentage was 16% compared to the 19% in 1968. If one allocates a proportionate share of the "housewives" and considers them as the spouses of these high-level white-collar workers, we might estimate that about 27% of the voters are in the *families* of those white-collar workers.

Of course, that leaves about 73% who are *not* in such families, still the vast majority; all *those* voters are in families where the earners are working with their hands. When one realizes that fact, the rhetoric of George Wallace can be fully savored, at least for its demographic accuracy:

> Now what are the real issues that exist today in these United States? It is the trend of pseudo-intellectual government, where a select, elite group have written guidelines in bureaus and court decisions, have spoken from some pulpits, some college campuses, some newspaper offices, looking down their noses at the average man on the street, *the glassworker, the steelworker, the autoworker, and the textile worker, the farmer, the policeman, the beautician and the barber, and the little businessman,* saying to him that you do not know how to get up in the morning or go to bed at night unless we write you a guideline. . . .

Furthermore, consider for a moment that "policeman" falls into the "work with hands" category. When the "cops" clashed with the "kids" at the 1968 Democratic Convention in Chicago, the journalists and many liberal politicians (high-level white-collars both), picked up the cry, "They're beating up our children." This was accurate: Most of the "kids" came from high-level white-collar homes. On the other hand, the other 73% of the voters could say, "Those student punks are beating up *our* children, or *our* husbands, or *our* fathers." That, too, would be accurate if one considers the policeman as a respected part of the nonelite.

After the convention, the opinion pollsters asked the public what they thought about the Chicago confrontation, and about two of every three Americans said they thought the police acted correctly, which coincides rather well with the occupational categorizations above. The old political axiom applies: "It depends on whose ox is being gored," or, in other words, "It depends on who is the clobberer and who the clobberee."

The confrontation at Chicago probably etched the lines of social class as sharply as they have ever been drawn in America. The fight in the streets was not between hawks and doves. For many it was perceived as between "elitists" and "plain people." There are more plain people than elitists in America.

Finally, and paradoxically, how do these "high-level" families vote? Despite all the recent comment about elitist Democratic intellectuals, the cold fact remains that the elite in America has a Republican majority. They are the doctors, bankers, and businessmen, with a good proportion of the lawyers and scientists as well. Only the vocal minority of the high-level voters are generally Democratic leaners. In the 1968 election the "professional and business" group went 56–34% for Nixon over Humphrey. The Democrats, despite the Agnew hoopla about the Democratic elitist establishmentarians, are those "plain people who work with their hands." Manual workers went 50–35% for Humphrey over Nixon.

That the Democrats have held the allegiance of most of the "plain people" has been the critical fact in American Presidential politics for more than a third of a century. That is why Democrats have won so often. Now, upon the shoals of the Social Issue, there seems to be the possibility of a rupture in that pattern. If it happens, it will be bad news for Democrats. If it can be prevented from happening, if it can be reversed, it will by happy days again for Democrats.

Next, don't forget the farmer. Although, numerically, there are many more voting blacks than voting farmers, this is somewhat misleading. While the numbers of farmers has decreased strikingly in recent years,* there remains a substantial part of the population whose work is directly related to farming. A rural town in the Midwest may have few "farmers," but the townsfolk sell and repair tractors and reapers, store grain, work as agricultural extension agents, publish weekly newspapers for farmers, and give loans to farmers or all the people whose work is related to farming. The analogy might be to a "mining town." Perhaps no more than 20 to 30% of the population work as "miners," but close down the mine, and you've rather effectively closed down the town. In short, the "farm vote," in its broad sense, is still with us, particularly in the states of the Midwest and South.

Next item: More than half the voters are women—51.9% to be precise. They show up in the preceding table not only as

---

* Compared to the 3% farmers in 1968, in the election of 1900 the percentage of farmers in the population was 38.

housewives, but as substantial parts of both the large employed groups: clerks, secretaries, teachers, etc. In America today, 43% of the women are working.

Since the advent of woman suffrage, no candidate for President has been solidly identified as a "woman's candidate." Women vote pretty much as their men do, or vice versa. In the last five Presidential elections, the largest margin of variance between men and women voters was 6% in the 1956 election—with women more likely to vote for General Eisenhower than Adlai Stevenson. Curiously, despite the legend building that has gone on about John Kennedy's "appeal to women voters," he would have lost the 1960 election had only women voted. In 1960, men voted 52–48% for JFK; women voted 51–49% for Nixon. As solace to Mr. Nixon, had only women voted in 1968, Hubert Humphrey would have won the popular vote, but the differentials aren't great in either case.

Middle-income, middle-aged, middle-educated, white, and what else?

Protestant, mostly:

VOTERS, BY RELIGION
Percentage

Protestant	68%
Catholic	25
Jewish	4

Catholics in America are substantially more likely than Protestants to be first- and second-generation Americans (Italians, Poles, Mexicans, Puerto Ricans) and are more likely to be residents of big cities. Residents of big cities and so-called ethnic Americans have traditionally been more likely to vote Democratic. Accordingly, Catholics are somewhat more likely to vote Democratic than are Protestants, but with the single exception of 1960, when Catholicism itself became an issue, there is little recent evidence that Catholics vote heavily *as* Catholics. Catholics will usually vote a few extra points for a Catholic candidate, but not always:

McCARTHY vs HUMPHREY, JULY, 1968

	McCarthy	Humphrey
National	48%	40%
Catholics	47	41
Protestants	49	39

(*Gallup*)

It is interesting to note how fast an issue can be laid to rest in American politics. Such results—Protestants outvoting Catholics for a Catholic candidate—would have been wholly inconceivable in the years between the defeat of Al Smith in 1928 and the victory of John F. Kennedy in 1960. In November, 1928, a Midwestern newspaper reported the defeat of Al Smith, a Catholic, under the banner headline THANK GOD, AMERICA IS SAVED. Today Catholicism seems thoroughly dead as a political issue. An interesting parlor game to demonstrate this is to ask: "Is Spiro Agnew a Catholic?" (He is Episcopalian.)

Two of every three voters are Protestant. Less likely to be big-city urban, less likely to be first- or second-generation Americans, Protestants are somewhat more likely than Catholics to vote Republican in Presidential races. But with the apparent disappearance of Catholicism as an issue, no national candidate has been able to figure out a way to be the Protestant candidate.

Will religion be an issue if a Jew runs for President in the 1970's? Perhaps less so than we might imagine. A Gallup Poll in 1969 showed that only 8% would not vote for a candidate *because* he was Jewish. Gallup data from 1937 showed 46% would not vote for a candidate because he was Jewish. Of course, Barry Goldwater was born of a Jewish father, but as Harry Golden said ruefully: "I always knew the first Jewish President would be an Episcopalian."

With the exceptions of blacks and Latin Americans, the Jews in the United States are the most solidly liberal-Democratic bloc in the entire electorate. Thus, in 1968, Jews voted 81% for Humphrey. During the years of Franklin Roosevelt the proportion was even higher, according to the studies of Lawrence H. Fuchs in *The Political Behavior of American Jews*. Jewish voting patterns are generally unique in that the vote is usually a liberal and Democratic one even among the wealthy and well educated. Among the non-Jewish well-to-do the trend among the wealthy and well educated goes the other way: Republican.

The so-called ethnic vote is hard to calculate. For how many generations does an Italian-American family remain under the influence of the first half of the hyphenation? How does one classify the children of a Polish father and an Italian mother who moved recently from an in-city "Little Italy" to a suburban neighborhood called Piney Grove? Or, as the late Joseph P. Kennedy, Sr., said, "How long do I have to live here to be an American?"

Yet the ethnics exist, or at least there are many precincts where 70% or 80% of the voters are of Italian, or Slavic, or Mexican origin. For the most part, ethnics have tended to vote Democratic:

ETHNIC GROUPS, VOTE FOR PRESIDENT, 1968

	Humphrey %	Nixon %	Wallace %
Latin Americans			
East (mostly Puerto Ricans)	81	16	3
South (mostly Mexican Americans)	92	7	1
West (mostly Mexican Americans)	81	17	2
Slavic	65	24	11
Italian	51	39	10

(NBC data)

The "solid" Democratic-liberal group is clearly the "Latin-American" one.

Of more than passing psephological interest is the fact that ethnics are dying out in America and becoming a smaller percentage of the total population. In 1940, Americans of foreign stock (*i.e.*, first- or second-generation) constituted 26% of the population. Twenty years later, in 1960, the foreign stock constituted 18% of the population. An estimate for 1970 shows the foreign stock at 15%, and in ethnic neighborhoods all over America the remark one hears is the same: "All the kids are moving out to the suburbs."

On the surface of it, at least, this data would tend to say that as the masses of immigrants and their children breed and die out, then it may be said that ethnicism in American political life may be dying out also. A first-generation Polish stevedore from Brooklyn via Krakow may feel "Polish." His grandson, the electrician who lives in Hempstead, Long Island, may feel more like an "electrician from Hempstead" than like a "Pole." But even this is too simple. As Nathan Glazer and Daniel Moynihan have pointed out in *Beyond the Melting Pot,* the ethnic feelings may last for far longer than the point when, after two generations, the Census stops classifying people as "foreign stock." Surely, tens of millions of Americans still feel deep ties and ethnic, racial, or religious allegiance as Poles, Hungarians, Jews, blacks, Italians, Mexicans—as well as "just plain Americans." And frequently they still vote along these ethnic lines, and politicians can still attempt all the ethnic appeals with some success. In certain areas, a politician can do worse than to be found with his mouth full of blintzes and knishes, or kielbasa, or soul food.

A middle-aged, middle-income, high-school-educated, white Protestant, who works with his hands, decreasingly ethnic—our portrait of the Middle Voter is beginning to emerge. What else? Generally metropolitan, and increasingly suburban, following the pattern of the American postwar hegira: from farms to cities, from cities to suburbs.

U.S. POPULATION DISTRIBUTION

	1950 %	1960 %	1968 %	*Gain in Population, 1950–68*
Central cities	35%	32%	29%	6 million
Suburb	24	31	35	32 million (!)
Small cities, towns and rural	41	37	36	9 million

Those are population figures; the *voting* figures are about the same, but give the suburbanite a one-point bonus for a higher participation rate:

VOTERS BY PLACE OF RESIDENCE, 1968

	% of Electorate
Central cities	29.6%
Suburbs	35.6%
Small cities, towns and farms	34.8%

Among many of the biggest, and oldest, metropolitan areas the voting figures etch in sharp relief this demographic movement from city to suburb. Comparing the 1948 election to the 1968 election, one finds that New York City *lost* more than half a million voters, while the suburbs around New York City (Westchester, Nassau, and Suffolk counties) gained 750,000 voters. The city of Chicago *lost* 400,000 voters; the Chicago suburbs *gained* 500,000. The city of Minneapolis: down 40,000; the Minneapolis suburbs: up 160,000. The term "central cities" refers to cities with populations of 50,000 or more. Accordingly, 2 of every 3 American voters live in or near (suburb) a large city. About an additional 15% live in cities of between 10,000 and 50,000. Accordingly, it is fair to view most of the American electorate as metropolitan or, alternately, as urban.

And where are these metropolitan areas? On the next page is a map that shows where Americans live:

Because, at least through 1968, the state has been the basic unit of Presidential politics, it is very important to note in which *states* these metropolitan areas lie. And unless a national popular vote replaces the electoral college,* then the *state* will remain of vital importance to political strategists.

There has been much talk of a Southern Strategy, a Border State Strategy, a Sun State Strategy, each supposedly designed to corral enough states to win an election for Republicans. Those are excellent strategies to convince your opponents to use. As for the authors, our geographic strategy is an elementary one called Quadcali. It is the essence of simplicity. If one draws a *quad*rangle from Massachusetts to Washington, D.C., to Illinois, to Wisconsin, and then adds in *Cali*fornia, it includes a majority

---

* Which is doubtful for 1972, possible for 1976.

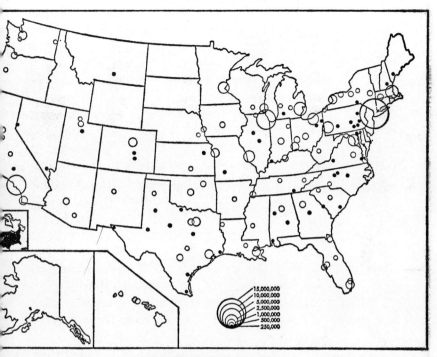

POPULATION DISTRIBUTION: 1960

of Americans. Where Americans live, they vote. Where a majority of them live and vote is where Presidents are elected.

In all, 266 electoral votes are needed to win. It is estimated that Quadcali will comprise about 300 electoral votes after the 1970 census.

Of the sixteen states in Quadcali, all but one (Indiana*) are either Democratic or close—the Republican margin of victory being no higher than 4.5% and usually slimmer than that. In a tidal year, all those close states can drop like a row of falling dominoes—a familiar image. Carry Quadcali—win the election. Lose Quadcali—lose the election. Split Quadcali close—and it

---

* Which is more than balanced by Minnesota, Maine, Hawaii, Texas, and the state of Washington, all non-Quadcalian states that voted Democratic.

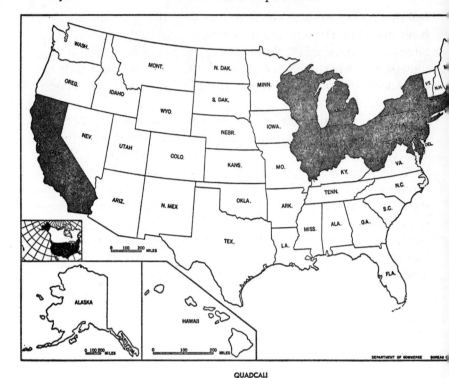

QUADCALI

will be a close election that no book can tell you about in advance.

So there you have it: Middle Voter. A metropolitan Quadcalian, middle-aged, middle-income, middle-educated, Protestant,* in a family whose working members work more likely with hands than abstractly with head.

Think about that picture when you consider the American power structure. Middle Voter is a forty-seven-year-old housewife from the outskirts of Dayton, Ohio, whose husband is a machinist. She very likely has a somewhat different view of life and politics from that of a twenty-four-year-old instructor of political science at Yale. Now the young man from Yale may

---

* Quadcalians would tend to be more Catholic than the rest of the country, but still predominantly Protestant.

feel that he *knows* more about politics than the machinist's wife from suburban Dayton, and of course, in one sense he does. But he does not know much about politics, or psephology, unless he understands what is bothering that lady in Dayton and unless he understands that her circumstances in large measure dictate her concerns.

To know that the lady in Dayton is afraid to walk the streets alone at night, to know that she has a mixed view about blacks and civil rights because before moving to the suburbs she lived in a neighborhood that became all black, to know that her brother-in-law is a policeman, to know that she does not have the money to move if her new neighborhood deteriorates, to know that she is deeply distressed that her son is going to a community junior college where LSD was found on the campus —to know all this is the beginning of contemporary political wisdom.

6

The Center

Having noted a few of the seminal events that have affected voters (like riots and student disruptions), having touched on the life circumstances of the voters (the middle-agedness and middle-classness of the woman in Dayton), we can now consider a related area: the swirling pool of voter attitudes.

It is attitudes, or ideology, that play a large part in motivating voters when they enter the voting booth. It is attitudes that can form an electoral tide. And the swirling attitudinal pool, as we will see, is a pool of paradox.

In terms of political viewpoints, we may look at Gallup Poll results from the fall of 1963 and from the summer of 1969, polls in which voters were asked to place themselves in those much-used and much misused categories: liberal and conservative. Here are the results:

	Conservative	Liberal	No Opinion
Summer, 1969*	51%	33%	16%
Fall, 1963	46%	49%	5%
			(Gallup)

* Confirmed by roughly comparable Gallup data in April, 1970.

The percentage of liberals has dropped sharply, while the conservative view has risen slightly; results, incidentally, that are backed up by other polling data. Those of "no opinion" have tripled. These "no opinions" include, we presume, the plain confused—a not necessarily illogical choice in a confused era.

But the 1969 data can also be seen in a somewhat more sophisticated way:

Summer, 1969

Conservative	Moderately Conservative	Moderately Liberal	Liberal	No Opinion
23%	28%	18%	15%	16%
				(Gallup)

which shows clearly the power of the political center, even in an allegedly conservative era. A candidate perceived of as purely a liberal or purely a conservative is relatively weak. Only with the added weight of the "moderate" label does a candidate come to even a mildly powerful position. The moderate conservatives plus the straight conservatives have the highest combined total (51%), while the combination of moderate conservatives and moderate liberals are close behind with 46%. The two liberal groupings, reflecting the recent liberal nose dive, trail well behind at 33%.

Note above that the highest single group is moderate conservative. Now in the normal order of things in America—at least in modern Presidential politics—moderate conservative spells *Republican*, while moderate liberal spells *Democratic*. Unfortunately, for those who seek neatness in political life, it doesn't seem to work out that way:

POLITICAL PARTY IDENTIFICATION

Question: "In politics, as of today, do you consider yourself a Republican, Democrat or Independent?"

	Republican	Democrat	Independent
July 1969	28%	42%	30%
July 1968	27%	46%	27%
			(Gallup)

The Democrats, generally perceived as the more liberal party in America, are still far ahead of the less liberal Republicans, even though the percentage of Democrats has declined somewhat in recent years.

There is, then, an apparent *non sequitur* between political ideology and party allegiance. When it comes to a specific issue, which holds sway: ideology or partisanship?

Question: "When new appointments are made by the President to the Supreme Court, would you like to have these people be people who are liberal or conservative in their political views?"

	Liberal	Conservative	No Opinion
April 1970	27%	49%	24%

Political ideology would seem to be of overriding importance, which then leads us to ask: What does "conservative" mean in the context of the 1970's? And in answering that, we come to a paradox within a paradox.

On the more obvious Social Issue problems, public opinion is massively arrayed on the so-called conservative side:

Question: "In general, would you like to see college administrations take a stronger stand on student disorders, or not?"

	Yes	No	No Opinion
Early June 1969	94%	3%	3%

Question: "A Negro organization is asking American churches and synagogues to pay 500 million dollars to Negroes because of past injustices. How do you feel about this—would you favor or oppose this being done?"

	Favor	Oppose	No Opinion
Late June 1969	4%	90%	6%

Question: "Here are some questions about obscene literature sent through the mails . . . would you like to see stricter State and local laws dealing with such literature, or not?"

	Yes	No	No Opinion
Late May 1969	85%	8%	7%

Question: "Do you think the use of marijuana should be made legal or not?"

	Should	Should Not	No Opinion
October 1969	12%	84%	4%

(Gallup)

So one-sided are these results that we may predicate that it may well be the feeling about the Social Issue that has been moving voters to say they are "conservative."

But on the non-Social Issues there seems to have been a move toward liberal, not conservative, attitudes. For example, Harris asked the public what they "felt bad about":

Say They "Often Feel Bad" Over the Way:

	1965	1969
Some people in U.S. still go hungry	50%	63%
Older people have been neglected	35%	52%
American Indian has been treated	24%	42%
Some people in big cities still live in slums	31%	37%
Negroes have been treated	31%	35%

(Harris, June 1, 1969)

These feelings of guilt are translatable into feelings about programs. President Nixon's welfare program was generally hailed by liberals and by a wide plurality of the public as well.

Question: "All in all, do you tend to favor or to oppose President Nixon's new welfare program?"

	Total Public
Favor	47%
Oppose	17%
Not Sure	36%

(Harris, October 1969)

And these feelings are translated into priorities:

Question: "I want to give you this list of government programs. Which ONE of these government programs would you most like to see kept or even increased, if you had to choose one?"

	Keep or Increase %	Cut First %
Anti-crime, law enforcement programs	22	1
Aid to education	19	1
Anti-poverty program	17	6
Medicaid	9	2
Anti-air and anti-water pollution programs	8	2
Welfare and relief	8	10
Aid to cities	3	5
Subsidies to farmers	4	7
Financing Vietnam war	4	18
Build for highways	2	9
Space program	2	39

(*Harris, February 1969*)

a generally "liberal" set of priorities. "Crime" is number one, but about tripled by combining the traditional social welfare items: education, poverty, medical care, pollution, etc.

Some of these, such as Medicaid, poverty programs, aid to cities, are issues that five or ten or fifteen years ago would have been considered rather far out for middle-of-the-roaders. Today they are clearly in the mainstream. Today the voters are all for coping with the crisis of the cities, for fighting pollution, for better health care—all the liberal goals of only a few years ago.

Insofar as the political eye can see, this is the apparent paradox of attitude in the seventies: conservative on the Social Issue, liberal on the bread-and-butter issues. Barring for a moment any unforeseen events or issues, it would seem that the party and candidates that will best understand how to cope with these apparently contrary public attitudes will be well on the way toward a strategy for victory.

Now strategies are easy to come by in politics. For example, the reader of the previous chapters on demography may feel qualified now to give strategic advice to a potential Presidential candidate as follows: "Mr. Candidate," the reader may say, "I read a book that says forget blacks, poor people, young people, Jews, intellectuals, Catholics, ethnic minorities, Southerners, and the residents of thirty-five states."

As our reader finds himself unhired and unwanted as adviser

to Presidents, he may brood on the fact that he has made two mistakes—misguided the candidate and misread the chapter.

Granted, as demonstrated, that many of the blocs are either too small, or not solidly deliverable, or probably unswitchable, suppose one were to start putting together some pieces? A nickel here, a dime there, can it add up to the fare to 1600 Pennsylvania Avenue?

There is a phrase for that nickel-and-dime strategy: the politics of coalition. And around that phrase hums the liveliest of the current political debates—and perhaps the most misunderstood. The first step toward understanding is to realize that "coalition" is not a dirty word, for politicians, old or new; in a diverse nation of 205,000,000 people, no majority can be formed unless groups coalesce behind a single leader.

During the 1968 primary campaign Senator McCarthy taunted Senator Kennedy for resorting to Old Politics in that year of New Politics. High on McCarthy's grievance list was the fact that the Kennedy organization had established, as McCarthy put it, "twenty-six separate varieties of Americans—like twenty-six varieties of ice cream."

It was indeed so. Here is the alphabetical list of RFK campaign committees:

Academic
Architects and Engineers
Arts
Businessmen
Communications
Doctors
Editors and Publishers
Entertainment
Farmers
Former Public Officials
Labor-Civil Service
Law Enforcement Officials
Lawyers
Philanthropoids
Republicans

Scientists and Engineers
Senior Citizens
Sports
State and Local Public Officials
Teachers
Clergy
Indians
Nationalities
Negroes
Social Workers
Spanish Speaking
Students
Veterans
Women's Groups
Ex-Peace Corps-Ex-VISTA

This sort of demographic politics is indeed Old Politics* and coalition politics, but that is not the relevant question. Far more important is this: Is it effective coalition politics?

Senator McCarthy's strategic alternative to what he saw as "jigsaw puzzle" politics was what he called a "constituency of conscience." This would be an appeal to Americans, not as Italians or Jews or blacks or union members, but as thoughtful citizens concerned with certain issues that affect *all* Americans. In our lexicon that would be a Voting Issue referred to in Chapter 3, although Senator McCarthy may not necessarily have seen the same issue the authors saw.

It is the judgment of the authors that there are no two strategies for victory—they are the same strategy with different rhetoric. This single strategy involves a drive toward the center of the electorate, a drive to gain the vote of the forty-seven-year-old woman from Dayton, Ohio, or, if you prefer, a *coalition that incorporates a large piece of the attitudinal center,* understanding that this attitudinal center can move from year to year. As described in this chapter, and elaborated on in the remainder of this book, this moving attitudinal center today involves progressivism on economic issues and toughness on the Social Issue. Clean up the slums; clean up the environment. Clean out the criminals; clean out the drugs.

The drive toward the attitudinal center is crucial in politics because it produces the maximum number of votes, and, as is well known, the man with the most votes wins. That is, perhaps, too obvious to mention here, but it is surprising how often it is forgotten. When a candidate or a party takes noncentrist positions, he or it is vulnerable to attack by a centrist, and he will lose votes. In a most simplistic way for the moment: On a total scale of 100, a candidate taking a position of 25 on an attitudinal question gives his opponent all the votes from 26 to 100. On the other hand, a candidate taking a position at 49 or 50 or even 51 begins to cut into his opponent's vote.

---

* And bipartisan politics. The Republicans had similar organizations in 1968. So did the Humphrey campaign.

This becomes more complicated in a three- or four-man race (as will be seen). It becomes further complicated when we understand that a politician can often change public attitudes, as well as follow them; he can sometimes move the center. But the principle remains valid. A candidate announcing that he favors legalization of pot allows his opponent to say that while he is against legalizing pot, he is for "reducing punishment for pot smoking" and also for appointing a "study commission to examine the possibility of legalization," as well as a "broad program of education and medical care for the addicted."

Such a centrist position cuts the flank of the extremist and produces a maximum amount of support. On the other extreme, a conservative candidate might foolishly take a position espousing concentration camps for pot smokers. This would allow the liberal candidate to come out with the centrist position and say that while he is against concentration camps for pot smokers, he "deplores the use of pot," but he understands the problem and *he* is for a "commission to study the problem" as well as a "broad program of education and medical care for the addicted."

This may sound cynical; it is not. The jousting for the center in politics is only a craven way of expressing a far nobler sentiment: Politicians in a democratic form of government are in business to represent the will of the majority of the people (without trampling on minority rights). Politicians represent the public by establishing a position that most of the public can accept or by educating and convincing the public that their position is best—usually a mixture of both. A politician must either go to where the ducks are or convince the ducks he is where they want to be. But the final choice is the choice of the ducks, not of the politicians.

The most important practical characteristic of a potentially winning "coalition of attitude" is that it must occupy a substantial part of the middle ground. Leapfrogging doesn't usually work, although even the hoariest of political professionals occasionally give it a whirl.

In 1968 candidate Nixon tried his hand at it. He noted all the New Left rhetoric about decentralization and giving people "control of their own destiny"—and he said, in effect, "Join the Republican Party; that's what we've believed in all along." But it didn't work: Anti-Establishment hyperliberals were not about to team up with the Republican bankers in blue suits. They don't think alike, even if their rhetoric occasionally coincides.

There has also been much speculation about a new coalition of intellectuals, the urban poor, and the suburban affluent. This is a doubtful mix because there is a lack of common attitudes on many issues and because the opposition can take the vast quantity of unpoor, unrich votes—the middle-class votes that constitute the substantial majority of the electorate.

To understand attitudinal coalition-making is to understand that the Wallace right is not about to team up with the Cleaver left. As shown later, the Reagan right will not likely coalesce with the Rockefeller left at a Republican convention, save for the most ephemeral of political goals. The "coalitions" that politicians talk about are, after all, composed of people, not idiots. Coalitions are formed when different groups of voters have common attitudes and can benefit themselves by uniting around a candidate or a party that responds to such common attitudes. Coalitions can rarely be formed artificially, or arbitrarily, or mechanistically. The vaunted FDR Coalition was not a collection of stray political animals herded unsuspectingly into a corral by canny political cowboys. They were tens of millions of Americans who *felt* commonly about certain issues—mostly economic issues—and voted for the man who they felt acted in their interest. That this coalition could be described demographically—*i.e.,* blacks, union labor, Jews, etc.—was because demography influences attitude, not because some political boss could deliver a bloc vote.

We repeat: The winning coalition in America is the one that holds the center ground on an attitudinal battlefield. In the years until the election of 1968, the battlefield had been mostly an economic battlefield, and the Democrats held the ideological allegiance of the machinist and his wife from the suburbs of Dayton, and tens of millions of other middle-income, middle-educated, middle-aged voters who wanted a high minimum wage, Social Security, Medicare, union protection, and so on. That seems to be changing. For the seventies, the battlefield shows signs of splitting into two battlefields: the old economic one and the new social one that deals with crime, drugs, racial pressure, and disruption. To the extent that this transformation occurs, then the party and the candidate that can best occupy the center ground of the two battlefields will win the Presidency.

PART THREE

The Ideas at Work

7

Spring Training:

Lyndon Johnson Against Everyone

An American Presidential election involves a three-step prome-
nade: primaries; conventions; general election. At each step the
ideas we have discussed—the Social Issue, the middle-class electorate, the drive for the center—can be observed at work.

Consider, first, the New Hampshire primary, held on a cold
and gusty Tuesday, March 12, 1968. To begin to understand
what happened in New Hampshire, one must understand the
complicated New Hampshire primary ballot* and something of
the strange nature of the American primary system.

To begin, the ballot in New Hampshire is composed of two
parts. Most of the attention is paid to the second part, known
formally as the preference primary and known generically in
the political trade as the beauty contest. It is a straight popularity test: The voter expresses only a *preference* and no commitment or assignment of delegates is involved. At one and the

---

* By no means the most complicated in America. The Scammon-Wattenberg
award for the most complicated and interesting primary ballot goes to Oregon.
That ballot in 1968 offered roughly 220 separate choices, with a no-more-than-
12-word slogan to go with each choice of candidate. Classic slogans demonstrating
the politics of controversy at its fever pitch: "What my fellow Democrats want,
I want" and "Put the U.S. in the driver's seat" and Wayne Morse's "As always,
principle above politics."

same time, then, the beauty contest is the most meaningful and least meaningful part of the ballot in New Hampshire. Defeat in the beauty contest can brand a candidate as an electoral ugly duckling, yet victory brings no branded delegates to the convention floor.

In March, 1968, the Democratic beauty contest in New Hampshire looked this way:

CANDIDATE OF THE

DEMOCRATIC PARTY

FOR

PRESIDENT

OF THE UNITED STATES

I HEREBY DECLARE MY PREFERENCE FOR CANDIDATE FOR THE OFFICE OF PRESIDENT OF THE UNITED STATES TO BE AS FOLLOWS:

JOHN G. CROMMELIN.   ☐

JACOB J. GORDON   ☐

RICHARD E. LEE   ☐

EUGENE J. McCARTHY   ☐

Mr. John G. Crommelin received 186 votes on March 12.
Mr. Jacob J. Gordon received 77 votes.
Mr. Richard E. Lee received 170 votes.
The fourth and final listed candidate in the New Hampshire Democratic beauty contest was the senior Senator from Min-

nesota, Eugene J. McCarthy. He swamped Messrs. Crommelin, Gordon, and Lee—receiving 23,263 votes.

The winner of the Democratic beauty contest appeared in the next spot on the ballot marked _____, where 27,520 voters wrote in the name of President Lyndon B. Johnson.

The percentages of that vote came out to 50% for President Johnson, 42% for Senator McCarthy, with the remaining 8% divided among the minor candidates and the other write-ins, including 2,532 for a Republican, Richard M. Nixon.

Meanwhile, on the *other* side of the New Hampshire Democratic ballot, something else was going on. Twenty-four delegates were being chosen to represent New Hampshire at the Democratic National Convention to be held in August in Chicago.

Using common sense, once considered a hallmark of the Old Politics, the McCarthy New Politicians put up a slate of twenty-four names for the twenty-four vacancies. Eschewing same, the "political pros" running the Johnson campaign allowed forty-five candidates favorable to Johnson to appear on the ballot. The Johnson vote, which went 50–42% on the beauty contest, was split forty-five ways on the delegate selection ballot, and accordingly, McCarthy won almost all the New Hampshire delegates.

Mr. Scammon spent several days in New Hampshire at the time of the primary. The efficient McCarthy organization was visible not only on the ballot, reports Scammon, but all over the state. Every town had its McCarthy headquarters; every headquarters was manned by lean young volunteers. On the other hand, the Johnson effort was dreary, at least in part owing to the President. Johnson himself had not formally announced his candidacy, he did not campaign personally in the state, and there was general disorganization and discombobulation among the organization regulars.

In the Republican beauty contest, the results were clearer:

Nixon	78%
Romney	2%
Others	1%

[*Write-ins*]

Rockefeller	11%
McCarthy	5%
Johnson	2%
Others	1%

Nixon was the landslide victor. In absolute numbers, he received 80,666 votes in the Republican primary, compared to the fewer than 30,000 each that Johnson and McCarthy had received on the Democratic side. Governor George Romney, it should be recalled, had announced several days before the primary that he was withdrawing from the Presidential race. This followed his examination of some private poll results in New Hampshire that indicated he would be a lopsided loser to Nixon.

The write-in results were interesting. Governor Ronald Reagan got only 362 votes. Nelson Rockefeller, who at that point was unannounced for the Presidency, received 11,241. Eugene McCarthy got 5,511 *Republican* votes. Lyndon B. Johnson got 1,778 *Republican* votes.

And so ended the voting: Nixon swamping the Republican field; Johnson edging out McCarthy in the Democratic heat; McCarthy getting most of the Democratic delegates; Nixon winning the Republican delegates.

The most important part of the primary began *after* the votes were counted: the interpretation of the vote and its effect around the country. For Presidential primaries are a thing apart on the American political scene. In a primary for local office, or in a general election, or in a convention election, there are certifiable legal victors. But a Presidential primary in America can be won—legitimately won—by the candidate who claims most effectively that he won, *regardless of vote totals*. And at the root of that notion is the question: What was being contested?

In New Hampshire, in 1968, several items were at issue—perhaps the least of which was the political allegiance of the comparative handful of convention delegates who would represent New Hampshire at the Democratic National Convention in Chicago.

There is an ancient political axiom that goes "You can't beat someone with no one." That constituted the first hurdle that Eugene McCarthy had to leap in 1968, and he did it most effectively in New Hampshire. Announcing for the Presidency in November, 1967, McCarthy was a "no one." An early opinion poll showed that running against a "someone" (Lyndon Johnson), McCarthy would get only 11% of the vote. By coming quite close to the Johnson total, by capturing headlines and television time, McCarthy became a "someone." That is a crucial step in American Presidential politics.

The process by which a potential candidate becomes "someone" is usually performed by the press and certified by public opinion polls well in advance of any Presidential primaries. Only occasionally, as in the McCarthy campaign of 1968, is the process of becoming someone done with skill and gusto by the candidate himself through primary campaigns.*

Score one victory for McCarthy.

The corollary to "You can't beat someone with no one" is, obviously, "You can beat someone with someone." And there is not too much distance between that thought and the idea of challenging another ancient political axiom: "You can't beat a sitting President if he wants renomination," an axiom that has much solid historical weight behind it.

For McCarthy's campaign (and subsequently, Kennedy's campaign) to become serious, the notion that a sitting President could not be denied nomination had to be challenged. This was a second item at issue in New Hampshire.

In New Hampshire that notion *was* challenged by McCarthy's strong showing. Not *refuted*, by any means, for many observers still think that President Johnson probably could have been renominated had he stayed in the race, but the notion was certainly *challenged*. There was doubt about the proposition where before there was surety, and that doubt was essential to both the McCarthy and Kennedy campaigns.

Score two solid victories for McCarthy.

---

* Senator Estes Kefauver and Senator John Kennedy were better known than Senator McCarthy, but they, too, became "household words" by running the gauntlet of Presidential primaries.

There was a third proposition also being tested in the New Hampshire primary. Senator McCarthy claimed to have scored on this one as well, indeed as Senator Kennedy claimed later to score on it. The proposition was this: "The primaries represented a yes-no referendum on Vietnam, and the American people voted no."

It is our contention that this McCarthy/Kennedy contention was wrong—that the New Hampshire primary, or any other subsequent primary, demonstrated neither a substantive no vote nor a substantive yes vote on Vietnam. In fact, quite a different substantive item was on the electoral anvil during much of the 1968 election season: the Social Issue.

Obviously, the determination of whether it was Vietnam or the Social Issue that motivated the voters in 1968 is crucial to the thesis of this book. If American voting behavior in the 1968 primaries was based on "Vietnam—Yes" versus "Vietnam—No," then the 1968 situation might well be viewed as a one-wave election *à la* the 1964 Goldwater defeat, certainly so if by 1972 American troops are no longer dying in Vietnam. If, on the other hand, the Social Issue was being tested in 1968, we were conceivably watching the beginning of a tide. Waves make interesting history. Tides can tell us something about the future.

The dove perspective of the 1968 election has been widely chronicled in a host of books. It can be summed up briefly here: McCarthy ran stronger than expected in New Hampshire. He won the primary in Wisconsin. In Indiana, Nebraska, Oregon, and California, the combined votes of McCarthy and Kennedy ranged between 70% and 87%. Because it was opposition to the war in Vietnam that brought both McCarthy and Kennedy into the race, because it was opposition to the war in Vietnam that fired up their supporters, ergo, it was opposition to Vietnam that was being voiced by the American electorate.

The view of the authors is different.

First, let us examine some data about Vietnam accumulated about the time of the New Hampshire primary. What were Americans thinking about the war?

Item: In the aftermath of the Tet offensive, as the New Hampshire primary approached, dove sentiment was growing:

	"Hawk"	*"Dove"*	*"No Opinion"*
March	41%	42%	17%
February	60%	24%	16%
			(Gallup)

but doves were at best about half the population.

Item: Another series of polls taken throughout the election season showed that Vietnam was the "number one problem" in America. (At the end of 1967, Gallup showed almost 60% indicating that Vietnam was the number one problem.)

Item: Assuming that McCarthy, alone on the New Hampshire ballot, represented a "peace candidate," he received only 18% of the *combined* Democratic and Republican vote:

NEW HAMPSHIRE PRIMARY TOTAL VOTE

	Votes Received	*Percent of Total Vote*
Nixon	83,198	52.2%
Johnson	29,298	18.4%
McCarthy	28,774	18.1%
Others	18,132	11.4%

If peace was the driving issue, the Voting Issue as it were, Republican voters anxious to cast a peace ballot could write in McCarthy—5,511 did, in fact, do so. (Mr. Nixon, we should remember, as of the date of the New Hampshire primary, was considered at least as much of a hawk as President Johnson.)

Item: The University of Michigan Survey Research Center polls show that three out of five *of the McCarthy supporters* in New Hampshire believed that the Johnson administration was wrong on Vietnam because it was not hawkish *enough,* not because it was *too* hawkish.

What can we make of all this? The first two items are *national* data and not likely to reflect precisely the feeling in New Hampshire. Still, neither are New Hampshire attitudes likely to be far off the national norms on such a major issue. So, then, there are some apparent contradictions. The dove attitude was held by somewhere between 24% and 42% of the people. Yet, as we have seen among New Hampshiremen, only 18% voted for the only "peace candidate" in the New Hampshire race, Eugene McCarthy. Clearly, then, some dovish voters went for Nixon, or Johnson, both nondoves. And McCarthy's support came more from hawks than doves, according to the Survey Research Center data. Yet Gallup shows that Americans regarded Vietnam as the number one problem, and clearly McCarthy and Kennedy were drawn into an anti-Johnson challenge because of Vietnam policy.

In sorting it out, three thoughts emerge that seem to fill the round holes with round pegs. There is, first, the *policy* judgment that Americans seem to have made about Vietnam during 1968. Basically, the data seem to show that the voters were prepared to go glumly along with the Johnson military policy. About a quarter (27% in mid-March, Gallup) felt the United States should go all out with atomic weapons and "win" in Vietnam. These were the strong hawks. About a sixth (17% in mid-March, Harris) felt that unilateral withdrawal was the answer. These were the committed doves. But the vast middle of the population gave grudging acquiescence to the President's middle course on the war whether they told the pollster that they were hawks or told him they were doves. They apparently had no better solutions than the Commander in Chief, but this didn't necessarily make them happy about it all. This general malaise about the war—not an ideological hawk versus dove feeling—was to be one factor among several that were to lead to the generalized anti-Johnson feeling that will be examined in a moment.

The second thought is *political*. The Vietnam War *did* raise an eloquent challenge within the Democratic Party and did bring into the Presidential contest two able and charismatic political personalities, McCarthy and Robert Kennedy. Later, with the same essential motivation, George McGovern announced his candidacy. Vietnam, then, was a powerful political catalyst, most powerful in the manner in which it caused turmoil within the Democratic Party.

The third thought is *psephological*. Although Americans in massive numbers felt that Vietnam was our most serious problem—which it likely was—and although McCarthy and later Robert Kennedy were running because of Vietnam, it was not the essential issue on which votes swung yea or nay. Vietnam was not the Voting Issue of 1968. This is not an unfamiliar paradox. World War II was certainly our number one issue, but while it was in progress, it was not the issue over which people voted for or against President Roosevelt. And so too with Vietnam (although, obviously, there was far greater dissatisfaction with Vietnam than with World War II).

Johnson did not get his slim New Hampshire write-in victory because New Hampshiremen were pro-Vietnam. Nixon did not get his victory because New Hampshiremen were pro-Vietnam. McCarthy did not get his 42% in New Hampshire or later his 56% vote in Wisconsin because the voters were anti-Vietnam. If Vietnam *were* the Voting Issue, Johnson would have won, not lost, in Wisconsin (as we shall see); hawks would not have voted for McCarthy; Nixon would not have so conclusively trounced his more dovish competition (Romney, Rockefeller, and McCarthy Republican write-ins). Finally, in a jump way ahead of our story, had "80% of the American people been voting dovish" (the dove claim), one could wager his last psephological dollar on the idea that either Mr. Nixon, Mr. Humphrey, or Mr. Wallace—or all three—would have emerged as dove candidates. Politicians respond to 80% desires of the electorate—and respond fast. Briefly, then, the candidates and the press were talking Vietnam; the voters were not voting it.

A crucial question now presents itself. If Americans, in 1968, weren't essentially voting no to the ideology of our military involvement in Vietnam, why did McCarthy run so well in New Hampshire, win in Wisconsin, and, with Kennedy, get a combined vote of between 70% and 87% in the remaining four major primaries?

Beyond the previously mentioned feeling of nonideological malaise on Vietnam, there are (at least) two answers, each intertwined with the other, each variously and selectively operative in the key 1968 primaries. First, there was another issue that was motivating voters—an extremely potent one—the Social Issue. This included deep concern about crime, race, narcotics, alienation. It also included a feeling against the dissent and disruption engendered by the Vietnam protesters. In New Hampshire and Wisconsin this intense feeling about the full range of the Social Issue concerns became fully mixed in with Vietnam malaise, crystallized, and took a political half step to surface clearly with a different label: "anti-Johnsonism."

Second, after Wisconsin, Kennedy and McCarthy were essentially the only active candidates on the Democratic primary ballots.

For evidence concerning the Social Issue one can look to the opinion polls. At about the time of the New Hampshire primary, when Mr. Gallup's pollsters were asking voters about their opinions on Vietnam, they were also asking other questions. And on February 28, 1968, the Gallup organization released the results of a survey whose headline read as follows: CRIME TOPS ALL DOMESTIC WORRIES FOR FIRST TIME IN POLLING HISTORY.

The question asked was: "What do you think is the most important problem facing this country today?"

The top two domestic problems listed by Gallup were (1) "Crime and lawlessness (including riots, looting, juvenile delinquency)" and (2) "Civil Rights."

It is fruitful now to look at the "problems" of crime and race at greater length.

In the same February, 1968, survey, Gallup also asked a question that he had polled three years earlier: *"In general, do you think the courts in this area deal too harshly, or not harshly enough with criminals?"* The response:

	April 1965	Feb. 1968
"Not harshly enough"	48%	63%
"Too harshly"	2%	2%
"About right"	34%	19%
"No Opinion"	16%	16%

A sharp rise in the "not harshly enough" category. But that criminals were being treated too leniently is really only an abstract thought to most Americans. However, Gallup also asked a more personal question: *"Is there any area around here—that is, within a mile—where you would be afraid to walk alone at night?"*

The yes vote was:

National	35%*
By Sex:	
Men	19%
Women	50%

* Thirty-eight percent in the East. New Hampshire is in the East.

One way of verbalizing the social dynamite inherent in these figures is to phrase it this way: *Half the husbands in America have wives who are afraid to go out at night.*

Or to put that thought in Mr. Wallace's mouth and watch it become even more volatile:

> If you walk out of this hotel tonight and someone knocks you on the head, he'll be out of jail before you're out of the hospital, and on Monday morning, they'll try the policeman instead of the criminal.
> . . . But some psychologist says, "Well, he's not to blame—society's to blame. His father didn't take him to see the Pittsburgh Pirates when he was a little boy." Well, I was raised in a house that didn't even have an indoor toilet. My mama couldn't even buy me a dollar and fifteen cent cowboy suit that I saw in the Sears Roebuck window. But I didn't go and bust the window out to get it.

Clearly tens of millions of Americans were upset by crime and violence. Somewhat later in the year, Harris surveyed a more general pair of questions on the same subject that gives further definition of the magnitude of the feeling as well as a clue to "who is to blame," as perceived by the public:

	Agree	*Disagree*	*Not Sure*
"Law and order has broken down in this country"	81%	14%	5%
"A strong President can make a big difference in directly preserving law and order"	84%	10%	6%

(Harris, September, 1968)

At the time this poll was taken Richard Nixon was not President. Neither was Eugene McCarthy President. Lyndon Johnson was.

It is, of course, highly debatable whether, in fact, a President, who has no control of local or state police, can indeed do much to preserve the day-to-day law and order of a community. But when one views the numbers above, it is not debatable that the electorate *feels* that way, for 84% believe Presidents "can make a big difference." Mayors, who actually control the local constabulary, would probably rate even higher than Presidents on this "can make a big difference" scale, and this was reflected in many mayoralty races in 1969. But mayors were not running in New Hampshire. Lyndon Johnson was.

An appropriate syllogism to view Johnson's position, as his New Hampshire write-in drive was mounted, might be this one, as perceived from a voter's-eye-view:

1. Law and order have broken down.
2. I am against law and order breaking down.
3. Presidents make a big difference in preserving law and order.
4. Johnson is President.
5. It's his fault.
6. I'll vote for the other guy.

This is a little simple, of course. But clearly, too, "law and order" was working against Johnson. Whenever a couple from the suburbs voted with their feet and decided not to come into the city for dinner on Saturday night because of "crime," whenever a city family moved to the suburbs because of "crime," one of the political losers was the incumbent President.

If the public's attitude toward the number one domestic problem ("crime") is clear enough, the public attitude concerning the number two domestic problem ("civil rights") is much more complex. Inordinately more complex.

There was a time during the election of 1968 when it was fashionable to maintain that "law and order" was a code phrase for "racism" or, alternately, "crime in the streets" was a code phrase for "I hate niggers."

There is a measure of truth to that. There was, and is, a clear attitudinal spillover and linkage from the crime issue to the race issue. Thus, in Harris's early September, 1968, poll, fully 59% of American voters indicated that "Negroes who start riots" are one of the "major causes" in the "breakdown of law and order in this country." Harris also showed that 42% of whites felt that blacks are "more violent than whites" and that 33% of whites believe that blacks "breed crime."

There is, in addition to the crime linkage, out-and-out prejudice in the United States. In September, 1968, Harris asked American voters whether they agreed with certain statements about blacks. Harris found that about a quarter (24%) of all whites felt that blacks are *"inferior to whites."* Not quite half of all whites (44%) felt that blacks have *"less native intelligence than whites."* Somewhat more than six in ten whites felt that blacks have *"less ambition than whites."*

That is the measure of undiluted race feeling in America. None of those racial stereotypes has, in itself, any immediate and necessary contact point with the political system. No longer do politicians in America run on a stated platform of white supremacy, not even in the deepest South. But also on the Harris scale of stereotypes was this statement about blacks: *"[They] are asking for more than [they are] ready for."* That statement was agreed with by fully two-thirds of the whites (67%). And that statement, clearly, *has* a direct and immediate political contest point—*i.e.,* if they're *asking,* we're *denying.*

Expressing that idea somewhat more programmatically, Harris, in October, asked if *"the progress in civil rights should be speeded up."*

72% of Negroes said yes
28% of Whites said yes

There is also a specific partisan cast to the race issue. In May, one part of a Harris questionnaire asked the voters to identify whether or not specific candidates were in favor of "speeding up" racial progress. The results:

PUBLIC'S VIEWS OF CANDIDATES VIEWS ON "SPEED-UP" OF RACIAL PROGRESS

	Is in favor of racial progress speed-up
George Wallace (Am. Ind.)	5%
Ronald Reagan (Rep.)	15%
Richard Nixon (Rep.)	21%
Eugene McCarthy (Dem.)	34%
Nelson Rockefeller (Rep.)	38%
Hubert Humphrey (Dem.)	46%
Robert Kennedy (Dem.)	69%

Democrats, clearly, are more in favor of "racial progress speed-up" than are Republicans. There is only one major political personality missing from that survey—when the poll was taken in May, 1968, Lyndon Johnson was no longer a candidate. But if there is any doubt about which part of the spectrum he would fall into, note that another Harris poll showed these results to the question of *whether President Johnson was doing a good job:*

Negroes	85%
Whites	39%

It would seem, then, like a bad season for Democrats. Crime is linked to blacks, blacks are linked to Democrats—that would seem to spell disaster.

But there is a great paradox to the American public's view about the racial situation, and it is this paradox that draws the lines around the Voting Issue of our electoral era.

It is easy, and easily verifiable, to say, as President Nixon has said, "that Americans have had it up to here with lawlessness," but it is neither easy nor verifiable to say that "Americans have had it up to here with blacks."

For at the same time the Harris data showed that there is still a measure of white racism, that whites link blacks to crime, and that whites feel blacks want too much, other Harris data showed a different face of the white American's view of blacks.

Thus Harris asked for agreement or disagreement on the statement that *"Until there is justice for minorities, there will not be law and order."* By a vote of 63% to 27% Americans agreed. *Agreed.*

In the same poll that showed that 66% of whites felt that Negroes had gone too far in their demands, there were also 58% that agreed that *"America has discriminated against Negroes for too long."*

In early 1970, Harris found that 53% favored open housing—compared to 35% three years earlier.

And if there is a rising tide of racism in America, it would be very difficult to discern it in a historical analysis of a Gallup Poll question that asks: ". . . if your party nominated a generally well-qualified man for President and he happened to be a Negro, would you vote for him?"

The results:

	Yes, would vote for a Negro President
1958	38%
1969	67%

The great center of the American public is, clearly, not clear about its racial feelings.

REFLECTIVE: What kind of candidate would mesh with this ambivalent American attitude on the racial question?

Certainly a candidate who came through as a white racist extremist would be rejected by the guilty two-thirds of all American voters who felt that "America has discriminated against Negroes for too long." That would rule out much of the potential centrist base for George Wallace. It was Mr. Wallace, after

*all, who had stood in the schoolhouse door and whose call to
arms was: "Segregation now, segregation tomorrow, segregation
forever."*

*Certainly a candidate like Robert Kennedy or Hubert
Humphrey would encounter voter resistance on this issue. Only
28% of the public was for a "racial progress speed-up," but 46%
of American voters thought Humphrey wanted to speed up
racial progress, and 69% thought RFK was for a speedup.*

*Ideally, then, the candidate to score most heavily on the race
issue would be one who was identified with a middle position.
Musing a bit on that, we might say that most Americans felt
that there was already a good deal of racial progress going on—
civil rights laws, open housing, war on poverty. They might not
like it but they probably thought it was "right." This attitudinal schizophrenia might well balance out at a point of status
quo—that is, keeping the rate of racial progress "as is"—no slow-
down, but no speedup either.*

*Now, what candidate filled that niche in 1968? Earlier, on
pages 97–98, an excerpt from a Harris Poll was shown to demonstrate voter attitudes only on "speed up" of race progress as tied
to specific candidates. Here is the full attitudinal range from
that Harris Poll:*

PUBLIC'S VIEWS OF CANDIDATE VIEWS ON RACIAL PROGRESS

	Slow Down %	Keep as Is %	Speed Up %	Not Sure %
George Wallace	61	8	5	26
Ronald Reagan	24	14	15	47
Richard Nixon	22	*30*	21	27
Eugene McCarthy	8	17	34	41
Nelson Rockefeller	8	19	38	35
Hubert Humphrey	4	24	46	26
Robert Kennedy	4	8	69	19

Note that Richard Nixon is the only *candidate whose "keep
as is" rating is higher than both his "slow down" and "speed
up" rating. Also note that Richard Nixon is the only candidate
whose "keep as is" rating is higher than his "not sure" rating.
The voters, then, were pretty certain about Richard Nixon. He
was in the middle of the road. He is now President.*

It is correct to say, as the Gallup Poll indicated, that Americans viewed crime and race as the number one and number two domestic problems. But to say that crime and race are the sole components of what's bothering Americans would be far too narrow a description.

In November, 1968, as the Presidential year reached its crescendo, Gallup asked Americans, *"Do you believe that life today is getting better or worse in terms of morals?"*
The answer:

Better	Worse	No Change	Don't Know
8%	78%	12%	2%

Gallup asked the same question in eleven other countries. Everywhere the question was asked, people responded "worse" —but nowhere by as high a proportion as in America.

Gallup asked, *"Do you believe that life is getting better or worse in terms of honesty?"* and 61% of Americans said "worse," again the highest of the twelve countries.

Gallup asked, *"Do you believe that life is getting better or worse in terms of happiness?"* The American response—in a land of the highest per capita income, of great prosperity—was:

Better	Worse	No Change	No Opinion
26%	49%	18%	7%

Americans felt "worse" about the happiness thing than any other country except Uruguay.

Gallup asked, *"Do you believe that life today is getting better or worse in terms of peace of mind?"* France, the Netherlands, and Finland had somewhat more people who were unpeaceful of mind, but Americans were still not tranquil by any means:

Better	Worse	No Change	Don't Know
15%	69%	10%	6%

Thus, the "malaise" factor. Americans were unhappy about criminality and about racial problems. They were unhappy about inflation. They were unhappy about Vietnam. They were unhappy with people who were unhappy about Vietnam. They were unhappy about morality, unhappy with hippies, drug takers, students who took over colleges, and, perhaps most of all, unhappy about being unhappy.

Americans were in a bad mood.

And yet, lest anything be stated definitely here, it must be pointed out that even "bad mood" was an ambivalent feeling. When pinned down to certain *specifics* concerning their own well-being, Americans were generally "more satisfied" than they had previously been. Here are Gallup results* published in April, 1969:

Regarding *work,* Americans were satisfied in high proportions, as the numbers show:

	SATISFIED
1969	88%
1949	69%

People generally aren't pleased with their paychecks, nor are their wives; still, the "satisfied with *income*" trend is up:

	SATISFIED
1969	67%
1949	50%

Satisfaction with *housing* also increased:

	SATISFIED
1969	80%
1949	67%

And of course, Americans had some good reasons for satisfaction. By election day of 1968 American voters could look back at eight years of uninterrupted prosperity (since the 1960 recession). Personal incomes had gone up at a record rate, by

---

* Data for whites only.

far offsetting any inflationary rises, and in 1968 unemployment dropped to an eighteen-year low of 3.6%. Americans were more likely than ever before to be working at skilled and interesting jobs, and more young Americans than ever before were being graduated from high school and going on to college. Americans were far less likely to be living in substandard housing, and they were much more likely to be living in suburbs, owning their own houses, surrounded by nice green lawns.

So there is the paradox: Americans had more of the measurable good things in life and apparently were enjoying them less.*

What is moot about this state of affairs is whether or not people generally are *always* dissatisfied and, if that is so, whether they were more dissatisfied in the late 1960's than at other times in America. The field of attitudinal polling is very much in its infancy, and there are no sure answers. The intuitive feeling one gets is that societies, like people, have a cyclical run of "bad moods." Sometimes these moods are related to clear external factors, such as a depression. Sometimes the "bad mood" may be related to factors somewhat less definite, like the Social Issue. And sometimes people are just plain glum for no wholly explicable reason.

Suffice it to say that Americans in 1968 were glum, riled, and rattled—and are so today. Whether this malaise is a common and recurrent phenomenon, whether it is particularly intense now, is debatable. But what does seem to be clear from the data is that the general disquietude has attached itself to certain lightning rods of dissatisfaction: crime, race, morals, disruption—and with the "cost of living" a perennially blooming factor. Vietnam was an additional concern, to be sure, but not entirely an ideological concern, as in "America shouldn't be the world's policeman" or even as in "We ought to bomb them

---

* It was pseudopsephologist Charles Dickens who wrote in 1859: "It was the best of times, it was the worst of times, it was the age of wisdom, it was the age of foolishness, it was the epoch of belief, it was the epoch of incredulity, it was the season of Light, it was the season of Darkness, it was the spring of hope, it was the winter of despair." (*A Tale of Two Cities*, 1859.)

back to the Stone Age." Of probably greater impact was the distress about disruption and disquiet that was caused by the Vietnam situation. Strangely, this disruption worked against LBJ, even though LBJ was the target of this disruption. The President, like it or not, is blamed when the nation is in turmoil. Between crime, race, morals, disruption, and dissent, there was a turmoil in the land, and voters didn't like it, and when they had a chance to vote against the government that was perceived as "at fault," they did so. It was to be a "progovernment" or "antigovernment" vote, reminiscent of the atmosphere of nineteenth-century British politics when Members of Parliament, sitting on opposite sides of the House of Commons, were labeled by the press ministerialists (in favor of the government) and oppositionists (who were in favor of replacing the government). This would be the fashion of the 1968 election: the ministerialists versus the oppositionists, or, in the American style, the ins versus the outs.

This, then, was the paradox of America going into 1968: dissatisfaction amid plenty, discontent with things as they were. As this book goes to press in mid-1970, that description is still valid—and there is no end in sight.

Understanding all this, we can now return to the frosty battlegrounds of New Hampshire and offer a reinterpretation of the ministerialist and oppositionist vote in New Hampshire.

New Hampshiremen, like many Americans, were dissatisfied. The crime rate is low in New Hampshire, but there are plenty of television sets, and in the evening the television sets had for years been showing riots, disruption, racial turmoil, and sounding the rhetoric of social turbulence. There are data indicating that voters living in "safe" neighborhoods may be more upset by "crime" than people living in comparatively "unsafe" neighborhoods. And it is a safe assumption that if 81% of all Americans believed that "law and order has broken down," then a great majority of New Hampshiremen also felt the same way. If 84% of all Americans believed that "the President can make a big difference in directly preserving law and order," then a great majority of New Hampshiremen could be assumed to feel similarly.

New Hampshiremen—mostly unyoung, unpoor, unblack; mostly middle-aged, middle-income folks—were upset by "crime"; they were upset by "race"; they were upset by "morals" and by "youth disruption." New Hampshiremen, like most Americans, were concerned about the rising cost of living, and the McCarthy campaigners were astute enough to exploit it. The "Be Clean for Gene" door-to-door canvassers were advised to remind voters that the war in Vietnam was causing inflation. McCarthy's demeanor, too, worked in his favor as he competed for the psephological center. He was calm, cool, understated, and quiet—the personal antithesis of the very idea of social turbulence.

All these factors, and more, worked against President Johnson, canceling out much of the progress of his administration. A growing anti-Johnson feeling was apparent. In February, 1966, two years before the New Hampshire primary, Gallup reported that by 61% to 27% the voters "approved of the way Johnson is handling his job as President." In February, 1967, one year before the New Hampshire primary, voters approved by a 46% to 37% margin. In February, 1968, about a month before the New Hampshire primary, only 41% approved, while 47% disapproved. And it was to get worse before it got better, as we will see in Wisconsin.

Finally, on March 12, 1968, when New Hampshire Democrats were given a choice on the ballot between Things-as-They-Are (a Johnson write-in) or I-Don't-Like-What-I-See-in-America (a McCarthy check mark), many New Hampshire voters (but not a majority) voted for McCarthy. The soft-spoken Senator from Minnesota, in this analysis, got votes not primarily from Vietniks, but from Fed-up-niks. McCarthy, as the saying goes, was a choice, not an echo. He was also the *only* nonecho on the Democratic ballot; as such, he got votes from New Hampshiremen who were hawkier than LBJ, dovier than LBJ, angry about crime, at blacks, at disruption—angry about almost anything at all.

8

Spring Training:

Exhibition Game Number Two: Wisconsin

The Wisconsin primary on April 2, 1968, was a different cup of tea—but not so different as might appear at first tasting.

On the Democratic side, McCarthy beat Johnson this time, beat him big, and beat him when Johnson's name *was* on the ballot. The final tally was resounding and emphatic:

DEMOCRATIC RESULTS, WISCONSIN PRESIDENTIAL
PREFERENCE PRIMARY, APRIL, 1968

McCarthy	56%
Johnson	35%
Kennedy	6%
Others	3%

It is true that two days before the election President Johnson announced that he would not be a candidate for President, but it is also true that privately taken polls showed Johnson running well behind McCarthy even before his March 31 withdrawal speech. There is every reason to believe that the voting patterns that actually appeared on primary day closely resembled what the totals would have shown had Johnson not dropped out two days before the election.

The McCarthy victory in Wisconsin was striking in many respects. Six months prior to April 2, 1968, Senator McCarthy was virtually unknown as a national politician. On April 2, 1968, the recently unknown Senator beat the incumbent President of the United States by better than a 3 to 2 margin!

There is no tarnishing a victory of that magnitude, nor can the velocity of McCarthy's climb to national prominence be deprecated in any way; it was a meteoric ascent rarely matched in American political annals.

Why did McCarthy win? There are some simple reasons and some not so simple, and in order to understand the Wisconsin results more fully, it is important to look behind the numbers and attempt to assess what the voters were trying to say. The voters decide only who wins; the election observers declare mandates.

First, two simple reasons for McCarthy's impressive Wisconsin showing. One: On a very elementary level, it should be noted that McCarthy ran even stronger in Wisconsin than in New Hampshire precisely because he had run as strong as he had in New Hampshire. In Wisconsin, in a speech to a professional journalism fraternity, McCarthy pointed out that the television stations had stopped running his name under his face during the film clips of his speeches that appeared on the news broadcasts. Robert Walters of the Washington *Star* covered McCarthy in Wisconsin and reported this: "Where once he went unnoticed, people now stop him on the street. When he visited a local television station last week to participate in a news show, the secretaries in the office lined a stairwell to shake his hand as he left the building." That sort of prominence is a major plus for any candidate for any office.

Two: Wisconsin was probably among the most dovish states in the United States. This dovishness derives in large measure from a long heritage of isolationism that goes back at least to the political dominance of Robert La Follette in the early part of this century. "Isolationism," of course, is not necessarily the same as what in 1968 was called dovishness, but both doves and isolationists would vote for McCarthy because he was against American involvement in Vietnam.

But there was a good deal more going on behind the election data than merely McCarthy's new prominence and a dovish propensity in the state. Not quite as obvious as the obvious factors, the Social Issue was apparently percolating in Wisconsin as it was in every other state in America, it was percolating in part as a feeling called anti-Johnson, and it was helping Mc-Carthy.

Consider, first, four somewhat disparate items.

Item: In Madison, home of the University of Wisconsin and probably the most dovish city in a dovish state, an antiwar referendum was on the ballot. On Wednesday morning, April 3, the day after the primary election, this story appeared in the Milwaukee *Journal:*

MADISON TURNS DOWN ANTI-WAR REFERENDUM

Madison, Wis.—A city referendum calling for an immediate cease fire and a withdrawal of United States troops from Vietnam was rejected by almost 7,000 votes here Tuesday.

Madison residents voted 27,533 to 20,679 (58% to 42%) against the proposal. The "yes" vote won in only 10 of the city's 41 precincts.

Strongest support for a "yes" vote came from the University of Wisconsin campus area, where thousands of student voters turned out.

Sen. Eugene McCarthy won all 41 precincts, most strongly in campus area wards.

Item: In mid-March, 1968, shortly before the primary in Wisconsin, the Gallup Poll matched Johnson with McCarthy among *Democratic* voters from *all over the nation.* Johnson led 59% to 29%.

Item: In Milwaukee, there was an election for mayor. From the Milwaukee *Journal,* April 3, 1968:

MAIER WINS, RECEIVED 86% OF VOTES

Mayor Henry W. Maier soared Tuesday to the greatest victory of his twenty year political career, winning re-election to his third four-year term with a record 86% of the vote.

Maier, who gained national prominence last summer for choking off a riot, smashed David L. Walther, a young, liberal attorney, in a victory unprecedented in Milwaukee history. The totals:

Henry W. Maier 172,156
David L. Walther 27,936

The Maier margin was greater than any Milwaukee mayor has achieved.

Maier, who received 86% of the vote in Milwaukee, *was a strong Johnson supporter.* His opponent, David Walther, who received 14% of the vote, *was a McCarthy supporter.* President Johnson ran strong in Milwaukee, getting 53% of the vote, but about 33% behind Mayor Maier.

Item: The Wisconsin primary is completely open; any voter can vote for either the Republican candidate or the Democratic candidate, and the candidates' names appear side by side on the same row of the ballot. The voter need not preregister for either party or even request a special ballot (as in New Hampshire). The ballot in Wisconsin on primary day is illustrated on page 110.

Reagan did not campaign in the state; Stassen did—ineffectively. Essentially, Nixon was unopposed as the Republican candidate. There was no real contest among Republicans, nothing to vote "for," nothing to vote "against"—and the voters knew it.

These were the Republican results:

Nixon	80%
Reagan	10%
Stassen	6%
Others	4%

Another resounding Nixon victory. But note the crossover effect. Wisconsin is normally a marginally Republican state, about 52% in recent gubernatorial and Senatorial races. In November, 1968, Nixon, running true to form, got 52%. Yet in

City of Wauwatosa—Ward 1, Precinct 1

Instructions for Voting on the Voting Machine

1. Move the Red Handle to the Right.
2. Turn Down a Voting Pointer over the "Yes" or "No" of the Referenda, and *LEAVE IT DOWN.*
3. For the Presidential Preference Vote, you may only vote for one party and make one choice. For further information, read the instructions for Presidential Preference Ballot (Republican and Democratic Party) in the instructions below.
4. Turn Down Voting Pointer OVER THE NAME of the Candidate of your choice.

Leave Voting Pointer DOWN.

5. To cast write-in vote — Raise Metal Slide Above Corresponding Office Column Number and Write the Name of Your Personal Choice on Exposed Paper.
6. Move the Red Handle to the Left.
(This returns your voting pointers, counts your vote, and then opens the curtains.)

SAMPLE BALLOT
Milwaukee County, Wisconsin
Presidential Preference, Judicial, County Executive, County Supervisor, Municipal and Referenda Elections
April 2, 1968

If you Change Your Mind, Turn UP a Voting Pointer and Turn DOWN Another FOR THE SAME OFFICE.

the primary in April, 705,000 Wisconsin voters cast Democratic ballots, but only 475,000 voted Republican. This represents only a 40% Republican vote. The assumption is that the other 12%, which would amount to 140,000 voters, crossed to vote in the Democratic primary. Many a voter who was to vote for Nixon in November voted in April in the more exciting Democratic primary, where the action was.*

*A common practice in recent Wisconsin primaries—for both parties. John Kennedy and Hubert Humphrey each outpolled Nixon in the 1960 primary when Nixon ran unopposed, but Nixon carried the state in November. Republican Robert Taft and Earl Warren each outpolled the unopposed Estes Kefauver in 1952. In 1948 the Wisconsin primary was won by Harold Stassen running against Thomas Dewey and General Douglas McArthur—each of whom outpolled Harry Truman, who was unopposed. Stassen, while something of a joke candidate in the 1968 primaries, was once one of the hottest political names in the country—young, dynamic, and even charismatic before charisma was discovered in U.S. politics. Political moral of the Stassen story and of most political stories: Almost anything can happen—and usually does.

Four facts, then, to go along with McCarthy's big win: an anti-antiwar vote in Madison; Johnson leading McCarthy two to one among Democrats nationally; a "law-and-order" pro-Johnson mayor winning a lopsided victory in Milwaukee; a sizable Republican crossover.

What does it mean? The colors are mixed, mottled, and muddy, and the ultimate hue comes out that perennial quadrennial blend, electoral gray, a muted shade allowing for many interpretations.

Still, we can speculate as well as the next man, and these are our speculations:

As in New Hampshire, the Wisconsin vote for McCarthy was not essentially an antiwar vote. Even in a city as ostensibly dovish as Madison, the antiwar referendum *lost* 58 to 42, while McCarthy (plus some few Kennedy write-ins) received 72% of the Democratic vote.

Who were all those voters who were *not* antiwar but *were* pro-McCarthy?

In the largest city of the state (Milwaukee) a Johnson supporter with a voter perception as a tough pro-blue (Mayor Maier), got 86% of the vote, while Johnson himself got 53% of that Milwaukee vote.

Who were those 33% who were for Maier and against Johnson—and why? They were anti things as they were and blamed on Washington. Translated to psephological terms, they became anti-Johnson votes.

Johnson was ahead 59% to 29% among national Democrats, according to Gallup, but lost 56% to 35% in Wisconsin. Some of that differential is no doubt attributable to Wisconsin dovishness as mentioned. Some of the differential is attributable to those Republican crossover voters who wanted to vote where the action was. Some of these crossovers were voting dove, but many were voting against things as they are or, psephologically speaking, anti-Johnson. Some of the differential was that McCarthy campaigned diligently and effectively in Wisconsin and became known to a greater degree than in the nation as a whole. Once he became known, once it was apparent that he was a reasonable man, once it was clear that he could responsibly be voted for and that it was all right to be "pro-McCarthy," those voters with even a vague anti-Johnson feeling had someplace to go, and the anti-Johnson vote materialized with a vengeance.

It is important, then, to look again at the anti-Johnson phenomenon.

The President, just prior to his March 31 speech withdrawing from the race, had sunk to a low ebb in the popularity polls: Only 36% of American voters approved of the way Johnson was handling his job as President. That was an all-time low figure for Lyndon Johnson and was down from the 41% approval rate registered just a month earlier prior to the New Hampshire primary. (The lowest rating a sitting President ever scored was the 23% approval rate registered by Harry Truman in November, 1951.)

What caused the heavy anti-Johnson feeling? One notion that has been put forth to account for President Johnson's fall in the popularity polls has been that Lyndon Johnson was not charismatic, that he was not a very good television personality, that he was not a "likable" man, and that he accordingly never had the deep or fervent national personal constituency of the sort that Presidents Eisenhower and Kennedy had.

In assessing this idea—and the whole idea of the politics of charisma—a personal illustrative anecdote may be in order.

For several months after beginning work at the White House in 1966, Mr. Wattenberg commuted on weekends back to his home in Stamford, Connecticut.

When friends in Connecticut asked what kind of man was Lyndon Johnson, Mr. Wattenberg allowed that from what little he had seen of the President at various meetings, he was (1) extremely articulate, (2) extremely bright, (3) humorous, (4) pungent, and (5) as "charismatic" as any man he had ever seen.

Mr. Wattenberg was treated sympathetically, as one might treat a deranged relative. His listeners knew the gray, solemn, and boring Johnson reading a speech on television, they had read that when he wasn't gray, and solemn, and boring, he was "cornpone" and trigger-tempered—and that was that.

This gap was never bridged. Johnson, one of the most exciting of private personalities, never was able to come across that way to the voters. And because this was so, President Johnson's popularity did indeed suffer.

So there was a charisma gap, and as the White House press corps convened daily on the green leather furniture in the lobby of the West Wing, they nodded knowledgeably to one another and said, "Johnson has no charisma; his problem is that he's not communicating to the people."

But that is far too simple; there is much more to the popularity of a political figure than the ability to transfer private persuasiveness or attractiveness into public charisma. The ordeal of John Lindsay is a case in point. When elected mayor of New York City in 1965, John Lindsay was possibly the most publicly charismatic politician in all America. Tall, handsome, articulate, he ran on a Republican/Fusion ticket in a Democratic city, won, and was apparently the darling of the biggest city in the nation. Four years later—after subway strikes, garbage strikes, teacher strikes, and a growing feeling by many white voters that he was paying too much attention to the black and Puerto Rican population in New York—John Lindsay found himself in grave political trouble. What saved his political life was not charisma, which he still had, but an opposition that was divided between two other candidates. Lindsay had angered the voters, millions of them; they did not like what was happening in New York City, and they weren't going to vote for John Lindsay come hell, high water, or the highest charisma count in all recorded political history. Lindsay managed to win the election, but almost three out of five New Yorkers voted against him. Despite charisma.

It is interesting to note that when a politician falls from public grace, his image may tarnish most at exactly the point it was once strongest. Thus, one of the anti-Lindsay slogans was: "Do we need a movie star for mayor?" Lyndon Johnson, when popular, was popular because he was active, always on the phone, and could get things done. Later, when the decline started, he was known as a wheeler-dealer and a manipulator.

Or to show the same point about charisma versus issues, imagine for a moment a line of bearded, sandaled pickets in front of the White House in the year 1967, chanting in unison, *"Hey, hey, JFK, how many kids did you kill today?"* Suppose, in other words, President John Kennedy had lived and had pursued the Johnson course in Vietnam. Suppose, in addition, Watts and Newark and Harlem and Detroit burned up during JFK's Presidency. Suppose all the civil rights laws had been passed during a JFK second term. Suppose crime and the perception of crime had gone up during JFK's Presidency. Would Kennedy's popularity have survived?*

Now John Kennedy did not suffer from Lyndon Johnson's lack of ability to transmit charisma. He was as good on television as any politician in recent memory, as good as John Lindsay.

And that is precisely the point. Very often events and a politician's substantive response to events will steal away the personal popularity of a politician in office, charisma or no. In Lyndon Johnson's first six months as President, his popularity rating was higher than John Kennedy's, and one of the highest in recent history—an average of 76%. When he began his first full term, in January, 1965, his rating was still 71%. The Johnson victory over Senator Barry Goldwater in 1964, it should be remembered, was by the biggest popular majority in American history. It was aided, to be sure, by the popular perception of Goldwater as an extremist, but it must be counted as a great personal victory as well.

So, it is events—and the public attitudes formed in response to events—that are most crucial in eroding or boosting a politician's stock with the public. Had the events of the mid-1960's occurred during the Presidency of John Kennedy, he likely would have seen much of his popularity fade, and all the charisma would have been of limited value. But the events of

---

* Or suppose Booth missed and it was Lincoln, not Andrew Johnson, who attempted the agonizing task of stitching the Union together "with malice toward none." Perhaps, then, Lincoln, not Andrew Johnson, would have been impeached.

the mid-sixties occurred during the Presidency of Lyndon Johnson, and his popularity and charisma count fell, probably more rapidly because he was not a charismatic, stirring, public personality to begin with, but primarily because of events. Sinking charisma, sinking popularity, is mostly a symptom of events—not, at first, a cause of events.

Reviewing: The anti-Johnsonism apparent in Wisconsin was a code feeling for "against things as they were." Thus, while a part of Johnson's sinking poll rating may have come from Johnson's essential lack of charisma, it was largely events that caused much of Johnson's unpopularity. Now, which were the events that eroded Johnson's popularity? One such "event" certainly was the course of the war in Vietnam which was opposed by doves, by hawks, and was frustrating even to supporters of the President. A second "event" was inflation and the rising cost of living, beginning to become a serious problem by the spring of 1968. Another "event"—probably of greater psephological importance—was the growth of deep feeling about the various facets of the Social Issue. We have seen in the previous chapter that the President is held accountable for crime. Now we can note too that he lost support on the Social Issue question of race.

When Johnson became President after John Kennedy's assassination, the Gallup pollsters asked Americans what they thought Johnson's position would be in the cause of racial integration. Most Americans thought he would either slow down the pace or keep it about the same:

"Of course, it's too early to have a definite opinion, but just your best guess—do you think that integration will now be pushed faster, or not so fast?"

The results:

Will be pushed faster 16%
Not so fast 29%
About the same 43%
No opinion 12%

(*Gallup, December, 1963*)

In May, 1965, Americans were asked if racial integration was proceeding too fast:

Question: "Do you think the Johnson Administration is pushing integration too fast or not fast enough?"

Too Fast 45%
Not Fast Enough 14%
About Right 32%
No Opinion 9%

(Gallup)

In just a year and a half, American perception of Johnson and integration went starkly from "about the same" to "too fast."

Gallup continued to ask the question over the years. Consistently, the public replied "too fast." And whose fault was it? The President's, of course. Presidents are to blame for wars, for crime, for depressions, recessions and inflations—why shouldn't they be faulted for a tortured racial situation 300 years in the making? In this instance, there was even good reason for blaming Johnson: He *had* led the fight for civil rights legislation; he *had* initiated the legislative programs that had helped poor blacks get jobs and some power in their communities. When George Wallace had been saying "never" and Richard Nixon had been saying "maybe soon," Johnson stood before Congress and said, "We shall overcome." This stand gained him plaudits from liberals, general approval from the public, and some sullen response from a few. But when the "event" of city riots came in full force, the sullen became angry, the general public became sullen, the liberals were talking about an immoral war, and Johnson was holding the civil rights bag all alone. As a guess, for every vote Johnson lost because he was a "hawk," he lost substantially more for being problack. That is a statement that is supportable by Survey Research Center data showing that Wallace was pulling far more votes from Johnson than was McCarthy.

When we consider the previously noted feelings about crime, some rhyme and reason can be attributed on why the tough-on-black-rioters Mayor Maier of Milwaukee, who supported LBJ, could run 33% ahead of Johnson. Maier was perceived as "tough." Johnson, while probably also perceived as personally tough, was perceived as the chief of a government that was "soft on race," as well as "soft on crime," and this hurt him politically, garbed as anti-Johnsonism.

Add it all up, and most of the anti-Johnson feeling can be diagrammed psephologically as what happened when the lines of the new Social Issue converged with the lines of the old Officeholding Syndrome. This familiar political disease afflicts a politician as he antagonizes segments of the electorate by making unpopular decisions that can be weighed only as a "lesser of two alternate evils." Regardless of cause, the key symptom in the Officeholding Syndrome is that when things go bad in the city or state or nation, the blame is most likely to be heaped on the man in power—and sometimes on the party in power as well.

It is Mr. Scammon's view, not wholly shared by Mr. Wattenberg, that President Johnson's decline in popularity was perhaps more precipitous than might normally be expected. This is due, Mr. Scammon feels, to the fact that President Johnson never had a wide or deep personal political base and that, despite his leadership in programs to combat urban problems, despite his racial liberalism, to many the Johnson image remained that of a Texas politician. When events began to erode Johnson's popularity, it was extremely erodable—and was sharply eroded. Scammon notes that if Eisenhower had faced a similar set of circumstances, his popularity, too, would have eroded—but probably more slowly. Wattenberg is somewhat more of a fatalist: Given the circumstances, any President doing his job in the mid-1960's would have suffered a severe reversal in the popularity polls.

But in either event, what struck Lyndon Johnson was an occupational disease. Presidents get elected by occupying the center territory. But once they are inaugurated, it is no simple matter to stay there. Presidents doing their job must attempt to lead as well as follow, must try to move the center, as well as respond to it, must find wisdom in the center, and give wisdom to the center.

It is a dilemma that Johnson had to face. As we shall see later, it is a dilemma that Nixon now faces. This grand Presidential dilemma is the most imponderable factor in the politics and psephology of the Presidency and the factor most frequently overlooked by pundits. When it comes down to the hard and important decisions, Presidents most often do what they think is right for the nation and not what is best for themselves or their party. Presidents will frequently "occupy the center" because that is not only good politics, but responsive politics and politics that is accordingly best for the nation. But when a President feels that the national interest is not where the center is, he will try to move the center and be willing to suffer a sinking popularity poll in order to do it. This is a major point to consider when Pundit A says Nixon will end the war in 1972 in order to reelect Republicans and Richard Nixon or when Pundit B says that Nixon will pander to racism for the same reasons. That is bunk. It is the authors' judgment that Nixon, like Johnson, will scale down the war, or end the war, or change strategies, or escalate the war, or change the tactics of integration basically along the lines of what he considers the best interest of the nation, not of self or party. He may turn out to be tactically wrong on big decisions, he may turn out to be morally wrong on big decisions—but not because he was a partisan obsessed by reelection or popularity.

Returning to Wisconsin: The anti-Johnson feeling and the reasons that led to it accounted for much of the discrepancies in the Wisconsin primary: McCarthy doubling the peace vote in Madison; nondove Republican crossovers for McCarthy; Maier sharply outpolling Johnson. "Anti-Johnson" was the code phrase for "I'm displeased."

In terms of what subsequently happened in 1968, what happened in 1969, and in terms of what the authors believe will be happening in the 1970's, it is of only passing interest that the "I'm displeased" feeling found early expression under the label "anti-Johnson." What is important, vitally important, is that the motivating feeling was "I'm displeased," and not "I'm a dove," and that when Johnson decided not to run, the "I'm displeased" feeling was seen to be deeper than just a personal anti-Johnson feeling and instead was applied to the Democratic Party as a whole and was transmuted into an oppositionist feeling that worked against the candidacy of Hubert Humphrey. In 1969, this same feeling helped elect a series of "law-and-order" candidates. This same feeling, in the 1970's, may well be one of the most important political issues of our time.

To recapitulate what was happening in the Wisconsin primary, read the text of three advertisements that appeared in Wisconsin newspapers toward the end of the campaign:

From the Nixon camp:

THE NATION WATCHES
as Wisconsin Reacts to the President's Decision

Now we must choose new leadership; it is now clear that we will have a new President next year. No longer are we asked to compare the new with the old; there will be change.

Wisconsin votes first. Never before has a vote counted for so much. Republican or Democrat, every Wisconsin citizen must make his vote count. It is a decision to think through seriously.

Yesterday's idea of jumping party to vote *against* someone doesn't make sense today. Today, the choice is clear and precise for Wisconsin. Today, we must decide to vote *for* a man; a man who will be on his way to becoming the next President.

One Man is Better Prepared for the Presidency than Any Other Challenger in American History

One man has the background, the experience, the preparation needed for the world's biggest job; the one who has spent a lifetime getting ready.

One man stands above the rest at this point in our history; a man who has been at the center of world events for more than 20 years; world traveler, student of world and domestic affairs; tested and prepared. It's a new election—a new ball game. Now we must nominate the one man who can deal with *all* the nation's problems, for all the people.

For times like these   NIXON'S THE ONE

From the Johnson camp:

The important thing for every man who occupies this place is to search as best he can to get the right answer; to try to find out what is right; and then do it without regard to polls or without regard to criticism.

> President Johnson
> News Conference
> November 17, 1967

This can be a nation of greatness for all; if we only work together; if we have the common will to rise above trial; if we have the matching strength to carry our responsibilities abroad; if we have the unity, the good judgment, and the sound common sense to persevere in the greatest purpose of all—the work of peace on earth.

> President Johnson
> NRECA Convention in Dallas
> February 27, 1968

COURAGE . . . COMPASSION . . . WISDOM . . . AND
EXPERIENCE THE MARKS OF LEADERSHIP
THE MARKS OF A GREAT PRESIDENT!

Today the federal government is doing more than three times as much in the field of education as it did four years ago when this administration began . . . the objective and the goal of this administration—to give every boy and girl in the country all the education that he or she can take.

> President Johnson
> A Conversation at the White House
> February 3, 1968

No society can tolerate massive violence, any more than a body can tolerate a massive disease. And we in America shall not tolerate it . . . Today slum conditions are producing serious crime problems . . . We have dedicated ourselves to change those conditions . . .

President Johnson
Message to Congress
February 7, 1968

VOTE LYNDON B. JOHNSON/APRIL 2

From the McCarthy camp:

YOUR VOTE IS IMPORTANT

Tomorrow the voters of Wisconsin will show that the arrogant and unsuccessful policies of Lyndon Johnson have been repudiated by the American people in favor of the courage, dignity and humanity of Senator Eugene McCarthy.

All voters—Republicans and Independents as well as Democrats—can join in a demonstration of the vitality of the American political system that gives the citizens the right to replace a president.

JOIN the SWING to McCARTHY

"I am very grateful to him . . . for giving people the power to voice their feelings through him"—Mrs. Warren G. Knowles

"He was there when we needed him"—John Kenneth Galbraith

"It is important now that he achieve the largest possible majority in Wisconsin. I urge all my friends to give him their help and their votes"—Senator Robert F. Kennedy.

"Vote for Senator McCarthy"—Paul Newman

McCARTHY FOR PRESIDENT

Notice, carefully, the little word that isn't there—isn't there in any of these statements, the word that the contemporary media viewed as the key to the Wisconsin primary: Vietnam.

9

The Prove-Little Primaries—1

The spring of 1968 has already become mummified in the wrappings of political legend. The mythology has it that the "kids," and McCarthy, and Kennedy, and Allard Lowenstein all combined to swat the nasty Johnson a mighty blow and were successful in dumping Johnson. The legend-making process has also enshrined the notion that in the later primaries the Kennedy/McCarthy forces swept bright-eyed across the nation, leading the vast majority of the American public to an antiwar position.

But that is not what happened. When reality set in, after LBJ's withdrawal, both the Kennedy and McCarthy camps became aware—publicly aware it should be noted—that suddenly they had no one to run against and that Johnson's withdrawal would be a blow to each of their candidacies. For if the Wisconsin and New Hampshire primaries can be viewed as spring training exhibition games, the remaining primaries can be viewed only as *intramural* spring training games. They were exciting, colorful—and meant little.

When Johnson was a candidate, voters had a choice between things as they were (Johnson) or against things as they were (McCarthy in Wisconsin and New Hampshire; McCarthy or

Kennedy in the remaining primaries had LBJ stayed in). Even
that choice was not a clear and simple sort of choice: Johnson
did not actively campaign, and the non-Democratic candidates
who were also against things as they were were not really yet in
the race; Wallace was not in the primaries, and Nixon was
running unopposed in Republican, not Democratic, primaries.
But when Johnson announced his decision not to run, Mc-
Carthy and Kennedy essentially were fighting it out only for
who would hold the "against" banner on the *left* side of things
as they were. Nixon and Wallace would ultimately be tested on
the right-wing side of the "against" position, but not until
November. Humphrey would ultimately run his campaign
pretty much along the lines of a centrist things-as-they-were-but-
better theme, but he would not be tested formally on this
position until the Chicago convention and not formally by
voters until November.

Meanwhile, Eugene McCarthy and Robert Kennedy slugged
it out intramurally. McCarthy did not bring up the fact that
Kennedy had said he was in favor of sending blood to North
Vietnam; Kennedy did not challenge McCarthy's statements
that the war in Vietnam was an immoral, illegal adventure;
neither candidate disagreed with the Kerner Commission's
allegation that white racism was to blame for riots in the cities
—and so on. There were nuances of difference in the positions
espoused by the candidates, but they were only nuances.

In none of the remaining primaries was there an honest-to-
goodness choice against McCarthy or Kennedy. This was so
because Humphrey did not appear on any primary ballot running as President (in most instances because he *could* not run
owing to his late entry into the race; in some instances because
he *would* not run for tactical reasons). Now it has been argued
that the Humphrey candidacy *was,* in fact, represented in these
primary contests through a series of stand-in candidates or
administration slates, but let us see how that worked out in
practice in the first post-Johnson-withdrawal primary—Indiana.

Imagine for a moment that you are an Indiana Democrat on
the evening of May 6, 1968. Tomorrow you will go to your

polling place and, after properly identifying yourself, be handed a paper ballot or step into a voting booth. Several offices, including county recorder and county surveyor, are being contested for. The top line of the ballot says:

PRESIDENT OF THE UNITED STATES OF AMERICA
(Vote for one)

There are three candidates listed and no space for a write-in vote.

One candidate is Senator Robert F. Kennedy of New York. Senator Kennedy is one of the three or four most "famous" men in America. Seven weeks earlier he announced his candidacy for the Presidency. As he has traveled around the country in those eight weeks Senator Kennedy has been a prime attraction on prime-time television news shows; he has been on the front pages of newspapers and on the covers of magazines. *Senator Kennedy is running in the Indiana primary because he wants to be President.*

A second candidate in the race is Senator Eugene McCarthy. He has been an announced candidate for President for five months. One month earlier he had resoundingly beaten the President of the United States in a primary in Wisconsin. Not as well known as Robert Kennedy, he is nonetheless becoming very well known indeed. His picture and his words have been splashed on the media. *Senator McCarthy is running in the Indiana primary because he wants to be President.*

There is a third candidate in the Indiana primary, Governor Roger Branigin. *He is not running in Indiana because he wants to be President. He is running, he says, to keep Indiana's votes in a Hoosier's hands at the Democratic Convention.*

Branigin originally annouced his candidacy on March 17 as a stand-in for President Johnson. When the President withdrew, and the Indiana race heated up, Branigin denied he was a stand-in for Hubert Humphrey. He did, however, acknowledge his *preference* for Humphrey. Then he reversed field a bit and also intimated that he might become a more serious Presidential candidate if he won the primary, and finally, there were balloons floated that Branigin was among several men under consideration for the Democratic *Vice Presidential* nomination. Further, Hubert Humphrey did not campaign in the state for Branigin. Finally, a Harris poll at the time showed that only 44% of Indiana voters viewed Branigin as a Humphrey stand-in.

So here you are. It is May 6; there is a Presidential primary in your home state. Your choice is between two famous men, each running for the office listed, and a third man, your governor, running to stop the others from walking off with the Indiana delegates. You make up your mind for whom to vote,* you go to the polls, and these are the results:

Kennedy	42%
Branigin	31%
McCarthy	27%

Those were the candidates and the results, but as with the New Hampshire primary we must now ask: What was being contested?

As the primaries wore on, and after the primaries ended, one consistent theme was sounded by the anti-Humphrey forces: "Seventy percent [roughly] of the American people have re-

---

* It is just six months before a *real* President will be chosen, and it should be pointed out that Indianans, like many other Americans, have many things on their minds, and the primary elections are not the most important. Here is Robert Walters of the Washington *Star* reporting from Indianapolis two days before the primary:

. . . One would think, for example, that here in Indianapolis—the state's largest city, its capital and political nerve center—the primary would be foremost in the minds of voters.

Not so. What the locals are really talking about these days is "the race" and "the track."

The references, of course, are to the event for which the city is best known—the annual 500 mile auto race on Memorial Day.

Politicians are being unceremoniously removed from their hotel and motel rooms to make space available for "the crews"; residents worry far more about "the time trials" and "the tryouts" than about the millions of dollars being lavished upon them by the politicians.

pudiated the administration [*i.e.*, Humphrey]." It was this notion, in some measure, that led later to the feeling that the McCarthy forces had been "cheated" by the "boss-dominated" convention in Chicago. It is wise, therefore, to examine the notion carefully. Was this really being tested in Indiana?

The basic premise of the antiadministration notion was that the votes for Robert Kennedy and the votes for Eugene McCarthy could be added together and interpreted as antiwar.

There is solid evidence to indicate that this was not so.

In Indiana the choices that Democrats had were three. To repeat the results:

Kennedy	McCarthy	Branigin
42%	27%	31%

If one adds Kennedy and McCarthy votes together as anti-administration, then the numbers will support the statement "Seventy percent were against the administration." But . . . at that same time Gallup asked a national cross section of Democrats their preference and got these results:

Kennedy	McCarthy	Humphrey	No Opinion
31%	19%	40%	10%

Furthermore, earlier Gallup data showed that even in a two-man race Humphrey could do well. If McCarthy was dropped out of the poll, about one-third of his vote went for Humphrey and two-thirds for RFK. That would put Humphrey ahead of RFK by a few points. If Kennedy was dropped out of the poll, then his votes went to *Humphrey* by about 3 to 2, putting Humphrey far, far ahead of McCarthy in a two-man race.

What is clear about these data is that the McCarthy votes and the Kennedy votes were not bonded votes sealed to an antiwar, antiadministration position. Obviously the three-fifths of the RFK vote that would go for Humphrey if RFK weren't running were not dove votes. If they were, if the war were the issue they were voting on, they would have switched to McCarthy, not Humphrey. It wasn't. They didn't.

The moral of these numbers is very simple: Roger Branigin wasn't Hubert Humphrey. To some Indiana voters, certainly, a vote for Branigin was a vote for Humphrey, or a vote for the administration, or a prowar vote. To some Indiana voters, to be sure, a vote for Kennedy or McCarthy was an anti-Vietnam or antiadministration vote. But to many others, as the data would indicate, the voting carried no such connotations. Primary day merely offered a choice of voting for one of the three candidates on the ballot. Two of these candidates were charismatic, attractive, high-spending, national figures, each of whom was able to draw votes from people who were not necessarily doves, not necessarily hawks, not necessarily more interested in the primary than in the Indianapolis 500—but simply people who went out to choose between the available choices as those choices were perceived in the eye of the voter. With no real issues separating Kennedy from McCarthy, some Indiana voters may have voted for Robert Kennedy because he was a tough guy, a former Attorney General, who could cope with crime. Some voters may have voted for McCarthy because he was quiet and staid; he could cope with all the unruliness in America. Blacks and low-to-middle-income whites trended toward Kennedy; suburban, more affluent whites trended to McCarthy. But in most cases this sort of voting analysis of the Kennedy-McCarthy primaries is meaningless. Kennedy didn't have to fight for those factory workers against Wallace or even against Humphrey. McCarthy didn't have to fight for his suburban voters against Nixon or Humphrey. The Indiana contest was an intramural affair largely contested between men who were in at least general agreement with each other.

The only important question answered in Indiana and confirmed in subsequent primaries was this one: Was Robert F. Kennedy superman? The answer given by the voters was no; the answer given by the interpreters of the vote was "No—but," and that answer would seem to hold up in retrospect: "No, he was not a supercandidate, but he was a strong and potent vote getter."

Robert Kennedy, it should be remembered, had run for elective office only once before, for Senator of New York State. He won that race, from the very popular and able incumbent, Senator Kenneth Keating, by 719,693 votes, surely a good showing for a man's first crack at elective office. However, that was the Goldwater-Johnson year, and Johnson carried New York State by 2,669,543 votes. The prevailing political opinion was that Robert Kennedy won by coming in on the coattails of the pro-Johnson anti-Goldwater landslide, as did thousands of other politicians during that Republican plague year.

But the Kennedy *family* record for elective office, as opposed to Robert Kennedy's single pre-Indiana try, *was* close to political supermanism. Twenty-four general and primary elections—twenty-four victories. Some victories were close, some massive, such as John Kennedy's 1958 Senate victory or Edward Kennedy's 1964 Senate victory. In addition, there was the mystique about the "Kennedy team" of skilled political professionals who could quickly and skillfully organize all the physical paraphernalia, the fiscal wherewithal, and the human resources to mount an unbeatable juggernaut of a campaign.

The question, then, in Indiana was: How good was Robert Kennedy? Was he as good only as his decent but not spectacular 1964 Senate race, or was he as good as the family record, which in the then-current mythology was close to invincible?

The answer seems to be neither. Had Kennedy been able to come into Indiana and walk off with a Nixon-sized share (60%, 70%, 80%) of the three-man vote; had he been able to beat Humphrey big in the Gallup Polls, then the rest of the primaries would have been meaningless. Kennedy would have been Electoral Superman and likely would have won the nomination and very possibly the Presidency itself.

On the other hand, had he lost big to McCarthy and perhaps even to Branigin, he might have been finished.

As it turned out, he won. He won well. He did not, however, show up as invincible. That essential pattern (with the exception of Oregon, where Kennedy lost to McCarthy) carries through each of the remaining primaries: Kennedy was a good, tough, credible candidate, but not a miracle man. There was a

great pro-Kennedy feeling in America in 1968; there was also a
great anti-Kennedy feeling.

The battle in Indiana and in the ensuing primaries was
between two charismatic candidates contesting for the right to
carry the "against" banner the next time the "for" or "against"
was to be tested—in Chicago in August. With all credit to Gene
McCarthy, the primary results indicate that Robert F. Kennedy
won that right. He began winning that right in Indiana, and—
the phrase "New Politics" aside—he won it very much according
to the rules of the Old Politics or, perhaps more accurately
phrased, the Unchanging Politics. He won by strategically moving to the center, he won by stressing the Voting Issue, and he
won by understanding clearly the structure of the electorate.

Here are three political observers noting the changeover from
Kennedy the ideologue to Kennedy the campaigner:

First, John Herbers, reporting in the New York *Times* on
May 3:

> In his [Indiana] speeches, he is no longer the aggressive candi-
> date whipping up his audiences with emotional rhetoric. His
> approach is calm and reasoned, almost soft. If he answers
> charges hurled at him in the Indiana primary campaign at all
> he does so obliquely with humor.
>
> The "sock it to 'em Bobby" signs that appeared in abundance
> in the early stages of the campaign no longer seem appropriate
> and, in fact, are rarely seen in Indiana.
>
> Senator Kennedy's personal appearance, too, is more con-
> servative. His hair, though still full, has been clipped progres-
> sively shorter. . . .
>
> . . . in his first campaign speeches after announcing his can-
> didacy for President on March 16 . . . he spoke with raised
> voice. "Give me your help, give me your hand and we will build
> a new America." He smote the air with his fist for emphasis.
>
> He spoke then of American boys dying in swamps of South-
> east Asia and of the Johnson Administration appealing to "the
> darker impulse" of the American spirit. When he spoke of
> domestic violence he stressed the need to attack the causes of
> deprivation over the need for law and order.

The change to the new posture began even before President Johnson announced on March 31 that he would not seek re-election and would reduce the bombing of North Vietnam. In the Indiana campaign, the change has become pronounced.

Senator Kennedy's stand on the issues is not without continuity. It is still based largely on his Senate record. His appeal is still to restore a sense of destiny to the country through a new Kennedy Administration and to give hope to the alienated in the process. The change in posture is in emphasis rather than substance.

The Senator still chides the Administration for its Vietnam policy but his remarks are more balanced and more restrained. He still talks of the responsibility of the advantaged groups to help the disadvantaged and the rich to bear a greater share of the tax burden, but he talks more of strict law enforcement and reminds his audiences that for more than three years he was the nation's chief law enforcement officer, the Attorney General.

Next, David Broder in the Washington *Post* on April 30:

Kennedy has been talking mainly about the subjects that his polls tell him preoccupy the Indiana voters—fear of riots, fear of communism, fear of war. He tells them he is for law and order and against unilateral withdrawal from Vietnam. He invites them to discover that he has no tail, and that far from being coldly self-assured, he is quite ill-at-ease under their stares.

And, finally, Tom Wicker in the New York *Times,* just three days after the primary:

Senator Robert Kennedy offered his last campaign words to the people of Indiana in midnight television appearances just before the primary voting. Two themes dominated the half-hour color film.

One was his insistence on law and order, coupled with repeated assertions that violence in the cities was "unacceptable." The other was the idea that the Federal bureaucracy in Washington is too big and inflexible to meet the varied needs of the nation, and that government had to be returned to the people.

This was not exactly demagoguery. No one favors violence; and Kennedy and his Senate staff have done some advanced and useful thinking about the causes of riots and what to do about them, as well as the necessity for state, local and private responsibility in public affairs.

Nevertheless, this was not the emphasis Kennedy had displayed elsewhere. "Law and order" and "bureaucracy"—as well as another Kennedy campaign theme, the necessity to put welfare recipients to work—are well-known slogans guaranteed to evoke a sympathetic response from hard-working, conservative whites, of whom there are quite a few in this so-called "heartland" state.

There were those in the Kennedy camp, we are told, who viewed this appeal as the "bad Bobby" triumphing over the "good Bobby." That is nonsense; it was the "centrist Bobby" triumphing over the "extreme Bobby," and it can be noted again that centrists win elections and, having won elections, are in a position to make change. Acknowledging that voters are fearful of riots and disorders is not selling out to anything but the truth. Attempting to cope with those fears through programmatic efforts of crime control is not only allowed to a liberal candidate, but *demanded* of him in a nation where half the women are afraid to walk out at night.

In any event, with charisma, money, sound strategy, Senator Kennedy ran strong in Indiana. He captured a sizable piece of the center. He won.

So did Richard Nixon. He ran unopposed. He received 500,000 votes—more than Branigin and McCarthy put together and about half again as many as Kennedy.

10

The Prove-Little Primaries—2

The remaining contested primaries showed much the same pattern as the Indiana primary: a highly publicized intramural confrontation between two left-of-center Democrats, largely running against each other on the basis of personality. While this was going on, the real battle of 1968—the battle between the ministerialists and the oppositionists, between the ins and the outs, waged in part on the basis of the Social Issue—was slowly taking shape off the front pages. This major battle had seen more premature and somewhat distorted testing in New Hampshire and Wisconsin. When Johnson withdrew, when Humphrey did not enter the primaries, with Nixon and Wallace not really subject to test, the real substance of the campaign lay publicly dormant for many months.

To recall the situation in the spring of 1968: In polls among Democrats, Humphrey continued to lead Kennedy by a little and McCarthy by a lot. In the primaries Kennedy beat McCarthy everywhere but in Oregon, while a third entry in the race, usually identified by the press (but not by the authors) as an administration slate, ran well back.

On the Republican side, no real candidate opposed Nixon, and he just kept winning "meaningless" victories. That at least is what his opponents called them. In fact, these victories were loaded with meaning: They meant that Nixon was not "a loser," as his opponents described him, and they built a national base behind the idea that "Nixon's the One," as his campaign slogan went.

George Wallace kept up a fairly steady speaking schedule, and his organizers saw to it that the necessary legal steps were taken to get his name on the ballot in each of the fifty states. Just as the McCarthy kids were giving new definition to the role of participatory democracy, so, too, were the Wallace workers: raising money; collecting petitions; staging rallies. Both the Wallace and the McCarthy movements showed far greater political effectiveness than most observers would have thought possible.

For the record, and for a few brief psephological lessons, we can glance quickly at the results of the remaining spring primaries.

The Nebraska primary showed fine results from the Kennedy point of view. In a state where only 1% of the population is black and less than 20% are blue-collar workers, Kennedy decisively beat a Midwestern farm-oriented Senator:

DEMOCRATIC PREFERENCE VOTE, NEBRASKA, 1968

Robert F. Kennedy	52%
Eugene J. McCarthy	31%
Lyndon B. Johnson	6%
Hubert H. Humphrey write-ins	7%
Other write-ins	4%

There was no Roger Branigin in the Nebraska election, no one campaigning with any effectiveness as an anti-Kennedy/McCarthy candidate. As always, the voters chose essentially from those who were actively running and actively campaigning. The two active national candidates were Kennedy, who campaigned heavily in the state, and McCarthy, who conducted a rather desultory effort. Kennedy won.

Not for a change, Nixon won again. But Reagan, while on

the ballot, did not appear in the state, allowing pundits to note that Mr. Nixon's victory was "meaningless."

The Republican results:

REPUBLICAN PREFERENCE VOTE, NEBRASKA, 1968

Richard M. Nixon	70%
Ronald Reagan	21%
Others	2%
Nelson Rockefeller write-ins	5%
Other write-ins	2%

McCarthy's candidacy reached its apogee in the Oregon primary, two weeks later, when he solidly beat Kennedy:

DEMOCRATIC PREFERENCE VOTE, OREGON, 1968

McCarthy	44%
Kennedy	38%
Johnson	12%
Write-ins	6%

The strength of that showing should not be denied, as has been done, by deprecating Oregon as an atypically wealthy, white, and untroubled state, untarnished by the crisis of cities or other modern ailments. Be that as it may, it is by far outweighed by the fact that Somebody Beat a Kennedy Somewhere (first time anywhere, anytime). The fact that this same somebody had earlier beaten the incumbent President of the United States in a primary and that only six months earlier this somebody was a nobody is cause for a retrospective, retroactive, unencumbered, unmodified laurel wreath to be placed on Senator McCarthy's brow.

There was some talk at the time of the Oregon election that Humphrey supporters were urging their supporters to vote not for Johnson (who was on the ballot), but for McCarthy in order to help a "stop Bobby" movement. But like most such grand political machinations that the press finds so fascinating, the results among rank-and-file voters was probably somewhat less than small. It's a rare voter who will be directed *away* from a Johnson vote *to* a McCarthy vote in order to *stop* Kennedy and *help* Humphrey. Too cute. Far too cute to work. McCarthy won fair and square.

At the same time, it must also be stressed again that Senator McCarthy beat Senator Kennedy, not Vice President Humphrey. In national polls at about the time of the Oregon primary, Humphrey was beating McCarthy 56%–37% in a two-man race among Democrats.

That other fellow also won again. Governor Reagan was on the ballot, but he did not openly campaign in Oregon. Accordingly, Reagan's supporters were able to say that the contest was "meaningless" because Nixon was unopposed. But in fact, Nixon *was* opposed. Reagan, unlike Humphrey, *was* on the ballot. Reagan, unlike Johnson, by the time of the Oregon primary *was* a *de facto* candidate for President. If Oregon Republicans wanted to go the route of a right-wing candidate all they had to do was pull the little lever. They didn't. The fact that they didn't was to be clearly reflected at the Republican Convention in Miami.

The results:

REPUBLICAN PREFERENCE VOTE, OREGON, 1968

Nixon	73%
Reagan	23%
Rockefeller write-ins	4%

California. Same electoral story, with a different Democratic candidate the victor and terminated by a tragedy that changed the history of American politics.

After the defeat in Oregon, it was imperative for Robert Kennedy to win the preference primary (and California's 172 elected convention votes) in the most populous state of the Union. He did—barely.

Again, Kennedy's competition came from McCarthy and an amorphous third line on the ballot headed by Attorney General

Thomas Lynch, who chose to vacation in Hawaii for two weeks just prior to the primary. The Lynch candidacy in California was further complicated by the fact some of the delegates on the Lynch slate announced publicly that they were in support of Kennedy or McCarthy. By our reasoning, Attorney General Lynch represented, in California, what Governor Branigin represented in Indiana: a noncandidate for President, generally nonidentified by the voters with a real candidate for President. There was one essential difference: Branigin *campaigned* in his role as noncandidate; Lynch did not. Furthermore, Branigin had some help from a strong Democratic Party organization in Indiana; on the other hand, California is an organization man's nightmare.

The results:

Kennedy	46%
McCarthy	42%
Lynch	12%

The popular political mythology concerning California deals with its atypicality, and the impression is frequently gained that every second California voter wears a button labeled "I Am a Kook." Such voters, as we are informed, are interested in yoga, vegetarianism, or cryogenics. Many are said to be little old ladies in tennis shoes who consider Ronald Reagan a leftist and the John Birch Society as a middle-of-the-road group of political activists. More recently, to the much publicized roster of screwball Californians, there have been added gun-toting Black Panthers and shaggy, sandaled students whose political rhetoric deals with four-letter words, of which "vote" is not the most conspicuous.

It's a nice story, it makes good copy, and, of course, there are a lot of strange types in California (as elsewhere).

Yet California, viewed psephologically, is not really atypical, screwballs notwithstanding.

To begin with, the largest state—with more than 10% of the nation's total population—is unlikely to be very atypical, although there are no "typical" states. California, compared to other states, is slightly more urban, somewhat more wealthy, substantially more Mexican-American and Oriental-American, slightly less black, and it has proportionately fewer people residing there who were born in the state. It has first- and second-generation foreign stock and foreign born in proportions not very different from the nation as a whole.

Beyond that, in the small world of election analysts, California is known as an excellent *barometric* state. Among large states, Illinois and California are the two that vote most consistently like America as a whole. Since 1948 California had never been more than two percentage points away from the final national percentage for the Presidential winner.

It is important to note this as we watch how the three main notions of American elections were hard at work in the 1968 California primary. The California electorate was about as unyoung and unblack as elsewhere and only slightly more unpoor. One of the key issues of the election was the Social Issue. And despite the blossoming phrase "New Politics," the politicians were demonstrating the same old political tropism to that same old political center.

Here is the situation: The political writers were speculating avidly about which of the two left-of-center candidates had captured the hearts and minds of the New Left students, intellectuals, movie stars, blacks, and Mexican-Americans. Some of the younger, less savvy (and more smug) advisers and speech writers of the candidates were verifying to the press that indeed it was the leadership of the New Politics that the candidates were most deeply concerned about.

In the meanwhile, observe the candidates. Can we observe from their public actions that they were arguing about who would lead the New Politics to a brighter tomorrow? Hardly. They wanted to win an election, and lo and behold, the laws of political gravity were still working.

On June 1, McCarthy and Kennedy met in one of the less exciting political confrontations in American history. The debate, so called, was held under the auspices of ABC-TV and broadcast nationally, as well as in California. Commenting editorially on the televised tedium, the Washington *Post* noted:

> The "New Politics," it turned out, is very much like the "Old Politics." Peter Finley Dunne who caricatured American politicians at the turn of the century through his inspired character, Mr. Dooley, would have had no trouble adapting to the 1968 milieu. Dooley would have been delighted to discover that politicians today still favor larger appropriations and lower taxes; that they fearlessly affront small racial groups but deal respectfully with large, compact and articulate minorities; that they are for foreign policies when they succeed and against them when they fail; that they have an uncanny recollection of the good advice they have given and a short memory for the bad advice they have proffered.

But the Washington *Post* editorial did not note the one really fascinating bit of political interplay in the show—the part which concerned blacks.

Here is what the candidates said:

> SENATOR McCARTHY: . . . I don't think we ought to perpetuate the ghetto if we can help it, even by putting better houses there for them, or low-cost houses.
>
> What we have got to do is to try to break that up. Otherwise, we are adopting a kind of apartheid in this country, a practical apartheid. . . . Some of the housing has got to go out of the ghetto so there is a distribution of races throughout the whole structure of our cities and on into our rural areas.
>
> SENATOR KENNEDY: I am all in favor of moving people out of the ghettos. We have 40 million (*sic*) Negroes who are in the ghettos at the present time. We have here in the State of California a million Mexican-Americans whose poverty is even greater than many of the black people. *You say you are going to take 10,000 black people and move them into Orange County.* The people who graduate from high school, which are only three out of ten of the people, or children who go to these schools, only three out of ten graduate from high school, and the ones who graduate from high school have the equivalent of

an eighth grade education. So to take them out where 40 percent of them don't have any jobs at all—that is what you are talking about. *If you are talking about 100 people, that is one thing. But if you are talking about hitting this problem in a major way, to take those people out, put them in the suburbs where they can't afford the housing, where their children can't keep up with the schools, and where they don't have the skills for the jobs, it is just going to be catastrophic.* . . . [Our italics.]

McCarthy, idly fishing for some of Kennedy's black votes and seeking to give an earnest impression that his was not a one-issue candidacy, dips his toe into the water: He's for integration. Kennedy, sensing an opening to the center and looking for the bigger prize of McCarthy's suburban support, springs a rhetorical bear trap that grabs the Minnesota Senator at about the knee: He (RFK), too, is for integration, but not right now, it would appear, because blacks are underskilled and under-educated and not really quite ready to live in placid, crime-free, suburban Orange County. He has wrapped it all up: the Social Issue; the awareness that the great majority of the electorate is unyoung, unpoor and unblack; the need to drive to the center, gobbling up a maximum of the opposition's votes.

The following day Senator McCarthy attempts to loosen the jaws of the bear trap. He, too, knows who votes in California, knows what bothers the voters, knows where the center is. As reported by *Congressional Quarterly:*

Following the debate, McCarthy on June 2 accused Kennedy of injecting "scare tactics" into the campaign. Criticizing Kennedy's comment during the debate that McCarthy's new civil rights plan would "take 10,000 black people and move them into Orange County (Calif.)" McCarthy said Kennedy's comment was "a crude distortion of my proposals. It could increase suspicion and mistrust among the races." Orange County is a suburban area to Los Angeles with a history of right-wing political activity.

McCarthy, of course, could have said something different in rebuttal. "Yes," he might have noted, "I meant what I said, blacks should be moving into suburban white areas even if the suburban whites don't like it. As the Kerner Commission report said, it is white racism that causes the problems of the ghettos, and we will only solve the problems of the ghettos by dispersing the Negro population among white suburbs." Such a statement, following the Kennedy remarks, might well have cost McCarthy tens of thousands of votes; he contented himself with the "crude distortion" charge, minimizing a bad situation.

McCarthy also noted that it was perhaps more than coincidental that Senator Kennedy went campaigning in Orange County, of all places, right after the debate. And McCarthy supporters later claimed that Kennedy campaigners went out on election day in sound trucks to Orange County. They didn't play the RFK campaign song; they played back the tape of the "Orange County Remarks."

The results of both the District of Columbia Democratic primary and the South Dakota Democratic primary were largely eclipsed by far bigger primaries that were held on the same day: The D.C. primary was held at the same time as the Indiana primary; the South Dakota race was held simultaneously with the California primary.

The District primary provided the only point in the campaign where a slate of pro-Kennedy delegates directly faced a slate of pro-Humphrey delegates. (A pro-McCarthy slate withdrew from the race in favor of the pro-Kennedy slate.)

Kennedy clobbered Humphrey:

VOTE FOR DEMOCRATIC NATIONAL COMMITTEEMAN, DISTRICT OF COLUMBIA, 1968

Rev. Channing E. Phillips (pro-Kennedy)	62%
E. Franklin Jackson (pro-Humphrey)	36%
Byron N. Scott (independent pro-Humphrey)	2%

As an example of Kennedy electoral power, however, the results of the District primary were not of particular value to his candidacy.

The majority of the population of the District of Columbia in 1968 was black, compared to 11% for the country as a whole. What the District primary showed was great Kennedy strength among blacks—hardly a surprise.

It was in South Dakota that Robert Kennedy showed his most impressive political muscle of the 1968 campaign. Running in a proportionately whiter, more rural, more Protestant state even than Nebraska, Kennedy polled 50% in a three-slate race. Again Humphrey's name was *not* on the ballot, but South Dakota *was* his birthplace, and it was next door to Gene Mc-Carthy's home state.

The vote:

Kennedy slate	50%
Johnson slate	30%
McCarthy slate	20%

These South Dakota results would probably have been valuable to Kennedy in a stretch run to the convention. Viewing these South Dakota returns along with the relatively weaker California results, one can only say that Robert Kennedy was shot at a moment when his political future was uncertain.

Aside from the great personal tragedy involved, two political thoughts about the assassination occur.

The first is that one of the key factors in electoral politics is that we can never know all the key factors. After Herbert Hoover was landslided into office in 1928, it was "clear" to all the experts that the Democratic Party was finished in America—and then came the Depression. Mr. Scammon recalls a 1961 Washington dinner party at which some of the wisest political observers in the nation's capital sat around over cigars and brandy speculating on the forthcoming 1964 Presidential race between John Kennedy and Nelson Rockefeller.

The second thought is tangential to the first. Because the rule is "Expect the Unexpected," there is little real sense in playing the political "what if?" game—except that it is addictive. As addicts to this fruitless pastime, we ask the question: *What if* Robert Kennedy had not been killed; would he have been nominated in Chicago? Our answer, resounding and emphatic, delivered with all the courage we can muster is: "Probably not, but—"

Kennedy had won some primaries with substantial numbers of delegates, notably California and Indiana, but he had not beaten his main opponent, Humphrey, face-to-face in any direct competition. In point of fact, from the time the Vice President announced his candidacy *Humphrey led RFK among Democrats in each of the public opinion polls up until Kennedy's murder.* The last poll, as shown on page 126, showed Democrats voting 40%–31%–19%, for Humphrey, Kennedy, McCarthy, in that order. * *Furthermore, Humphrey was shown to run strongest against Nixon in those same polls.* The importance of these data cannot be underestimated, particularly in light of what happened in Chicago later. Here are the early May Gallup data:

NIXON-HUMPHREY-WALLACE "TEST ELECTION"

MAY, 1968

Nixon	Humphrey	Wallace	No Opinion
39%	36%	14%	11%

NIXON-KENNEDY-WALLACE "TEST ELECTION"

MAY, 1968

Nixon	Kennedy	Wallace	No Opinion
42%	32%	15%	11%

Humphrey's lead in the polls was reflected by his delegate strength in those states that did not have open and contested Presidential preference primary elections. Although there have been much subsequent comment and testimony about how "undemocratic" the no-primary system is, it has, in fact, been a rather good barometer of party sentiment over the years.

Because the system—if one chooses to dignify institutionalized

---

* And Humphrey was ahead when paired in a two-man race against either Kennedy or McCarthy. (See page 126.)

helter-skelterism with the word "system"—is so complicated, it is hard to say exactly *why* and *how* it ends up as responsive as it is. Some states have beauty contests and unbonded delegates. Some states have no beauty contest but elect pledged delegates. Some states choose delegates by caucus or convention. Some delegates in some states are chosen directly by the state committees. Some states have hybrid mixtures of these systems. Some states have all the mechanisms available for an open, contested primary but never reach a "democratic" choice because two competing candidates do not enter the contest. Some nonprimary states went to McCarthy, many more to Humphrey. Some nonprimary states went by a unit rule totally to Humphrey; some primary states went by unit rule totally to McCarthy; some states split their vote.

What can be said about the delegate selection system is this: Somehow it works. All the delegates are *elected* or, if not, are *selected* by people who *were elected* popularly or, in some cases, selected by people who were selected by people who were elected popularly at one time or another. There is, then, a democratic process, if far removed, behind each delegate. That there is also a good deal of democratic slippage in the system is unquestioned. Still, in convention after convention,* the choice the delegates ultimately make is the choice of the tens of millions of party voters. This will be examined at greater length in the next chapter.

When we consider why Hubert Humphrey was ahead of Kennedy and McCarthy in the polls, it is wise to remember (again) who votes in America and what these voters were mostly disturbed about. The voters are unyoung, unpoor, unblack; they are middle-aged, middle-class; they wanted a conservative for the next Supreme Court Justice; they were concerned about crime, race, kids, disruption, and dissent, as well as with Vietnam.

Now, it is true that both Kennedy and McCarthy were *against* the established order, as were tens of millions of the

---

* With the exception of the 1964 Republican Convention.

electorate. But they were against things as they were from a direction that was probably not in tune with mainstream thinking. McCarthy and RFK were perceived as somewhat more liberal than Humphrey and more liberal than the Establishment at a time when liberalism was declining in popularity as a political label. The voters generally were to the ideological *right* of things as they were, certainly on the Social Issue. Both McCarthy and Kennedy were generally perceived to be the ideological *left* of things as they were. Humphrey was in the middle, which, as we have noted, is a very good place for a politician to be. He was perceived as more representative and more responsive to the aspirations and fears of that Democratic lady from suburban Dayton. The polls show it.

Humphrey's problem was that while he was in the middle of the Democratic Party, it turned out that when *all* the candidates were in the poll—and all the voters, not just Democrats, were voting—he was not in the center, but a little off to the left.

But because of the way the campaign fell into place, it left the New Politics ideologues with the feeling that they had been euchred out of a fair shake in the psephological marketplace. First, Johnson withdrew, robbing them of someone to run against; then Humphrey opted not to run in the few primaries he could have entered, and he was not a candidate early enough to be pushed into running in the so-called force primaries*; finally, their most potent candidate was slain, eliminating their best hope to marshal public opinion behind their banner.

The conclusion drawn by the New Politicians was that the system was rigged and that the "bosses" denied the "people" the man they wanted or at least that the people never had a chance to pick their man. In the judgment of the authors, that is not what happened. The "people" did have a very eloquent, very powerful way of making their opinions felt. The advent of the accurate and speedy public opinion poll has probably done

---

* In Wisconsin, Nebraska, and Oregon a candidate's name appears on the primary ballot whether or not he wants it to if, in the judgment of state officials, he is a candidate. But the deadline had passed by the time Humphrey became a candidate.

more to advance the responsiveness of the democratic process than any invention since the secret ballot and the direct primary. When the Gallup pollster and the Harris pollster visited that machinist's wife in suburban Dayton, they were hearing the voice of the people, and a week or two later her voice thundered its message to politicians across the land. Had the Gallup Poll in May shown Kennedy clearly ahead of Humphrey among Democrats, had the Gallup Poll in July shown McCarthy clearly ahead of Humphrey among Democrats, then it is entirely likely the Democratic delegates would have (1) been different people, or (2) not selected Humphrey. But it was Humphrey who was ahead—and it was Humphrey who was selected.

In one sense, the New Politics operation may actually have received more power and attention from the system than its public support merited. Suppose Humphrey *had* run in some of those spring primaries and *won* against either Kennedy or McCarthy or both of them—as the polls indicated he would have. Suppose something else. Suppose George Wallace *and* Humphrey entered the Democratic primaries. Wallace, let us remember, captured 34% of the Wisconsin primary vote and 30% of the Indiana vote in *1964*, long before the full flowering of the Social Issue. Suppose Wallace ran in Indiana and took 30% of the primary vote and Humphrey took another 35%, leaving Kennedy and McCarthy to split up the remaining 35%. Suppose there was a Wallace-*Johnson*-McCarthy race in New Hampshire. The against-things-as-they-were voters might well have split between Wallace and McCarthy,* leaving Johnson with the 50% write-in vote he actually received and letting Wallace and McCarthy split up the rest.

Such speculations can go on indefinitely and can prove almost anything. That is why the speculations about RFK's ultimate success must remain only speculations about imponderables.

But as we now approach a short examination of the 1968 Democratic Convention, we must remember one central *fact*,

---

* Remember that most McCarthy voters were more hawkish than Johnson.

not a speculation, that would have affected RFK or any Democratic candidate who might have run for the Presidency in 1968. It is this: At no time during 1968 did a majority of the Americans ever vote "for." The prevailing sentiment was "against." When calculated as a Nixon-plus-Wallace vote against either a Johnson or a Humphrey vote, the "against" sentiment ranged from a low of about 55% in June to a high of about 70% in September. Moreover, this "against" pattern formed to the *right* of things as they were, certainly on the Social Issue. To suppose that any candidate, no matter how personally charismatic—Kennedy, McCarthy, McGovern—from the *left* of things as they were could surmount this lead seems to the authors to be highly unlikely.

With neither Nixon nor Wallace in the Democratic primaries in New Hampshire and Wisconsin, the "against" feeling helped McCarthy, making him appear stronger than he was. With Johnson out of the race and Humphrey not yet in it, the remaining primaries became meaningless, although the polls showed that the "againsts" were more against the leftist candidacies of RFK and McCarthy than against the centrist candidacy of HHH, and more against the left centrism of HHH than the combined feeling for the right centrism and extreme rightism of, respectively, Nixon and Wallace.

The sentiment, then, was *against;* for the Democrats it was only a question of how this "against" might split. For a politician, happiness is a divided opposition. Any Democratic victory in 1968 would be dependent on George Wallace biting into Nixon's potential vote.

In the meanwhile, each major party had to go through the ritual of certifying the people's choice.

11

The Psephology of Nonpsephological Conventions

Only in the loosest sense can an American national political convention be regarded as a psephological event. There is an "election," it is true, but it is an election where the "voters" (the delegates) are at least once removed from the great masses of the American public whose actions and feelings we have been chronicling heretofore. In this sense, the convention assemblage resembles an elected body such as the Congress or a state legislature. It is a *republican* sort of institution, while psephology tends to study the more *democratic* actions.

Still, in looking at the conventions there are some lessons to be learned or reinforced; there are psephological axioms that apply; and of course, there can be no real understanding of Presidential politics without some knowledge of the convention itself. And so we will look briefly at conventions present, past, future, in that order.

It was alleged in 1968 that both national conventions were "rigged" against the charismatic candidates: Eugene McCarthy and Nelson Rockefeller.

But this is not correct. What is correct is that by the time the two national conventions met, it was an odds-on conclusion that Richard Nixon and Hubert Humphrey would emerge as the standard-bearers of their party. The conventions, in effect, were coronations—not contests. However, in deviation from the New Left mythology, the preselection, or the "rigging," did not occur owing to the back-room deal, the influence of the power brokers, or, as we have seen, the nonparticipatory method of delegate selection.

The conventions were rigged—and most conventions are usually rigged—only insofar as they reflected the previously expressed views of the majority of the party constituency.

Observe first the Republican coronation at Miami Beach. In a survey taken just prior to the convention, Republicans around the nation showed these preferences:

CHOICES OF REPUBLICANS
(Survey conducted just before the 1968 GOP Convention)

Nixon 60%
Rockefeller 23%
Reagan 7%
Others, and No Preference 10%
(*Gallup*)

Clearly, then, people who identified themselves as Republicans wanted Nixon.

At the same time (late July), people identifying themselves as Democrats were also quite clear about their choice for the nomination:

McCarthy-Humphrey "Showdown," Late July 1968 (*Among Democrats*)

Humphrey 53%
McCarthy 38%
No Opinion 9%
(*Gallup*)

After the Republican convention, Humphrey lost seven points among Democrats, while McCarthy gained four points, providing this result in mid-August:

McCarthy-Humphrey "Showdown," Mid-August 1968 (*Among Democrats*)

Humphrey 46%
McCarthy 42%
No Opinion 12%
(*Gallup*)

But some days later, on the eve of the Democratic Convention, Harris found a Humphrey resurge:

McCarthy-Humphrey "Showdown," Late August 1968 (Among Democrats)

Humphrey 56%
McCarthy 38%
Not Sure 6%

So, it can be said that *in the conventions of 1968, as in every Presidential nominating convention of the past quarter of a century except one, the choice of the party's tens of millions of adherents across the nation has also been the selection of the national nominating convention.* The one exception was the nomination of Barry Goldwater in 1964—of which and of whom more later.

In 1968 the proponents of the idea that the conventions were rigged by the bosses claimed that even if the conventions—as shown—were responsive to the "party will," they were not reflective of the "public will." This is a familiar charge, and its equally familiar "proof" traditionally concerns the poll data that show the choice not only of the "party voter," but of the "general public" as well. Using the Gallup Polls to show party breakdowns, we can see the point clearly.

Here's how Nixon versus Rockefeller looked prior to the Republican Convention:

NIXON-ROCKEFELLER "SHOWDOWN"
(July, 1968)

	Nixon	Rockefeller	No Opinion
NATIONAL	46%	46%	8%
Republican	67	28	5
Democrat	31	60	9
Independent	45	44	11

(Gallup)

While Nixon was the overwhelming choice of Republicans, Nixon and Rockefeller were even-steven among the total public.

The "public" view of Humphrey-McCarthy showed the same pattern in July, and even more acutely in August as Humphrey's popularity nose-dived in the summer after relatively high ratings all during the spring. Democrats wanted Humphrey; the "general public" wanted McCarthy.

McCARTHY-HUMPHREY "SHOWDOWN"

	McCarthy	Humphrey	No Opinion
July, 1968			
NATIONAL	*48%*	*40%*	*12%*
Republican	59	28	13
Democrat	*38*	*53*	9
Independent	53	*32*	15
August, 1968			
NATIONAL	*48*	*36*	16
Republican	55	30	15
Democrat	*42*	*46*	12
Independent	49	29	22

(Gallup)

So much for the evidence. What does it mean?

The Republicans did not nominate the choice of the Democrats and independents.

The Democrats did not nominate the choice of Republicans and independents.

Essentially, this is the evidence that has been used to prove that the American political system is not "participatory," not "representative," not "responsive" in the choosing of a President. Or, as they said in 1968, the conventions were "rigged."

But questions arise: Are Democrats morally bound to nominate a candidate of whom Republicans particularly approve? Are Republicans morally bound to nominate a candidate of whom Democrats particularly approve? Surely on ideological grounds there is no reason.

But forget ideology. Forget political morality. Shouldn't McCarthy and Rockefeller have been nominated on the pragmatic grounds that they were the best vote getters, that they would be winners?

Perhaps so, if it were so. But the data do not show that it is so. What the data do show is that while both Republicans and

Democrats are more than willing to tell the pollster who the *other* party should nominate, they will *vote* for their *own* party's candidate when the crunch comes. Thus, when a Gallup pollster asked *Republicans* who they preferred for the *Democratic nomination,* many chose McCarthy over Humphrey. Similarly, most *Democrats* preferred Rockefeller over Nixon. But the key questions were: How many of the party faithful would have actually left their own party's choice when the real election came to pass? Do they love in November whom they say they love in May? And how many independents would swing which way in the event of specific pairings? Those were thoughts that had to be weighed by the delegates to national conventions in 1968—and in essence, they are the questions that face convention delegates, like clockwork, every four years.

If we look carefully at the last Gallup Poll prior to the beginning of either convention, the answers become clear, and the exercise reminds us again of that key rule of psephology: that in an election or a public opinion survey the voter or respondent *can choose only from among the choices offered.** It is a simple rule, but an inevitably potent one.

Thus, we can recall that in a Humphrey-McCarthy showdown Republicans, by 59%–28%, preferred McCarthy *as the opposition's nominee.* This led to the numbers that showed that McCarthy was the "people's choice." But when Gallup then asked the *same Republicans* for whom they would vote for *President* if Nixon and Wallace were running against McCarthy, these were the results:

	Nixon	McCarthy	Wallace	No Opinion
Republicans only	79	11 (!)	7	3

Between Democrats Humphrey and McCarthy—the Republicans were for McCarthy by 2 to 1. But the same Republican voters, when asked to indicate their November preference between Nixon and McCarthy, chose Nixon by 7 to 1.

---

* As we saw in the Kennedy versus McCarthy versus no-one primaries in the late spring of 1968.

The same pattern was applicable on the Democratic side. In a Nixon-Rockefeller showdown *for GOP nominee,* Democrats preferred the more liberal Rockefeller by about 2 to 1 (60%–31%). But the same Democrats were queried for whom they would vote for *President,* and these were the results:

	Rockefeller	Humphrey	Wallace	No Opinion
Democrats only	20%	59%	15%	6%

Again a clear question of "What were the choices?" Democrats vastly preferred Republican Rockefeller to Republican Nixon (by 2 to 1), but even more preferred Democrat Humphrey to Republican Rockefeller (by 3 to 1).

Both the Rockefeller forces in Miami and the McCarthy forces in Chicago had an identical pitch for their men, and it was the pitch of the Old Politics: "He can win because he can best bring over votes from the other side in November." The final Gallup Poll prior to the beginnings of the conventions, however, *did not bear this out:*

Nixon, not Rockefeller, ran strongest against Humphrey:

Nixon	Humphrey	Wallace	No Opinion
40%	38%	16%	6%

Rockefeller	Humphrey	Wallace	No Opinion
36%	36%	21%	7%

Notice that the big gainer in a Rockefeller entry into the race is Wallace, drawing off the Republican vote that could not stomach liberal Republicanism.

Nixon	Humphrey	Wallace	No Opinion
40%	38%	16%	6%

Nixon	McCarthy	Wallace	No Opinion
41%	36%	16%	7%

And Humphrey ran slightly *better* than McCarthy in a test election, even though McCarthy was beating Humphrey in a "showdown" for the *nomination* 48% to 40% *at the same time.* The McCarthy falloff is largely attributable to Republicans going back home.

It is, of course, very true that the men who are the delegates to national nominating conventions always have an open ear to the plea that "he can win." Had McCarthy or Rockefeller opened a major lead over Humphrey or Nixon* in the he-can-win pairings, it is conceivable, even likely, that the conventions might have turned to them. This, in fact, was the announced strategy of both McCarthy and Rockefeller campaigns: to open up such a lead in the public opinion polls in order to persuade delegates that only by nominating these men could the party win. In fact, as we have seen, neither candidate did open up such a lead. Accordingly, the conventions were not faced with the agonizing classic choice between a man whom the tens of millions of party faithfuls clearly wanted and a man who clearly "could win."

While the professional delegates are always interested in a winning candidate so that they will be helped at the top of the ticket in their own races for sewer commissioner, it is a grave mistake to assume that idealism or ideologuism is the exclusive concern of the "enlightened left," as they view themselves. The writer Arthur Miller was a delegate from Connecticut to the 1968 Democratic Convention, and this is how he viewed the proceedings:

> There had to be violence for many reasons, but one funda-
> mental cause was the two opposite ideas of politics in this
> Democratic party. The professionals—the ordinary Senator,
> Congressman, State Committeeman, Mayor, officeholder—see

---

* One Harris Poll immediately prior to the Republican Convention did show Rockefeller beating Humphrey and Nixon losing to him. The effect of that poll was thoroughly muted by the Gallup evidence offered here. To be effective, a he-can-win campaign for an underdog must be based on crystal-clear evidence, not muddied waters. Herewith the Law of Clear Blue Water: for poll evidence to be of value to an underdog candidate, the evidence must be massive and uncontradictable; there must be clear blue water between the underdog and the favorite, say 10 percentage points.

politics as a sort of game in which you win sometimes and sometimes you lose. Issues are not something you feel, like morality,
like good and evil, but something you succeed or fail to make
use of. To these men an issue is a segment of public opinion
which you either capitalize on or attempt to assuage according
to the present interests of the party. To the amateurs—the Mc-
Carthy people and some of the Kennedy adherents—an issue is
first of all moral, and embodies a vision of the country, even of
man and is not a counter in a game. [*"The Battle of Chicago:
From the Delegates' Side," The New York Times Magazine,
September 15, 1968.*]

Mr. Miller's elitism is suspect, we suspect. The traditionally
scorned so-called party hacks are about as ideological as Arthur
Miller, if not as articulate as he or in full agreement with him
on certain matters of substance. It was amusing to note that
during the "Vietnam debate" at the 1968 Democratic convention the cheering and shouting were loudest when Wayne Hays,
the Congressman from Ohio, denounced the dissenters over in
Grant Park as a minority who would choose to substitute
"anarchism for ambition . . . beards for brains, license for
liberty . . . pot for patriotism . . . sideburns instead of solutions . . . slogans instead of social reform . . . and . . . riots
for reason." The delegates who cheered these perhaps intem-
perate remarks were no less "ideological" than Arthur Miller or
the McCarthy delegate who allegedly bit the hand of a policeman he felt was impinging on his right to freedom of movement
on, off, and about the convention floor.

More toward the ideological center, those Democratic delegates who were essentially labor-union-oriented were ideologically at least as much pro-Humphrey as Arthur Miller was
ideologically pro-McCarthy. They felt Hubert Humphrey could
best continue the gains accrued by workingmen in America and
felt this as deeply and with as much relevance to their lives as
Arthur Miller felt that Thieu and Ky were corrupt U.S. pup-
pets. However, to judge it from much of the media, Humphrey's support was coming primarily from the "party hacks,"
from something called the machine, from the "power brokers,"

or, at best, from "the organization." Exactly why a Carl Albert*
elected every two years by Oklahomans for two decades is called
a party hack—while Arthur Miller who has not exactly made a
career of elective politics is a self-proclaimed voice of the people—
is somewhat a mystery to the authors. A good working definition for the phrase "party hack" and equally applicable to the
word "demagogue" is this: "a political personality that one
disagrees with."

Most of the delegates to a party convention want two things:
their man ideologically and a man they think can be a winner.
Usually the best possible satisfaction of both of these wishes
works out this way: *A convention will choose the candidate
nearest to the center of its own ideological spectrum.*

So, when we read that in 1968 the Republicans "almost"
nominated Ronald Reagan, we read that with a grain of salt—a
tricky literary accomplishment. What *is* possible is that had
Reagan and Rockefeller increased their first-ballot vote, then
the first-ballot nomination certainly could have been kept from
Nixon. But then what would have happened? Would the leftist
Rockefeller forces have crossed over the center to vote for the
rightist Reagan to put him over the top? Would the Reagan
forces have crossed over the center to vote for Rockefeller?
Certainly not. It is equally doubtful that the Nixon centrist
delegates would have flocked to Reagan. If you were running for
county commissioner and had to explain the presence of Barry
Goldwater at the top of your ticket in 1964, would you want
to have to explain to your moderate supporters the presence of
Ronald Reagan as standard-bearer in 1968? It is also doubtful
that a typical Republican centrist delegate would be particularly enthralled about the idea of going home with a big
"Rocky for President" button on his lapel—particularly when
he visualized his own right-wing supporters suddenly turning
up with buttons marked "Wallace." At best, our Republican
centrist could count on some of his most loyal party workers
deciding to "sit this one out" and letting someone else do the
tedious political work of the upcoming campaign.

---

* Permanent chairman of the 1968 Democratic Convention.

So had Nixon, the centrist, been denied the nomination on the first ballot, it is a good speculation to assume that his centrist delegates would not have vaulted either to the right or to the left. They might have stuck with Nixon and waited for the laws of political gravity to take effect—*i.e.*, both Reagan and Rockefeller backers would rather have seen Nixon get it than their polar rivals. Or the centrist forces would have come up with *another* candidate, a dark horse or a not-so-dark horse, but clearly a horse from a stall in the center of the barn.

The centrist tropism at conventions was also visible in Chicago when the Democrats met. The only difference was that the right wing of the Democratic Party never surfaced a candidate of its own, staying with the centrist Humphrey, albeit with occasionally itchy feet. But Governor John Connally and the Texas delegation and many of the Southern state delegations did represent a right-of-center power bloc at the Democratic Convention, just as the Reagan supporters made up a similar bloc in Miami. The Connally forces would no more have made a polar leap to support McCarthy or McGovern than the McCarthy or McGovern forces would have made a leap to support, say, John Connally or Richard Russell. The answer again—and not surprisingly—was a candidate of the party's center, in this case Humphrey, a candidate with substantial personal appeal and power among the middle-of-the-road Democrats. Had the centrist delegates taken the left-wing counsel of "Dump the Hump," it is likely that the Convention would have turned neither to McCarthy nor to McGovern, but to another centrist, perhaps a then-dark horse like Edmund Muskie. As in the Republican instance, neither wing could really live in comfort with a candidate of the opposite wing, making a centrist candidate almost an inevitability.

Senator Edward Kennedy, had he chosen to run, might have proved to be an exception. Had the Humphrey forces been denied a first-ballot victory and broken ranks, which is doubtful, it is conceivable that Senator Kennedy could have put together the middle and the left and received the nomination. In that instance, Kennedy could have expected to see some

Democrats on the right and center looking around for campaign buttons marked "Wallace" or "Nixon," depending on how rapidly the young Senator from Massachusetts could have himself moved centerward. Again, we can witness the all-pervading power of the center: When a candidate is to the left, he loses some of the right; when he is to the right, he loses from the left. The power position is in the center.

There is one group that *is* essentially unrepresented by the American convention system: the "independents." These voters have some effect on convention politics in terms of the "he can win" public opinion polls, but next to none in terms of center-of-the-party judgments also drawn from the polls. Had all the independents in 1968 opted to call themselves Democrats, then the center-of-the-party choice in 1968 would have been McCarthy, not Humphrey.

That independents are impotent is probably unfortunate in terms of the fidelity of the democratic process. However, it must be remembered that in almost all states a voter who chooses not to participate in party affairs does so of his own free will, knowingly disenfranchising himself from all direct electoral activity except a vote in November. Unregistered, unaffiliated, unwilling even to indicate to a pollster that he leans toward one party or the other, the "independent voter" is next to useless to a candidate, such as McCarthy, who seeks a party nomination but finds that his voter strength is especially significant with independent groups. There is a myth that the independent voter in America is the alert, aware citizen who "makes up his own mind on the issues." Not so, say Messrs. Campbell, Converse, Miller, and Stokes in the classic work *The American Voter:*

> Far from being more attentive, interested, and informed, Independents tend as a group to be somewhat less involved in politics. They have somewhat poorer knowledge of the issues, their image of the candidates is fainter, their interest in the campaign is less, their concern over the outcome is relatively slight, and their choice between competing candidates, although

it is indeed made later in the campaign, seems much less to spring from discoverable evaluations of the elements of national politics.

The applicable axiom might be: "The nonparticipant has little weight in participatory democracy." McCarthy, of course, had an alternative available. He could have run for President on a new-party ticket, and any independents who strongly approved of him could have voted for him as a choice over Nixon, Humphrey, and the man who did run on a new-party ticket, George Wallace. Senator McCarthy, of course, may well consider this course in 1972.

It is by no means a new development that conventions usually choose the candidate best representative of the party's centrist rank-and-file voters.

Thomas Dewey in 1948 had Harold Stassen to his left and Robert Taft to his right, and the polls and some key primaries showed him to be the choice of the majority of Republican voters. He was nominated.

In 1952 Eisenhower occupied the left *and* the center of his party while Taft held the right. Eisenhower was the overwhelming choice of the voters who called themselves Republican, and he was nominated in 1952 even though Taft was admired by many delegates who respected the political credentials that led Mr. Taft to hold the soubriquet "Mr. Republican."

Richard Nixon was nominated in 1960 and 1968 because he held the support of the vast center of his party—expressed both numerically and ideologically.

In 1952 Adlai Stevenson started out as an unknown on the national scene, whose major support came from "party bosses" like Jake Arvey of Chicago and David Lawrence of Pittsburgh. As he became known in 1952, he came to occupy both the center and much of the left ground of the party, challenged by another centrist, Estes Kefauver, and a candidate of the Southern right, Richard Russell. Since Henry Wallace had left the political scene after 1948, there was no leftist candidate in 1952, and the activist centrist Kefauver battled the reluctant centrist Stevenson on the issue of what was once known as popularity and is now known as charisma. Charisma, or popularity, is a crucial factor for a man who wants to win an election or a nomination, provided, first, that he is perceived to be a man of the center. A person with a brilliant political personality will not be elected to anything if he is perceived to be a brilliant political personality who is also Fascist or a Communist.

By convention time Stevenson was the clear choice of those Americans who called themselves Democrats. He was nominated, actually drafted, in 1952 and then fought for and won the nomination in 1956.

In 1960, after a stunning series of primary victories, John Kennedy was shown in polls to be the choice of Democrats. He was perceived as a candidate of the center with high personal appeal contrasted with Humphrey and Stevenson on the moderate-center left and Lyndon Johnson and Stuart Symington on the moderate-center right. He was nominated.

With the exception of incumbent Presidents, who received almost automatic nomination, that accounts for all the candidates since World War II except one: Barry Goldwater.

In 1964 Barry Goldwater was neither the candidate of the center nor the choice of party members. Shortly before the 1964 Republican Convention in San Francisco, this is what the polls showed:

CHOICE OF REPUBLICANS

Lodge	26%
Nixon	25%
Goldwater	*21%*
Rockefeller	10%
Scranton	9%
Romney	5%
Others, no preference	4%

(*Gallup*)

When the moderates ultimately pooled their support behind Governor Scranton of Pennsylvania, the pairing looked like this:

(Pairing, 6/28/64)

Scranton	55%
Goldwater	*34%*
Undecided	11%

(*Gallup*)

Yet in defiance of all psephological rules, laws, axioms, and precepts set forth in this book, Barry Goldwater was nominated. In further defiance of the rules, Goldwater sought, or was at least perceived to seek, an ideological right-wing victory instead of a compromise victory of the center. After charging his followers to go "where the ducks are" for votes, he immediately got caught in one of the most marshy, duck-free thickets in American politics—the kooky right. Goldwater received a devastatingly low 38.5% of the vote.

What does the Goldwater experience prove? First, that conventions *can* be rigged against the will of the party. It doesn't happen often, but it can happen. Goldwater was able to capture the nomination because for two years his followers had been quietly working to elect their people to positions of party power from which they could control delegations in those states where there were no primaries. What allowed this to happen was that middle-of-the-road Republicans were in a between-elections hibernation, waiting for a Choice from Gettysburg, and could not finally agree on a candidate until it was too late. Goldwater coupled this preprimary activity and the disarray of his opponents with *one* slender primary victory in California—and won the nomination.*

The second lesson of the Goldwater nomination is that men and parties violate the rules of psephology at their peril. A man or a party who forgets the center forgets the name of the game. He who forgets the name of the game loses the game.

While in many ways, the 1968 conventions were typical, some of what went on in Chicago was not. Two events, in particular, were innovative.

---

* It is interesting to speculate about whether Goldwater would have been nominated had he not had that one victory. Possibly, but it would have been much more difficult without *any* popular claim to electoral legitimacy.

The first innovation was the Vietnam debate. For three hours, while tens of millions of Americans watched on television, doves, hawks, and birds of less committed species told their story to the public. This was probably the first major issue to be so publicly and prominently debated at a party convention in recent American history. Originally demanded by the Mc-Carthy forces as a way of taking their case to the nation, the debates did that and more: They established a precedent for honest public discussion of matters of substance. It would seem to be a precedent that both Democrats and Republicans would do well to reinforce in forthcoming conventions.

The second innovation concerned the use of confrontation and disruption in the streets as a means of waging political combat. As much as the writers disapprove of the tactics involved, it must be conceded that the tactics were wildly successful in attracting the attention they were designed to achieve.* Accordingly, and perhaps dismally, one may expect that the same or other groups will attempt to resort to similar tactics in conventions to come. Once again, both parties will do well to consider plans to combat such attempts with vigor, but, it is hoped, with somewhat more finesse than was demonstrated in Chicago. The fact that Miami Beach is on an island with limited access would seem to give it a great advantage in the quadrennial battles over which city will get the plum of a convention that brings to a city tens of thousands of visitors and world attention.

As a final thought before we move on now to see the laws of elections at work in the general election of 1968, there is one tip-off from Chicago that deserves notice.

Not long after the confrontation between "our children" in the park and "the pigs" who hit them on the head, the Louis Harris organization had its interviewers ask American voters what they thought about it all:

---

* 1968 was not the first time that there was a threat to disrupt a national convention. In the 1912 Republican Convention the speakers' rostrum was partially ringed with handsome shrubbery. Inside the shrubbery was barbed wire. The threat of violence in the convention hall in 1912 did not materialize. It was perceived as coming from the Teddy Roosevelt Progressives. They thought the convention was rigged.

REACTION TO DEMOCRATIC CONVENTION

	Agree	Disagree	Not Sure
Mayor Daley was right the way he used police against demonstrators.	66	20	14
Anti-Vietnam demonstrators had protest rights taken away unlawfully.	14	66	20

Antiblue versus blue; kid versus pig; cop versus punk. Call it what you will, what the television sets across the country showed was that it was the melodrama of the Social Issue that was being enacted in the streets of Chicago. When the kids met the cops, they were perceived as challenging the very fabric of the social order. This confrontation seemed to separate the Social Issue into neat compartments, or, to use the more fashionable word, polarize. On the one side were the elite, long-haired students. On the other, "our children"—that is, the policemen, the children of the machinist's wife from suburban Dayton. When asked about it, the American public voted blue—and that vote illuminated the stage for the election of 1968.

12

The Return of Most of the Natives—
Humphrey '68

It was fall, and like football coaches all over the land, each of the major candidates looked over the field conditions and came up with a "game plan" designed to win. Because the teams (if not the players) will be generally the same in 1972 and 1976, it is instructive to examine the films of the 1968 game in slow motion. Watching, we can see who missed the blocks, who fumbled the ball, and who scored the touchdowns. In doing so, we and each of the teams may learn a good deal about how to construct a new and better game plan for the elections of the seventies.

The Humphrey plan came in two parts. First, he would attempt to get the leaders of his team together in the same huddle—a feat that had not been accomplished in Chicago. Second, he would march up the center of the field, actually perhaps a bit to the left, but at least where the center of the field used to be.

The Nixon plan was simple: a series of what used to be called line plunges over the three-hole, between right guard and right tackle—a spot that he perceived to be the new center of the field. This was sound strategy from Nixon's point of view. But it was almost foiled by a new fact about this strange football game: There were three teams on the field.

George Corley Wallace quarterbacked the third team. He started out on the right sideline with few experienced players or coaches and lacking even some rudimentary equipment such as shoulder pads or helmets. He did have a football, however—an extremely relevant political football—and in moments of extreme optimism he thought he might carry his football over the goal line with the help of his opponents' failures and an assist from the fans, whom he expected to swarm out of the grandstand. He got a good deal of support at one point, but ultimately Wallace learned that too many of his admirers felt that only two teams could play for keeps in the superbowl of political football.

First, let us see how the Democrats made out and why.

Humphrey came out of the Chicago convention at about the same level he went in—and that is a calamity for a Presidential candidate. A convention is designed to gain a candidate favorable exposure throughout the nation and through this exposure to gain popularity and votes. Nixon, indeed, had *gained* 14 percentage points on Humphrey immediately following the Republican Convention in Miami. But Humphrey did not do nearly as well. After the raucous, rioting Chicago Democratic Convention, Humphrey picked up only 4 percentage points. And in 1968 the 10-percentage-point differential between the two candidates represented more than *7,000,000* voters. By and large, these 7,000,000 voters had looked at the feuding, fighting, rioting Democrats on their television sets and said, "These guys couldn't be trusted to walk my dog and come back with the same animal."

The convention, designed to boost a candidate, did precious little boosting for Humphrey because of the public display of corrosive and bitter internal conflicts within the party over the issue of Vietnam. The first question we must ask, then, is: How did Humphrey manage to get his leadership team back into the huddle? And then: How did he manage to get the rank-and-file voter back into his camp?

Essentially, both groups came back largely because they realized there was no other huddle, no other team, with which they could feel comfortable. This political phenomenon is a common one, usually shorthanded into a question: Where else can you go?

Among the leadership, both doves and hawks were ultimately willing to accept Humphrey's "dawk" position because they had no other realistic choice left, and politics at its essence is the practical art of choice-making.

A dove who chose to reject Humphrey had the option of voting for Eldridge Cleaver or Dick Gregory in November, of wasting a write-in for Gene McCarthy, or of not voting. A hawk who rejected the Humphrey Vietnam position was left with the option of making bed with Richard Nixon or George Wallace. Some few Democratic doves did reject Humphrey. On the other side, some few Democratic hawks did find a home with Nixon or Wallace. But just how anxious the leadership was to get back together can be seen from the reaction to a speech Humphrey gave in Salt Lake City on September 30, which was broadcast over nationwide television.

A single paragraph—one that would have probably been rejected by hawks and doves alike if spoken six weeks earlier— seemed to serve temporarily to bury the hatchet and the Vietnam issue. The paragraph said:

> As President I would stop the bombing of North Vietnam as an acceptable risk for peace because I believe it could lead to success in the negotiations and thereby shorten the war. This would be the best protection of our troops. In weighing that risk, and *before taking action,* I would place key importance on the evidence of Communist willingness to restore the de-militarized zone between North and South Vietnam. Now if the government of North Vietnam were to show bad faith, I would reserve the right to resume the bombing. . . . [Italics ours.]

The speech raised as many questions as it tried to answer. Specifically, did it, or did it not, demand reciprocal enemy action in return for the bombing halt? The first sentence hints "no reciprocity necessary"; the third sentence hints "we want reciprocity." And at the time that *was* the issue: Hawks demanded reciprocity for a bombing halt; doves said gamble.

Democratic doves, looking for a way home, interpreted the paragraph as "a break with Johnson." Hawks, looking for a way home, interpreted the paragraph as, at worst, only a minuscule movement indicating that Humphrey was by no means selling out to the doves. Both groups, facing political realities, welcomed the statement and the idea that it laid to rest (temporarily) the thorny issue of the war.

In effect, what Humphrey did with an all-things-to-most-men paragraph on September 30 in Salt Lake City was the functional equivalent of a nominating convention: It established to the party leadership factions that the candidate was residing satisfactorily at the ideological center of his party. The super-doves, who had viewed Humphrey earlier as a creature with napalm in his veins, stopped heckling, stopped the "Dump the Hump" chanting. This allowed television to carry film footage of the candidate, not the hecklers. The hawks stopped their more subtle freeze-out. Humphrey, as a person, responded to this support and showed up as a far more attractive candidate.

From Humphrey's point of view, the tragedy was that his coronation occurred a full five weeks after convention time, with the election only five weeks away, and after the Democratic Party had been perceived as disrupted, ineffective, and very likely soft on the Social Issue—*viz.*, Chicago.

The rank-and-file voters who came back to Humphrey came back for the same essential reason the leadership came back. The clock kept ticking, and the realization that a choice must be made became stronger and stronger. Of the three real choices available, on the issues contested, these comeback voters concluded Humphrey was the best man for them. The choice was Humphrey or Nixon or Wallace or don't vote; it was that simple.

Elections are choices between candidates who represent a vast array of issues and who stir a vast array of emotions. Voters seek, but do not find, perfection. They seek a candidate with whom they agree 100% and whom they find 100% personally appealing. When they do not find that, when election day gets closer and closer, they choose from what is offered. They choose, usually, from among the candidates that they think have a chance of winning.*

Understanding all this, we look now at *why* so many rank-and-filers went from defector to loyalist and why some stayed as defectors. What was the substance behind the choice-making?

As Hubert Humphrey—with a great assist from a ticking clock—was establishing himself, finally, at the center of his party's leadership, he was also moving to establish himself at the center of the electorate as a whole. Accordingly, Mr. Humphrey's second major nationwide television speech, delivered in New York on October 12, dealt with law and order.

Not insignificantly, that was the week the Gallup headline released to newspapers said: CRIME IN STREETS IS REAL FEAR OF U.S. VOTERS.

But Humphrey's foray into the crime problem met with only partial success. It was in some ways an irony that Hubert Humphrey was unable to capitalize on the problem. As the very young mayor of Minneapolis from 1945 to 1948, Humphrey was perceived to be perhaps the toughest and most effective anti-crime mayor in America. He came down hard on the leaders of organized crime and was successful in driving them out of the city.

Accordingly, it might seem a bit unfair that Richard Nixon, a man who never served in any elective office that had anything directly to do with crime or criminals, reaped the harvest of the law-and-order vote. But he did. In September it looked this way:

"Which candidate do you feel could do the best job in handling law and order?"

Nixon	36%
Wallace	26%
Humphrey	23%
Not sure	15%

(*Gallup*)

---

* Just as most nonliberals chose either liberal McCarthy or liberal RFK in the spring primaries because those were the choices that were then available. Or as Jimmy Durante said, "Them is the conditions what prevail."

Humphrey's plight on the crime issue was exacerbated by some incredible ideological verbiage on the part of liberals. With half the women in America uptight about law and order, what was the liberal response? "Law and order," they said, "is a code word for racism." In other words, "Lady, you're not really afraid of being mugged; you're a bigot." The "code word for racism" was in fact a code phrase for first-water political ineptitude. Politically, liberal Democrats should actively have been trying to separate the crime issue from the race issue; instead, they were busy as beavers linking them. Instead of saying, "We are *for* civil rights and *against* crime," many seemed to feel that anyone against crime must also be against civil rights. Humphrey himself did not publicly use the "code word for racism." But this sort of thinking was clearly a part of the constellation of liberal clichés, and as such, it was identified with Humphrey and gained a good deal of public currency. Ultimately, liberals caught on to what was going on in America, and the new cliché —a much more satisfactory one—was "law and order *with justice.*"

In any event, September saw Humphrey in bad straits indeed. He was at least a month behind the normal political timetable of uniting the party. He was perceived as number three in a three-man race in regard to the ability to handle the number one issue. To these unhappy circumstances was added another: For two to three weeks after the convention, the simple mechanics of campaign organization was inexcusably lacking. Rally crowds were sparse; arrangements sloppy; schedules chaotic. And the press was riding Humphrey unmercifully.

Not all—perhaps not any—of these psephological catastrophes should be viewed as the fault of the candidate. But many observers think there was one major flaw in Humphrey's candidacy that probably was, at least partly, his own fault. This was what might be called the Wishy-Washy Issue.

For reasons discussed earlier, most American Presidential elections usually come down to being choices between centrists of the right and centrists of the left. Once both candidates are established as being centrist, the issue of personality can become paramount. And perhaps the one personal trait that most voters want to see in a Presidential aspirant is that he is resolute and decisive: a "take-charge guy."*

The Wishy-Washy perception by the voters of Hubert Humphrey was related in large part to the Vietnam trap in which he found himself, and for this reason it is perhaps unfair to pin blame on the candidate himself.

In the spring, after the announcement of his candidacy, Humphrey was perceived of as wholeheartedly backing the Johnson position on the war. At that point, Humphrey led Robert Kennedy and Gene McCarthy in a laundry list rating, and he *beat* Richard Nixon by 45%–40%–15% in a Nixon-Humphrey-Wallace heat. It is important to bear this in mind because the legend-making about 1968 seems to claim that Humphrey was never ahead and came up with a grand rush only at the very end. That is not what happened: Humphrey was ahead (although not with a majority); he fell behind; he recouped—almost.

But Humphrey's pro-Johnson Vietnam position of the spring did not satisfy a large dove faction of the Democratic Party. As the months wore on toward the convention, Humphrey was perceived as being more dovish than the President and still not dovish enough for the doves. Was he really "Johnson's puppet"; did he really believe in the Vietnam war? Or was he a secret dove; would he, could he, run on a peace plank?

Almost any position would have been better than the one he ultimately took, which was best described as "confused," "indecisive," or "wishy-washy." He could have gained respect from a forthright, positive endorsement of Johnson's policies—*i.e.,* "I know some of my respected fellow Democrats in good conscience disagree with the current course of the tragic war in Vietnam, but I think it is the best available one." He could have gained respect with the opposite point of view: "As much

---

* This is also the trait voters seem most to look for in a mayor. It is in part because of this similarity that extensive attention is paid here to the mayoralty races of 1969. See Chapters 16–18.

as I respect the judgment of President Johnson on most issues, on the issue of the war, I disagree with his judgment in the following ways and for the following reasons." He probably could even have finessed the issue—as he ultimately did in Salt Lake City—by taking a *definite stand* that he had no definite stand. This is essentially what Richard Nixon did: He said he would end the war honorably. He said he knew how he would do it—and then said no more.

Here is how the Wishy-Washy Issue stood in a Harris poll midway during the campaign:

"Candidate is too wishy-washy"

	Agree	Disagree	Not Sure
Humphrey	37%	46%	17%
Nixon	26%*	57%	17%

(*Harris, October, 1968*)

* Nobody in his right mind in 1968 ever accused Richard Nixon of coming across as a particularly decisive personality. But a high wishy-washy rating is not nearly as damaging to an out-party candidate as it is to an in-party candidate. It may even be helpful. One recalls Walter Lippmann's 1932 description of Franklin D. Roosevelt as "a pleasant young man who wants to be President." In fact, in 1932, it was in FDR's best interest to take few firm stands, to be wishy-washy, to be no more than a pleasant young man. His basic strength was that he was *not* Hoover. Any stand he took could alienate some support he already had in his pocket. Similarly, in 1968, Nixon's strength came from the fact that he was *not* Johnson, *not* Humphrey, and didn't have anything to do with anything that people were angry about.

In any event, by mid-September, between a disunited party, a stumbling campaign, trouble on the Social Issue, and a sinking charisma count, the candidacy of Hubert Humphrey was in grave trouble.

By the third week in September the Gallup Poll reported these results:

Nixon	43%
Humphrey	28% (!)
Wallace	21%
Undecided	8%

But Humphrey did have one big factor going for him. As September wore on, as September became October, as the leaves turned, as the World Series ended, the fact that Hubert Humphrey was a *Democrat*—and a good one—began to tell. Like children scattered wildly on a long and unsuccessful scavenger hunt, the Democrats began to come home and the independents who usually voted Democratic began to come home—just a few at first, but then in big numbers and with a great rush during October and early November.

At Humphrey's 28% low point in the campaign the oppositionists were riding high. About seven in ten Americans were saying no to Humphrey and the Democrats, and the press was beginning to speculate that Humphrey could finish with fewer electoral votes than Wallace and perhaps not many more popular votes. He went up a point to 29% in the September 27–30 Gallup Poll. After his two nationwide television speeches he climbed to 31% in polling done October 3–12. By October 17–21 he was at 36%; in the October 31–November 2 polling, he was at 40%. Gallup estimated that about 200,000 votes per day in October were flowing to Humphrey. On election day he received 43% of the vote.

The wanderers in a year-long political scavenger hunt were returning—most of them to home base, but some few to strange homes. One polling organization official said he had never seen anything like it in a lifetime of observing election trends.

Why did so many leave in the first place? Why did most of the natives return? Why did some go elsewhere? The answers to these questions tell us why the election went as it did and a great deal about what factors will be at work in the years to come.

In answering these questions, we shall see some of our earlier psephological axioms reemerge, and we will confront head on a whole new psephological area: the role of the party.

Here, to review, is the road map of what happened in 1968, derived from Gallup Polls after distributing the "undecided" vote in roughly the same proportion as the way the "decided" vote went:

	JUNE	JULY (pre-GOP Convention)	AUGUST (pre-Dem. Convention)	SEPTEMBER (post-Dem. Convention)	FINAL
Humphrey	45%	40.5%	31.5%	33%	43%
Nixon	40%	42.5%	48.5%	46%	43.5%
Wallace	15%	17%	20%	21%	13.5%
"Oppositionist" (total Nixon plus Wallace)	55%	59.5%	68.5%	67%	57%

Why did Humphrey fall? He hurt himself, as described; he was hurt by the Republican Convention which helped Nixon; he was *not* helped by the split at the Democratic Convention; he was damaged by Wallace's rise.

Why did Humphrey come back? Voters get more serious and less emotional as the real election approaches. It is one thing to tell the Gallup pollster in early September that your choice for President is George Wallace because you're angry at black militants and upset about crime. It is another thing to tell the pollster "Wallace" in late October when it means that Wallace is who you'll actually vote for. It is one thing to say "Wallace" among a choice of three names, and another to say it when you are fully aware that only one of *two* men can actually win, and Wallace isn't one of them.

To this must also be added the fact that the Humphrey campaign finally began "putting it together," that the Vietnam issue was muted, and that the candidate was perceived, finally, as hard-hitting, spunky, intelligent, and forceful, as well as a "nice guy."

Beyond all this, combined with all this, part of all this, in a sense surrounding all this, looms the strange magnetism of party loyalty. It is a phenomenon worthy of some careful thought, a phenomenon about which much can be said, some of it apparently contradictory.

In late September, 1968, Gallup asked a cross section of Americans:

"Generally speaking, do you think it is better to vote for the man or the party?"

"The Man"	"The Party"	No Opinion
84%	12%	4%

That, at least, is how people *think* they vote, and it would seem, accordingly, that "the party" bears little influence on how Americans vote.

On a Presidential level, there is some scant evidence that this is so and a great deal of evidence that it is *not* so.

Eisenhower was most popular as "the man" in 1956, when he received 58% of the total vote. But 85% of Democrats still voted for Adlai Stevenson. In 1964, Barry Goldwater was alienating Americans by tens of millions, yet 80% of Republicans still voted for him. Franklin Roosevelt was an extremely popular "man," yet even in his peak year of 1936, the great majority of Republicans voted for Alf Landon. Perhaps the best that can be said of the apparent discrepancies in the man versus party data is that partisan Americans tend to think it is *their party* that usually nominates the best *man*. That was the essence of Harry Truman's remark: "Of course I'm for the best man. He's a Democrat."

There is more than simple tautology in that statement. Partisan Americans have felt that there is a substantial difference between the two major parties. They vote accordingly. Democrats—on a national level—are viewed demographically as the party of the workingman, the intellectual, the Jews, the blacks, many ethnic Catholics, and, until recently, Southerners. Ideologically, Democrats have largely been viewed as the party of the "little guy." They are viewed as favoring relatively active social and economic reform and as against big business. Republicans—on a national level—are viewed as the party of the businessman, large and small, the professional, the farmer, the suburbanite, a largely white and Protestant party. They are for slower social change, lower taxes, and less federal power. These are stereotypes, to be sure, and not necessarily always so. But they are widely believed. (The stereotypes may also be changing. If they change to the direction of saying that Democrats are the party of permissiveness on the Social Issue, the Democrats will be in for trouble.)

It is a cliché of politics to say that most Americans vote "by habit" for a party or vote by habit "for the party of their fathers." That is not quite correct. What is correct is that most

Americans don't casually change their basic overview of politics. Basic changes do occasionally come, as in 1932, and temporary shifts (as in 1964) are not uncommon—but the American voters are not best seen as political Yo-Yos. In most instances, in most places, American voters have been creatures of political continuity.

Essentially, it was this pattern of party voting that enabled Humphrey to make his stretch run such a powerful one. He and his supporters raised the old banner of the Democratic Party, and most of the people who had saluted it in the past found they could not easily abandon it or the political overview that it had for so long represented. And back they came: the Jews; the blacks; the poor; the big-city ethnic Catholics; the union men who had toyed with supporting Wallace; the intellectuals who had been for Eugene McCarthy. The party they had supported in the past, they realized, involved more than a stand on crime and race or a stand on Vietnam.

The intellectuals saw that there was no better choice available on Vietnam and so went, grimly sometimes, to the man and the party they felt best represented their other interests: civil rights; aid to cities; aid to education; etc.

The labor unions, in particular, waged a massive campaign for Humphrey. The leadership of labor felt that while many Democratic leaders had been their friends, Humphrey was their blood brother. An intensive political effort that involved 50,000,000 pieces of campaign literature reminded union members that Hubert Humphrey and the Democratic Party had brought about Social Security and Medicare, had increased the minimum wage, and had ensured prosperity and dignity for the workingman. The union leadership, recognizing the threat of the Wallace campaign, made much of the low wage scales in Alabama and more of Wallace's alleged antilabor views. But this activity of the leadership would not have sufficed had not the rank-and-file members been attuned to the message, had they not believed it when they heard it. The campaign worked: Most of the workers were Democrats, and the "return of most of the natives" showed that the old Economic Issue, passionately and effectively voiced, could blunt much of the appeal of the Social Issue for millions of working-class Americans.

With only the one exception of the South, and despite all the hoopla about the "breakup" of the FDR Democratic coalition, the voting results of 1968 were not terribly different from the voting results of 1944. The majority of the poor voted for FDR—and for Hubert Humphrey. The majority of the rich voted for Tom Dewey—and for Richard Nixon. Blacks, Jews, and big-city Catholics were for Roosevelt and Humphrey. Outside the South, farmers were for Dewey and Nixon.

So the coalition was alive in America, and in 1968 that was a vital truth in the Humphrey "comeback."

As seen over the years, the rhetoric about the FDR Coalition resembles nothing so much as the rhetoric about "the theater is dying in New York." It has been decades now that the theater in New York has been "dying," according to all the theatrical *cognoscenti.* But every time one ventures into the theater district in New York, there are the lights and there are the shows. So too with the fabled FDR Coalition. For forty-seven months we hear about how it is "breaking up" or "disintegrating," yet every fourth year in November—presto! there it is again.

That having been smugly said, it is crucial to note that in 1968 the coalition, in losing the South, did this time *in fact* lose one vital piece and *did* show an erosion outside the South even though the *patterns* outside the South held fast. Whether these losses and erosions are small or large, whether they are one-time shifts or tidal movements, will determine the outcome of Presidential elections in the seventies. Accordingly, it is important to look carefully at the loss (the South) and the erosion (outside the South). It is equally important to attempt to ascribe reasons for the loss and the erosion.

How was the South lost to the Democrats? With 20–20 hindsight it can be seen that the defection away from Democrats in Presidential elections in the South had been building for a long time, but it was 1968 that drove the last nail into the coffin. The Solid South had remained solidly Democratic only through the years of Franklin Roosevelt, with Democratic percentages of

81%, 81%, 78%, and 72% in the 1932–44 elections. When it became increasingly clear that Democratic Presidential candidates would invariably and inevitably be "liberals" who did not reflect Southern conservative views on race, as well as other issues, the South began its bolt.

In the next five elections, Southern votes went from the Roosevelt-years 70%–80% pro-Democratic range to about the 50% range:

DEMOCRATIC PERCENTAGE IN THE SOUTH

1948	50%
1952	52%
1956	48%
1960	51%
1964	50%

And then—1968—31% (!)

But the handwriting was already on the wall in the election of 1964, although it was obscured in part by the strange nature of the Goldwater candidacy and the Democratic landslide. The first Democratic Presidential candidate in a century to hail from one of the states of the Old Confederacy—Lyndon Johnson—polled only 49.5% of the Southern vote while carrying *63.5%* of the non-Southern national vote. Goldwater carried 48.7% of the Southern vote compared to *36.3%* of the non-Southern national vote. Here, then, in a section of the nation that once went 20 or 30 percentage points *more for the Democrats* than the non-Southern national average, the vote was now 12 percentage points *more for the Republican candidate* in a year of a Democratic landslide.

What happened in 1968 confirmed, intensified, and probably ended the bulk of the Southern shift. The Democrats received only 30.9% of the Southern vote—*less* than either Republicans (34.6%) or American independents (34.3%).

So, in the course of twenty-four years—from Roosevelt to Humphrey—the Democratic vote in the South plummeted from 72% to 31%, a massive party movement in a land where people supposedly "vote the party of their fathers" or "vote by habit." The era of the Brass Collar Democrat is over.

Of all the states of the Old Confederacy, only Texas and its 25 electoral votes were to be found in the Democratic column. And Texas only gave Humphrey a 41% to 40% margin over Nixon, with Wallace getting 19%. Had Wallace not been in the race, it is likely Texas, too, would have gone Republican. That the Wallace vote would largely have gone for Nixon in 1968 is an important point, to be discussed in detail in a moment.

The defection of the South is clearly a staggering blow to the Democratic Party of the future. For the "political South," defined as the eleven states of the Old Confederacy,* is a potent bloc of political real estate. In 1968 it involved 128 electoral votes and 20% of the popular vote. When we look backward, it is significant to note that *had not at least some Southern states gone for John F. Kennedy and Harry S. Truman, they would not have gained enough electoral votes to be elected.*

That is a crucial fact, worth mulling. But so is this one which points up some of the vagaries of the electoral college: *Franklin D. Roosevelt would have won each of his four elections without a single Southern electoral vote.* And, in recalling that, let it also be remembered that FDR's last two victories were far from landslides with 54.7% and 53.4% of the vote. And of course, *Lyndon Johnson would have won in 1964 without a single Southern state.*

There is a twin rule that carries a clear message for both political parties and all psephologists. First part of rule: In a close election even a slight shift can change the result, and the South is more than "slight." Second part of rule: When the electoral tide is running your way, it can easily knock over enough dominoes to bring in victory without the South.

In 1968 the electoral tide was not running with Democrats. They were annihilated in the South. But there was attrition even in non-Southern Democratic strongholds—among those natives that did not return.

Note that:

---

* They are: Alabama, Arkansas, Florida, Georgia, Louisiana, Mississippi, North Carolina, South Carolina, Tennessee, Texas, and Virginia.

—Humphrey succeeded in carrying only six states with a clear majority—two being the "home" states of Humphrey and Muskie (Maine and Minnesota), two the non-Caucasian states (Hawaii and the District of Columbia), and two heavily Catholic states, the only Northern states that went for Al Smith in 1928 (Massachusetts and Rhode Island).

—If one looks at 1960 as a base-line 50–50 year, six non-Southern states shifted from the 1960 Democratic column to the 1968 Republican column: Delaware, Illinois, Missouri, Nevada, New Jersey, and New Mexico, representing 65 electoral votes.

—Only two non-Southern states went from Republican in 1960 to Democratic in 1968: Maine and Washington, representing 13 electoral votes. Outside the South, then, five times as many electoral votes switched to Nixon than to Humphrey.

An examination of the nationwide data of the Gallup Poll in the appendix of this volume shows the broad trending of the vote from 1960 to 1968 by electoral groups. Except for the black voter, the eight-year shifts favored Nixon, but not with large changes. The non-Southern switchers were not a massive number, only enough to change the outcome of the election. To borrow a cliché from baseball, politics is a game of inches.

To know just how close, picture a dinner party with 20 guests seated around the table. As can be determined from the election gazeteer in this volume, in four of the last seven Presidential elections the guests at that table would have split their votes by some fraction less than an 11 to 9 count. Only in the Johnson-Goldwater election of 1964 and the two Eisenhower-Stevenson elections did the winner receive more than a 55% vote. Even in the 1964 election, generally acknowledged to be a landslide, the split at the dinner table would have been only 12 to 8.

Now remember 1964. It was a year when the incumbent President Lyndon Johnson was at the height of his personal and political career, when Barry Goldwater was pilloried as a nuclear bomber who would take away hard-earned Social Security dollars and when psychiatrists who never met him hinted that Goldwater was mentally unfit for the Presidency. In that year, if one stopped a random *ten* Americans on the street, *four would have voted for Goldwater.*

This pattern of closeness is not unique to America. Around the world, most truly democratic elections are close. Certainly, if one follows the election results since World War II in nations such as Great Britain, Canada, France, and Italy, there is an almost unremitting succession of close elections.*

The reason for close elections has been discussed earlier: centrism. Politicians the world over bid for the support of the voters at the swinging center of the political spectrum. Usually they are somewhat successful. Accordingly, the voting is usually close.

It was close in the U.S. election of 1968 for the same reason: The two major-party candidates were competing for the large, uncommitted center of the electorate. As Hubert Humphrey's campaign finally jelled, as the candidate himself came on with a stirring rush, as Wallace was perceived more and more as extremist, as most of the Democratic natives returned to the fold, the poll readings became increasingly close. So close, in fact, that the day before the election Harris predicted a Humphrey popular vote victory, and both Harris and Gallup conceded that it was so close that the standard margin of error in their polls could give the popular vote victory to the other man.

Still, the Democrats did lose the election and clearly lost ground from base year 1960; they lost ground massively in the South and slightly, but significantly, elsewhere.

Why? Of what portent?

The counting of votes is a craft—sometimes a tricky one, sometimes a creative one, but always one that can ultimately be measured precisely. But ascribing *reasons* and *motives* to votes

---

* There are exceptions. The members of the House of Commons (and thus the Prime Minister) of Northern Ireland are elected by top-heavy majorities. This represents the no-compromise politics of theology in which Protestants vote for Protestant candidates and Catholics (the minority) vote for Catholic candidates. No coalition of Protestant and Catholic voters, formal or informal, has yet been successful.

is more an art than a craft and never wholly susceptible to precise measurement. Why did the machinist in Dayton vote for Wallace? Why did his wife stay with Humphrey?* Why did his brother-in-law go to Nixon? In all probability, they themselves do not fully know the answers. People vote, and change their vote, for a vast variety of reasons and emotions, counterreasons and counteremotions, one trading off against another in an often mystical, unmeasurable way. Still, given the fact that we have precious few facts, we do have many pointers, clues, hints, with which to beef up a postulation.

Postulating about the breakaway of the South from the Democratic Party is relatively easy because the shift has been so massive. When the Democratic vote goes from 72% in 1944 to 31% in 1968, something has happened, and it has been something tidal. In the case of the South the basic issue has been racial, although the other pressures of the Social Issue have also been present. John Kennedy could still take half of the Southern vote in 1960, when it was Dwight Eisenhower who had sent the troops to Little Rock. But when the sixties came, when it was John Kennedy who sent the troops to Oxford, Mississippi; when in 1968 Lyndon Johnson, after passing the Civil Rights and Voting Rights bills, could call a group of black lawyers, in honesty, "soul brothers," the marriage between the Democrats and the South was sundered—and sundered as far ahead as the psephological eye can see.

The Democrats in the South were hurt by being perceived (correctly) as a problack national party, but they were also hurt by the other nonracial aspects of the Social Issue that had become identified with liberal Democrats: soft on crime, "kidlash," morals, and disruption. Anachronistic evidence: In the late fall of 1969, Vice President Agnew lashed out against the "impudent corps of snobs," the long-haired kids marched on Washington, and a handful of them broke up Dupont Circle and made a run on the Justice Department. The villains in Agnew's tirade were almost exclusively *white*—but throughout

---

* Wallace polled higher among men than among women.

the South bumper stickers blossomed reading *"Spiro is my hero,"* and a Southern politician was quoted as saying he was voting for Agnew in 1972, and if that meant voting for Nixon also, so be it.

In the South today, the Democratic Party—in terms of national elections—is most often perceived as the party of blacks, plus a comparative handful of white Southern liberals. In no Southern state are there enough Presidential Democrats to put together a statewide majority.* Although the divorce decree may not be absolutely final, the question now is which of the two suitors the South will accept: Wallaceite or Republican. In the event that the affection for *each* remains strong, there is the possibility of the Democrats sneaking in the back door for some selective wooing of selected states. The Democrats carried Texas in 1968 with only 41% of the vote, and this might be repeated there or elsewhere in a close Republican-Wallaceite standoff.

So much, for the moment, for the reasons behind the Southern defection.

As the authors see the small but significant Democratic drop *outside* the South, we note again the fact of the return of (most of) the natives to a traditional Democratic loyalty. Save for the black vote, which was largely Democratic from the beginning of the campaign, the combination of events discussed earlier in this chapter turned a debacle (in September) into an extremely close race (in November). Unlike the Southern shift, which

---

* The Southern *white* Democratic vote for Humphrey was very low. As an example of Southern voting patterns in 1968, here is urban Fulton County, Georgia (including Atlanta), a county with more liberal-minded whites than in many Southern counties.

Fulton County (Atlanta), Georgia

Precinct Group	Nixon	Humphrey	Wallace
Precincts 95% + Black	2%	98%	0%
Precincts 95% + White	52%	22%	26%

It should be remembered that the New Deal Southern vote—in the 70%–80% range for Democrats—was largely an *all-white* vote. Now the *white* Presidential Democratic vote is probably below 20%, well below in *rural* white areas.

was tidal, the shift outside the South seemed tidal at Labor Day but subsided to an apparent ripple by election day. It was enough of a ripple to shift key states and elect Nixon, but a ripple nonetheless.

The anti-Humphrey tide that rose in September showed the vast potential power of the Social Issue. Exacerbated by the turmoil in Chicago, the Wallace vote (almost wholly a Social Issue vote) climbed to 21%, and the Humphrey vote plummeted. But then other factors came into play as discussed here: the successful finesse of Vietnam by candidate Humphrey; the gradual recession of the Wishy-Washy Issue as Humphrey became more and more his own man; the return of labor as the Economic Issue showed much of its old clout; and the realization that the choice between Nixon and Humphrey was the crude, rough, real choice of 1968, not some high-level option between clouds nine and fourteen. All these factors played a part in the return of most of the Democratic natives and in the apparently razor-thin election results.

We say "apparently" razor-thin because of the presence of the Wallace vote. There are a variety of views about what would have happened in 1968 had George Wallace not been on the ballot. Lou Harris in his polling found that "Richard Nixon would have won a two-way election going away," while the University of Michigan Survey Research Center also suggests that Nixon's lead over Humphrey might have been larger had Wallace not been on the ballot, but that the lead would perhaps not have been as massive as Harris suggests.

One or two writers have indicated their belief that *Humphrey* would have won with Wallace out. This latter view seems to the authors to be based more upon generalized voter profession of Democratic or Republican preferences than upon the specific circumstances of the 1968 election. That Alabama or Mississippi voters—although nominally Democratic—would have gone to Humphrey if Wallace had not run in 1968 seems to us very unlikely. After all, these voters went massively for Goldwater in 1964.

In general, the authors have taken as a rule-of-thumb premise that the *national* vote for Wallace would have split about 70 to 30 for Nixon. The Wallace vote was largely a Social Issue vote, and that vote was trending to Nixon. This 70–30 split would break down roughly to an 80–20 split for Nixon in the *South* and about 60–40 *outside the South*. These rough splits are used in subsequent calculations in this book.

Further, the authors feel that there was a significant difference between the character of the Wallace vote at 21% in the early fall of 1968 and the character of the Wallace vote at 13.5% in November. Those who considered voting for Wallace in September but did not finally do so appear to have had a considerably larger potentially pro-Humphrey component than did the remaining hard-core Wallace supporters on election day. These were in part the "union workers" discussed earlier.

Most of the natives returned, but not all. Put the South and the non-South together and allocate the Wallace/Social Issue vote as above—and one arrives at a not-so-razor-thin 53% to 47% victory for the Republicans. This is compared to a 50–50 vote in 1960. A spread of zero points becomes a spread of six points.

Why? Why did the Republicans gain? Many reasons, of course, many imponderables, many immeasurables, but we look toward the Social Issue as the new factor and the key change.* Many Democratic natives—South and non-South—left because of it at various times, and not quite as many returned to the fold on election day. The differential was likely the margin of difference.

In a football summation:

In the South, under the accumulated pressure of race and the Social Issue, the Democratic line was charged, it collapsed, and the quarterback was smothered.

Outside the South, under the accumulated pressure of the Social Issue, as well as other issues, the Democratic line was

---

* The Harris survey issued in the final week before the election said: "LAW AND ORDER: Perhaps more than any other, this issue finds Humphrey on the defensive." On who would handle it best in the White House, Nixon emerged as the choice of 35%, followed by Humphrey at 26% and Wallace close behind with 24%.

charged; it trembled, fell back, then rallied and basically held, allowing the quarterback to get his pass off, which was good for a long gain, but not a touchdown.

The key election *fact* of the seventies is that Democrats, by carrying non-Southern states of Quadcali,* can win national elections without the South, although it is more difficult than it used to be. Assuming that Republicans stay near the center, the key electoral *question* of the seventies is whether the Democrats will be able to cope with the Social Issue electoral forces at work in the society and, by coping, hold together the FDR Coalition and build upon it.

As this book is written in the early part of the year 1970, the votes of the unyoung, unpoor, unblack Quadcalians are still very much up for grabs. The machinist's wife in Dayton may decide to leave the Democratic reservation in 1972 and vote for Nixon or Wallace or their ideological descendants. If she thinks that Democrats feel that she isn't scared of crime but that she's really a bigot, if she thinks that Democrats feel the police are Fascist pigs and that the Black Panthers and the Weathermen are just poor, misunderstood, picked-upon kids, if she thinks that Democrats are for the hip drug culture and that she, the machinist's wife, is not only a bigot, but a square, then good-bye, lady—and good-bye, Democrats.

But the ripples, the waves, the big waves, are not necessarily yet a tide. There is no inevitable emerging Republican majority. Politics is not mechanistic. Political history concerns a number of organic trends that can be changed; it does not proceed ploddingly, arithmetically, with no relation to the living world of voters. That there have been tidal shifts in American politics every third of a century for the past century or so is a quaint historical fact. If there is another tidal shift that shows up in the seventies, it will not be because a third of a century has elapsed, but because one political party is responding with more fidelity to the considered wishes of the people— and that, after all, is what democracy is about.

---

* See page 70 for Quadcali map.

13

Straying Natives—Wallace '68

Without much question, the third-party movement of George C. Wallace constituted the most unusual feature of the 1968 presidential election. While this movement failed by a substantial margin in its audacious attempt to throw the presidential contest into the House of Representatives, in any other terms it was a striking success. It represented the first noteworthy intrusion on a two-party election in twenty years. The Wallace ticket drew a larger proportion of electoral votes than any such movement for more than a century, back to the curiously divided election of 1860. Indeed, the spectre of an electoral college stalemate loomed sufficiently large that serious efforts at reform have since taken root.

> "Continuity and Change in American Politics:
> Parties and Issues in the 1968 Election"
> PHILIP E. CONVERSE, WARREN E. MILLER,
> JERROLD G. RUSK, ARTHUR C. WOLFE,
> University of Michigan

As this is written in mid-1970, the position of George Wallace in Alabama politics is not known, many electoral wise men are predicting that Wallace will not be reelected governor of Alabama, and many pundits are saying that if Wallace is not reelected, he will be finished as a national political force.

In the opinion of the authors, the Alabama political situation is not nearly so important as claimed. If Wallace wins, nothing is changed. If Wallace loses, it may be marginally more difficult for him to run for President in 1972, but only marginally more difficult. Richard Nixon, let us recall, also lost for governor once.

Moreover, even if Wallace were not to run for President again, there are many reasons to believe that the Wallace movement will continue. Like the legions of the New Politics, the Wallace supporters are numerous and are ideologically committed to their own vision of life and politics. There is no reason to think that they will fade away if Wallace is not present to lead them. In short, one not only must view *George Wallace* as a strong political force in America, but remember that *Wallace-ism* is also strong.

A discussion of George Wallace and his role in American politics should start with three ideas, all of which are not quite what they seem, some of which are apparently contradictory.

The three ideas: Wallace is *young;* he is *shrewd;* he is *perceived as a racist and extremist.*

George Wallace was forty-nine years old in 1968. In 1972 he will be fifty-three years old. For Presidential hopefuls, that is young. He can be a candidate in 1976 and in 1980 and in 1984 and still be, in 1984, younger than the age at which Dwight Eisenhower was elected for a second term. Wallace can be a candidate for President conceivably four more times, and certainly three more times.

George Wallace is shrewd. He knows politics. Talk to Southern politicians about George Wallace, and the operative phrase one hears is "Ol' George is sharp" and there is evidence that "Ol' George" is, indeed, sharp, and smart, too, in that the record shows that he learns from his mistakes.

George Wallace is racist or, at the least, is *perceived* to be a racist and on the far right of national politics. It was George Wallace who vowed "segregation now, segregation tomorrow, segregation forever." He has not yet retracted that statement, although he makes it no longer.

Young. Smart. Perceived racist/extremist. Each of these three ideas must be examined, for each is at the root of an important part of the Wallace phenomenon: past, present, and future.

Let us consider, first, the present and the future and then gradually meander back to the 1968 election.

Wallace, as the *young* head of an ideological movement, has time to let the movement grow, to let it take advantage of the political terrain as it may form in the years to come. Accordingly, it is the opinion of the authors that had Wallace received enough electoral votes in 1968 to throw the election into the House of Representatives, he would have instructed his delegates to vote for *Nixon* and vote for him *before* the contest got to the House (where Wallace would have little, if any, power). Why would Wallace have selected Nixon and not Humphrey? Perhaps partly on the grounds that he was somewhat closer, ideologically, to Nixon, but primarily because of 1972, or 1976, or 1980. In those Presidential years, following at least some Republican time in office and with crime still present, with racial tension still present, with student disrupters still present, with pointy-headed guideline writers still present, George Wallace could then go to the American people and say, "You've had Democrats, and they couldn't control it; you've had Republicans, and they couldn't control it. Let George do it."

Wallace's youth allows him to encourage the growth of his movement, and it is important, then, to look at the movement.

The nature of the political structure that Wallace put together in 1968 is sometimes misunderstood. Though not a "political party" in the usual sense, the American Independent Party was able to get itself put on the ballot in all fifty states in 1968.

It should have no difficulty in doing so in 1972 again, even if it is still largely a Presidential-election-oriented quadrennial political group rather than a true national party. To do so will involve again, in many states, a large petition-signing campaign.

In a sense this activity will be an asset to the Wallace forces. Every political organization is hampered by the problem of giving its troops some meaningful work to do. The phrase normally used is "stuffing envelopes"—never really that time-consuming or important a job and now, with the advent of automatic folders, sealers, and stampers, even less important than before. But getting tens of thousands of political organizers out into the streets to get hundreds of thousands—even millions —of voters to sign a petition to get your candidate on the ballot is both time-consuming and important political work. It identifies the party workers early and can serve to instill real spirit. The petition-getting efforts of the Wallace troops and the door-to-door work of the McCarthy student cadremen were two major mass-participation movements in 1968 that added up to a hill of psephological beans. Because Wallace will have this forced activism working for—not against—him in 1972, that should be counted as a plus for his campaign.

There is one point where the Wallace movement is sometimes thought to be weak and spongy. Largely because of the impact of the primary system in America, there seems little possibility of the American Independent Party's successfully running large numbers of candidates for state or local office. Obviously, this is not because there are no states or localities where a majority of the electorate is pro-Wallace—because part of the Southern electorate certainly is. But the primary system allows that a pro-Wallace candidate in a pro-Wallace area can run in, and win, the Democratic primary—or the Republican primary for that matter. Accordingly, why should such a candidate bother establishing himself on a new party line, possibly alienating some Brass Collar Democrats and losing such patronage and seniority benefits that automatically accrue to an office-holder in a major national party? In this connection, it is interesting to remember that Wallace himself ran on a Democratic* line on the Alabama ballot. But this lack of a full vertical party is also not really a weakness for Wallace or a potential successor. What does it mean? No patronage problems, no division of money and work resources with local candidates,

---

* Wallace's line on the ballot carried the "official" Alabama Democratic symbol of the rooster and the label "Democratic." Humphrey ran on two separate lines, one with a symbol of an eagle and the label "The National Democratic Party of Alabama" and another with the symbol of a kicking donkey labeled "Alabama Independent Democratic."

no mayors, governors, Congressmen, and Senators bugging the candidate to trim a sail here, cut a corner there, pay a campaign visit, appoint a postmaster. Not a loss—provided there is a popular movement behind Wallace. And there is.

What is important to bear in mind, then, is that if Wallace or Wallaceism remains a serious force in American politics, it will likely be as a quadrennial, ideological Presidential movement that can lend some support to state and local candidates, but not as a broad-based, year-in, year-out, "new" party. Traditionally, in America, people who want to form a new party are lured away from such actions by the ease with which nominations within the old parties can be captured in primaries. This rule holds sway at all levels of American political life, bar one: the Presidential level. Because the Presidential nomination system has only scattered state primaries, Wallace would find little value in any attempt to "capture the national party," even in the unlikely event that he won in the primaries. Any such attempt would be blocked by the bosses—in this instance "liberal" bosses, who would certainly be able to find some intellectual rationale for not listening to the voice of the people as expressed in a few state primaries.

So, in all, there would seem to be every reason to expect the American Independence Party to continue in business, probably with still-young George Wallace leading it.

Now, what of the last two of the three characteristics listed earlier about Mr. Wallace: He is shrewd and knows politics, and he is racist, or, at least, he is perceived as racist. As we look at what happened to Mr. Wallace in 1968, it can be said that in national political terms *a man cannot be both "shrewd" and "racist."* For racism in American politics equals extremism, and extremism loses votes. Shrewd politicians are not running around the country in order to lose votes.

Wallace, it would seem, is aware of all this. He apparently chose retired General Curtis LeMay as his running mate in part to escape the Southern and racist and extremist image—and then turned pale at the Pittsburgh press conference when the general casually discoursed on the efficacy of nuclear weapons in

a manner that Wallace knew would be interpreted as extremist.
As the New York *Times* recorded it:

> By Walter Rugaber
> Special to the New York Times
>
> PITTSBURGH, Oct. 3—Gen. Curtis E. LeMay, the former Air
> Force Chief of Staff, became George C. Wallace's Vice-Presi-
> dential running mate today and promptly dropped some politi-
> cal bombs in the third-party campaign.
>
> "If I found it necessary [in the Vietnam war]," the General
> said, "I would use anything that we could dream up, including
> nuclear weapons, if it was necessary." But he added, "I don't
> think it's necessary in this case or this war to use it."
>
> Mr. Wallace who has taken great pains to assure audiences
> in his Presidential bid that he would use only conventional
> weapons in Vietnam, appeared markedly perturbed by all the
> General's talk of nuclear bombs.
>
> As his campaign plane left Pittsburgh for stops in Indianap-
> olis and Toledo, the former Alabama Governor insisted to re-
> porters aboard that the General also flatly ruled out a nuclear
> war in Vietnam.
>
> #### An Angry Response
>
> The General was presented by Mr. Wallace at a nationally
> televised news conference in the Pittsburgh Hilton Hotel.
>
> When Jack Nelson, southern correspondent of The Los
> Angeles Times, asked Mr. Wallace whether he agreed with the
> General's position, the Alabamian, obviously nettled, snapped
> back:
>
> "What you're doing, Mr. Nelson, is typical of The Los
> Angeles Times. You're trying to say that if the time ever came
> that it was necessary to use any sort of weapon in the vital
> interests of our national security, you wouldn't use them.
>
> "All General LeMay has said—and I know you fellows better
> than he does because I've had to deal with you—he said that if
> the security of the country depended on the use of any weapon
> in the future he would use it. But he said he prefers not to use
> any sort of weapon. He prefers to negotiate."

Wallace did not want to be viewed as an extremist on nuclear
bombs any more than he wanted to be viewed as an extremist
on race.

As it turned out, Wallace *was* perceived as an extremist, and this, in part, led to his decline. Here is the chronicle of his rise and fall:

WALLACE, PERCENT OF VOTE, 1968

April	9%
May	14%
June	14%
July	16%
August	18%
Sept. 3–7	19%
Sept. 20–22	21%
Sept. 27–30	20%
Oct. 3–12	20%
Oct. 17–21	15%
Oct. 31–Nov. 2	14%
Final Result	13.5%

Why did Wallace fall? One set of reasons, mentioned in the previous chapter, concerns the return of Democratic natives to a now-tough, now-forceful Hubert Humphrey. Another key set of reasons for the erosion of the Wallace vote concerns the third-party nature of his candidacy. Both Nixon and Humphrey went after the Wallace voter on the basis of "he can't win." Nixon, particularly in the South, made hay with "A Vote for Wallace Is a Vote for Humphrey."

But by no means all the Wallace erosion was due to the Wasted Vote Syndrome or the Return of the Native Syndrome. A good part of the Wallace drop-off was likely due to the fact that as the campaign drew to a close, Wallace was increasingly perceived as a regional candidate, a racist candidate, an extremist candidate, and one who would *not* handle the law-and-order problem effectively. Wallace, in short, went over the far side of the Social Issue*—if the American people want order and an end to discombobulation, they do not want it from a man perceived as an extremist or a racist.

Here is what Louis Harris said in a November, 1968, address in Atlanta, Georgia:

---

* There is a lesson here, probably most applicable today to Vice President Agnew. The Social Issue is a good issue until one goes too far with it. If carried to a point where pro-Social Issuism becomes in itself a disrupting and chaotic influence, it can begin to be a vote loser, not a vote gainer.

By the last week in October, the number who thought Wallace could handle law and order shrunk from 53 to 43 to 33 to 24 to 21% in consecutive polls. The number who viewed him solely as a regional candidate had grown from 34 to 39 to 44 to 49 to 57%. By the same token, the percentage who viewed him as a "racist" jumped from 40 to 51 to 59 to 67%, and those who looked on him as an "extremist" rose from 51 to 56 to 62 to 69%. Conversely, his vote began to drop precipitously from 21 to 18 to 16 to 13%.

All this points the way of the future for Wallace or for a Wallace successor. Wallace's strength, like the strength of any national political figure, is in direct relation to his proximity to the center. Stray away from the center, away from the "beauticians, cabdrivers, farmers, and shopkeepers" that Wallace said he represented, be viewed as an "extremist," a "racist," or a "regionalist"—and watch the votes disappear.

Wallace knows this. It should be remembered that he made a point of mentioning in his speeches that blacks in Alabama had voted for his wife,* that he was a great friend of blacks, etc., etc. Wallace, since his 1968 campaign, had made a continuing point of never directly attacking blacks *as* blacks.†

---

* A half-truth. Blacks voted against the late Lurleen Wallace in her primary race against a liberal opponent. They voted for her only in the general election when her opponent showed up as even less desirable than the Wallaces.
† Here is the way the *George C. Wallace Newsletter* of September, 1969, described Governor Wallace's reaction to the black versus labor union contretemps:

APPRENTICE, SENIORITY LISTS THREATENED

"Members of the great trade organizations in America have exerted tremendous influence on the economic and social life of this nation. Their efforts have brought us to a standard of living above all other nations.

"For this reason, I view with concern the recent events in Pittsburgh which, in effect, threaten the apprenticeship system and the seniority program of our skilled crafts unions."

These were the comments of Gov. George C. Wallace in regard to demands of some unqualified workers in Pittsburgh that more be employed on construction jobs regardless of qualifications. . . .

"The skilled crafts organizations should be permitted to come up with a solution to the problem. They are aware that people of every race are entitled to work and of the need for more skilled workmen.

Now politics is a funny game. Suppose George Wallace, for all his youth, died or was disabled or was scandalized. In either of those instances, one can easily predict a new AIP candidate, and the strongest image position for such a new AIP candidate would be to be perceived as a "non-Southern, nonracist non-extremist George Wallace." One can also predict that such a candidate would be stronger than the perceived George Wallace: extremist, racist, Southern. But what is fascinating is to consider the idea of George Wallace himself taking the appropriate steps to appear more and more "non-Southern, nonracist, and nonextremist." We presume that the Wallace of the seventies will do just that: move toward the center—not *to* it, but certainly *toward* it. Wallace, for example, could transfer his AIP headquarters from Montgomery to Washington or a "heartland city" like St. Louis. He could make even prettier noises about equal rights for all—and still maintain his basic constituency, all the while attempting to bite off the Social Issue flank of both the Republican and the Democratic parties. In his more recent public appearances, Wallace's emphasis on preserving the public schools and getting tax relief for the "little man" seem to predict just such a course.

Following the doctrine of push to the center, Wallace has great freedom to move to the center; he can look over his shoulder and see no one there. That, as we shall see, is not a statement that Mr. Humphrey can make, nor any Democrat. It is certainly not a statement that Mr. Nixon could make. But Wallace can do it more easily; he can move to the center until that point when his original supporters start calling *him* pro-black. And there is a lot of political distance on the trail before that happens.

Wallace, of course, would not be the first national politician to change a stand or an image. Nelson Rockefeller went from

---

They have an apprenticeship program for training skilled craftsmen," Gov. Wallace said.

He further pointed out that crafts unions adhere to a national non-discriminatory policy of employment of qualified workers.

Notice that there is no mention of "Negroes" or "blacks" in the statement that "People of every race are entitled to work . . ."

hawk to semidove without ever really announcing a change of position; Lyndon Johnson went from a moderate to a liberal as soon as he became Vice President; and who can forget the "new" Nixon?

The classic Wallace story concerns his reaction to his defeat in the 1958 Alabama gubernatorial primary race. Wallace was defeated by an arch-segregationist candidate, John Patterson, and his response was: "Boys, I'm never going to get outniggered again." Now if, as they say, "Ol' George is a sharp fellow," he will push toward the center, saying, "Boys, I'm never going to get outextremed again." At which point, the Wallace movement could conceivably be a real threat to the two-party Presidential system in America.

The importance of the Wallace movement or perhaps more accurately the "Wallace feeling" cannot be underestimated in looking ahead at the future of American politics. Wallace received almost 10,000,000 votes in 1968. At his high-water mark in late September, 1968, he was the choice of more than 1 in 5 Americans. About half his strength was from the South; about half outside it.

Any attempt to dismiss these votes as "deviant" or as "out of the mainstream" is just unreal. These were 10,000,000 votes, roughly 15,000,000 pollees in mid-September, 1968; the *drop-off alone* in the Wallace vote in the last six weeks of the campaign was about equal to the total number of black votes cast in the same election.

Furthermore, the nature of both the actual Wallace voter and the Wallace dropper* seems to epitomize the nature of the psephological struggle that has been going on in America and that gives every indication of continuing and possibly even intensifying as the years go on.

The profile of the Wallace voter shows with devastating clearness the schism between the new Social Issues and the old Economic Issues—each powerful and potent, each showing one face of the key that unlocks the door to political victory in the seventies.

---

* Designating those voters who at one time indicated they would vote for Wallace and then voted for others.

The peculiarity of the Wallace voter is that there does not seem to be a convenient traditional pigeonhole in which to place him. The old linear political placements have no good spot for the Wallace voter. Typically, the Wallace voters are to the *right* of Republicans on race, law and order, and big government—the Social Issues. But they are to the *left* of Republicans on the bread-and-butter Economic Issues.

Arthur C. Wolfe of the University of Michigan examined the Survey Research Center data concerning the 1968 election and wrote this: "Wallace voters are more likely than Nixon voters to favor the Federal Government's helping people to get doctors and hospital care at low cost and to believe that the Federal Government should see to it that every person has a job and a good standard of living."

Here are data backing up that statement:

SOCIAL WELFARE VIEWS OF HUMPHREY, NIXON, AND WALLACE VOTERS

	Humphrey Voters %	Wallace Voters %	Nixon Voters %
Favor federal medical help	68	48	35
Favor federal job assistance	41	27	20

(Survey Research Center, University of Michigan, 1968)

In terms of "class feeling" and occupational status, the Wallaceites also tend to correlate more with Democrats than with Republicans. From the same Survey Research data:

SOCIO-ECONOMIC BACKGROUND OF HUMPHREY, NIXON, AND WALLACE VOTERS

	Wallace Voters %	Humphrey Voters %	Nixon Voters %
Feel identified with a class	77	68	61
Identify with the working class	64	55	44
Family was working class	80	68	57
Union member in household	29	29	20
Manual occupation	40	36	28

(Survey Research Center, University of Michigan, 1968)

So, on the *class* and *economic* issues the Wallaceites would view Democrats as the "party of the center" where they could find compromise, if not total solace. This apparently is where, in the 1968 election, much of the last-month Humphrey surge came from—Wallace droppers who came back and voted on what they perceived to be the bread-and-butter issues.

But the Democrats are *not* the party of the center for the Wallaceites on the newer, *social* sorts of issues:

DIFFERENCES IN CIVIL RIGHTS AND URBAN UNREST
ATTITUDES OF HUMPHREY, NIXON, AND WALLACE VOTERS

	Wallace Voters %	Nixon Voters %	Humphrey Voters %
Disapprove of permitting protest marches	65	49	42
Federal government getting too powerful	65	54	24
Federal government wastes a lot of money	85	63	50
Against federal push to school integration	75	48	28
Civil rights people pushing too fast	87	66	49
Black actions seen as mostly violent	83	72	58
In favor of strict segregation	38	11	9

(*Survey Research Center, University of Michigan, 1968*)

On race, on social disruption, on federal intrusion, the Wallaceite finds himself closer to the Republican voter than to the Democrat.

And when there is an issue that can be viewed as in the bread-and-butter syndrome *and* in the law-and-order syndrome, what then? The case in point is federal aid to education. On the surface it is a good Democratic issue: Help local schools with federal dollars. On the surface it ought to correlate with an issue like federal aid to medical services. But the school question, of course, involves a major social component—school integration, busing, etc. And faced with the conflict, here is how the Wallace voter reacted:

SOCIAL WELFARE VIEWS OF
HUMPHREY, NIXON, AND WALLACE VOTERS

	Humphrey Voters %	Wallace Voters %	Nixon Voters %
Favor federal medical help	68	48	35
Favor federal aid to education	42	*11* (!)	19

(*Survey Research Center, University of Michigan, 1968*)

"Law and order" beats "bread and butter"; social beats economic. Keep your tainted federal dollars if it means putting my kid in school with the colored. That was the view of the *Wallaceites*. But, as we have seen in the previous chapter, the *Wallace droppers* ultimately went the other way: bread and butter beat law and order, Humphrey over Wallace. What will happen in 1972 and 1976 when the Social Issue faces new events, new circumstances, new personalities, remains to be seen. The issue is up for grabs. There is nothing on the horizon, however, that says it will vanish.

Looking again at the movement and the makeup of the Wallace constituency during the 1968 campaign shows in stark relief why its vote is so crucial in the politics of the seventies for both Democrats and Republicans.

The 10,000,000 who voted for Wallace (13.5%) did so largely on the basis of the Social Issue. The additional 7% or so who dropped Wallace were tempted largely on the basis of the Social Issue. There are likely another 5–10% who were always for either Nixon or Humphrey in the polls but may have had the beginnings of the Social Issue itch. We are talking, then, about somewhere between a fifth and a third of the electorate that is up for grabs largely on the basis of the Social Issue and is potentially willing to break party ranks, if necessary. Needless to say, that is quite a massive swing vote. Who are they? Mostly the unyoung, unpoor, unblack; the middle-aged, middle-class, middle-educated, working with their hands, etc. Capture a good share of those tens of millions of voters, and you have likely captured the Presidency—provided only that you haven't alienated more voters in the process.

In attempting to capture the free-floating Wallaceite, what strategies suggest themselves to the major political parties?

FOR THE DEMOCRATS

Capitalize on the economic issues and even expand on them: Be for a higher minimum wage, higher Social Security benefits, expanded Medicare for children ("Kiddicare") and eventually for the entire population; be anti-inflation, antirecession, (standard out-party economic themes) ; be for the little guy, white and black. Say, "It's time to get America moving again."

Neutralize the Social Issue. Democrats—national Democrats vying for public office, that is—cannot, should not, and will not conduct a campaign with even an undertone of racism. This may inevitably mean some relatively unpopular positions on issues like school integration and job slots in white unions. But aside from the racial facet of the Social Issue, Democrats must campaign against crime, against student disruption, against violent black militancy, against riots—and mean it. As will be pointed out at some length in the concluding section of this book, it is the judgment of the authors that such a strategy is not only tactically wise, but one that is fully consistent with the time-honored goals of liberal Democrats.

For the Democrats—recall that while Mussolini was for making the trains run on time, one can be in favor of trains running on time without being for Mussolini. Stalin was in favor of increasing agricultural productivity—but one can be in favor of increasing agricultural productivity without being pro-Stalin. Democrats of the seventies can be for law and order without being pro-Wallace, or racist, or repressionist. That Wallace and Goldwater first sounded forth the law-and-order theme has by now become irrelevant. That "law and order" is now clearly seen as a legitimate demand of the American people is very relevant.

FOR THE REPUBLICANS

The strategy is a mirror image. Hold fast on the easier Social Issues, like law enforcement. Attempt to reinforce the notion that crime, the perceived breakdown of law and order, permissiveness, student and black rebels all are problems started by Democrats—and crying for Republican solutions. Finesse the tricky social issues like school integration by indicating that Republicans are all for civil rights and actually move ahead—but at a slower, more "reasonable" pace than those frenzied Democratic social engineers would like. Be for moderate integration and against busing.

On the Economic Issues show that Republicans, too, can be the party of the workingman. Programs designed to help the middle-income working class are desirable: tax relief; aid to schools (somewhat less tied to racial issues than earlier Democratic programs); tax sharing with states and cities and counties and suburbs; etc. Say, "It's time to get America moving again."

There is a shorthand for all this, applicable not only to both major parties, but to the Wallaceites as well. It is this: *Go to the center*. There is evidence to suggest that there are elements in each of the three parties that currently advocate a move to the fringes and away from the center. There is a shorthand for that, too: *defeat*.

14

The Man in the Middle—Nixon '68

Certainly, of the three major campaigns, the Nixon model was the least exciting. Such is the fate of professional centrists, and that is exactly what Richard Nixon was—and is. Moreover, he was further bedeviled: a professional centrist in a three-man race.

With Humphrey to his presumptive left, with Wallace to his presumptive right, there wasn't terribly much of substance Mr. Nixon could say or do. A move to the left, to swipe a few of Humphrey's votes, could cause slippage to the right. After all, George Wallace was saying, about the two parties: "There's not a dime's worth of difference." A move right, toward Wallace, could easily cause slippage among the Rockefeller-style Republicans.

So there was Nixon in a two-way stretch—and there, as this is written in 1970, he remains.

The major thesis of this book is that the center is the only position of political power. But that is a notion that is more easily applicable in a two-party model than in a three-party model. With three parties contending, the coalition of the attitudinal center can theoretically be weak, not strong. It can, for example, command the allegiance only of the middle 20% of the electorate, conceivably leaving 40% to the right and 40% to the left. Such, indeed, is the traditional position of the British Liberal Party, boxed in on the right (by the Conservatives), and on the left (by the Labour Party).

Accordingly, Mr. Nixon's problem in 1968 was somewhat more complex than the standard "capture the center" doctrine. It is more complex today, too.

He had in 1968, and has today, the center position on the attitudinal spectrum. His problem—then and now—is to see that he not only retains that position, but retains at least the plurality position as well. To do this, Mr. Nixon must prevent erosion from right and left and hopefully expand his center position to either right or left or both. This would seem to make even more attractive the normally attractive politics of caution. A little push left, a little push right, always expanding the center base, trying not to antagonize the rightists when moving left or the leftists when moving right. All this may seem very convenient and comfortable. But today, as President, Mr. Nixon is burdened by that hauntingly antipolitical thing—the moral imperative of "doing what is best for the country."

Not an easy position, after all.

That Richard Nixon did hold the center spot in 1968 is most easily demonstrated by noting that the Democrats did not. It is of major significance to realize that at no time in 1968 did any Democrat—Johnson, Humphrey, Kennedy, McCarthy—ever poll as much as 50% of the vote against Wallace and Nixon.

This is *not* to say that Nixon was *ahead*—only that the Democrats never had a majority, never held the center point. Once again, in English political terms, it can be said that all during early 1968 it was clear that the oppositionists (Nixon and Wallace) had a lead over the ministerialists (first Johnson, then Humphrey) by about 55–60% versus 45–40%.

Further evidence: Although many more Americans are registered *Democratic* than Republican, the Gallup Polls in 1968 found in every instance that when Americans were asked, "Which party is best able to handle the top problems?" there was a *Republican* preference by a slight margin. Thus, while Nixon never rose above the 50% mark himself, oppositionist feeling was over the halfway mark.

For Nixon, then, the question was a simple one: *How would the oppositionists split their votes?* Let us say that Humphrey would get 43% (which he ultimately did). If the remaining 57% of the voters went 50% for Nixon and 7% for Wallace, then Nixon would be a massive winner. On the other hand, if the remaining 57% was distributed 37% for Nixon and 20% for Wallace, then Humphrey would be a big winner. Who, then, was the joker in the deck? Wallace. How his Social Issue voters moved determined who would be President.

As we have noted earlier, Nixon was the overwhelming choice of Republicans for the nomination. By the time September rolled around, with the Humphrey candidacy floundering, Nixon held an overwhelming lead for the Presidency itself; the September 20–22 Gallup tally read Nixon 43%, Humphrey 28%, Wallace 21%, undecided 8%. The differential of 15% between Nixon and Humphrey was a wide, wide margin as these things go, representing close to 11,000,000 votes. Still, it should be recognized that even at that high point Nixon did not have a majority of the vote; technically at least he was still at the mercy of "how would the oppositionists split."

But he was way ahead. In examining Mr. Nixon's campaign in the fall of 1968, then, we will do well first to ask ourselves one quick question: How do you campaign when you are way out in front?

The rules of psephology answer: "Safely." Or: "Don't rock the vote."

Accordingly, Nixon chose not to debate with Humphrey, chose not to gamble for extra votes by campaigning mercilessly from dawn till midnight, chose to do just enough pressing the flesh and face-to-face "unrehearsed" television as was necessary to attempt to try to avoid the charge that he wasn't "taking his case to the people."

This sort of campaign strategy also dovetailed neatly with another important element of the Nixon effort: lack of frenzy.

Nixon (correctly) felt that the feeling of frenzy—the jumpers and screamers, the confrontations—was distressing many Americans. Accordingly, there was a conscious attempt to run a low-key campaign.

We must now ask—or reask—the critical questions of the campaign: *Why* were the oppositionists ahead? And *why* did they stay ahead?

We can begin by eliminating some dubious phrases that do not explain the oppositionist strength.

There is first the notion of a Southern Strategy. It has been alleged in countless news stories, articles, essays, and books that it was the Southern Strategy that built the Nixon lead and won the election for him. On the face of it, the notion is preposterous. When examined closely, it remains preposterous.

There are eleven politically "Southern" states (the Old Confederacy). If a candidate carried *all* of them in 1968, he would corral 128 electoral votes. That is less than half of the 270 necessary for election. Mr. Nixon did *not* carry *all* the Southern states. He carried five of eleven with a total of 57 votes, less than one-fifth of his total of 301—and less than half the available Southern electoral votes. The last Republican Presidential aspirant who waged a Southern Strategy reveals how successful that approach is: Barry Goldwater, in 1964, carried five Southern states. And Arizona. And that was all.

As an alternate, it has been suggested that Nixon's victory and his strength came from a Border State Strategy. Again, nonsense. There are five Border States (Missouri, Kentucky, West Virginia, Maryland, Oklahoma). Collectively, they cast 46 electoral votes. Of the 46 votes, Nixon got 29, and Humphrey got 17. Of the popular vote, Nixon won Kentucky by 65,000 but lost West Virginia by 67,000. Nixon won Missouri by 20,000 votes but lost Maryland by 20,000 votes. Only in Oklahoma did Nixon win a fairly big plurality: 148,000 votes.

There is, next, the notion that Nixon was packaged well. This argument concerns how many millions of dollars were spent on television time, how the videotape was spliced to make the candidate look better than he was—and so on. What else is new? Caesar brought grain from North Africa to the citizens of Rome to influence an election; an intellectual, introspective lawyer from Springfield made psephological hay as "Honest Abe, the Rail Splitter"; Mark Hanna packaged Presidential aspirant William McKinley by keeping him on his "front porch" in Canton, Ohio, talking face-to-face with Americans from all over the country who wanted to see him. As William Safire points out in a fine book, *The New Language of Politics:*

> McKinley, especially, had good reason to stay at home and entertain delegations to Canton, Ohio—he was not the stem-winding orator that his opponent, William Jennings Bryan was. It made more political sense to play to his strength, which was a homely, conservative, heartland-of-American stability.

Of course, candidates are packaged. Most people are packaged—psychiatrists call it role playing.

If anything, it may well be that television and extensive newspaper and magazine coverage has given Americans more of a chance than existed before to observe the "real" Presidential candidate. In earlier days, after all, Americans had to judge their candidate by what the few newspapers in their area had to say about him, in addition to "word of mouth" and the word of the local party proselytizer. Today voters get a fix on their man not only through a few newspapers, but through radio, weekly national newsmagazines, and daily television news broadcasts. The voter sees far more of the unpackaged candidate.

The fact of packaging candidates is this: It is easy to use cash and media to bring home a winner when he's the best horse on the track. Nelson Rockefeller's spectacular comeback in 1966 to win the New York governorship was in part due to the fact that he spent many millions of dollars on a sagacious campaign that stressed imaginative television spots. But Nelson Rockefeller had also been a dynamic governor of New York for eight years, he is an attractive, appealing, and intelligent man, and he was running against opposition split between a somewhat lackluster Democrat, Frank O'Connor, and Liberal and Conservative splinter party candidates, who each polled half a million votes.

In the same year, another millionaire in an adjacent state tried a similar exercise in big-money-big-television campaigning. A millionaire named Milton Shapp was the Democratic gubernatorial candidate in Pennsylvania. A nonexciting campaigner, Shapp was beaten by Republican Raymond Shafer—in a state that Democrat Hubert Humphrey carried by 170,000 votes in 1968.

The examples of how money and TV are not the be-all and end-all of political victory are many. Charles Stenvig won the Minneapolis mayoralty primary in 1969 with a budget of $3,400 and next to no paid television commercials. On the national scene, it may be recalled that while the Humphrey staff was complaining that it was running so poorly in the polls because Nixon had all the money and all the TV and radio time, a Harris survey showed that the equally underfinanced Ed Muskie was running 17% points ahead of Spiro Agnew, and Mr. Agnew was as well financed as Richard Nixon.

In the meanwhile, the fully operative dictum regarding the importance of money and media remains to be made by some brilliant political scientist. When it finally emerges, our guess is that it will lean heavily on the ancient adage concerning sow's ears and silk purses. And on Lincoln's remark about fooling the people. And on the notion that the voters, corporately, are smart and not hoodwinkable by manufactured personalities or by personalities who claim they can manufacture personalities.* Voters are not nitwits.

There was, finally, the notion in mid-September that the bandwagon effect would kill off any possibility of a Humphrey comeback. The bandwagonists make a point of noting every four years that voters like to go with a winner, and once the polls show who's ahead, that candidate will go farther ahead.

---

* In the fall of 1969 the American Association of Political Consultants met in New York. They, too, came to the conclusion that if the medium was the message, it was the candidate who was the medium. As one conferee noted, "Mr. Lincoln would be spectacular on television. He'd write his own stuff. He'd be short, and his unprofessional, personal power is the greatest thing in the world." The general feeling was that it is hard enough to make a silk purse out of silk.

That is a discredited theory—discredited again in 1968 when Humphrey wagonbanded back into contention after trailing far, far behind.

So, then, Nixon wasn't ahead because of Southern Strategy, Border State Strategy, packaging, money, or bandwagonism.

Why was he ahead?

He was ahead for the same simple reason most candidates are ahead in most elections: He was more closely attuned to the temper of a larger segment of the electorate than was his opposition. He was a man for the season. That may sound simplistic. It is simplistic—and accurate.

The question then arises, why was (and is) Nixon attuned to the electorate? And that, in turn, begs the question once again: Who is the electorate; what kind of people are they?

Three spokes off the wheel of an idea:

—Some months after the election, John Ehrlichman, by then the Counsel to President Nixon, was asked by a newspaperman about the liberal criticism that President Nixon was receiving regarding a certain piece of relatively conservative legislation. "Don't worry about it," Ehrlichman was quoted as saying, "it'll play in Peoria. . . ."

—The late Everett Dirksen was fond of telling stories about his youth in Pekin, Illinois—at that time a city of some 10,000. Dirksen recalled how he and most of his teen-age contemporaries were perfectly content to spend their evenings and weekends right at home in Pekin enjoying the church suppers and hayrides. "Of course," he said, "there were always a few young rakehells who were drawn away like moths to the bright lights and licentiousness—of Peoria."

—Finally, attitudinally speaking, Peoria is in the Bronx, even in Manhattan. Pekin is in Los Angeles, even in San Francisco. There is a common assumption found in much political writing that sharply different attitudes are held by different groups of Americans. We hear of "big-city" voters from industrial states, of "rich suburban voters," of the "Southern mentality," of "farm voters," of the "college-educated voter," and, oh, so often, of the "Eastern seaboard intellectuals." This leads to the idea of attitudinal coalitions that can combine the "intellectual vote" with the "black vote" or the "young vote" and the "wealthy vote" to produce majorities that are at variance with that mythical group called Middle America or the equally mythical Silent Majority. Conservatives play the same games with "Southern votes," "ethnic backlash votes," "new suburbanites," and so on. Yet when one examines the attitudinal data on the sorts of Social Issues we have been talking about, the striking fact is how *similarly* Americans feel about these issues regardless of age, region, sex, education, occupation, religion, politics, unions, community size, or almost any other cross-index one might come up with.

On the next page, for a particularly sharp example, are the results of a Gallup Poll taken in June, 1969. The subject is student disorders.

The maximum range of difference occurs between young people ("21–29 years") at 89% and farmers at 97%. *All* the standard Gallup groups overwhelmingly want college administrations to get tougher. That is the attitude of voters in Pekin and Peoria—and in the Bronx, and Los Angeles, and San Francisco, and even probably in Berkeley, Madison, and Cambridge —of men and women, white collar and blue collar, rich and poor, North, East, South and West, big city and small, old, middle-aged, and young, too (89% of young people said yes). There is accordingly little leeway in such an attitudinal mix for a candidate for office to be perceived as being "soft on student disorders." To the extent that he is so perceived, he will lose votes.

The same rough pattern holds true for other issues. In February, 1969, Gallup asked: "In general, do you think the courts in this area deal too harshly, or not harshly enough, with criminals?" and the choices were "too harshly," "not harshly enough," or "about right." Not one of the thirty-two Gallup groupings

Question: *"In general would you like to see college administrations take a stronger stand on student disorders, or not?"*

	Yes %		Yes %
National	94		
SEX		**POLITICS**	
Men	94	Republican	96
Women	93	Democrat	93
RACE		Independent	93
White	95	**REGION**	
Non-white	X*	East	90
EDUCATION		Midwest	95
College	91	South	96
High School	95	West	96
Grade School	93	**INCOME**	
OCCUPATION		$10,000 & over	94
Prof. & Bus.	94	$ 7,000 & over	95
White Collar	94	$ 5,000–$6,999	94
Farmers	97	$ 3,000–$4,999	93
Manual	94	Under $3,000	90
AGE		**COMMUNITY SIZE**	
21–29 years	89	1,000,000 & over	92
30–49 years	95	500,000 & over	91
50 & over	94	50,000–499,999	93
RELIGION		2,500–49,999	96
Protestant	96	Under 2,500,	
Catholic	94	Rural	96
Jewish	X*		

* Insufficient Sample

was recorded at more than 4% "too harshly." Every Gallup grouping was recorded as above 60% for "not harshly enough."

Again, a candidate can be viewed as "soft on law and order," but if he is so viewed, he will be going against the grain of the voting public—everywhere from Pekin to Park Avenue.

The same sort of lopsided, all-over-the-nation result is observable regarding the issue of speed of integration. In October, 1968, for example, all the Gallup groupings for "not fast enough" fell into the 10% to 23% range, while the "too fast" range was from 42% to 63%.

Similar one-sided results are observable on issues like morals, marijuana, pornography, and indeed many of the other social issues that are at the cutting edge of today's politics.

Getting back, now, to Mr. Nixon and the Republicans in 1968: It is the opinion of the authors that on the Social Issues that disturbed the nation—crime, race, student disorders, among others—the Republicans were perceived as somewhat "tougher" than the Democrats, somewhat more in tune with the attitudes of the electorate, and they accordingly gathered some very critical votes on these issues. Many of the votes they gathered were in the South; many of the votes were only half votes—*i.e.,* Wallace votes from people nominally Democratic. Many of the votes and half votes did not come from the South. The Social Issues permeated every nook and cranny of American life— every region, every religion, every age group, every political persuasion, every income group, every area. The feelings that Nixon capitalized upon were not part of a Southern Strategy or a Border State Strategy—they were part of a national strategy that was attuned to the national malaise we have discussed earlier.

Perhaps the clearest indication Nixon gave that he understood these factors (as well as some of the earlier psephological notions discussed here) was his choice of Spiro Agnew as Vice President. It may be said, in fact, that *Agnewism* as a social thought won the election for Nixon, while Agnew, the individual, almost lost it for him.

Here was Agnew. First and foremost, he was a creature of the Republican center. Strom Thurmond may have liked to have had John Tower on the ticket; Nelson Rockefeller might have liked to have had Mark Hatfield on the ticket—but Thurmond couldn't go home with Hatfield; Rockefeller couldn't go home with Tower. Everyone could go home with Agnew—maybe grumpily, as in Rockefeller's case—but it was a livable arrangement.

Why? Because Agnew at the time of the convention was perceived as a liberal conservative or, if you prefer, a conservative liberal. After all, Agnew won Maryland's gubernatorial race in 1966 with liberal Democratic support, running against the anti-open-housing appeals of George Mahoney, the Democratic nominee. Agnew was originally a big Rockefeller supporter. Yet it was Agnew who got tough on "race" and "law and order" after the April, 1968, riots in Baltimore.

Agnew seemed (before he started campaigning) the quintessential embodiment of the attitudes just discussed. Could such a man be "soft" on student disturbances? Would he be easy on criminals? Or hippies? Would he ram integration down anyone's throat? Would he be for nudity in movies? Would he, on the other hand, be associated with racist bigots? Would he cavort with extremists? Hell, no.

That's Agnewism, or call it social stolidity. Call it what you will, but it is unquestionably in conformity with the attitudes of the "plain folks" who are the great majority of voters*—those called most recently the Silent Majority.

That Agnew turned out to be a less than total success and, in fact, almost a disaster as a campaigner is almost irrelevant—if almost changing the outcome of a Presidential election can ever be called an irrelevancy. The importance of selecting Agnew was symbolic; it was Nixon's clear choice of a centrist path.

That's why Nixon was ahead or, more properly, why the oppositionists were ahead of the ministerialists. And it is important to remember again that the oppositionists *were ahead all year long,* before and after Chicago, before and after RFK's murder, before and after Hubert Humphrey's drop in the polls and his subsequent revival. The final election results of oppositionists† 57% versus ministerialists 43% were not terribly different in November from those in May, June, and July. A five poll average from May to July (after distributing the "undecided") shows Humphrey 42.5%, Nixon 40.5% and Wallace 16.5%. Except for the minor point of who won the election, these totals are all within 3% of the final vote. In August and

---

* Let there be no romanticization of these "plain folks," either. They are against pornography and smut, they say, but count the cars at the drive-in for a special midnight feature of the nudie movie *Sex on Sale.* The nudies do very well all over America. All over America, as in Peoria and Pekin. Perhaps the most accurate portrayal of the morality of life in small-town America concerns another town with a *P*—Peyton Place.

† Nixon-Wallace combination. Figuring the Wallace vote as 70–30 for Nixon if Wallace was not running, you get an oppositionist-ministerialist count of 53%–47%.

September, Humphrey plunged to a point where the oppositionists were leading by almost 70–30; then he dramatically
recouped and came close to winning the election.

Having indicated why Nixon won, it is now instructive to
note why Nixon almost lost.

—He almost lost because the second oppositionist (Wallace)
  drained many of his potential votes.
—He almost lost because the second oppositionist created
  two psephological battlegrounds for him to fight on. This
  left him in somewhat of a box, a box in which he remains.
—He almost lost because of charismatic and personalistic
  factors. Nixon was a lackluster candidate in 1968. It is hard
  now to remember the gags about Nixon "being out of
  synchronization," with gestures not matching words, hard
  to remember the artificial laughs and smiles that were so
  painfully visible on television.

And so the election of 1968 passed into history. A tide rose in
the South; some whitecaps were seen elsewhere.

15

Campaigning and Wednesday-Morning Calculations

When the votes were finally tallied, in the actual three-man race of 1968, Richard Nixon received 43.4% of the vote to Hubert Humphrey's 42.7%, a difference of less than 1 percentage point. Wallace received 13.5% of the vote. In the absolute vote count, Nixon's plurality was 510,000, meaning that if 255,000 votes— about 1/280th of the electorate—had switched from Nixon to Humphrey, then Humphrey would have been the popular vote winner. Along with the election of 1960, the 1968 vote was one of the closest Presidential races in American history.

In an election that close, almost any group can be viewed as the swing vote that (1) elected Richard Nixon or (2) defeated Hubert Humphrey. It can be said, in fact, that any swinging group of votes numbering 255,000 would have given the popular vote to Hubert Humphrey.

But it gets somewhat more complicated when one attempts to figure the *electoral* swing vote. Humphrey, who received 191 electoral votes, needed 79 more to go over the majority total needed to become President. If one switched 112,000 Nixon votes to Humphrey in California; 68,000 Nixon votes to Humphrey in Illinois; and 32,000 Nixon votes to Humphrey in New Jersey, then Humphrey would be President. That is to say,

then, that any group or bloc of only 212,000 Americans switch·
ing their votes in those three states in correct proportions would
have changed the Presidential outcome. Speaking demographic·
ally, one can say that Italians, or Slavs, or Jews, or Negroes, or
farmers, or Poles, or Catholics, or white-collar workers, or sub·
urbanites, or Catholic suburbanites, or white-collar Catholic
suburbanites, or white-collar Irish Catholic suburbanites swung
the election.

The problem with this sort of electoral vote juggling that is
so popular among Monday-morning psephologists—or should it
be Wednesday-morning psephologists?—is that elections and
election campaigning do not occur in separate, airtight state
compartments. It is extremely difficult, and probably impos·
sible, to move 32,000 votes in a New Jersey Presidential election
without moving thousands and tens of thousands of votes in
each of the other forty-nine states. The day of the pinpoint
sectional or statewide campaign is gone—if it ever existed—and
the fact that votes cannot be garnered in bushels on specific
street corners is of crucial significance when one looks at the
arithmetic of the future.

As an example, let us examine the idea put forward by some
that had Hubert Humphrey campaigned diligently in New
Jersey in the final week of the campaign, he could have switched
enough votes to carry New Jersey's seventeen electoral votes.
This sort of electoral calculation is familiar fare in the syndi·
cated political columns. Just take political ratchet Q, apply to
voting bloc R, place a few drops of political oil on the gears of
the political machine, twist four turns, and—presto! victory.

Once again, this sort of analysis almost invariably suffers from
the familiar political malady of Too Cute.

Observe the premises at work in the New Jersey assumption:

First, if the candidate is to spend two days in New Jersey,
where does he *not* spend two days? The answer is simple
enough: He does not spend those two days in California, where,
in fact, Humphrey did spend the final two days of the cam·
paign. Why does he not go to California? Obviously, because he
will lose California anyway. Of course, it turned out that

Humphrey *did* lose California, but who knew *that* before the election? The much-respected Muchmore Poll in California said that as of election eve, Humphrey was running neck and neck with Nixon. So it is always easy to design a candidate's schedule *after* an election.

A second premise is that a candidate *gains* votes when he appears personally. Who says so? Who comes out to a political rally? A great majority of the people who attend political rallies are usually partisans who will vote for the candidate whether or not he appears at a rally. When Humphrey spoke in Southern and Border states in 1968, he attracted large and enthusiastic crowds, leading his advisers to suspect that there was much greater Humphrey support than their polls indicated. In fact, what was happening was that Humphrey supporters were coming to rallies from 50 to 100 miles away, making a nice crowd; they were, however, unable to make much of a dent in November. Of the nonfaithful at a typical political rally, some few are already committed to vote for the opposition candidate. That doesn't leave many who are "undecided." In a crowd at a shopping center of 3,000 people, at most a few hundred are theoretically switchable. But how many voters will decide to vote for a candidate just because he saw him give a ten-minute speech? And how many, upon hearing him speak, might switch the other way, deciding that he didn't really like what he heard or saw and might now vote for the opposition candidate instead? How many of the undecided voters couldn't find a parking place, or got jostled in the crowd, or never did like the Democratic mayor of the city, and now, seeing Hubert Humphrey shaking hands with that same mayor, decide that they'll vote for Nixon?

And how many people can be assembled to hear or even glimpse a candidate in the flesh on a given day? Twenty-five thousand? Fifty thousand? A hundred thousand? Two hundred and fifty thousand? A two-minute clip on each of the three network news shows during the campaign will yield the candidate an audience of many tens of million Americans! Hubert Humphrey or Richard Nixon will be seen by more residents of

New Jersey if he says something fairly noteworthy in Oregon than if he says something banal in Trenton, Montclair, Newark, Camden, and Tenafly all in the same day.

Furthermore, because of the impact of television and the national news media, a candidate can no longer effectively perform that ancient political parlor trick of "saying one thing in the South and another in the North." Not that many candidates might not do so if they could—but they can't. Talk tough on race in North Carolina, and the liberals and blacks in Illinois will hear and *see* you say it that night in their own living room. Advocate busing schoolchildren at a stump speech in Harlem, and white suburbanites in Tallahassee *see* you say it that night in *their* living rooms. Come out for dropping oil quotas in Maine, and there you are on Huntley-Brinkley saying it in Dallas.*

Candidates in recent years have learned this lesson well and have been adroit in making the best of necessity. Count in 1972 how many times each candidate is introduced as "a man who has the courage of his convictions . . . a man who will say the same things in the North as in the South." So be it.

When confronted with this sort of evidence regarding the limited value of extensive local campaigning, the party professionals will respond by saying that the appearance of the candidate will give "a shot in the arm" to local party workers, who will work extra hard to get out the vote on election day. There is probably some limited truth to this, but again, one must remember that far more party workers throughout the nation are enthused seeing their candidate in an effective two-minute spot on a news-broadcast appearance on television than can be enthused by a candidate's visit to Weehawken, Union City, Bergen, and Short Hills.

As a matter of fact, in the New Jersey situation, where the state gets television reception from New York City and Philadelphia stations, a candidate may actually reach more New

---

* There is *some* leeway allowed in local and regional television. Nuances can be changed, but any major shift will be reported as news all over the country.

Jerseyites—party workers and citizens—by appearing on local television in Philadelphia and New York City.

So, when an unsuspecting newspaper reader scans the wire service story datelined Trenton and reads, "Candidate X brought his campaign to New Jersey today in an attempt to capture the Garden State's 17 electoral votes . . ." the story should be read with caution. No candidate in a general national election in a country of 210,000,000–220,000,000 people in the decade to come will "capture" a single state's electoral votes just by local campaigning, by handshaking, by motorcades, or whistle-stopping or prop-stopping. Any calculations of whether New Jersey will go Democratic in 1972 will involve a basic *national* movement of voters, of which New Jerseyites will be a part. The people in New Jersey, like the rest of the Americans, will be judging their Presidential choices largely on the basis of national television, national magazines, national columnists, and national reporters appearing in their local newspapers and largely on national issues and national images.

This leads, then, to the question: Does campaigning—even on a national basis—have any real value to a candidate?

The critics of the American-style campaign complain of its length, its banality, and its drain on the stamina of the candidate, in addition to some of the drawbacks just mentioned.

And yet . . . and yet . . . there are some solid reasons for campaigning, and beyond them there is something grandiose and good about American campaigns that ought to be mentioned here.

A candidate does get some extra local publicity in the area where he appears, both in newspapers and on television. This is usually helpful. If he appears with *popular* local politicians, there can be some rub-off.* There is also certainly some local benefit from the point of view "He cared enough to come."†

---

* Humphrey's campaign in Texas was no doubt helped by his appearance at the Astrodome on the Sunday before election in company with President Johnson, Governor John Connally, and Senator Ralph Yarborough, the latter two especially sharp political rivals who temporarily buried the hatchet to help get Texas' vote for Humphrey—successfully.

† Which was Rockefeller's campaign slogan in Oregon during 1964.

And of course, the campaign is important in providing the candidate with *something to do* that can be televised, photographed, and written about for national consumption. Appearing in a motorcade and a shopping center in Bloomfield, New Jersey, may not provide a particularly strong bonus in New Jersey, but it will be televised all over the country (including New Jersey). If, in Bloomfield, the candidate kisses a baby, dons an Indian headdress, swings a baseball bat, or perhaps even says something new about Vietnam or school busing, the coverage will cross the nation that evening. Further, if a candidate does *not* campaign at all, his opposition will criticize him for "not taking his case to the people."

Beyond all that, however, is a certain extremely valuable democratic symbolism that underlies all the flesh pressing, baby kissing, hurly-burly of a campaign. There is great value in a system that somehow demands that a candidate get sweaty and dirty and exhausted, his hands bleeding, his hair messed by the masses of people whom he wants to represent. The successful candidate in America must *touch* the people, figuratively and literally. It is the sweaty crowds, the long receiving lines, the workers at factory gates from whom power flows, and it is to the benefit of both the voter and the candidate to understand that blunt fact about the political system.

It has been suggested that the flying three-ring circus that makes up the fall of an election year could be replaced by another set of baffles and hurdles for a candidate, for all the relevance the campaigning has to reveal the real qualification of a candidate for the Presidency. It has been sarcastically suggested, for example, that a candidate could simply be tested by wind sprints, hand strength (right hand), and vocal timbre, letting the Presidency go to the man who scored highest. But the cynics miss the point of what the trade calls pressing the flesh. The sweaty, grasping people are the taproot of power, and if a politician cannot cope with or relate to a crowd, he is in political trouble and for good reason. He may make a good Secretary of State, a good chairman of the Interstate Commerce Commission, even a good Supreme Court Justice, but he will be missing one of the key attributes and key understandings that a President—or any *elected* officeholder—should have.

The institutionalized hurly-burly and flesh pressing of American politics is probably unmatched anywhere in the world —although there is evidence that the style may be spreading. The idea that people can push politicians around—instead of the reverse—is a contagious thought.

In October, 1966, President Johnson arrived at the airport at the far outskirts of Canberra, Australia, on his way to the Manila Summit Conference. He was met by the Prime Minister of Australia, Harold Holt, a popular leader who was himself running for reelection that December. After brief welcoming and arrival remarks, the two chiefs of state entered a limousine and headed for the city, tailed by scores of limousines with other VIP's and a complement of several buses carrying the hundreds of journalists covering the President's journey.

The route of the motorcade had been announced in advance, and at major intersections hundreds of people were waiting to wave American flags to welcome the President. As the motorcade reached the first knot of people, Johnson ordered the limousine stopped, got out of the car, grabbed an electronic bullhorn, stepped onto the running board, made a short speech, and then shook every hand in sight. This was not standard procedure in Australia, and the people in the crowd were delighted at the idea of having their hand shaken by the man the Australian press continually referred to as "the most powerful man in the world." While this went on, Prime Minister Holt viewed the proceedings from the sidelines with somewhat amused detachment.

It was late in the evening, but the crowds kept swelling, apparently having heard on their radios about this crazy American and his strange habits. Again and again the motorcade was stopped at Johnson's instruction; again and again some weary scribe in the press bus said, "He's loose; let's go."

The attention was on Johnson, but the man for the psephologically minded to watch was Holt. The screamers and jumpers were Australians. *Potential voters for* Holt. *Soon he got the idea. When Johnson went into the crowd to press the flesh, so did Holt, probably surprising himself as much as the Australians. When Johnson finished his little speech, he'd hand the bullhorn to Holt, and his first remark concerned how glad he was to welcome Johnson to Australia, and his next remark was that he certainly was glad that President Johnson wasn't standing for election against Holt in December. In the December election Holt won a big victory, and the Australian press noted with interest the Prime Minister's new personalized and aggressive campaign style.*

Paradox again. On the one hand, campaigning American-style plays at least a key symbolic role in our system; on the other hand, much of the hoopla of campaigning is useless, its value far overrated and overpublicized—particularly in terms of its ability to move specific states.

But in any event, returning to those missing 32,000 votes in New Jersey, we do know that they cannot be moved *alone* to give Humphrey those extra electoral votes. They must be moved *in concert* with *national* totals.

Well, then, *how many* votes, nationwide, would have had to have been moved for enough *states* to go Democratic so that a Democrat would have been elected? That is an idle historical question when concerned with 1968. But if one asks the same question regarding the election of 1972 (but using 1968 as a model), then the answer concerns the most basic arithmetic of the Presidential election.

It will not take much.

The key to such calculations concerns how the Wallace vote goes in the elections to come, and there are many ways to calculate that. But if we assume for a moment that Wallace is in the race in 1972 and that he draws the same number of votes as he did in 1968 and in the same places, that means Wallace would take 7 potential Nixon votes for every 3 potential Humphrey votes. That will keep the race close, and then the Democratic candidate would have to take only 1½ percentage points off the Nixon vote to switch enough states to surpass the 270 electoral votes necessary for election. That involves changing about 1,000,000 votes out of the 70,000,000 cast. *That is not such a big switch.* By that calculation, it's still very much an open race in the seventies. Whether it remains open and why it may remain open will be examined shortly.

Before we explore more fully the tides and waves that were seen in 1968—and that the authors expect to see in the 1970's—it is important to fill in one missing gap. That would be the elections of 1969, and they deserve scrutiny. For if the psephological patterns we have been talking about were not replicated—even in the off-year non-Presidential elections of 1969—then perhaps they were not patterns, not tides, but only random happenings. On the other hand, if there was continuity and replication, then, perhaps, there is a pattern, maybe a tide that bears watching for the seventies.

There *was* replication.

PART FOUR

The Ideas Confirmed: The Elections of 1969

16

Immoderating Elections:

Minneapolis, Los Angeles, New York

In September, 1969, an astonishing headline appeared on the front page of the Washington *Post*. It read: WORKING AMERICANS ARE REDISCOVERED.

Beneath the headline was a perceptive article by the *Post*'s Richard Harwood that dealt with the problems of Mayor John Lindsay in New York. An excerpt from Harwood's piece:

> Truck drivers, dock workers, factory hands and shoe clerks are being rediscovered as an enormous political force that may be bent on counter-revolution. Like specimens in a laboratory, they are being classified and labeled: "The Forgotten American," "The Other American," "The Ethnic American" or, more simply, "The Working American."
>
> The Harvard-MIT Joint Center for Urban Studies has set out to learn what makes him tick. The American Jewish Committee is sponsoring seminars, and literature to illuminate his concerns. The children of SDS want to entice him into a "student-worker alliance." Magazines, newspapers and television networks are exploring his world. Politicians of every description are pondering his anger and alienation.
>
> "We're trying to find out what is bothering them," said David Garth, Lindsay's principal television adviser. "Our problem is

that we never had contact with those neighborhoods until last year."

Perhaps the most fascinating political question of recent years is: Who lost the forgotten Americans so that they had to be rediscovered by John Lindsay, by his principal television adviser, by the Washington *Post*, by assorted other media, by assorted other politicians who forgot where the votes came from, and by assembled foundations all in a row? And the answer is: The people who forgot them are the same people who are now remembering them. In all fairness, the present authors think they didn't forget them, and of more importance, most elected officials didn't forget them. Most important, the so-called forgotten Americans didn't forget; they knew they were there all along.

But somehow, that is how the Press-Political Complex works. Peter Viereck has called it "ritualized chic." And so, for several years, it was impossible to pick up a Sunday supplement or a national magazine and not read about student radicals and hippies who were spawned by middle-class affluence, attuned to a drug culture, nudity, and pornography, who were sexually promiscuous, and who were, as they say, gapped generation-wise. The young were liberal, very liberal; they wanted peace and participatory democracy; the candidates who could harness the thrust of this new politics would be in fine fettle indeed. The issues that concerned all right-thinking citizens—young and old—were poverty, white racism, urban slums, black ghettos, Indians, Mexican-Americans, grapes, and so on. The historian Eric Goldman stated that President Johnson lost his hold over the American people when he lost contact with those whom Goldman called Metro-Americans and who were described by Professor Goldman as "youthful, educated, affluent . . . liberal but without ideology . . . articulate and powerful . . . especially important in determining national attitudes because of their dominance in the world of books, magazines, radio and television." These, we were informed, were the shakers and the movers. And indeed, in some ways, they were—and are.

But as the elections of 1968 drew to a close, it became apparent that neither the students, nor the poor, nor the militants, nor the intellectuals, nor the Metro-Americans were a particularly strong *electoral* force in America. The bottom of the iceberg was dubbed Middle America, and suddenly, as Mr. Harwood pointed out, everyone was writing about it and studying it. The Middle Americans sat in their undershirts drinking beer; they worked in factories; they were antiblack; they bought guns; they were alienated; they felt they didn't have power over their lives; they were for law and order; they were fanning an incipient taxpayers' revolt and a brewing white revolution; they were against sex education; they saw America and its traditional values crumbling; they said, "I worked my way up, why don't the niggers?"; and they elected some nasty or ignorant people who had tapped this feeling of national malaise.

In the course of a couple of years, then, we have been told that America has changed from pot to potbelly, from liberal radicalism to conservative repressionism, from Metro-Americans to Middle Americans. The new unwashed (hippies) have been submerged; the old unwashed (ethnics) have surfaced again and are cracking their political backlash.

It might be well before beginning this chapter about the elections of 1969 to make an attempt to put the politics—and the people—of America in some reasonable perspective.

The fact is this: *Most voters, most often, are not primarily political beings.* Thus, neither New Politics, nor Old Politics, nor malaise, nor hatred is the most important thing in the lives of most American voters. In shorthand, the American voter is typically unyoung, unpoor, unblack, *and* unpolitical. But consider the problem of the reporter who went out on assignment to feel the pulse of America and came back to his editor with this story:

I asked people all over the country what was most on their mind.

A fellow in Cleveland was hoping to get a raise and a promotion, but thought it would go to someone else.

A woman in Bloomington, Indiana, was dreading her forthcoming 40th birthday, because she felt that would really be the end of her youth.

A fifty year-old carpenter in Canton, Ohio, was worried about arthritis in his hands. He is black.

A farm housewife in Belvidere, New Jersey, was deeply concerned about her six-year-old son who stuttered badly.

In Springfield, Missouri, a 28-year-old bachelor was beginning to think he'd never get married, and he didn't like the idea.

A woman in Sacramento thought her husband was seeing another woman.

A couple in Roseburg, Oregon, were concerned that they couldn't seem to make ends meet; they blamed high prices, high taxes. They had bought a 50 h.p. power boat last year.

A college girl in New York State felt she was unattractive to boys. . . .

An insurance salesman in Great Falls, Montana, said he didn't particularly have anything particular on his mind; everything was o.k.

Naturally, such a report would not find its way into the news—because it isn't "news." And yet it is, precisely because most Americans are most deeply and immediately concerned about themselves and their families and about nonpolitical concerns that so much of the talk about the seething white majority, the seething black minority, the rebellion of this, the counterrebellion of that, is totally out of perspective.

We can look at Americans—or any people—on at least three levels. On a *personal* level, their deepest concerns are probably along the lines itemized above: sickness, self-esteem, financial problems, etc.

On a *family* level, a Gallup survey from November, 1967, shows that adults are concerned mostly about making ends meet:

MOST URGENT PROBLEM FACING FAMILY

Question: "What do you consider to be the MOST urgent problem facing *you and your family* today?"

Financial: the high cost of living, taxes, cost of education	60%
No problems—"everything's fine"	16

Miscellaneous	10
Sickness, health problems	8
Vietnam: concern over relatives in Vietnam or the possibility of his going	5
Racial problems: integrated neighborhoods, riots	4
Employment problems: hard to find a good job	3
Old age: proper housing and care	3
No opinion, no answer	2

(NOTE: Table adds to more than 100 percent because
some persons named more than one problem.)

Finally, there is the *political* level, and the findings of this sort of poll are familiar. Here is what Gallup showed in March, 1969, as the various campaigns of 1969 began to move into gear:

MOST IMPORTANT PROBLEM

Question: "What do you think is the most important problem facing *this country* today?"

Vietnam war	40%
Crime and lawlessness (including riots, looting, juvenile delinquency)	17
Race relations	16
Inflation, high cost of living	9
College demonstrations	4
Poverty	3
Unrest in nation	3
Other problems	16
Don't know, no answer	2

(NOTE: Total adds to more than 100% since some
persons gave more than one answer.)

The comparisons between family problems and national problems are most instructive. Forty percent view Vietnam as the most important *national* problem; 5% view it as the most urgent *family* problem. Race relations, including riots, draw 4% as a *family* problem, while race and crime (including riots) draw a combined total of 33% as a *national* or political problem.

It is only politicians, political spear carriers, and political writers who view the political and programmatic issues as the ones that must be on everyone's mind. And the higher up the political ladder one goes, the more entrenched is this idea. At any given moment, some staffman for a Congressman, for a

Senator, for a President, is cannily figuring out just how many votes Title 4 of a certain new piece of legislation is worth— only to find out, eventually, that almost no one will ever hear of his bill, let alone Title 4.

This is all by way of introduction to the voting behavior of the American voter in the year 1969—and most likely the years of the 1970's. American voters should be seen as moderate people: moderately concerned, reasonable, and not wildly back-lashing with rifle in one hand and broken beer bottle in the other. There is no mass revolution brewing—not by ethnics, not by blacks—and there are far more Americans who know about the Mets' Tom Seaver than about the Panthers' Eldridge Cleaver. *Politics and the issues of politics are not normally the most important things in the lives of most Americans.*

Having said that, we can come now to the paradoxical, almost contradictory point of the matter at hand—the elections of 1969. And the point is this: Confront even a moderate man with an immoderate issue, and he may well respond in a manner that seems immoderate.

In the scattered tests of 1969 this is the rule which seems to have emerged: When the Social Issue was raised dramatically— almost to a point of referendum—it was psephologically potent, sometimes to a point that it appeared immoderate. But by no means was the Social Issue brought to referendum level every-where; when it was not, Americans voted sensibly and sanely, moving with almost uncanny accuracy to the "man in the middle."

On the surface, there would seem to be an element of tau-tology in this analysis: The issue was potent except when it wasn't potent. But this is not the point at all. When the issue was not potent, it was not impotent because it was rejected, but because no single candidate captured it or had it pinned on him. No candidate in America won when perceived as being *against* law and order, or being *for* disruption, or *for* narcotics.

Thus, consider for a moment a *moderate* man. He is deeply interested in his family, his home, his financial position. He is moderately interested in politics. Now, ask Moderate Man whether he is for crime in the streets in his neighborhood or

Black Panthers or white Weathermen burning down his city, and he will immoderately say no. If you are then able to convince the moderate man that Candidate A will *eliminate* crime in the streets, while Candidate B is *responsible* for it, you have a winner in Candidate A.

On the other hand, if you approach a moderate man and indicate to him that *all* the candidates, just like himself, are very concerned about crime in the streets and that they'll all do their best to cure or control it, then Moderate Man will vote for the candidate who is most experienced, or who has a better plan for garbage disposal, or who is a Democrat or a Republican, or who went to high school with his brother, or who is of Polish stock—depending on his particular political sympathies and political motivations. He may even decide not to bother to vote at all.

By these lights we can look at the elections of 1969. By these lights, too, we shall later look ahead to the elections of the 1970's. There may be psephological tides at work in the political ocean and some lesser ripples, too, but there are no tidal waves visible that will smash the nation in a crest of frenzy, backlash, riot, or rebellion. Not so long as people can vote their future and, by voting it, direct it.

Now we can look briefly at some of the municipal elections of 1969.

In our judgment, mayoralty elections are excellent weather vanes for the future, particularly when we attempt to look ahead to a Presidential race and most particularly in trying to assess the impact of the Social Issue. Mayors and Presidents are the public officials held most accountable by the voters for the maintenance of law and order (see Gallup data, Chapter 7). Governors, although *executives* like mayors and the President, seem somehow to be held less accountable for social stability, probably because they have control over neither day-to-day police work nor matters of broad national policy. Congressmen, Senators, and other *legislators* are perceived (correctly) as the least accountable of all, once removed from the immediacy of the problem.

In looking at these city elections, then let us keep an eye on the Presidential future, on 1972, on 1976, to see what is relevant and what is not.

First, let us look at three municipal elections, which may be grouped together under the heading of "Immoderating": Minneapolis, Los Angeles, New York.

Between the Atlantic coast and the Pacific coast, Minneapolis is generally thought to be the most liberal major city in America. In recent years, a small legion of nationally prominent liberals have come forth from the Twin City area: Hubert Humphrey, Eugene McCarthy, Orville Freeman, Walter Heller, Harold Stassen, Eric Sevareid, Congressman Don Fraser (chairman of the liberal Democratic Study Group), and the nationally regarded immediate past mayor of Minneapolis, Arthur Naftalin.

In this seedbed of Midwestern liberalism one Charles Stenvig ran for mayor in 1969, when Mayor Naftalin declared he would not run to succeed himself.

Stenvig was a burglary squad detective and head of the Police Federation. He ran, with almost no financial support, on a campaign "to take the handcuffs off the police . . . to protect law-abiding citizens from hoodlums" and to curb black militancy. Minneapolis has only a few blacks but had some burning and looting early in 1969 and some highly publicized black militancy. Mayor Naftalin, according to the New York *Times,* was perceived of by at least part of the electorate in this way: "Many citizens in the city thought Mayor Arthur Naftalin had not been tough enough with militants and held the police in too tight a rein."

Stenvig picked up the law-and-order issue as his sole theme very early in the campaign, became thoroughly identified with it, and won the nonpartisan primary going away.

Stenvig (Independent, law-and-order)	30,230
Cohen (Republican endorsee)	21,899
Hegstrom (Democratic-Farmer-Labor endorsee)	19,210
Others	1,662

In the runoff Mr. Cohen was endorsed by Eugene McCarthy, the Central Labor Union, the Minneapolis *Star and Tribune,* and Hegstrom. Mr. Cohen was also endorsed by Richard M. Nixon, the President of the United States, who said that Cohen was the man who would "prevail over reaction and extremism." But it was Stenvig who won in a landslide, 76,000 to 47,000.

Joseph Alsop, no knee-jerk liberal he, summed it up rather neatly:

> At his victory celebration, Stenvig was asked who his chief adviser would be.
> "God," he replied, with beautiful simplicity. "God first of all."
> The Almighty will have his work cut out for him. During the campaign, when asked about complex modern city problems like urban renewal, Stenvig had a way of answering that he hoped to learn about all those matters after he had been elected as mayor. Yet, this was the man who reduced to ruins the once-powerful Democratic-Farmer-Labor Coalition, and ended nearly a quarter of a century of almost uninterrupted liberal rule in Minneapolis.

It is instructive to take a retrospective look at just what happened to generate the defeat of the liberals in Minneapolis, for it seems to have a national application.

Essentially, it can be said that the liberal elements in Minneapolis allowed a severe fracture of the Roosevelt coalition and that all the political horses and all the political men couldn't put the coalition together again. The original Democratic-Farmer-Labor candidate Gerard Hegstrom was perceived by the voters as being a candidate of the "university liberals."* His campaign was run largely by McCarthy types of the New Politics, and his stance was one that tended to pooh-pooh the Social Issue. When challenged by the allegedly immoderate law-and-order pitch of Stenvig, the liberal Hegstrom had little credi-

---

* Even though, ironically, he was a former FBI investigator. In New York City, later in the year, the same stripe of politician was dubbed the "limousine liberal."

bility in saying he, too, was for order. This let Stenvig run to daylight on the Social Issue, and he scored heavily in the middle- and working-class wards.

When Stenvig met the Republican Cohen, the election went pretty well along class lines: poor and lower-middle-class workers for Stenvig, middle-middle-class workers also for Stenvig, with only the blacks, the intellectuals, straight-line Republicans, upper-middle-class gentry, and the wealthy, for Cohen—by then perceived as the Establishment candidate. Interestingly, the Republican Cohen was "conservative" enough to carry the relatively wealthy and conservative areas that went to Goldwater in 1964. But the presumptive "conservative" Stenvig, by then, was in an ideal position: He had the scare vote on the Social Issue and got the workingman vote on the economic issue by virtue of his image as "a man of the people." Stenvig ran best in the same wards in which the Socialist mayor of Minneapolis, Tom Van Lear, did well fifty years ago, in 1919. Stenvig carried the wards that voted for FDR and Hubert Humphrey.

The fact that "intellectual liberals" and the city's few blacks switched to the Republican candidate made very little difference. Stenvig still won in a landslide.

This all leads to a thought that will be repeated and elaborated on in later pages. Picture, if you will, the FDR Coalition as an automobile, and remember that an automobile needs an engine to run. Accordingly, when a political pundit comes onto the showroom floor to tell you about a flashy new-style coalition composed of the poor, the young, the blacks, the browns, the Jews, the intellectuals, then beware. What he is saying is this: "My friends, here is this wonderful new model. It's got fantastic windshield wipers. It's got ashtrays that you wouldn't believe. The seat covers are astonishing. Its hubcaps gleam in the sunlight." Unfortunately, when the prospective buyer lifts up the hood, there is no engine. The engine, the salesman explains, is in the back room, and it's considered optional equipment on this particular model. And the engine, of course, is the "Labor vote" or, if one wishes to expand it, the "plain people vote," or "Middle Americans," or "unyoung, unpoor, unblack." The

Democratic car just doesn't run without it, and the Minneapolis election places this in stark relief. You can knock the "liberal intellectuals" out of the Democratic coalition, and you've lost the front bumper; knock out the black vote, and you've lost the fenders and the back seat; but knock out labor, Middle America, or the unyoung, unpoor, unblack, and you've lost the engine, and the car won't run. This is an unpleasant fact to some, but fact it is.

What happened in Minneapolis was that moderate men were faced with an immoderate choice. Stenvig phrased the issue of the election early and was perceived as the only man who could cope with it. Once that was established, the fact that Stenvig was inexperienced in municipal affairs or that he was opposed by all the Establishment's movers and shakers made no difference.

In Minneapolis, in an anti-Establishment time, the liberals and progressives were handicapped by the feeling that they were the rascals who ought to be thrown out. Mr. Hegstrom of Minneapolis was not formally the incumbent, nor was Mr. Cohen, but Detective Stenvig artfully managed to pin the "Establishment" label on both.

In Los Angeles, on the other hand, the forces of liberalism had a golden chance. The incumbent was the conservative Sam Yorty, a mayor in whose city the Watts riots flared, a mayor whose administration was charged with corruption, a mayor many regarded as somewhat of an incompetent.

And the liberals had a good candidate, a black ex-policeman, who was calm, bright, and articulate. But Tom Bradley lost because the Social Issue slipped through his fingers. Admittedly, this is all said with the remarkable 20-20 psephological hindsight that is permitted to authors, but unfortunately denied to active candidates. And when Bradley, after beating Yorty in the primary, went into the final week of the campaign, the polls showed him ahead.

Retrospectively, however, it would seem that Bradley had the opportunity to fill a slot that could well be one of the most politically profitable in contemporary America: the tough, but well-educated, black cop who will be mayor of all the people. Bradley filled this prescription with only one exception—the image of *toughness*.

Suppose Bradley had opened up his campaign by saying, "I served on the police force of this city for many years, and let me tell you something, my friends: When I am mayor, there won't be a single junkie or dope peddler left on the streets. Not on streets where blacks live. Not on streets where Mexican-Americans live. Not on streets where whites live. No more will our children—black, white, or tan—be sucked into crime by these human scum." Suppose then Bradley endorsed the tough-on-crime platform set forth by the Harlem branch of the NAACP a few years ago: minimum of five years in jail for muggers, minimum of ten years for dope pushers, thirty years for murder—with no time off for good behavior.* And then suppose he said, "My friends, let me assure you of something else. When I am mayor of Los Angeles, the college students of this city—black, white, and tan—will not have to fear that their colleges will be shut down—not by black militants and not by white radicals. I have been a professional lawman, and I know my business; this can be done. Sam Yorty couldn't do it or wouldn't do it; but I can, and I will, with your help."

Well, now. That's a pretty tough law-and-order speech. It might have antagonized a few professional liberals and a few militant blacks who would quickly label Bradley as a "black Stenvig," but who were they going to vote for—Sam Yorty?

More important, would such a speech say anything that Tom Bradley doesn't believe? Has it said anything with which any decent liberal or decent human being disagrees? Who is for dope peddlers? Who is for black or white anarchists disrupting colleges? Is there anything for a liberal, black or white, to be ashamed of when he comes out against crime in the streets, or anarchy in academia? (Anything that is, except the self-inflicted guilt by association that George Wallace is also against it?)

---

* In March, 1970, Gallup reported that 71% favored a minimum punishment of ten years in jail for heroin pushers; 65% favored such a minimum for marijuana sellers.

But Tom Bradley and his supporters opted not to play their ace of trumps and decided, instead, to hand the card over to Sam Yorty to use as he saw fit. The Bradleyites were perceived, in effect, to accept the standard liberal dogma that " 'law and order' is a code phrase for racism." By doing that, they allowed law and order and all the Social Issues to become the paramount issues of a campaign. Had the Bradley supporters beaten Yorty to the law-and-order issue, Bradley would have won, in the opinion of the authors. *Likely he would have won without crime and race becoming the dominant issue. The issue would have been co-opted. Two candidates, each vigorously for law and order, equals no issue.*

Instead, when Yorty finished a bad second to Bradley in the primary, he played his gift trump card with a vengeance. Yorty was able to charge that Bradley, of all people, was "antipolice." Yorty was able to charge that Bradley was the candidate of "black militants and left-wing extremists."

Bradley, not having co-opted the issue, was vulnerable to it. He was particularly vulnerable to it because he is a black and the thought of "crime/disruption" and the thought of "black" are unfortunately somewhat intertwined.* Accordingly, when Yorty ran a thinly disguised racist campaign against Bradley, he was able to score just well enough to win the election. The final results were fairly close:

Yorty 53%
Bradley 47%

A resounding gain for Yorty from the primary, when Bradley got 42% and Yorty 26%, with the balance scattered among twelve candidates. Bradley came close to his full potential in the first primary and was unable to increase his total by many votes.

Los Angeles, it should be remembered, is only 17% black, so

---

*Ethnic or racial stereotypes in a political campaign are, of course, nothing new. John Lindsay got some votes in New York from people who refused to believe that an Italian politician could not be associated with the Mafia—and Lindsay's two opponents were Italian.

it was vital that Bradley gain the support of many nonblacks. As his final vote total attests, he did, to his great credit as a candidate. In this respect, he ran far better than the two other black big-city mayoralty candidates in 1969, Carl Stokes in Cleveland (who won) and Richard Austin in Detroit (who lost), each of whom got only about 20% of the white vote, but in cities where the proportion of black voters is much higher than in Los Angeles. Bradley ran fairly well in the Mexican-American district, and about 14% of the Los Angeles population is of Mexican-American background. In some solid Latin districts the vote total looked like this:

> Yorty 54%
> Bradley 46%

That is a pretty fair turnout for Bradley, but compared to the vote in the same precincts for Hubert Humphrey in 1968:

> Humphrey 83%
> Nixon 15
> Wallace 2

it wasn't good at all. In fact, if the Mexican-American vote had gone for Bradley as it had for Humphrey, Tom Bradley would be mayor of Los Angeles.

This data would seem to cast at least some doubt on the prevailing notion that either the "poor" or "minority groups" are particularly monolithic or "coalesceable" in their voting habits when it comes to supporting minority group candidates other than their own.

In fact, they are probably not. Bradley got almost 100% of the black vote because he was a black, clearly cashing in on the standard "one of our boys made it" feeling. One of the reasons he got only 40% of the Mexican-American vote was the same: He was a black. Had a Mexican-American run for mayor, he might well have received 100% of the Mexican-American vote and 40% of the black vote.

Did some of the Mexican-Americans vote against Bradley because he was black and they were prejudiced? Probably so; most Americans are antisomebody, and it even finally caught up to the WASP's in New York in 1969, when Lindsay lost some votes because he was *not* ethnic in a city that was. That much is normal. Also, Yorty had courted the Mexican-American vote over many years. Also normal. But there is another very important question to consider: Did those Mexican-Americans vote against Bradley because Yorty made points—not only on the race issue, not only on the friendship/incumbency issue, but also on the law-and-order issue, just as he got other Angeleno votes on the law-and-order issue? The answer to that is probably yes. In the previous chapter we noted that on certain gut aspects of the Social Issue, attitudes all over America were overwhelmingly one-sided and were overwhelmingly one-sided in every region, among every income group, every occupation group, in every age bracket, of both sexes. The standard Gallup groupings of the electorate are not able, however, to give cross tabulations on blacks, Mexican-Americans, or Jews, because the normal Gallup sample is not large enough to include enough interviews among these minority groups to make them statistically valid.

But the Los Angeles evidence would seem to indicate that Mexican-Americans, like all the other Gallup-grouped Americans, have the same susceptibility to a Social Issue campaign. And, indeed, is there any reason why they shouldn't have such a susceptibility? For the most part, the Mexican-American districts are in the inner city where there are high crime rates. Furthermore, the parents of a Mexican-American teen-ager, who are working hard so that their son can attend a state university, say, like San Francisco State, are going to be less than pleased when black or white militants close down the school. And so, when a Sam Yorty plays that familiar social string on his political fiddle, the Mexican-Americans hear it and perhaps hear it even more clearly than the basic breadbasket, pocketbook, and good-government issues that a candidate like Bradley might be said to represent.

Much the same sort of an analysis can be drawn from the

Jewish vote. Probably no group in American history has voted more consistently "liberal" than Jews. Yet when confronted with a referendum-type Social Issue election (which is what the Los Angeles election turned out to be), many Jews defected from the "liberal" candidate (Bradley) to the more conservative candidate Yorty. Here are the figures for some selected heavily Jewish precincts:

JEWISH VOTING IN LOS ANGELES, 1968, 1969 (selected precincts)

1968	Humphrey	86%	Nixon	13%	Wallace	1%
1969	Bradley	51%	Yorty	49%		

Notice that the Jews did go for Bradley, but not nearly by the same proportions as before. Much the same sort of liberal Jewish defection can be detected in the Lindsay election in New York in 1969—another election where the Social Issue was paramount. So, while the Gallup Poll does not normally carry cross tabulations by religion other than by Protestant and Catholic, it can be seen that Jews, like Mexican-Americans—*and everyone else in America*—are responsive to the law-and-order issue.*

Finally, and conclusively, be it noted that blacks, too, will buy many of the aspects of the Social Issue when properly presented. Obviously, they disagree with the antiblack biases held by whites that have been discussed here. But race and race prejudice are only one aspect of the Social Issue. On the non-racial aspects of the Social Issue, blacks and whites share many

---

* If Yorty was able to cash in on the Social Issue among Mexican-Americans and Jews against Bradley, why wasn't Nixon able similarly to cash in against Humphrey, who was also being hurt by the Social Issue? Several reasons. The Presidential race was Democrat versus Republican; the LA mayoralty race was a "nonpartisan" race. (Yorty and Bradley are both Democrats, although Yorty is a strange kind of Democrat.) The Mexican-Americans and Jews in 1968 were voting more Democratic than Social Issue—as discussed in Chapter 12. They were voting economics and history. The Social Issue, like everything else in politics, is a question of degree and a question of location. It cut deeply for Nixon and Wallace in the South in 1968 and less so—but still significantly—among non-Southern areas. It cut deeply against Bradley in Los Angeles when it was perceived as the major issue in a referendum-style election, far more deeply than it hurt Humphrey a year earlier. As we shall see, it also cut deeply against John Lindsay in New York.

attitudes. It is instructive in this regard to recall the results of the Milwaukee mayoralty race held in April, 1968—on the same day as the Wisconsin Presidential preference primary. In that election, the mayor of Milwaukee, Henry Maier, ran for reelection after a downtown riot had raged briefly in Milwaukee. Maier had responded by calling in police (and the National Guard) and moving forcefully and early to stop the riot. He was the first mayor to slap on a "curfew system" to combat a riot. He was criticized by militant blacks and liberal whites for "repression," "brutality," "hardness," etc.

In the election, Mayor Maier ran against David Walther, a liberal white attorney. Maier was elected by a landslide: 86% to 14%. *Most interestingly, he did not run at all badly in the black precincts in Milwaukee, despite the fact that his opponent was clearly against "repression" of black rioters.* Walther carried these precincts, but Maier polled 35%–40% of the vote, quite a respectable showing.

It would seem, then, that blacks, too, are responsive to the law-and-order issue. Mayor Maier was known as a decent and effective liberal on economic matters, and he was known not to be racist. To that image he added a new facet, toughness. There is no evidence that this posture hurt him badly in the black community; nor, when one thinks about it, is there any reason that it should. The crime rate is highest in black areas; the riots destroy black property; dope pushers cripple black youth. Why shouldn't a law-and-order message, delivered not as a code word for racism but on its own merits, why shouldn't such a pitch be successful?

Some years ago, columnist Murray Kempton wrote a piece that described the creeping growth of the white Anglo-Saxon Protestant Establishment in America. Kempton perceptively noted that one didn't have to be either white, Anglo-Saxon, or Protestant to be part of the WASP Establishment. The Kennedys, said Kempton, were CASP's (Catholic white Anglo-Saxon Protestant). Herbert Lehman was a JASP (Jewish white Anglo-Saxon Protestant). And there were NASP's, too, said Kempton, like Carl Rowan (Negro white Anglo-Saxon Protestant).

The authors would like to now make a contribution to the Kempton syndrome. As follows: *Blacks are a part of white Middle America.* Not totally, not everywhere, not everyone, not on every issue, but enough so as to be psephologically significant. As a matter of fact, based on the old principle that no one is more middle class than the new middle class, some feel there is probably no community in America that is more bourgeois, more addicted to those "middle-class values," than the growing number of blacks now reaching middle-income status. Black voters, like all other groups of voters, have not shown any delight at campus disruptions, or hippies on drugs, or crime in the streets, or pornography on the newsstand.

The campaign strategists of the seventies, then, must be prepared to accept a strange notion: Blacks, too, are "plain people"; they, too, are "forgotten Americans"; they, too, belong in the Silent Majority—and many, too, are unyoung and unpoor. The implications of this idea will be discussed in the final chapter.

And now for New York, and the bittersweet victory defeat of John V. Lindsay. We say "victory defeat" because there seems to be no other phrase that expresses the reality of the situation with quite such precision. What other phrase better describes the results of an election in which the only liberal candidate— running in the most liberal big city in the nation—pulls only four out of ten votes? What other phrase better describes the results of an election in which a politician with national aspirations pulls only one in four votes of the "white workingman," or if one chooses to look at Lindsay specifically as a potential *Democratic* candidate, what kind of recommendation is it to say that he received *fewer* than half of the Jewish votes the last time out?

Of course, with all that, John Lindsay and his family still occupy Gracie Mansion, he did receive more votes than either of his opponents, he is still the mayor of New York, and so on. But he won on the basis of an ancient political rule: "Happiness is a divided opposition." The fact is that John Lindsay won on a fluke, just as if Hubert Humphrey had won the Presidency in 1968, he would have won on a fluke. (Humphrey, in fact, got a greater percentage of the national vote than Lindsay did for mayor of New York.) In Humphrey's case, the oppositionists split in a lopsided way: Nixon 43.4%, Wallace 13.5%, and so Nixon is President. In Lindsay's case, the oppositionists split more evenly: John Lindsay 42%, Mario Procaccino 35%, John Marchi 23%—and so, Lindsay is mayor.

Why did Lindsay run so poorly? Because he, like Hegstrom and Bradley, allowed the election to be phrased as a referendum on law and order/race/crime. In all fairness to John Lindsay, it must be remembered that it took him four years as mayor of a difficult city to put himself in the same social quicksand that Bradley and Hegstrom managed to fall into merely by running an election campaign. On the other hand, Lindsay was at one point sunk up to his lower lip in the swamp of the Social Issue, while the others might be adjudged as only mired waist-deep.

An opinion often heard from voters in New York in 1969 was that John Lindsay "had turned the city over to the blacks and Puerto Ricans" and that among other things this was contributing to the rise in crime.

There is the poignant story of a New Yorker who would, of necessity, venture out in the streets of the city at night—but only with exactly $30 in his pocket. Why exactly $30? His reasoning was this: If you got mugged and had only a couple of dollars on your person, the muggers would not only take your money but beat you up for having so little money to give them. On the other hand, if you carried $100 or $200, you would be wasting a lot of money if you got mugged. So our pragmatic New Yorker carries three $10 bills with him.

Fear such as this was compounded with a school strike, a garbagemen's strike, a snow removal crisis, and a transit strike, which served to give Lindsay an image of executive incompetence.

Perhaps Lindsay's most tragic mistake came simultaneously with his greatest achievements. When, in the "hot" summers of 1966 and 1967, Lindsay went out in shirt sleeves to walk the streets of Harlem, Spanish Harlem, and Bedford-Stuyvesant—he was courageously doing what ought to have been done. He was attempting to keep the city cool, and he gained a great deal of respect and attention because New York did not blow up the way Newark, or Detroit, or Washington did. Whether Lindsay's walking the slums indeed was instrumental in defusing potential riots or whether it was only *perceived* to have defused riots is not terribly important. It showed that the charismatic mayor had concern for the ghettos, as well as personal guts and flair.

Unfortunately, John Lindsay did not go the next day to Bensonhurst or Kew Gardens. He did not go to Kingsbridge, or Flushing, or Washington Heights, or Brooklyn Heights. Not going there, he did not eat a blintz, go to an Italian block party, attend an Irish wake, or visit with the Polish Falcons. As the New York voter perceived it, he went to Lincoln Center to watch the ballet in the company of the beautiful people. To put it once again in the words of David Garth, "Lindsay's principal television adviser," "We are trying to find out what is bothering them. Our problem is that we never had contact with those neighborhoods until last year."

And so, alas, the Italians and Irishmen and Jews began to feel that Lindsay was mayor exclusively for the blacks, the Puerto Ricans, and the "limousine liberals"—the wealthy do-gooders who had twenty-four-hour doorman service at the front of their apartment houses and whose children were sent to private schools.

And that was the unfortunate phrasing of the New York 1969 mayoralty race: Lindsay and crime, race, and permissiveness— versus two candidates, each allegedly representing the "little man" or the "plain people" or, if you prefer, the Silent Majority. Given such phrasing, Lindsay was in deep trouble.

To see *how* deep, we can compare the New York City returns from 1968 and 1969. Hubert Humphrey, himself on the edge of trouble on the Social Issue, also ran against two candidates perceived as conservatives—Nixon and Wallace. Yet, in New York City, the liberal Humphrey received 61% of the vote. Exactly one year later, in far deeper Social Issue trouble, the liberal John Lindsay received 42% of the vote. In other words, about one in every three liberal voters left the liberal camp to vote against Lindsay. This happened, in our judgment, because the city election was almost entirely a referendum on the Social Issue, while the Presidential race was a vast mixture of social, economic, and international issues.*

In point of fact, the pattern of the Lindsay election most closely resembled an earlier New York City election that was purely Social Issue. That was the 1966 referendum concerning the establishment of a Police Review Board staffed by civilians and designed to curb "police brutality."

Just as in the Lindsay 1969 election, all the forces favoring good government—the leading public figures, clergy, business-men, artists, labor leaders, politicians—lined up in favor of the new Police Review Board. And as in 1969, the Irish, Italians, and many Jews voted down the Police Review Board 65%–35%, just as they voted against Lindsay.

That Lindsay did somewhat better than the Police Review Board—enough better to be reelected—is due in some measure to personalism. Lindsay is handsome, articulate, telegenic—but how much good that was doing him can be judged by the fact that in February, 1969, a poll commissioned by Lindsay showed that 74% of the voters disapproved of his administration.

But personalism helped John Lindsay in a negative way: His major opponent, Procaccino, said the *wrong* things, in the *wrong* way, at the *wrong* time.† Procaccino was finally perceived as somewhat of a political clown; as this happened, his poll ratings shrank enough to give Lindsay a victory on the basis of a close oppositionist split.

There was another interesting factor in the Lindsay election. Despite a three-man race, there was no center candidate. Procaccino had won the Democratic primary as the most conserva-

---

* Some have suggested that Lindsay's drop from the Humphrey 1968 percentage was due to his running as a third-party (*i.e.,* Liberal) nominee. But New York's mayors have often been mavericks, and voters are willing to cross party lines. Fiorello LaGuardia was elected under a great variety of political labels. Vincent Impelliteri won with only the label of the Experience Party.
† The classic example, to a black audience: "My heart is as black as yours."

tive of Democrats—because the moderate/liberal opposition cut each other's throats. Consequently, Lindsay was running against two opponents conceived of as conservative, instead of one conservative and one moderate, which would have been the case had Robert Wagner won the Democratic primary, as many observers had expected. This allowed Lindsay to make a last-minute charge toward the center—"Look at me, I put on extra policemen; look at me, I wear a yarmulke at a synagogue in Bensonhurst"—and this helped him.

Finally, because this volume looks ahead to the remainder of the decade, and because John Lindsay has been mentioned as a possible Presidential candidate, some further comment is in order about his status as Presidential timber in a forest of potential candidates. After Lindsay's victory defeat in 1969, Jack Newfield, the chronicler of the New Left, wrote in *Life* about the backlash vote in 1969 and said:

> . . . Most significantly, John Lindsay has stopped it at the banks of the Hudson River with his New Politics combination of an independent political campaign, expert media, hundreds of student activists and antiwar conviction. *There are those in his inner circle and among his army of college canvassers who believe John Lindsay has invented, in cynical, fragmented New York, the scale model for a national New Politics campaign in 1972.* [Italics ours.]

Rebuttal: If John Lindsay's 1969 vote in New York were projected on a national canvass—properly weighting black, Puerto Rican, Jewish, Italian, Irish, WASP, etc., votes—it is doubtful that he would poll as well as Barry Goldwater in 1964.

Should John Lindsay switch his party allegiance to the Democrats,* be nominated for President in 1972, and be perceived by the voters nationwide as he was in 1969 in New York City, he would lose massively to centrist Richard Nixon or any other middle-of-the-road Republican. If by some quirk of fate, he

---

* Which, in our judgment, would be wise; his future as a Republican seems very, very dim.

received the Republican nomination and ran as a liberal Republican against a liberal Democrat, he might conceivably succeed in electing George Wallace as President.

Having said that, let us backtrack: Lindsay can change; the country can change. Expect the unexpected. Lindsay—an attractive and bright man—can head back into the center and can "rediscover the workingman," not just during election years, but throughout his term as mayor of the largest, most exciting city in America. If he does that, he can still go far.

Summing up: Lindsay got into trouble in New York because he allowed the Social Issue to phrase the election: It became a referendum. He won on a fluke. If the lesson sinks in, the rules of politics allow him the power of self-regeneration.

17

Moderating Elections:

Seattle, Detroit, Pittsburgh

Elections phrased as referenda on the Social Issue did not follow a consistent pattern throughout the nation in 1969. Nor will such elections *necessarily* be the rule in the Presidential contests of 1972 or 1976.

For example, consider the 1969 mayoralty elections in Seattle, Detroit, and Pittsburgh. In each campaign, race and law and order played a role, but not the decisive role.

In Seattle, ten candidates competed in the first round of the nonpartisan mayoralty race. Impressed by earlier law-and-order victories in Los Angeles, Minneapolis, and the New York primary, several of the Seattle mayoralty candidates attempted to run a straight, tough, one-issue, law-and-order campaign. But their campaigns never jelled because there was no incumbent*
identified as a softie to run against (as in New York), and it soon became apparent that *all ten candidates were in favor of law and order*. That issue, accordingly, became a "motherhood issue": Everyone was for it, and you can't run a promotherhood campaign unless someone is running against motherhood.

Accordingly, the campaign shifted to other issues, and the Seattle *Post-Intelligencer* could write on the day after the election:

---

* Seattle's mayor, J. D. Braman, had taken a job in the Nixon administration.

AFTERMATH OF ELECTION: IRONY, CLASS

By Shelby Scates
P-I Political Writer

Seattle flashed its class Tuesday in that primary election.

They rap us back east as provincial; cut-off if not cloddish. Around Los Angeles, it's chic to sneer through tinted eyeshades at the square scene along Puget Sound. Besides, it rains too much.

Okay. It's not hip enough for the jet-set. But stack Mort Frayn and Wes Uhlman against Sam Yorty, and Seattle comes out first class.

It could have come out the other way. There were Yorty-like exhortations in the primary election to "make Seattle safe again" and insure "law and order." Naked raids on fear.

Instead the voters showed their concern with more than the single, simple, issue. In the process, they picked a pair of competent, balanced, politicians to meet in the November 4 general election.

The irony—and Seattle seemed to sense it—is that Frayn and Uhlman probably have greater capacity to handle crime and civil disorder than those who shouted loudest about it.

They are vivid contrasts in style, but not so different in the substance of their ideas.

Uhlman made a quantum leap in the election. From a respected, but relatively unknown state legislator, he is suddenly a ranking new star in the State Democratic party—win or lose Nov. 4. He is 34.

Frayn's style is as old shoe as Uhlman's is telegenic, a fact that firmly establishes him as the under-dog, despite his enormous number of friends and his backing from the downtown business community.

He is 63, rumpled as a Dutch uncle. A book publisher, he learned his political ropes as House speaker and a leader in the 1964 Rockefeller for President campaign.

If, taking a cue from Los Angeles and Minneapolis, Seattle's primary campaign opened with a predominant "law and order" theme, it's expected to finish with talk on total environmental quality.

That covers more ground than safe streets. It includes the need for a balanced transportation system, increased city services and tax reform. [Italics ours.]

In Detroit, too, the law-and-order issue was largely co-opted by moderates in the primary election. When one remembers that Detroit suffered the worst of riots in the summer of 1967 and that in late March, 1969, a much-heralded shoot-out occurred between police and black militants (killing one policeman), it is not surprising that a white candidate would make a run for mayor on the classic lines of a law-and-order campaign. Such a candidate was Councilwoman Mary V. Beck. As the Detroit *Free Press* noted after the election: "Miss Beck, 61, ran virtually a one-issue campaign: She would sweep the streets clean of crime, corruption and every form of pollution. . . ."

But on the day before the July 26 filing date, six weeks before the election, Miss Beck lost her bid. She had the center cut out from her constituency when Roman S. Gribbs announced his candidacy. Mr. Gribbs was a self-proclaimed middle-of-the-roader, with two very great advantages: He was of Polish origin, like Miss Beck, and he was the sheriff of Wayne County, unlike Miss Beck. He was tough enough so that he didn't have to act tough.* As the *Free Press* noted:

> Gribbs, who remained vague on most issues throughout the campaign, appeared to benefit from a dual image: He was a moderate, and he was a professional lawman.
>
> He ran well in both low-income white areas where the fear of crime is strong, and in more affluent white areas where the "law and order" theme of Miss Beck was apparently too strident.

It was this image that allowed Mr. Gribbs to head into the center. The *Free Press* again:

> Only days before the primary election, he announced a 19-point program that stressed *upgrading the police department and improving housing conditions in the Inner City.* [Italics ours; there is a hint here of strategies to come.]

---

* Or, as General David Shoup said shortly after assuming command of the U.S. Marine Corp: "Any Marine officer who feels the need to carry a swagger stick, may do so." Shoup holds the Congressional Medal of Honor.

Gribbs was able to preempt the law-and-order issue and move on to other things.

The third mayoralty candidate in the nonpartisan primary was the Wayne County auditor, Richard Austin. Mr. Austin is a black. He, like Sheriff Gribbs, ran as a moderate, to the dismay of some of the more militant black community. The *Free Press:*

> In an ambitious schedule of campaign appearances—the most ambitious of the primary—Austin offered himself as the man who could stem the flow of people and business to the suburbs.
>
> Austin's campaign strategy was twofold: To allay the fears of whites and convince them that a responsible black man can successfully govern Detroit. . . .

Mr. Austin, the moderate black, won the primary as the white vote split:

Austin (moderate black)	38%
Gribbs (moderate white)	32%
Beck (law-and-order white)	21%
Others	9%

Austin, running in a city that is 45% black, but where blacks traditionally cast only about 25% of the vote, understood that he needed white as well as black support. The *Free Press* reported: "Austin wanted 15% of the city's white vote. Returns from the primary showed he got less than 10%." Undoubtedly, one of the reasons he didn't get as much of the white vote as he had hoped for was that Gribbs' moderate stance siphoned off some potential white liberal support.

After the primary, the black community rallied to its man:

> In spite of the discouraging signs on the November horizon, Austin counted major pluses last night as he greeted jubilant supporters at a downtown hotel.
>
> First, his first-place finish brought belated promises of support from some of the important black community leaders who had preferred a more militant candidate—or none at all. Many

of these leaders had sat on their hands during the primary campaign and a few had even undermined Austin's campaign in the black community.

Secondly, the city's black community demonstrated it can play a powerful role in Detroit politics—and only half of its potential was realized in the Tuesday primary.

Austin believes he can nearly double the number of black voters with a massive registration drive, full cooperation from former foes and the money, volunteer help and new endorsements that his top of the ticket victory are likely to bring.

And the *Free Press* concluded:

In the one-month primary campaign neither Gribbs nor Austin made racist appeals to Detroit voters. It seems unlikely that the campaign ahead will be any different.

This is not to say that race played only a small role in the Detroit election. In the larger sense, it was the determining factor in Gribbs' ultimate victory—whites voting for a white candidate, blacks for a black candidate, in a manner starker, but not wholly dissimilar from Jews voting for a Jewish candidate, Poles voting for a Polish candidate, and willing to cross party lines to do so.

The final count:

Gribbs (moderate, white)	51%
Austin (moderate, black)	49%

But the Detroit election was essentially a moderating, bring-us-together affair, with two centrist candidates who appreciated each other's position. Accordingly, the venom count was low, and an already polarized city was not further embittered. As a matter of fact, the black voters of Detroit, while "losing" the mayorality, did win additional seats of the nine-member Common Council, and the successful black council candidates gained appreciable white support.

Retrospectively, both black and white Detroiters finessed the potentially exacerbating Social Issue confrontation by putting up good candidates of the center, candidates who were not perceived either as softies or as militants, candidates who would pull extremists into the center. The other choice—putting up extreme candidates—could force the moderate center to choose between black and white militants. By co-opting the Social Issue, candidates in Detroit, as in Seattle, defused the Social Issue—much to the benefit of their communities.

Finally, we come to Pittsburgh, as a third example of a moderating, rather than a divisive, election. The Pittsburgh scene was by no means as simple or as clear-cut as either the Detroit or the Seattle mayoralty races.

The contenders in the Democratic primary were Harry A. Kramer and Pete Flaherty. They ran in a city that has a 3 to 1 Democratic registration edge and that had a longtime powerful Democratic mayor, Joseph Barr.

Kramer was generally regarded as Barr's "handpicked successor," and it was understood that he had the support of the "Democratic machine."

Pete Flaherty, a liberal, was a telegenic forty-four-year-old attorney when he announced for Pittsburgh's mayorality. Flaherty ran his Pittsburgh primary campaign "against the machine"—as a New Politics candidate versus the Old Politics. Here is the text of Flaherty's newspaper advertisement on the eve of the May 21, 1969, primary election:

TOMORROW IT'S UP TO YOU . . .

PETE OR THE MACHINE

For a change the people have a chance to own the Mayor. For a change he'll belong to all 208,000 Democrats. This scares City Hall. During the campaign they acted like politicians. They worried about the future of their "machines," not the future of our City. They forgot to worry about spending and high taxes and the needs of the people. Now, they're worried about the secret ballot . . . your vote. The choice is up to you. A Democratic Party for the "few" or for the people. More of the same or a new hope for the future. A machine or a man. Pete. Nobody owns him . . . just the people. All it takes is one vote . . . yours. Tomorrow.

PETE
   FLAHERTY
FOR MAYOR
Your Democratic Candidate

Kramer attempted to run a law-and-order campaign, but this is generally a difficult route for a man representing the established political structure, a man perceived of as almost an incumbent and therefore held responsible for any earlier perceived permissiveness. Flaherty, on the other hand, was charismatic, antimachine—and that was enough. He won a whopping victory.

Flaherty (New Politics, liberal)	59%
Kramer (Old Politics, "machine candidate")	41%

As for Flaherty's appeal as a New Politics man, McCarthy/Kennedy style, that support was there to be sure, but it came with some strange bedfellows, according to the Pittsburgh *Press:*

At one stage in the night the oldest person to be found in a Flaherty vote counting room was 18 years old.

Typical of the youthful Flaherty followers was Barbara Lembersky, 19, a Pitt student from Squirrel Hill.

She's been typing, stuffing envelopes and talking up her man for months.

"I like the way he responds to people," was the reason she gave for her loyalty.

And then there was the 55-year old man who voted George Wallace for president and then threw his support to Pete for mayor.

"I just wanted to rock the boat," he explained. [Italics ours.]

And this admixture was reflected in the vote tallies as well. Here is James Helbert, the politics editor of the *Press:*

Mr. Flaherty enjoyed support from former backers of Sen. Eugene McCarthy, but he won handily in wards that never gave the Minnesota senator's presidential campaign or his intellectual backers the time of day.*

Mr. Flaherty even won in such hard-nosed organization wards as the South Side's 16th and 17th and in all the North Side wards except for the dead heat in the 23rd.

So Flaherty breezed home, a primary winner in a moderating election bringing blacks, liberals, moderates, and Wallace supporters together in a fascinating coalition. With a 3 to 1 Democratic majority in Pittsburgh, the Flaherty forces anticipated little difficulty in beating the Republican candidate, John Tabor, in the November general elections.

But the moment of psephological truth for Pete Flaherty was yet to come. In August a great potential crack appeared in Pete Flaherty's coalition, a potential crack that could easily have turned a moderating election into an immoderating election.

The issue concerned the admittance of blacks into the construction unions in Pittsburgh. The Pittsburgh Black Coalition, angry that blacks held only a tiny fraction of the skilled construction jobs in the city, picketed several building sites in the Pittsburgh area—most notably the sites of the Three Rivers Stadium and the United States Steel building in the downtown area. Acrimony and some violence flared on the picket line as white unionists and some white police showed intense distaste for the black picketers. Mayor Barr, attempting to maintain civil peace, temporarily closed down all construction jobs in the city. White unionists lost several days' work. Whites then counterdemonstrated, marching on City Hall with signs reading WE'RE THE MAJORITY, LABOR AND WHITE POLICE UNITY, and WE BUILD UP THE CITY, NOT BURN IT DOWN.

Quickly, an election that seemed to be a nonracist, noncrime

---

* This is not wholly accurate. McCarthy's vocal and visible supporters were the young doves. But a large part of his invisible support came precisely from hard-nosed blue-collar voters who wanted to rock the boat. As the University of Michigan survey revealed, many McCarthy supporters switched to George Wallace in the November, 1968, elections. (See Chapter 7.)

election showed the potential of escalating into the referendum type of election witnessed in New York, Minneapolis, and Los Angeles. Tabor, the Republican underdog, immediately announced that he was opposed to the black demands. He sent out a mailing stating his position to union groups; he began escalating the crime-on-the-streets issue, although in a relatively responsible manner.

Flaherty had a problem. His white liberal, New Politics supporters wanted him to show sympathy with the black demands. Naturally, Flaherty's black supporters also wanted a show of allegiance.

But what about the ex-George Wallace supporter who had been for Flaherty in order to "rock the boat"? What about all those hard-nosed wards? What about the fact that blacks constituted less than 25% of the population and an even lesser fraction of the voters. What about the fact that Pittsburgh is probably one of the strongest union towns in America?

Even if he wanted to, Pete Flaherty could not delude himself that a candidate representing a coalition of blacks and white liberals could ever triumph in Pittsburgh if that candidate were perceived as against the white working class. Furthermore, there is equity on both sides of the issue. Blacks clearly do not have a decent share of skilled union slots. But unionists have a right to demand that any new members of their union go through what they themselves went through, a full apprenticeship program.

The blacks say, truthfully, that they've had the short end of the stick for 300 years in America; the unionists respond with a variant of John Marchi's statement: "I don't feel guilty for three hundred years of injustice to blacks in America—forty years ago my family was eating spaghetti in Italy."

Psephologically, Flaherty had three choices, and they were crystal clear.

Choice One: Go left, fully endorse the black position—and very likely lose an election that would immediately turn into a race referendum. Pure as the driven snow, he could return to his law practice and remember his purity while his Republican opponent governed Pittsburgh.

Choice Two: Go right, fully endorse the union, completely antagonize his liberal and black supporters, violate fully what were probably his own principles, possibly hurt his ultimate vote because of his transparent insincerity, and, perhaps worse, remain with that awful taste in his soul for years to come.

Choice Three: Finesse it. Keep quiet. Take the heat from his liberals and his blacks. Run his campaign on his youth, his ability, his intelligence, his antiestablishmentarianism—and hope that when he becomes mayor, he can help the blacks *and* the unionists settle their difference.

Flaherty, the New Politics advocate, opted for Choice Three, otherwise known as Old Liberalism, Old Politics, or Moving Toward the Center. He clammed up on the black versus union issue and was only a moving target for Tabor's modified law-and-order campaign. His liberals and his blacks temporarily thought him somewhat of a fink—but where did they have to go? They ultimately voted for him. He was elected by a large margin and managed to marry Old Liberalism with New Politics. He had found the center. In the process, he kept a moderating election from becoming a polarizing election and may have set himself up as a Young Man to Watch.

Seattle. Detroit. Pittsburgh. In different ways, these cities avoided the rancor and the risk of elections that could become referenda on crime/race. By finessing the issue, by co-opting it, by defusing it, by preempting it, each city ended up with a mayoralty campaign that centered on proposals for building a better city for whites and for blacks, with ideas for coping with the urban problems rather than exacerbating them. These results were ensured long before election day.

It was so as well in Louisville. There an incumbent Republican administration was overturned by a Democratic challenge team at the city and county level. But it was *not* a fire-eating, hammer-and-tongs, law-and-order election because no one was soft on crime. Moreover, wingers had never had much success in Louisville, and they did not do so in 1969. Though there was an American Party candidate for mayor, he finished a very poor third, with but 2% of the vote. As the Washington *Post's*

William Greider put it, Louisville ". . . turned away from extremes and toward a graceful middle course."

It may have been luck, happenstance, planned political strategy, or personal courage, but there was a common factor in each
election. In each instance, no candidate was perceived as soft on
crime or, our way, soft on the Social Issue. With no softness
perceived, softness was not an issue, and the Social Issue was not
elevated to referendum status. The city was likely to be the
better for it.

Moderate men were not forced—or even allowed in some
instances—to vote on immoderate issues. There is a lesson there.

18

Complications:

Denver, Atlanta

The Social Issue, unfortunately, does not always frame itself in a "law and order" or a "disruption" context. Those sorts of issues, as we saw in the moderating elections, can be frequently co-opted by hard-nosed liberalism.

But the issue in Denver in the spring of 1969 was not as simple as crime or disruption. It was busing. And it may well be on just such complicated issues that the politics of the center will face its most difficult dilemmas in the decade of the 1970's.

The busing issue is complex, and there is certainly equity on both sides.

The classic strong busing position has stressed the fact that there can be no real racial integration in schools while neighborhoods remained segregated—unless black children are transported to schools in white neighborhoods. Furthermore, as the position goes, some white children should be transported into the schools in black neighborhoods—both to fill all those empty desks in the black schools and to "enrich" white children with a "real learning experience" by seeing life as it is outside of their treelined, private-house, residential neighborhoods.

The antibusing position comes in two varieties. The first is a straight racist view: "No nigger's going to go to school with my kids." The other variety makes a sound point: Why send white children from middle-class environments into black slum neighborhoods? This question is followed by horror stories. Tales of children whose lunch money was systematically extorted by ghetto toughs, tales of dope peddling in the slums. The antibusers ask: Is the cause of better education served by sending white children into poor black neighborhoods? And they answer, no, their children will get a worse education.

Furthermore, they usually oppose the idea of busing large numbers of black children into white neighborhoods. Black children from deprived homes, they say, are educationally far behind white children from middle-class areas. Bringing slum black children into white middle-class schools can only slow down the educational process for white children and, moreover, make black children feel inferior. The responsible antibusers say that cities ought to try to make *all* schools better, slum schools and middle-class schools. This would improve educational quality and would prevent innocent children from being used as pawns in the turbulent racial situation.*

In Denver, in the spring of 1969, there was a direct confrontation between the busers and the antibusers. It took the form of a school board election held after the board had already enacted a strong busing policy. School board candidates A. Edgar Benton and Monte Pascoe waged their campaign favoring the busing policy. School board candidates Frank K. Southworth and James C. Perrill waged their campaign against the busing policy.

Rarely, in America, does an election of *men* so clearly reflect opinions on an *issue*. The Denver school board election was understood by all to be a referendum on the issue of crisscross school busing.

How deeply the community felt about the issue can be gauged by the number of voters who turned out for what is normally an innocuous school board election, with not even a mayoralty race to draw voters to the polls.

---

* In the spring of 1970 Gallup found that 81% of the parents in the United States ". . . oppose the busing of Negro and white school children from one school district to another."

The last time the Denver voters had an election with only school board candidates on the ballot, 51,000 voters came to the polls. In 1969, with roughly the same electorate, 110,000 turned out! And this is how they voted:

Southworth (antibusing)	75,596
Perill (antibusing)	73,932
Benton (probusing)	31,098
Pascoe (probusing)	28,948

Blacks in Denver voted heavily probusing, but they are a minority of the Denver population, and the busing proposal lost by about 2½ to 1. Not even close.

Thus spake the majority. The ads of Perrill and Southworth had been blunt: "James Perrill and Frank Southworth are dedicated to retaining and improving the neighborhood school concept. They are opposed to driving school children all over Denver. . . . The opposition candidates are pledged to force two-way busing of your children. Vote to keep them out."

Here was an aspect of the Social Issue brought to a clearly defined referendum. As has usually been the case during the last decade, when the Social Issue is brought to referendum level, the antis won. This has been apparent in the busing referenda, in referenda concerning civilian review boards to monitor police, and, in most instances, in open-housing referenda around the nation over the past half decade.

REFLECTIVE: DENVER AND BEYOND

When these sorts of election results were coupled with the results of the Nixon-Wallace showing and with what has come to be called the conservative revival, liberals became quite despondent as the 1960's ended and the 1970's began. Their despondency was reinforced by polling results such as the Gallup survey cited on page 72 and an even more clear-cut set of results emanating from a survey taken by the Field Poll in California in August, 1969:

ALL VOTERS—CALIFORNIA STATEWIDE

	Jan. 1964	*Aug. 1969*
Described themselves as:		
Conservative	32%	42%
Middle-of-road	30%	27%
Liberal	28%	24%
Don't know	10%	7%

The data would clearly seem to show that Californians are indeed becoming more conservative. And California, as discussed earlier, is an excellent political barometer.

Yet, not for a change, we are faced with somewhat of a paradox in this situation. The paradox seems to stem from the changing content of what it is that Americans now consider conservative and what they now consider liberal. As pointed out earlier, the center moves.

For example, one can assume that most of the 32% of the Californians who classified themselves as conservatives in *1964* were against that scheme of "socialized medicine" that went under the name of Medicare. That scheme passed the Congress in *1965* over much Republican opposition. By *1966* not a Republican candidate in the nation was saying that he would *repeal* Medicare. Today about 20,000,000 elderly Americans are covered by Medicare, and today it is doubtful that very many of the now 42% of Californians who consider themselves conservative would be *against* Medicare.

Much the same can be said about the once-flaming issue of federal aid to education. Today, only a few years after the passage of major federal legislation, no politician now campaigns against federal aid to education. There is, to be sure, opposition to the manner and the restrictions with which such federal aid is dispensed. Southerners, in particular, don't like guidelines that tie federal money to desegregation. But George Wallace only campaigned against the *guidelines* for dispensing money; *he did not campaign against the programs or the money.*

The instance of civil rights is another case in point. Even with all the current black-white discord, there is clear evidence of some sharp changes in attitude—toward the liberal side, and even in conservative bastions. The University of Michigan Survey Research Center polled white Southerners in 1964 and 1968 and found a drop of 20% in those favoring segregation.

These liberalizing attitudes on Medicare, on education, on race, are fully consistent with other changing liberalizing attitudes now held by most Americans. Gallup data show that two-thirds of all Americans approved of President Nixon's welfare plan which would triple the number of welfare recipients and make it a largely *federal* program.

Harris Poll data of 1969 show that Americans believe that the federal government ought to spend the necessary money to "clean up the slums":

VIEWS ON CITIES
Commitments of Federal Funds for Cities

	Agree Percent	Disagree Percent	Not Sure Percent
Slums in cities should be wiped out so people there can live decently	83%	11%	6%
America cannot survive unless the problems of the cities are worked out	73%	18%	9%
If we neglect the cities, we will have a racial explosion on our hands	68%	19%	13%

This is conservatism?

It is not, but yet we have the data shown earlier that Americans are substantially more likely to *consider* themselves conservative and that the referendum-type elections we have been discussing usually turn up antibusing, anti-civilian review boards, anti-open housing.

How is all this reconcilable? Is it, indeed, reconcilable?

We believe that it is and that its reconciliation points the way for liberally minded Americans to make some headway in the years ahead.

First: The labels change. What is conservative today may

have been liberal ten years ago. Moreover, labels may tarnish at the same time that much of the substance that the labels originally represented becomes accepted. A voter can say today that he is conservative and yet not be against Medicare, federal aid to slums, education, and welfare. He may be "conservative" only because he thinks "liberals" have been the ones who have let the students get out of hand at Berkeley or let rioters burn down Watts.

Second: Much of the liberalization of attitudes that has occurred has come about in fields that are perceived as not directly relevant to the Social Issue: medical care, Social Security, better schools, aid to cities. But, on crime, on drugs, on promiscuity, on student disruption, the mood has been for law and order and no nonsense, not for increased "liberalization." The race question and the school integration question fall in between, and the attitudinal picture is muddied, as has been noted.

Third: The center moves. We have discussed in this book, again and again, the notion of the psephological center. What must be understood again is that the "center" is not a stationary place. It moves as the opinions of the electorate move. Furthermore, the center can often be moved by persuasion by political leaders and by public education, sometimes quickly, sometimes not so quickly. And finally, not only can politicians educate the public, but the public can educate political leaders as well. Thus, while liberal Democrats were successfully selling their programs for Medicare, education and civil rights, they were also hearing about crime, disruption, and riot from the public. For a while some politicians pooh-poohed it all as "a code word for racism," but it was not, and ultimately the politicians came around, learning from the public in one area while leading in another.

All this represents the beginnings of a strategy for liberals in the seventies. Beware of the "liberal" label, but do not be despondent about the liberal program. The center may be moving your way after all, or it can be persuaded to move your way. Beware of the Social Issue. It cuts deep and must be approached on little cat feet. There is learning as well as leading to do. There can be no pandering to disruption or crime; the public is not buying the notion that there are no bad boys, only bad environments, but they may well accept the idea that there are bad boys *and* there are bad environments—and each must be dealt with.

What, then, about Denver and the schools; what about the educational gray area between the Social Issue and the Economic Issue? Even there, hope can be seen on the horizon for liberals, for there, too, the center has been moving.

In viewing the Denver situation, perhaps the first thought that should be brought up is that it never could have happened fifteen years ago, or ten years ago, and probably not even five years ago.

Roughly fifteen years ago, 1954, the Supreme Court handed down the *Brown v. Board of Education* decision that declared that "separate but equal" school facilities were unconstitutional. The "Board of Education" in the suit was not in Birmingham or Biloxi. It was not even in Louisville or Nashville. *Linda Brown attended a legally segregated school in Wichita, Kansas, a non-Southern state.*

Roughly ten years ago—call it the early 1960's—the big education battles concerned getting *one* Negro into the University of Mississippi.

Not until the mid-1960's did the phrase "de facto segregation" come into common currency, and not until then were real efforts made to integrate school systems north of the Mason-Dixon Line.

Denver today has a fine public school system where some major steps toward integration have already been taken—and where one further new step was contemplated, passed by the school board, and then rejected by the voters.

That Denver's educational policy today is not what it was fifteen years ago or ten years ago or even five years ago is very important, and it ought to be very much on the minds of both old and new liberals as they ponder their strategy for the future.

What was actually voted on in Denver? It was a proposition

that white parents viewed as directly threatening to the physical and educational well-being of their children: busing them into slum neighborhoods and into schools that they perceived to be inferior. Part of their feeling, to be sure, was that the slums involved were *black* slums and the schools were pupiled by *black* students. But poll data might suggest that the feeling against "crossbusing" is more than just racism. Here are Gallup data taken in July, 1969:

Question: "Would you, yourself, have any objection to sending your children to a school where *a few* of the children are Negroes?"

Yes	No	No Opinion
11%	89%	—

Question: "Would you, yourself, have any objection to sending your children to a school where *half* of the children are Negroes?"

32%	64%	4%

Question: "Would you, yourself, have any objection to sending your children to a school where *more than half* of the children are Negroes?"

55%	36%	9%

To be sure, those opinions would be in different proportions if all the respondents actually had to make a choice of physically sending a child from an all-white school to a half-black school. It is obviously much pleasanter to tell the nice Gallup lady that there is no bigotry in this household than it is to act on principles which may be only loosely held. *Still, by 8 to 1, Americans say they reject total segregation; by 2 to 1, they say they would send children to a school where half of the students are black.* A third of Americans say they would not object to sending their children to schools which have a black majority.

So, as the social scientists say, those are the parameters of the situation. On the one hand, we have seen that the white majority—as in Denver—will not stand for sending their children into black slum schools and probably not into white slum schools either. On the other hand, white Americans at least *say* they are not against having their children in school with blacks, even when there are relatively sizable proportions of black students in the classroom.

Within that attitudinal framework, there are a number of solutions, or partial solutions, to the problem of integrated schools: voluntary one-way busing; mandatory one-way busing; one-way busing to only certain schools; redrawing of school district lines (in smaller cities). All these plans or other variants can bring about the beginnings of a school system that is fairer to minority groups than the ones now existing in many areas of the nation. Indeed, some of these policies were already in effect in Denver prior to the "mandatory cross-busing" election. Those policies were not opposed by the new (antibusing) school board members, and they indicated that they did not expect to roll back the clock.*

And ultimately? Who knows? Perhaps the white citizens of Denver—after considerable liberal tutelage—will one day accept a plan of mandatory crossbusing as the best kind of public education for all Denver. Such stark attitudinal change has happened before. But perhaps liberals—after considerable study of the election returns from 1969 and perhaps of future school board elections—will recognize that the stand against mandatory crossbusing is a nonnegotiable middle-class demand, and maybe even a wise one, in which case they might look for other ways to skin the cat.

To begin, it should be noted that integrated schooling and the so-called neighborhood school are not mutually exclusive ideas. As a matter of fact, they come together rather neatly under the concept of the "integrated neighborhood"—an older idea, currently in disfavor among some militant blacks, but an idea that is increasingly acceptable to whites in America and that has always been desired by the vast majority of blacks in America. If a black man can afford a decent house in a decent neighborhood, most Americans today would agree that he should be able to buy it and send his children to the local

---

* What they did do, when elected, was to rescind the cross-busing policy. This action was challenged in the courts by busers, and after a series of court actions, the busers won. The crisscross plan was reinstated, although further legal action was under way as this book went to press. For the record, the citizens of Denver were not happy at the court's overruling what they had voted by 2 to 1. It can be expected that the matter will be alive and bubbling in Denver —and other cities—for years to come.

school. It is a compromise, of course: Neither white nor black suburban children will get "enriched" in the slums, but that may not be such a steep price to pay. It is also a compromise that may become more commonplace as black incomes continue to rise and larger numbers of black middle-class families will be found in suburban areas.

From another flank comes another thought: the "autonomous" local school board within a big-city system. Some experimentation along these lines has been attempted with mixed results. Some organizations, like CORE (the Congress of Racial Equality), have urged what are essentially separate school boards, white and black, arguing that only with such an arrangement can black youngsters really get a quality education apart from the "plantationism" of alleged "good" white education rubbing off on alleged "bad" black education.

Another proposal, predating the CORE suggestion: Gild the ghetto. Keep the neighborhood school concept, admitting this means *de facto* segregation in some cases, but make the schools in black neighborhoods as good as or better than white schools.

And so on. The point here, obviously, is not to make substantive educational recommendations, but only to notice that there are many alternate solutions or semisolutions to the question of school integration. The cliché that has described politics, at least since the time of Bismarck, is "the art of the possible." The attitudinal data of recent years would suggest that there is a wide area of compromise now available, that attitudinal trends in some aspects may perhaps be widening the area of compromise in the middle, while at the same time there is a hardening of viewpoints out at the extremes. There is, at least, operating room for men of good faith who want to explore the center ground of a semi-Social Issue like school integration. Liberals, willing only to accept a label change to "moderate," still have fertile fields to hoe.

For a city where just such a "moderate" stance has represented a relatively liberal program over the years, we can turn now to Atlanta and note briefly some recent history and the results of the 1969 election.

The big law-and-order battle in Atlanta was waged more than a decade ago in 1957, when the political coalition put together by longtime Mayor William Hartsfield was challenged by a young restaurateur named Lester Maddox.

Hartsfield's coalition had been formed by uniting a growing black population with the few liberal whites and a greater number of whites who were conservatively oriented but interested most in a good municipal climate in which to go about their business. A psychic "deal" was struck. If the blacks cooled it, in terms of violence and commotion, the municipal government would pursue a relatively liberal course that would help blacks on the bread-and-butter issues like decent low-cost public housing.* The Hartsfield coalition bypassed the low-income white backlash vote.

The deal worked. When Maddox challenged Hartsfield's mayoralty coalition, Hartsfield referred to Maddox as the "fried chicken man," to his supporters as the "Outhouse Gang"—and beat the pants off of Maddox in the 1957 vote for mayor 63% to 37%. Hartsfield carried the city's black precincts by such votes as 1,843 to 46, but he won the white majority as well.

Because the Atlanta deal was shown to be impervious to challenge by the Yahoos, Atlanta was the first major Southern city to desegregate its public schools, and Atlanta's no-nonsense police chief, Herbert Jenkins, saw to it that no red-neck demonstrations would stain Atlanta on Integration Day. When the time came to desegregate eating places and Lester Maddox stood in the door of his restaurant with an ax handle, the Atlanta police arrested Maddox.

Mayor Hartsfield retired in 1961 and was replaced by another moderate, Ivan Allen, who beat the "fried chicken man" with 64% in a 1961 nonpartisan runoff election. Under Allen, as under Hartsfield, Atlanta moved ahead about as quickly as could be expected, given the demographic, economic, political, and regional situation of the city.

The deal was strong enough so that it could handle not only substance, but symbols as well, which in an emotionally charged

* While Hartsfield was mayor, Atlanta was honored by *Fortune* magazine as "one of the best managed cities in the United States."

climate is sometimes even more difficult. In 1964 the Nobel Prize for Peace was awarded to Martin Luther King, Jr. Now the Reverend Dr. King was an Atlanta native,* but to say the least, his cause was not very popular among most Southern whites. And Atlanta, for all its cosmopolitanism, is still a Southern white city. But the black leadership in Atlanta organized a testimonial dinner for King and asked Mayor Allen to see to it that the white leadership, as well as the black, turned out to honor King. Pressure was exerted on Allen, and Allen cajoled and pleaded and twisted arms—and the affair was indeed biracial, with the White Establishment present in full regalia.

The deal, in fact, was shown to have a life of its own, stronger than even its proponents believed. In 1963, President Kennedy needed some Southern support for the proposed public accommodations section of his civil rights bill. He asked Mayor Allen to come to Washington and testify for the law. Here is Allen's account of what transpired, as it appeared some years later in the New York *Times:*

"President Kennedy sent Morris B. Abram, who was formerly from Atlanta and then a prominent New York attorney, to see me.

"Mr. Abram requested that I testify on behalf of public accommodations, saying that they had to have some public official from the South. Well, of course, the advice of the white community in Atlanta was almost unanimous for me not to do it.

"And I was torn in great indecision, and I told Morris Abram that I hoped he realized that if I did it, why I didn't have a chance of being re-elected. And he agreed with me and said he would take it back to the President.

"The President called me and said that he didn't think it would cause my defeat, that he thought things would change, but regardless of that, he needed testimony.

"I told him I would try to do it. But when I presented my testimony to 25 Negro leaders in Atlanta, 21 of them advised

---

* His father, Martin Luther King, Sr., is the respected spiritual leader of the Ebenezer Baptist Church. He is a leader of Atlanta's comparatively well-to-do black community and very much a part of the political coalition described above.

me not to do it because they said I couldn't be re-elected and it wouldn't pass the bill either."

At this point, Mr. Allen took his indecision to his wife, who had no indecision at all.

"Mrs. Allen," the Mayor continued, "said that I had committed myself to doing what I thought was right and I felt this was right, and go ahead and do what you thought was right and let the chips fall where they may, and I'd at least be happy and could live with myself the rest of my life."

The testimony that was a triumph in Washington was something else in Georgia, he noted.

"Well, I came back to a holocaust in Atlanta," Mr. Allen said. "I have never seen such violent opposition. The white community rose up in righteous indignation. Of course the Negro community was tremendously pleased.

"And then it began to change—one of the most precipitous changes I have ever seen in political life. The New York Times wrote a magnificent editorial. It started out by saying that the oratorical fog on Capitol Hill is occasionally penetrated by a clear voice. This was the first break I got.

"The local papers were impressed by the national response to my testimony, and they printed The New York Times's editorial and my testimony, which was a full page.

"Within six months the business community said that I did the right thing, and that this was the only solution for it, and when I had to run again, I was on the right side."

And indeed, when Ivan Allen ran for reelection in 1965, it looked for a while as if he wouldn't have any opposition at all. Finally, he was challenged in the primary by a man named Smith. When the returns were counted, Ivan Allen had 70% of the votes, which is pretty good in a business where 60% qualifies as a landslide. And Mr. Smith did not bother to bring up the race issue.

What happened in the 1969 election, when Ivan Allen retired, showed that the deal had become a way of life in Atlanta. The election also prefigured that the deal would be tested deeply again in the future.

First, the results of the vote in the nonpartisan October

primary for *vice-mayor* between Maynard Jackson, a very young thirty-one-year-old black lawyer, and Milton G. Farris, a middle-aged white alderman:

>   Jackson (black) 48,785
>   Farris (white) 33,715

in a city where only 40% of the voters are black—but up from 23% black in 1957.

Mr. Jackson, in a victory statement, gave thanks to blacks and whites in Atlanta and noted that his victory was in keeping with "the dream for which Martin Luther King, Jr., gave his life."

The mayoralty race was more complicated, involving the primary in October and then a runoff election in November. Four men competed in the primary. Sam Massell, described as a "liberal Democrat," had been vice-mayor for eight years. Rodney Cook is a Republican who described himself as a "moderate." Horace Tate, a respected educator, was the first black man to make a serious run for mayor of Atlanta. G. Everett Millican, seventy-two, has been a fixture in Atlanta municipal politics for decades and ran as a "law-and-order" candidate, but showed some moderation in his stand. The turnout at the polls was relatively light, with these results:

>   Massell (liberal Democrat, white)   29,971
>   Cook (moderate Republican, white)   25,830
>   Tate (liberal Democrat, black)   22,193
>   Millican ("law-and-order," white)   17,481

forcing a runoff between Massell and Cook.

An examination of the primary voting results shows some remarkable things. In the year of law and order, Mr. Millican was only able to get 18% of the vote—about half of what the fried chicken man got in 1957 and 1961. The black mayoral candidate (Tate) did not get all the black vote even though he was endorsed by Mrs. Martin Luther King and the Reverend Ralph Abernathy. Other black leaders endorsed either Massell or Cook, and the black vote split three ways, with Democrat Massell getting a larger share than Republican Cook, and in some black precincts even larger than Tate, the black candidate. Finally, in the vice-mayoralty race, Jackson, a black man, got not only all the black vote, but a substantial fraction of the white vote. In one all-white district, Jackson polled 40% of the all-white vote, an outstanding performance for a black running for citywide office in any American city in 1969, but incredibly high in a Southern city.

Now, why did law and order lose in Atlanta? Because Atlanta, in some ways like Seattle, Detroit, and Pittsburgh, had co-opted the Social Issue. *All* the candidates were for law and order, and the voter's perception of the Establishment as represented in the past by Hartsfield and Allen was also one of law and order— with justice, as they say.

Having established their centrist positions, the candidates were able to compete on that good old American issue: personalities. Two days before election, Massell was accused of countenancing the fact that his brother sought campaign contributions from nightclub owners in the company of a police officer. Massell, a Jew, charged anti-Semitism and said that Cook got his money from the big bankers. When the torn fur had settled, Massell won by a majority of 11,000, with 55% of the vote.

So far so good. But while both candidates were centrists, there is evidence to suggest that perhaps the deal was not totally the victor and that perhaps the politics of centrism can give way to the politics of polarization in the seventies. For the first time in recent mayoralty elections the white majority in Atlanta voted for the loser, for Republican Rodney Cook. Where previously the winners' vote had run well over 60% because the majority of whites joined blacks to vote for Hartsfield and Allen, this time white precincts such as those in wealthy Ward 8 in north Atlanta went along with the blue-collar areas and voted for Cook, reducing winner Massell's margin to 55%, in a city whose voters are now 40% black. The black precincts in Atlanta voted overwhelmingly for Massell. The old coalition of blacks and whites was partially cracked, as fried-chicken-man whites and moderate whites found themselves backing the same candidate.

What may happen to the deal, to political centrism in Atlanta, no one can say. It has worked for a political generation, though less effectively in 1969 than in earlier years. By co-opting the Social Issue via an "arrangement," Atlantans have built themselves an enviable position in the South by centrism rather than the volatile extremism represented by George Wallace, or the fried chicken man, or black militants, or student radicals.

But the black share of Atlanta's population has risen and is now rising, as the white exodus to the suburbs increases. The question for the future is: Will centrism and moderation on the Social Issue survive when a black man runs for mayor or if a candidate like Massell is pushed into a corner to run as a quasi-black candidate? Will the deal, in effect, split into right dealers and left dealers or black dealers and white dealers, which could unravel the whole thing?

There are thorny issues in Atlanta that will test this. Right now there are proposals to merge Atlanta with its surrounding Fulton County suburbs, thereby reducing the black component of the new jurisdiction. There are other problems looming in the area of school desegregation which might lead to trouble. Whether the generation of political moderation has immunized the community from extremism and disruption remains to be seen.

To show that just about every combination and permutation are possible in elections, we can take a very brief look at the 1969 election in Buffalo. There a tough law-and-order mayoralty candidate *did* make it through the primaries—and lost. Mrs. Alfreda Slominski was the Republican anti-crime-in-the-streets candidate against incumbent Democratic Mayor Frank Sedita and an independent black candidate, Ambrose Lane. In the often ethnic politics of Buffalo, the Polish Mrs. Slominski and black Ambrose Lane had obvious appeals, but neither had the basic appeal to the center which Mayor Sedita could—and did—make. As long as the mayor could not be faulted on the fundamentals of law and order, as long as he was not perceived as being soft on crime, he could campaign as a moderate. Indeed the very presence on the ballot of a candidate "to the right" and one "to the left" probably helped the mayor's centrist image. In November Sedita won, and won handily, with a plurality of 20,000 over Mrs. Slominski, 54% to her 42%, with 5% for Lane.

Though we have been discussing mayors, one might add a word about the two 1969 gubernatorial elections. Both New Jersey and Virginia chose their state leadership at the same time many of the mayors described in this and earlier chapters were being elected. But there is an interesting problem about these two elections for governor. The four candidates (Cahill and Meyner in New Jersey; Holton and Battle in Virginia) were all so close to the political center as to make useful political analysis almost impossible. That the Republicans won both elections seems of little significance.*

All the candidates were for moving their state forward; all were for the better life for their citizens; all urged vigorous programs against crime, pollution, and the bad things. All seemed to campaign with that new political trademark, the suit jacket slung casually over the shoulder, revealing the candidate as an informal, athletic, regular fellow. In each of these gubernatorial elections one came away with the impression of an elephant and a donkey struggling to place all eight legs on a single thin dime placed exactly on the 50-yard line, equidistant from each sideline. Which is not such a bad definition of American politics.

---

* Equally insignificant is the fact that Democrats won five out of seven widely scattered Congressional special elections in 1969. Major evidence of these elections was that a popular member can build incumbency to a value of 10 or 15 percentage points over his party's normal strength. When he isn't the candidate, the regular party vote prevails.

19

Hear What They Say

There is a story about a little seven-year-old boy who had never in his life said a single word. His parents, naturally distressed, had taken the child to a series of doctors, all of whom found no physiological cause for the child's muteness. One day at the breakfast table, after seven years of total silence, the boy suddenly said, "Mom, these damn pancakes are cold."

Flabbergasted and delighted, the mother finally said, "Son, son, why haven't you spoken in all these years?"

And the boy answered, "I didn't have anything to say."

We believe that in the 1969 municipal elections, unlike some years, the American voters *had* something to say that transcended local issues. We believe they said it clearly. We believe that what they said was largely in concert with what was said in 1968. We believe that in electing their chief city executives, the voters set up a partial model that is useful to look at in considering how the electorate can be expected to respond when electing their chief national executives in the decade to come. Beyond that, we believe that what the voters said will have relevance to the state, local, and Congressional elections that will be held in the seventies.

What, then, are the message and the mood that Americans

were trying to get through to their politicians on the eve of the 1970's? If one could amass all the votes and all the attitudes behind all the votes in all the diverse elections of 1969, what would they show? The authors believe the voter was saying:

"I am a moderate man, but I must tell you that I have been unnerved in recent years. I am upset by crime; I am distressed about drugs; I am against disruptions and riots; I disapprove of the change in morality; I am against forced busing of my children into slum neighborhoods; I am concerned, with mixed feelings, about the racial situation.

"I do not expect that a politician, any politician, can make these conditions disappear overnight. I even understand that some of the problems aren't strictly political problems. But I do expect that any politician I vote for will *be on my side.*

"If I am offered a choice where both men seek harmony and order in the center, I'd choose by party or by personality or by program, and maybe even a pretty liberal or progressive program at that. But if I am offered a choice where one of the candidates seems to be soft on these issues that concern me, I'll vote for the other man.

"If civil liberties for criminals becomes civil license for criminals and becomes more important than my civil liberty to walk the streets of my neighborhood, then I'll vote against the man I perceive as providing license for criminality. I've got nothing against integration, but I do if it means sending my children to school in a slum school—black slum school or white slum school —and I'll vote against a man who wants to do that. The drug situation scares me; so do violent demonstrations and disruptions. Obviously, I'll vote against a man who *favors* drugs and disruptions, but I'll also vote against a man who isn't clearly *against* drugs and disruption.

"Beyond that, I'm flexible. I don't want a decayed city or traffic jams or bad schools, polluted rivers or racial conflict or crowded national parks any more than you do. Who do you think goes out in those campers to those national parks?

"I'm a liberal or a progressive in the sense that FDR and JFK and maybe even LBJ were liberal. I'm for unions and for Social

Security, Medicare, and aid to education. But if liberal now means coddling crime, student anarchy, and pot, then I'm conservative after all."

Now, as political theoreticians, how do we deal with that attitude in the future?

PART FIVE

The Fourth Idea

20

Looking Ahead:

To Move the Moving Center

Three ideas of contemporary psephology have been enunciated and elaborated on. The first concerns the new potency of the Social Issue when and if it is brought to a referendum level. The second concerns the middle-class, middle-aged, middle-minded, unyoung, unpoor, unblack nature of the electorate. The third concerns the one essential political strategy: the drive toward the center.

The implementation of these three ideas, we believe, will be critical factors in the Presidential elections of the 1970's. The implementation of these ideas will also be critical in many other elections in the 1970's. A good deal of what we describe Presidentially is also operative on other levels. Accordingly, the astute psephologist in the 1970's will not only note how many Congressional seats the Democrats or Republicans gained or lost, but also carefully try to determine *how the winners won.* Did they come on tough, or did they play Pity the Panther? Did they stress their support by activist college students or their support by labor unions? Were the conservatives running as *social* conservatives or as *economic* conservatives? How many Republican candidates ran on platforms opposing the nasty social engineering programs instituted by Democrats—such as

Medicare? These criteria may well be the way-station pointers that will indicate to the psephologist how lays the electoral land of the 1970's.

As we look ahead to the politics and psephology of the 1970's, a fourth idea is now ready for discussion. It is this: Those who would violate the first three precepts are known by a simple word—losers. That, for the moment at least, is not a moral or ideological judgment, only a psephological one.

What makes this simplistic fourth notion relevant today is that *there are forces in each of the major parties that are counseling sharp deviation from some or all of the first three concepts.*

In the Republican Party, voices are heard that success lies in moving to the right, toward a Southern Strategy, toward capitalizing on antiblack feelings, toward capturing the Wallace vote to build "an emerging Republican majority." As Independent Democrats the authors might welcome just such a course by President Nixon: Leave the center; move rightward; turn over the center to the Democrats. As citizens, however, we would recoil from such actions, and as psephologists we must point out that such a strategy would probably be disastrous for Republicans. Most Republicans old enough to remember 1964 are aware of the disaster inherent in such a course. There is a possibility, but a slim one, that the Republicans will trod that path again in the near future.

In the Democratic Party, similar voices are heard, but with designs toward a leftward movement. Under the banner of New Politics there is talk of forming a new coalition of the left, composed of the young, the black, the poor, the well educated, the socially alienated, minority groups, and intellectuals—while relegating Middle America and especially white union labor to the ranks of "racists." This position manages to violate *all* the axioms described in this book. Accordingly, if the search of the right-leaning Republicans can lead only to psephological fool's gold, then the march of the left-leaning Democrats must certainly yield up a prize of some new, even baser political nonmetal; perhaps we might call it jackass pyrite.

There would seem to be a greater likelihood of the Democrats doing themselves in than the Republicans. First, the Republican right is not nearly as powerful in its milieu as is the Lemming Left within the Democratic Party. There are several reasons for this. Democrats have not recently gone down the Goldwater path—the catastrophe of political extremism is a textbook lesson to Democrats, not a personal scar. Today, accordingly, the young ideologues of the Democratic left can spout rhetoric so astonishingly close to Goldwaterism—"we need a choice, not an echo," "hidden majorities"—and yet be regarded as idealistic, pleasant young men rather than as walking political catastrophes. Second, the Republicans have the built-in moderating force of an incumbent President in the White House who, of necessity, usually takes a centrist position. It is the out party that will normally tend toward a more extremist position, as did the out-party Republicans in 1964.

But an immediate caveat must be offered that would seem to the authors to set out the true shape of the competitive politics of the seventies: If the Democrats do not commit suicide by throwing themselves upon the knife-edge of the Social Issue, they can lead a long life struggling to capture the center. This nonsuicidal scenario can easily include a Democrat in the White House in the not-too-distant future.

Beyond the two major parties, what of the other two important political forces in America: the Wallaceites and the Radical Left? How do they fare in the political seventies in the electoral ambiance of the middle class, of centrism, of a socially concerned electorate?

As with the major parties, their power and influence depends on whether they can stay within hailing distance of the center or whether they march off the side of the cliff, in lock-step, Minutemen and Weathermen, hand in hand, smiling as they plummet, saying, "Only I am pure."

They face an additional problem—or maybe it is not such a problem. So responsive are the major parties that they unabashedly swipe the appealing parts from the winger positions, leaving the wingers partial ideological winners, but relatively impotent as major political forces. The case can be made, for example, that the two ideological winners of the 1968 election were Wallace and the Radical Left. Their respective issues (crime for Wallace; limited international disengagement for the New Left) have in part been adopted by President Nixon and the American public.

In all, then, with all the pushes, all the counterpushes, who will be doing what in the decade to come? We can look at them here one by one: Democrats, Republicans, Wallaceites, and the Radical Left.

Politics, like military tactics, is always subject to the "terrain and situation," and of course, there is much of the terrain and situations of the future that are largely unpredictable. Who could have foretold the political effects of events like wars in Vietnam or Korea, riots in the cities, the Depression, FDR's death, John Kennedy's assassination—all events that sharply altered subsequent electoral history?

Still, even after acknowledging the unpredictable, there are certain elements of the future that seem to be both clear and relevant to the future direction of American political life. Before attempting to assess the national future of the four political forces, it is important now to note briefly some few of the most important likely conditions.

One, of course, is the Social Issue. There is no evidence that it will go away. It is with us now, and if someone sees the decade ahead without voter perception of racial problems, crime as an issue, student disruption, pot, pornography, morals, school integration, and raucous dissent, let him speak up. To the authors it seems clear that the issue will remain. The only thing that is not at all clear about the Social Issue is who it cuts and why.

Another is the older, perennial Economic Issue, specifically, inflation, the high cost of living, recession, unemployment, jobs, housing, the tax bite, minimum wage—collectively usually gathered together under a more commonplace rubric: "pocketbook issues." Politically, the Economic Issue tends to be a "Ping-Pong" issue—that is, when conditions are bad it is the "fault" of the people in power (a "Ping"), and works for the people out of power (a "Pong"). When Republicans are in office, high taxes and inflation are their fault; when Democrats are in office, high taxes and inflation are *their* fault. There are some few constant ideological overtones: Republicans are for business, the Democrats are for the little people, or . . . Republicans can watch the pennies, while Democrats are big spenders. But largely it is a matter of Ping and Pong, in party and out party, and there can be little doubt that serious economic difficulties in the seventies would severely hurt any administration in power—that is, Republicans to 1972 and whoever thereafter. A real depression, even a major recession over a long time, could conceivably wipe out the Social Issue as a major issue. Understanding this, the assumption here is that President Nixon's economic policies will be generally sound, that the American economy will be in generally healthy shape over the course of the decade. If it is not, all bets are off.

A new horse in the field is the Ecological Issue. It is stirring great commotion as this is written, and no one yet knows how potent a political force it may be. Our guess is that it will be limited *as an issue* but important, of course, as public policy. As an issue ecology will likely rank with motherhood. No one will be unopposed to pollution; ergo there will be no issue to vote on.

Finally, the International Issue. Not usually a major political issue, this changes if American soldiers, particularly *drafted* soldiers, are dying somewhere. Perhaps the most accurate single statement that came from the Vietnam protesters was emblazoned on a placard held aloft at the Chicago convention. It read: NOT WITH MY LIFE, YOU DON'T. Barring this sort of Vietnam situation, international issues will not likely be the voting issues for most Americans in the seventies. Accordingly the parties have a good measure of policy leeway in this field.

Now, considering these basic issues, how stand the four political forces for the seventies?

THE DEMOCRATS

In the last Presidential election the Social Issue worked against the "liberal Democratic Establishment incumbents." The question before the house is whether it worked against the Democrats because they were liberal or because they were in power or, most likely, both. A secondary question is this: Is there a way that Democrats can remain "liberal" and yet not get the social albatross draped on their shoulders? After all, some of the tenets sometimes challenged by the Social Issue—like civil liberties—are bedrock tenets of American liberalism, and it is not much of a solution to tell liberal Democrats they can win elections if only they behave like conservative Republicans. How, then, do Democrats deal with the Social Issue?

To begin, it should be clear to any practicing political type that the keynote address at the 1972 Democratic Convention will include a passage to this effect: "Fellow Americans, in the past four years crime in America has gone up by __, while the population has increased by only __%."

Of course, this same paragraph was recited several hundred times by Candidate Nixon in 1968, who pointed the accusing finger at eight years of Democratic rule. In 1972, however, the accusing finger will be pointed toward four years of *Republican* rule.

Crucial Question: Will the Social Issue become a Ping-Pong issue?

To which there are two possible answers:

Answer: No, not if Richard Nixon can help it. He will point with pride at the steps his administration has taken to curb the crime that had become a major problem during Democratic misrule. He will have Spiro Agnew on the hustings attacking the effete corps of impudent snobs.

Answer: Yes, if the Democrats are astute and adroit. They will view with alarm the fact that crime continues to rise.

The difficulty for Mr. Nixon's answer is that crime will in all likelihood continue to be a problem as will all the other facets of the Social Issue. For how long can he blame Democrats and liberals? Probably not for too long, unless Democrats and liberals help him out.

But it is a thorny and complex matter for Democrats. For the Social Issue, as perceived by the voter, is deeply intertwined with the whole racial problem in America. And the national Democratic Party is perceived by the voter as being the champion of blacks over recent years. Furthermore, it is neither likely, nor proper, nor potentially profitable for Democrats to nominate a candidate who would be, or would be perceived as, antiblack. Morality aside, for the moment, any such candidacy would destroy itself on the rocks of credibility; the national party of Stevenson, Kennedy, Johnson and Humphrey will not be believed as a party advocating a go-slow-on-civil-rights policy; a party that attracted so much of the black vote in 1968 will not be perceived as the line on the ballot to voice antiblack sentiments, certainly not with a Republican and an American Independent also on the ballot to choose from.

What to do? The Social Issue, when unchecked, is psephologically potent. The problack stance of liberal Democrats can link them to the wrong side of the Social Issue.

Stating the problem points toward its solution. Liberal Democrats must attempt to split off the Race Issue from the Social Issue.

This split-off of race from crime may not be as difficult as it seems. To begin, it is inherently a phony linkup. The Social Issue would be present in America if every black American vanished tomorrow morning; not only would the Social Issue be present, but it would still be rubbing raw the psephological nerve endings all over the nation. Campus disruptions, drugs, pornography, Vietnam dissent, the generation gap certainly are not caused by blacks. There would still be a crime problem without blacks—white crime rates are increasing, too. There are poverty and urban decay in inner-city neighborhoods that are neither black nor threatened by blacks, and there are middle-class whites who are distinctly unhappy when poor whites begin to move into a neighborhood, "destroying property values." To some extent, then, blacks in America have become only a lightning rod that attracts white resentment over already existent problems.

If the Social Issue and the Race Issue are *not* the same, then Democrats, if prudent, should be able to remain a pro-civil-rights party without being an anti-law-and-order party or a pro-mugger party. The law-and-order issue can be finessed as it was in Detroit, Pittsburgh, and Seattle. Or it can be turned partially into a Ping-Pong issue working against the party in power: Republicans.

The rhetoric for such a position is not hard to imagine:

—Do *not* say, "Well, I don't agree with the Students for a Democratic Society when they invade a college president's office, but I can understand their deep sense of frustration."
—*Do* say, "When students break laws they will be treated as lawbreakers."

—Do *not* say, "Crime is a complicated sociological phenomenon and we'll never be able to solve the problem until we get at the root causes of poverty and racism."
—*Do* say, "I am going to make our neighborhoods safe again for decent citizens of every color. I am also in favor of job training, eradication of poverty, etc., etc."

. . . and so on. After each utterance, it is further suggested to add this rhetorical suffix: "and what have Richard Nixon and the Republicans done about it? Nothing!"

This, in the authors' opinion, is more than opportunistic political rhetoric. It is viable rhetoric because it is valid, and it should be a *Democratic* issue. If there is to be a political party in America deeply concerned about law and order, then by logic and history, it most certainly ought to be the Democratic Party.

—The law-and-order issue today is essentially a civil libertarian's issue and the question that must be asked is: What about the civil liberties of hardworking, crime-scared Americans today, black and white—many of whom happen to be *Democrats?*

—It is black *Democrats* who face the worst crime rates in America, and who have the most legitimate fears of mugging, rape, robbery, and drugs. It is white *Democrats* in inner-city neighborhoods—the so-called ethnics—who are also more than casually threatened by violent crime.

—It is *Democratic* intellectuals in all those colleges and universities whose way of life is disrupted, bulldozed, and brutalized by student anarchists.

That being "liberal" should equate with being soft on mugging or soft on disruption is absurd. In point of fact, being liberal *demands* a firm stand on freedom from fear in society. Democrats have made a major national issue of the "environment." Fine. Let them include in that position the key element of a decent urban environment: safety of the citizenry from the pollution of violence.

No doubt, there will be some of the Radical Left who will view this as merely a cover-up for a neofascist, cryptomonarchial, repressive, imperialistic, racist plot. No matter. The extremists are the best enemy a political party could hope to have.

In attempting to separate the crime problem from the black problem, Democrats could do worse than to refer to their firm law-and-order stance as the "tough NAACP law-and-order program" (see page 234). That stance, by the bye, should also get more black votes than any endorsement of Swahili as a language to be taught in public schools.

As we have noted here, "law and order"—which is a partial code phrase for the Social Issue—has become a nonnegotiable demand by voting Americans. If Democratic liberal politicians accept it as such, it can be an issue finessed, or an issue Ping-Ponged, or an issue endorsed, or a little bit of all three. After the lessons of Hubert Humphrey and Tom Bradley it seems unlikely that Democrats will once again limply hand over the psephological trump card to their opponents—unless they are bent on suicide, Republican-style, vintage 1964.

The key to turning the tables on the Social Issue is an elementary one: belief. Liberal Democrats have to *believe* that the Social Issue is important, is distressing to their constituents, and rightly so. Politicians are bad liars. They are convincing only when they are convinced. Rhetoric alone is never enough.

On balance, as we look ahead to the seventies, this much can be said: If the Democrats are not wise, the Social Issue can cut them even deeper than heretofore. In 1968, after all, Hubert Humphrey was not perceived as the candidate of the beard-and-sandal set. He was a centrist. He was hurt on the Social Issue, but not massively. It could get worse for Democrats, but there is at least a strong hope that the cutting edge of the Social Issue can be blunted.

It is the judgment of the authors that the manner in which the Democratic Party handles the Social Issue will largely determine how potent a political force the party will be in America in the years to come. Visualizing a party that is not in total ideological disarray over an issue that can and should be laid to rest, the remainder of the party's problems are either soluble or subject to a sort of political compromise that all sides can live with.

For in many respects, events would seem to be working in favor of a rejuvenated national Presidential Democratic Party. There is a strong likelihood to believe that the Vietnam War will not be a major issue by election time in 1972.

As Vietnam passes from a "not with my life" situation to a somewhat more academic problem, it should help Democrats as they attempt to re-form their political legions. Those who supported the war may not be viewed so clearly as "war criminals who committed genocide"; those who rejected the war may not be seen as "traitors in league with Hanoi"—each militant group as seen by the other. The gradual disappearance of this burr beneath the saddle can do nothing but help Democrats.

The demise of Vietnam as an issue should also help Democrats on the Social Issue. For plainly, the demise of Vietnam as an issue will also lead to the demise of Vietnam *dissent* as an issue—an end to draft-card burnings, American flag burnings, blood pouring on draft records, etc. As noted earlier, this home-front facet of the Vietnam War may well have been more harmful to Democrats than the actual substance of the war itself. Although President Johnson and later Vice President Humphrey were the *targets* of the demonstrators, they were also *in office* and therefore held vaguely accountable for the start of all and any disruption and disarray. Further, of course, the young demonstrators were largely perceived of as identified with the Democratic Party or, at least, Democratic leaners.

If national Democrats cease being losers on the Social Issue—and cease being double losers on both Vietnam Substantive and Vietnam Dissent—then perhaps things aren't quite as bad as prophets of new emerging Republican majorities may have us believe. We will return shortly to the problems and possibilities of Democrats in the seventies. But first we must see where and why the Republicans stand, in order to see the byplay.

THE REPUBLICANS

Politics seems often to be like a tennis game—the player doesn't so much win as watch as his opponent makes errors and throws the game away. The Republicans of the seventies may do well to wait for their Democratic opponents to hit the ball conclusively into the net of the Social Issue, handing over point, set, and match to the GOP. Republicans today chortle with glee watching Democrats debate intramurally whether Abbie Hoffman or Judge Hoffman is a bigger damn fool.*

But even beyond that defensive posture, the Republicans have some new power strokes for offense available as they survey the picture of the next decade.

Basically, their opportunity lies in the somewhat unglued nature of current Presidential politics. It has been a cliché of

* A Harris Poll in April, 1970, showed that by 71% to 19% the American people felt that the "Chicago 7" had received a fair trial.

our times to say that there is a Democratic majority among the voters, but it just isn't so, at least in Presidential voting. Many respondents to public opinion surveys will say they are Democrats, but in the six Presidential elections since World War II, the Democrats have won a clear majority only once—in 1964, just as Richard Nixon has failed twice to get half the voters to support him. It has been a tideless time. If anything, the Presidential campaign of 1968 further unglued the magnitude and the intensity of the old FDR Coalition, leaving Republicans running room to set themselves up as the Grand New Party, with a new coalition that conceivably could lock them into the potent political center for a long time to come.

The South is clearly the beginning of the New Republican Coalition. The Republicans did well in the Southland in 1968 and will score some points there in 1972 and 1976, with or without Wallace in the race.

But the South is not the fifty states. If our electorate is unpoor, unyoung, and unblack, it is also un-Southern. A solid Southern vote would do the Nixon Grand New Party of the center no good if other strengths couldn't be mobilized along with it. A purely Southern Strategy is a losing strategy. Quadcali counts. A national political party that does not have the allegiance of the machinist's wife in Dayton will have difficulty capturing the center.

In 1968 this center was shaken loose from its moorings, and most, but not all, voters returned to its Democratic home base. The Republican job in the seventies is to shake loose more of this vote and to see to it that it goes to the Republican side.

It is conceivable the Republicans may be hampered in this shake-and-hold operation by the situation that develops in Vietnam and Southeast Asia in the early years of the 1970's. President Nixon, once elected, made a firm commitment to wind down the war and has stated unequivocally that he expects to be held politically accountable for keeping that promise.

Most of the plausible scenarios, however, seem to indicate that, barring catastrophe, Vietnam will be neither a great plus nor a great minus for President Nixon.

There are four basic possibilities to consider.

The war, in terms of a high-level American involvement with combat troops, will be over. This, it is true, will allow Republicans to say, "We ended the Vietnam War," but gratitude is the scarcest of psephological quantities. On balance, an end to the war should help Republicans in 1972 to about the extent that English gratitude for Churchill's heroic leadership during World War II helped in his race with Clement Attlee in 1945—not at all. Despite the remarkable validity of all the novel axioms and precepts set forth in these pages, there is none that is as invariably accurate and relevant as the ancient political question: "What have you done for me lately?"

The second possibility in Vietnam is that some limited American presence will remain: some volunteer troops, air cover, naval forces, etc. Certainly, the dove element of both parties will strongly demand pulling out such troops as are there, while the more hawkish Democrats will support President Nixon. But it would likely be a comparatively small issue once no large quantities of American lives were being lost—to be more precise, no *drafted* American lives were being lost. Once that aspect of the Vietnam War is over, America's foreign policy will likely become a matter that can be intelligently debated intraparty, interparty and bipartisanly—but without the emotionalism of street demonstrations. It should be a lively and interesting debate, particularly so because the nature of the world's future depends on the outcome. To venture a guess, America is ready for a change in many aspects of its foreign policy, and perhaps all political persuasions will be receptive to creative new ideas reasonably presented.

A third possibility, a slim one only, is that the American involvement in Vietnam or in Cambodia will again involve high U.S. casualties among draftees. In that event Mr. Nixon will be in trouble at home, and we imagine no one knows it better than he.

A fourth possibility concerns what happens if Americans leave Vietnam and Vietnam then falls under Communist control. This will also hurt Mr. Nixon at home, although, as a guess, the great emergence of the right-wing "stab-in-the-back" movement will not materialize. If it does, Republicans will be able to neutralize much of its impact by noting that America's pull out of Vietnam was forced largely by *Democratic* dove pressure.

Assuming Vietnam is to be reduced as an issue for the seventies—and assuming it is not replaced by some other major unforeseen international problem area—Republicans will then be free to do their best in the domestic garden, and it is this garden to which Americans normally pay the greater part of their political attention.

There can be no question that a good deal of Republican gardening will be done on the Social Issue. When Vice President Agnew says: "The rank-and-file Democrat in this country does not share the philosophy of permissiveness expressed by the best publicized moral and intellectual leaders of our society. He reads with disgust all the rave reviews the press gives the latest dirty movie or dirty book" then it is clear that the Republicans are aware of this strategy.

But it is not enough. The Grand New Party must also move on the bread-and-butter issues. Just as Democrats must move on the Social Issue to keep in tune with the center, so Republicans must move on the Economic Issue to capture the center. A Republican Party perceived of as go-slow on the problems of unemployment or the cities or transportation or pollution or against Medicare or Social Security will be vulnerable. America has problems; Americans of the center are aware that America has problems; Americans of the center in the seventies will want an activist problem-solving government. Republicans must offer up such an image or face trouble; they cannot keep the image of the party of the small-town banker. There aren't enough small-town bankers to elect a President. Their rhetoric, too, ought to be predictable:

—Do *not* say, "The great American system of free enterprise will take care of our problems if we let it."

—*Do* say, "The American workingman is the backbone of America; we must help him help America."

—Do *not* say, "We ought to return to the good old days when people lived in big houses in small towns."
—*Do* say, "America must look to the future."

Democrats and Republicans

The major party strategies for the seventies, then, are mirror images: Hold where you are strong; beef up where you are weak. That is the nature of centrism. Democrats must heal the wound of the Social Issue; Republicans must prove that they are the party of Middle America and not of the fat cats. Cynics may ask what is the sense of parties that must always move toward the other-party position to gain political strength. They may be answered by noting that this is the procedure that guarantees the *responsiveness* of the American system. It must also be understood that *within the center* the parties do stand for differing political philosophies: the Republicans basically right of center; the Democrats basically left of center. The party that looks to Haynsworth and Carswell for the Supreme Court is not the ideological twin of the party that chooses Fortas and Thurgood Marshall.

In examining the battleground of the center in the seventies, it may be useful to particularize it somewhat. While it will be occurring all over America, the battle for the hearts and minds of the electorate will probably be most acute and most significant in the suburbs.

Some Republican strategists have noted that the potential for more Republican voters increases as more Americans live in suburbia. These Republicans view the new suburbanites as a surfeit of honey, an embarrassment of psephological riches.

There is a premise behind that reasoning that is probably dubious. The dubiety might be viewed as equating with the old line: "You can take the boy out of the country, but you can't take the country out of the boy." The applicable switch might be: "You can take the Democrat out of the city, but you don't necessarily make him a Republican." In short, there is no evidence that Democratic-oriented voters switch parties simply because they move from the cities or become more affluent. The "old affluent" are traditionally Republican; the new suburbanite is neither so affluent nor so Republican. In fact, there is evidence that many suburbs once solidly Republican are now toss-ups between Democrats and Republicans or, in some instances, already solidly Democratic. The example of Macomb County, just north of Detroit, comes most immediately to mind: As white union auto workers moved out of Detroit into a Republican suburb, suburbia became Democratic.

Suburbia will indeed be the major psephological battle-ground in the years to come but will probably be the major battleground only because so many Americans will be living there. Anyone who automatically deeds that turf to Republicans does so at his peril.

How, then, will the lines form in suburbia? We can ask first: Who are these new suburbanites? They have been described, not wholly accurately, as the "platinum-plated proletariat." They live not in the $70,000 homes in Darien, Connecticut, a 40-mile-distant exurb of New York City, but in the $20,000 houses of Parma, Ohio, immediately abutting Cleveland. They are plumbers. They are foremen. They are airplane mechanics. They are small merchants. They are union workers in an automobile plant. They are telephone repairmen with a second job or with wives who work. They are mostly white, but there are some black busdrivers whose wives are schoolteachers who are moving in. The lady from Dayton is counted in their number.

But they are platinum-plated only in the eyes of the analytical beholder, who may compare their new surroundings to where "workers" used to live in America or to where "workers" still do live in Europe. A house on a quarter of an acre of creeping crabgrass is quite a step up from a tenement, let us say, in Baltimore. But when family income is $8,000 per year, or $10,000 per year, or $12,000 per year, or $15,000 per year, and there are three children, a car, and a mortgage to feed, the occupants do not *feel* platinum-plated or privileged. They feel pressed and pinched.

And which party in America is the party of the pressed and the pinched? In the past it has not been perceived as the Republican Party of the bankers, doctors, and merchants. The party that has spoken for a better economic break for the forgotten American (excuse that phrase) has usually been seen as the Democratic Party, and that is so in the suburbs, as well as in the city.

The Democrats have been the "little man" and the "plain people," all those laborers, cabdrivers, beauticians, and clerks whom George Wallace tried to pull away from the party of their parents, but with only mild success outside the South.

Nixon's Grand New Party must capture that "little man" feeling if it is to be successful; the Democrats must retain it if they want to win the Presidency.

The Democratic Party can remain credible in that role, particularly so if there is a recession, a rise in unemployment, or continuing inflation.

But this "party of the little man" feeling will be a potent Democratic weapon in the suburbs if, and only if, the Social Issue is defused by Democrats. The platinum-plated proletariat will not be wooed by the "limousine liberal" who is half apologizing for student take-overs of state universities whose classrooms are now filled with the sons and daughters of the new suburbanites. Neither will they be placated by any politician who is perceived as soft on crime. Public opinion poll data show that there is as much fear of crime in the suburbs as in the inner city, despite the fact that crime rates are lower (but rising) in the suburbs. Generally speaking, the new suburbanites are not pleased with a permissive attitude toward drugs, pornographic movies, or a hippie life-style—which are frequently perceived as threats that can corrupt their children.

But suppose, with not much more than a label change, that the liberal Democratic politician comes forth not as a "limousine liberal," but as a "moderate." First, he co-opts the Social Issue: He is tough on crime and has little sympathy with campus violence. If his own sons wear their hair long and their feet bare, he does not make a point of boasting about it. He is against black militants and white militants.

If he is successful in establishing credibility on this issue, there is hardly any limit to how "liberal" a Democrat can be on other issues. The moderate can then be for an immediate or near-immediate Vietnam withdrawal; he can be for an end to the draft; he can certainly be for a reduction of defense spending; he can be for increased aid to cities with the money saved from defense spending; he can be for higher welfare standards; he can be for decentralization ("all power to the people"); or centralization ("let's get America moving again"); and, most important, he can be for almost any degree of integration.

A credible candidate on crime and on other facets of the Social Issue has relatively little to fear from being "problack." As a matter of fact, it is probably impossible for any serious major candidate for office to be "antiblack," certainly outside the Deep South. Even George Wallace makes claim to being the black man's best friend. And while there may be some political profit in a wiffle-waffle approach to civil rights, it is a small profit. A credible moderate can gain as many points for "sticking to his beliefs" on civil rights as he can gain by waffling on the issue—again, and again, and again, provided that he has separated his beliefs on "race" from his beliefs on the Social Issue in general and "crime" in particular. The answer to the riddle on page 7 of this book is that the tough black cop wins the election. Crime is a more important issue than race.

It is a misreading of public sentiment to say, as many have, that America is in a mood of programmatic retrenchment following the frenetic blaze of social and economic legislation that went under the name of the Great Society. Not so. Americans *are* fed up with some relatively extraneous situations (riots, crime, violent dissent) and with a relatively few Social Issue situations that went hand in glove with some of the legislation. But job training, aid to education, Medicare, increased minimum wage, Social Security, most of the civil rights laws, even most of the War on Poverty programs of the Office of Economic

Opportunity are generally approved. The Job Corps is fine, but when angry blacks, funded under Community Action Programs, led disruptions, the American public drew a line. There was also a revulsion to welfare when it was perceived as "handouts," either to men who allegedly wouldn't work or to promiscuous women who allegedly had too many babies and not enough husbands. When President Nixon, however, proposed an expansion of welfare eligibility to the "working poor," there was little complaint.

For a while, Americans will accept, even welcome, President Nixon's go-slow, antifrenetic style of government. But such attitudes will not last terribly long, nor, in the guess of the authors, will President Nixon want them to last long.

Both major parties will be anxious to show that they are the ones who can solve America's problems; both parties will attempt to show that they can be firm on the Social Issue. Insofar as they are credible in these roles, to that extent will they be effective in helping their Presidential candidates reside in the White House.

There is a final thought about "Democrat versus Republican." As the 1972 election gets closer, the pundits will begin noting the "power of the incumbent President." In truth, it is limited; the mere fact of incumbency is no guarantee for a Nixon second-term victory. It worked for Eisenhower—but Eisenhower was something else in American politics; he carried the deep personal trust of the American people for eight years to an extent that has never been matched in recent American political history.

If we assume that Mr. Nixon will be a candidate to succeed himself in 1972, as Harry Dent has announced,* then it is fair to speculate about Nixon's merits as a candidate.

He will be the incumbent; he will fly around in Air Force One; he will draw large crowds because he is President; he will likely have a united party behind him; he will create, or time,

---

* Dent, a Nixon political lieutenant, told District of Columbia Young Republicans that things were going so well under Mr. Nixon's leadership that "I don't have much question now that his administration will be in for two terms."

certain events for his own benefit; he will have a certain amount of political arm-twisting power because of his position—all to the good for Mr. Nixon.

But we know more about him, as well. He has, after all, run for President twice, and in neither instance did he get a majority of the vote. In neither instance did he demonstrate that he was a particularly devastating television personality. In the first year of his Presidency he has shown some improvement as a television performer, but not enough to make an observer think that he will build up the huge and intense personal sort of following that President Eisenhower or President Kennedy had. His popularity seems somewhat hollow, a popularity that is extremely vulnerable to a bad turn of events.

So, if we assume that Mr. Nixon will be the candidate of the Republicans in 1972, we can assume *only* that the Republicans will have a competent, well-known, centrist candidate—but that's all. Not an Eisenhower.

Mr. Nixon was perhaps described best by his English adviser on Vietnam, Sir Robert Thompson. After meeting with Mr. Nixon, Sir Robert remarked upon how good it was that America now had a "professional President." Strange phrase, that. Probably accurate. But is a "professional President," a super-civil servant, a GS 100, is that an appealing political image? Not very, we'd venture. If the Democratic candidate in 1972 is a man of the center, he may do very well on a personality versus personality contest.

If these seem, then, to be the major perceivable lines of political action by the major parties, what then of Wallace and of the fringe left? How will they behave, why, and with what effect on the major parties?

WALLACEITES

Several years ago Leonard Hall, sometime chairman of the Republican National Committee, remarked that the longer he was in politics, the more he became convinced that events rather than people determine the course of politics. To this may be added that George Wallace is perhaps more the prisoner of events than any other contemporary political figure in America.

We have seen what lines of doctrine Republicans and Democrats might take for victory in the seventies. In the case of Wallace, he has already staked out his position on the political spectrum, a position we have sketched out in Chapter 12 on Wallace's 1968 campaign.

That Wallace will run in 1972 seems likely. That Wallace will move toward the center, toward the realities of political power in the seventies, seems obvious. But he can't really move far enough unless the character of the events of the seventies helps by moving the center toward him. If social turbulence and disorder, school problems, and riots deepen and intensify the Social Issue, Wallace might benefit from such circumstances, but even then only if *both* major parties were seen by the voters as mired deep in nonresponsive dogmas about these problems.

But the whole nature of American politics *is* responsive. Should the public attitude go so far as to come closer to Wallace policies or to what these policies may become, then in all probability one (or both) of the major parties will co-opt Wallace rhetoric or Wallace strategy. Mr. Agnew has already been called, pejoratively, a "white-collar Wallace," read as a "semidemagogue." Should the times and conditions demand it, some patriot in some party will step forward as a "white-collar Agnew," substantively in tune with an intensified Social Issue, but "nondemagogic," no doubt denouncing Wallace and Agnew while picking up their rhetoric.

In a very real sense it is because American two-party Presidential politics *is* so close to the people that Wallace's chances in the seventies seem dim. Wallace will likely be co-opted by the major parties. He personally will not likely be President. But because he may still carry many votes (10,000,000 in 1968), his electoral presence may well determine who the next Presidents are. The Wallace voter and the decrease or increase of Wallace voters may well be the kingmaking factors in the 1970's.

These votes are obviously an alluring target, particularly so for President Nixon, for we may recall that about seven of every ten Wallace voters would have gone for Nixon in 1968 had Wallace not run.

An alluring target, but a mixed blessing.

President Nixon might conceivably think of making a deal to keep Wallace from running, but then he'd think twice about it and realize that deals don't stay secret for long and that the spectacle of an American President dealing with a politician still perceived by many as a red-neck racist would undoubtedly cost more votes than it would gain.* Wallace, after all, drew only 46 electoral votes—about the number that California will have after the 1970 reapportionment of electoral seats that follows each decennial census. Nixon carried California by only 223,346 votes, a margin over Humphrey of about 3.1%. In any attempt to win some of the five Southern Wallace states, Mr. Nixon must be very careful not to lose 112,000 votes in California, or perhaps his margin for error is a bit more if he can get some of California's Wallace vote. In New Jersey, a switch of 32,000 gives 17 electoral votes to the Democrats; in Illinois 68,000 switches provide 26 votes to the Democrats. Just let the voters feel that their President is trying to outbid George Wallace in the South, and watch those slim non-Southern pluralities melt all over the nation. Let Richard Nixon say he's going to run over a demonstrator with his car, and watch the seepage from voters who might well like to run over demonstrators with *their* car but would find such rhetoric unseemly from a President.

Furthermore, there is another, but very potent, reason to believe that Nixon will not deal with Wallace, nor will he try any number of cute political tricks that the strategists will conjure up. Presidents, strange as it may seem, are honorable men, honestly trying to do their best for the nation. This notion is apparently indigestible to large segments of the political press that find cabals and conspiracies beneath every press release. But in fact, being President places very real constraints on political operations. A *candidate*—some candidates and some tacticians anyway—can plot a nifty antiblack ploy that will allow Nixon to pick up Wallace votes. But Richard Nixon is

---

* In effect, Goldwater made such a deal with Wallace in 1964; Wallace was implored not to split the conservative vote. He didn't. Goldwater got 39% of the total vote.

not only a *candidate,* but a *President* running for reelection. And no President who is responsible is going to play the race-hatred game in the already tense racial climate in America. That may seem to some to be a naïve view of the Presidency, but we submit it as a valid one, duly demonstrated by each of the recent Presidents in America: They do what they feel is in the best interests of the nation, even when it hurts them politically. Richard Nixon does not believe that turning back the clock on civil rights or that drumming upon antiblack sentiments is in the best interests of the nation. Accordingly, he will not so act.

THE RADICAL LEFT

If Wallace's chances in the seventies are dim, so too are those of the Radical Left.

The evidence concerning the universality of the Social Issue would seem to leave the theoreticians of the Democratic New Left somewhere between a rock and a hard place. The more radical aspects of the creed—the ideal of confrontation politics, of confusing cops with pigs, of justifying riots, of sympathy for muggers and rapists, of support of the drug culture or the gay culture—seem to have an extremely limited constituency. Not only are these ideas thoroughly and totally rejected by an overwhelming majority of Middle Americans, but they are rejected by a large portion of their supposed natural constituency as well: blacks, Mexican-Americans, poor people, Jews, young people. The more radical aspects of the New Left are a psephological fraud. It has no constituency worth counting. Furthermore, even sympathy for, let alone espousal of, those radical aspects can poison the well of any sincere candidate for public office.

This seems to leave the Radical Left with four basic choices:

Choice One: Back to the drawing boards. Rethink. Examine again the propositions; question the validity and justifications of radicalism versus the backlash it breeds. Take a deep breath of fresh air, and come up brainwashed—reconstituted as Old Liberals. An admittedly difficult choice.

Choice Two: Retain the radical beliefs, but sear into one's political soul the idea that they are psephological poison. Accordingly, clam up on the radical aspects of the Social Issue, and concentrate on making the best compromise possible with the Democratic center. The center of the Democratic Party supports most, if not all, of the nonradical substantive demands of the left. The issues of better housing, aid to education, low unemployment are not the exclusive province of radicals. Nor is integration a taboo issue. The center of the Democratic Party is receptive to demands for bettering the conditions of blacks in the United States. It is sometimes a difficult political issue these days, but not an impossible one.

Choice Three: Withdraw from major-party politics. Form a fourth party that is ideologically as pure as the driven snow, a party unwilling to compromise intellectually with the center of the national Democratic Party. Be prepared that such a fourth party will have a very limited appeal and won't elect anyone to anything and that it will probably split into several factions within three years. This choice is not offered facetiously. It is the choice that a peaceful man like Norman Thomas took, and Mr. Thomas eventually wielded great influence on political thought in America and lived to see many of his "radical" ideas enacted into law and become a beneficial part of American life. Remember, the center is a moving center and can be moved in many ways. The process of changing society does not always come about through the machinery of a political party in power. It can come simply from the articulation of an idea, whose time has come—or almost come—from a minor party or from no party at all. The Anti-Saloon League brought about Prohibition—but it was not a political party.

As a subvariant of Choice Three, a further choice is offered: Depoliticize completely. Perhaps politics is not the answer to the real problems that so much of the New Left is concerned with: alienation, identity, rootlessness, and the harsh fact that life is at least somewhat absurd. There is no denying that these are major human problems, but there is room to question whether there is any beneficial reason to clutter up major-party national politics with the distracting notion that living is not as easy as it seemed in high school.

It is unlikely that an extreme left party would meet with the same relative success that greeted the Wallace right. Because of the electoral college system, Wallace's strength in the South brought him electoral votes. An extreme left party would not be regional; would not, therefore, get any electoral votes; and would therefore be in a minimal bargaining position. (This would change in the event of the passage of a popular vote for President system.) Furthermore, unlike the Wallace situation, an extreme left party would take almost all of its votes from one party—the Democratic Party. If it ever got strong, then, it could only be a "spoiler" ensuring Republican victories. As a weak party, however, an extreme left party might be helpful to Democrats, by getting the crazies out of the tent, decreasing the identification of "Democrats" as "radicals."

A final possibility: If Senator McCarthy should be a fourth-party candidate he might try to go for the center rather than the extreme, attempting to bridge the Republican-Democratic gap. He had some Republican/surburban-type strength in 1968 and might try to take some of Nixon's vote and go for a 26%-type victory in a four-man race. It won't work. In a showdown, those Republican votes will stay with Nixon. (See page 151.)

Choice Four: Become real revolutionaries; attempt violently to take control of the national government, or the campus, or the city hall. Prepare against the possibility of languishing in jail for long periods of time under extremely inhospitable surroundings, sure only that a movement toward "real" revolution will trigger "real" repression.

So much for the radical fringe of the New Left. In fact, the choices and comments above are not terribly relevant to the future of the nation. The radical fringe has only a nuisance value in the broad political struggle of the United States. What is extremely relevant to the future of the nation, however, is the position that the rest of the Democratic Party will ultimately take toward the radical fringe, for it is a moving part of the Social Issue. Equally relevant is the stance the Republican Party will adopt. Who will say what about the next confrontation, the next disruption, the next eyeball-to-eyeball meeting of kids and cops? Who will say what about Justice Douglas' apologia for violence? How the Republican and Democratic postures are arranged and orchestrated on this issue can conceivably determine who the next Presidents will be, and the basic political direction of the nation in the decade of the 1970's.

Here is what Gerard Hegstrom, the liberal Democrat who lost to Charles Stenvig in Minneapolis, had to say after the dust settled:

> . . . For the liberal, the language of the radical left is often appealing. They speak of justice, equality, and human concern. Yet for the liberal politician the radical left is far more dangerous than any other political force. As the liberal identifies with the apparent causes he is, unfortunately, also identified with their means, including the apparently easy shift to violence. No liberal politician can hold the loyalty of the radicals for any length of time. The liberal is doubted by the Middle American and berated by the radical. Any liberal policy, . . . must include, especially for any new candidate, a clear separation from the radical left movement.

Readers, the electorate has spoken, and rather clearly over the past few years.

The voters have said, in Mr. Nixon's phrase, that they have had it "up to here" with the Social Issue. They have *not* said, "Turn back the clock" or "Down with progress" or "Hate."

In the judgment of the authors, this corporate voice of the voters over the past few years has generally been a voice of wisdom, although some of the candidates who first capitalized upon the new Voting Issue have been demagogic, rather than wise. It is now the task of responsible politicians to attune themselves honestly to the legitimate desires of the voters and, in attuning themselves, reestablish their ability to lead. For the first task of democracy is to be *responsive* to the real majority of voters—without being repressive to minorities.

To lead the people, to lead the people in wisdom, is a fine day's work, but a tricky business. One man's wisdom can be another man's Fascism. Perhaps the greatest contribution of our form of democracy is not that it is always right, but that it is usually responsive. In many ways, responsivity to the body politic *is* wisdom; it is responsivity that establishes both domestic tranquillity and justice, and it is to establish a balance of such tranquillity and justice that men come together into society. Responsivity bypasses revolution.

The people in our society speak through an imperfect loudspeaker—the ballot. The imperfections in the loudspeaker can sometimes garble the voice of the voter, but this does not seem to have been the case in recent years. The message is loud and clear; the ripples and the waves can become a tide. The only question is whether the candidates and the parties are willing to respond to the voice of the voter or, instead, to insist that their wisdom is of a higher order (and, in so insisting, ensure their own defeat at the polls).

The authors trust the people. We recommend to would-be leaders of the people that they trust the people and listen to the people before leading the people. Listen to the center before leading the center.

Those who listen best can lead best.

Epilogue

The Next President

Our book *The Real Majority* declared itself to be an exercise in psephology—that is, the study of elections. Somewhat more specifically, the book dealt in depth with *Presidential psephology*. Quoting ourselves, it was a guide to ". . . a fascinating political moment in America, a political moment framed in time by two Presidential elections—the last one and the next one." At one point, in fact, we even considered calling the book *The Next President*.

And now dawns a Presidential race, and it is a fascinating one for inveterate election watchers. Because *The Real Majority* received such wide attention when it was published in 1970 (the cliché had it that it was the "bible" for both political parties), it seems appropriate now to ask some questions about the book. Did it prove valid in 1970? Is it still valid for the 1972 Presidential race? Are there any necessary amendments, caveats, or new emphases that need stating in the light of a newer reality? Does the evidence of the 1970 campaigns confirm or deny our major ideas?

Briefly, to begin, we would answer the questions this way:

—The book was valid in 1970.
—It will, we believe, be valid in 1972.
—There are indeed some amendments, caveats, and new emphases.

THE 1970 ELECTION

What actually happened in 1970?

Six months before the election of 1970 there was evidence that led many

Democrats to dread the icy possibility of a major Republican victory—the real emergence of an emerging Republican majority.

One month before the election of 1970 there was evidence available that led some Republicans to fear the possibility of a major Democratic victory —a potential wipeout of any authentic claim by Republicans to coequal political status.

Now, as the postelection rhetorical volley about who-really-won-what-how-and-why has subsided, it is important to take notice of the single most critical fact of the 1970 elections. It is this: Neither party woke up on the morning of November 4 in a state of catastrophic defeat.

That is an admittedly unsensational claim. It is less newsworthy to be sure than head counts proving Republican "ideological gains"; it is less newsworthy than the manifestos showing that a new corps of Democratic incumbent governors will somehow deliver the Presidency to a Democrat in 1972. Less newsworthy and more accurate.

What happened was: The Republican did not win the Senate as they had hoped, but they did pick up a few seats. The Democrats did win several seats in the House, but their victory did not approach the magnitude that Foley's Law advocates had predicted (fifteen House seats Republican loss for every 1% rise in the unemployment rate). The governorships went Democratic, but if incumbent governorships are so valuable to faraway Presidential candidates, why weren't Republican incumbents even able to save their own statehouses in 1970?

If one must make a judgment on who won in 1970, it would probably be the Democrats. For when all is said and done, Republican *expectations* were higher, and when all those expectations lead only to a tie, there is at least a psychic loss.

But when you have said that, what have you said? Only that things remain roughly as they were. The nation's basic politics have not changed.

The 1970 elections show the powerful theme of stability and continuity in the ongoing American political process. After all the talk about the breakup of the two party system, about the new politics, about emerging Republican majorities and the disintegration of the FDR coalition, a look at the election data is positively startling as the familiar patterns reemerge.

The Democrats got 54% of the vote—compared to 51% in the last Congressional election. Labor went Democratic. The Chamber of Commerce types went Republican. Blacks, Jews, and Chicanos went Democratic. The majority of high-income voters, WASPs and suburbanites went Republican. What else is new?

The politics of the purge were relatively unsuccessful. Mr. Agnew, out to purge the Radic-Libs, got a few scalps ("we killed that son of a bitch . . ." is the way our Vice President put it), but not very many, because Radic-Libs wisely chose not to play with his ball on his field.

Mr. John Kenneth Galbraith and young Mr. Sam Brown, out to purge the majority of Democrats from the Democratic Party, were even less successful. Those who were to be purged—Senator Gale McGee, Senator Henry Jackson, former Vice President Hubert Humphrey, and Adlai Stevenson III —are in the U.S. Senate with big victories, while a surprising number of the erstwhile allies of the purgers didn't quite make it.

What were the factors at work?

There was first the Social Issue, an innocuous enough phrase when we first wrote it. Compounded of unequal parts of law and order, permissiveness, pot, pornography, disruption, and elements of the race problem, the Social Issue played a major role in just about every Senatorial campaign of 1970. In our judgment, it clearly took its place alongside economic concerns as a major political issue of our time.

Liberals who were able to credibly neutralize the Social Issue of 1970 were then able to run effective campaigns based on that hoary chestnut "It's time to get America moving again." Hoary. Old. And valid.

And so all over America, liberals showed their concern with the Social Issue, showed that a politician could be both pro-civil rights and anti-crime, and combatted the tough Nixon-Agnew attack that developed.

—John Tunney was last seen cruising in a police car in Los Angeles.
—Adlai Stevenson III filmed television commercials alongside a pot-bellied Southern Illinois sheriff. Stevenson also reminded the voters that he had been a combat tank commander in Korea.
—Senator Muskie's classic election eve nationwide television broadcast followed the basic outline of the analysis offered in *The Real Majority*: How dare they say we are soft, said Muskie, followed with, look how they've mangled the economy.
—Allard Lowenstein took to wearing an American flag in his lapel. He said, "It's my flag, too."

And so on. Liberals—properly and wisely—attempted to tell voters that they were not necessarily softies, that they understood what was bothering Americans. In the language of our book, *they moved to the attitudinal center* and talked directly to the real majority of Americans, demographically categorized mostly as unyoung, unpoor, unblack, middle-aged, middle-class, and middle-minded.

The map of the liberal hegira can be plainly seen if one looks at a pair of political clichés uttered by the same people but with two years' worth of turbulent political water under the bridge.

In 1968 liberals were saying, *"Law and order is a codeword for racism."*

In 1970 the same liberals were saying, *"Law and order is not a partisan issue."* There is, we would suggest, miles of political distance between these two statements.

The reason for this concentration by liberals on the Social Issue can be gleaned from the following Gallup data, gathered on the day before the 1970 elections in four barometric counties around the nation:

The Issue:	Yes	No
Legalize marijuana	14	86
Bus children to achieve racial balance	22	78
More money for police	91	9
Deny federal aid to colleges that do not expel students involved in campus riots	79	21

The Social Issue lives.

And what about economic issues?

Of course, they were important in 1970. They are always important. It is only the most simplistic of viewpoints that sees an election as hinging on a single issue. This happens occasionally to be sure, and when it does, it is big news indeed. But that is the exception: The rule is a trade-off of one issue against another or of one personality against another.

A high rate of inflation, a rising rate of unemployment—surely these factors hurt many Republican candidates across the nation in 1970.

But still, the Republicans were not trounced. One can speculate on why the Economic Issue was not more damaging to Republicans in 1970:

—The economy wasn't bad enough long enough. A rate of 5.6% (October, 1970) is not the 6.8% faced by Republicans in 1958. Unemployment benefits are higher and easier to come by than a decade ago. The really high unemployment (5% or over) was only operative for the last three months before the election.

—The election was "cross-tidal." The anti-Republican economic issue was muted by the force of the anti-Democratic Social Issue. And vice versa. Probably true, but with no real proof available.

—Off-year elections are usually nontidal in nature. Local issues, individual personalities take precedence. By this view one can say—with some accuracy—that the independents Harry Byrd, Jr., and James Buckley merely joined ninety-eight other independent Senators who, incidentally, carry a party label for convenience sake. The central misconception of American politics is that the United States has a national party system. In fact, with the exception of Presidential years, we usually don't.

And what about Vietnam as an Issue in the 1970 election? It is generally conceded that it was "defused." And we would agree with the consensus.

LOOKING AHEAD TO 1972

The Social Issue remains an issue. For doubters, let it be noted that in March, 1971, here is what a Gallup Poll showed:

Public's List of Most Important Problems

Vietnam; Indo-China	28%
Economic	24%
Other international	12%
Crime, lawlessness	7%
Race relations	7%
Pollution, ecology	7%
Drug addiction	6%
Division in America, polarization of views	6%
Poverty, welfare	5%
Education	2%
Lack of religion, moral decay	2%
Other responses	6%
No opinion	2%
	114%

(Tables add to more than 100 percent because of multiple responses.)

If one adds up the italicized items (giving half value for "poverty, welfare") they total 30%, higher than any other single issue. That is the sum of the Social Issue in March, 1971.

The Social Issue remains. This unpleasant event occurred in New York City in the spring of 1971, during midafternoon on the posh Upper East Side: A well-dressed black gentleman approached a white doctor who was standing on a busy street corner. "Do you have a match?" the black man asked. The doctor promptly took out his wallet and removed his watch, saying, "Take it all, I don't want any trouble." The black man looked at him strangely. "All I wanted was a match," he said.

The Social Issue remains. For tacticians who say Aha! but now it works against the Republicans because they are in power, we offer only scant solace. To be sure, Democrats will attempt to say this—as did Jess Unruh in California—and they may make a few points. But essentially, as Governor Reagan showed, it is still a pro-Republican issue and is likely to remain as such. Neither Muskie, Humphrey, Kennedy, McGovern, Harold Hughes, or Ramsey Clark will get very far calling Nixon, Agnew, and Mitchell soft and permissive. It fact, of the potential Democratic candidates, the only one who seems relatively immune on the issue would be Senator Henry Jackson.

The Social Issue remains. And it will be more potent in 1972 than in 1970 for one other reason. It is mostly perceived by voters as an *executive's* issue, one that mayors and the President are responsible for, not legislators. As an executive's issue, it might be remembered that executive Richard M. Nixon has run for President twice. One campaign was based on economic issues (1960). He lost. One campaign was based on the Social Issue (1968). He won.

By defusing the Social Issue, by demonstrating that concern for people afraid to walk their streets by day or night was not an illiberal concern, many liberals were able to win in 1970. If some liberals will now re-fuse the issue, they and their party and their party's candidate will suffer in 1972. Dismissing the Social Issue for 1972 is like saying, "There never was any danger of fire. Why did we bother to take the rags out of the closet?"

How about the Economic Issue in 1972?

To see an economic issue that cut really deeply one can look back to the elections during the recession of 1958. President Eisenhower had a Congress with 201 Republicans. He lost 48, ending up with 153! Interestingly, the loss cannot be attributed to the normal rubber-band effect that follows a big Presidential win. Ike's big victory two years earlier in 1956 had no coattail effect, actually costing the GOP a couple of seats.

The 48-seat loss in 1958 is what Republican strategists ought now to be ruminating about. That's how deeply a recession can cut politically when it does cut politically: Unemployment was 6.8% in 1958, up from 4.2% in 1956. Whether Dwight Eisenhower could have survived a 6.8% unemployment rate had 1958 been a Presidential election year is problematical. Whether a less charismatic personality, Richard Nixon, could survive that magnitude of unemployment is only theoretically problematical.

The President knows this, and one can assume with some surety that every effort will be made to reinvigorate the economy. This will not be done only for political purposes, of course. No one is for continued high unemployment and high inflation, politics notwithstanding. Whether these efforts on the part of the administration will be successful remains to be seen. If they are somewhat successful, it will be a horse race in 1972. If they are not, the Democrats will almost surely take over.

And what about the war as an issue? Here a clear differentiation must be made between an *issue* and a *concern*. In 1968—when 500,000 GI's were in Vietnam, when many of them were draftees, when 200 American soldiers were being killed each week—there was strong evidence to suggest that while the war was a paramount *concern*, it was not much of an *issue*. Each of the three candidates promised peace with honor. The polls showed that Nixon and Humphrey were viewed the same on a hawk-dove scale. There is no indication that many votes were *switched* in 1968 on the basis of the war. This was true not only in the general election, but in the primaries as well; McCarthy, the only dove candidate in New Hampshire, received only 18% of the two-party vote in a state where crossover write-ins are common. If the voters wanted to vote "dove" as a protest in 1968, they could have. They didn't.

Now, if the war was not an issue with 500,000 men overseas and 200 men per week dying, will it be an issue in 1972 if the troops number, say, 50,000 to 100,000, when the casualties are sharply lower and no draftees are involved? President Nixon thinks not. He has publicly stated that anyone running for President on the issue of the war "will have the rug pulled out from under him." He apparently feels that he will be able to go to the people and say he is delivering what he promised—*i.e.*, peace with honor—and that under those circumstances an opponent denouncing the war as an immoral lost cause will suffer.

Is the President correct in this judgment? It is hard to say. He has an excellent record of defusing the war as an issue since his election. On the other hand, public sentiment has moved against the war, partly no doubt because the President too is calling for withdrawal, albeit not quite as quickly as his opponents or the American majority would like.

Our judgment is that Nixon has a better than fair chance in continuing his defusing tactics. But in truth it is an unprecedented situation, and no one really knows.

Our guess is that many dove/liberals have mistaken the nature of the turn in public sentiment against the war. The 70%-odd of the American people who are now saying yes, bring out the last American soldier by December 31, 1971, are *not* saying, "Indict America!"

There is, to be sure, some of that feeling. But the attitudes that surfaced at the time of the Calley verdict are probably indicative. About 80% of the people said that the judgment against the confessed slayer of women and children was unfair. This attitude was not essentially one that favored slaying women and children. It reflected instead an inchoate anger and frustration over the idea that once again it was the little grunt who got shafted, while it was the big shots who were allowed the luxury of prattling on about war crimes. At this ugly point Vietnam can become an *issue* as well as a *concern*. And it will not be an issue that will help doves, if they be perceived of as anti-GI.

But one thing is known about the Vietnam conflict. If the war has re-escalated, if Americans are dying in great numbers in Vietnam in 1972, then certainly President Nixon will lose.

Another major concern that has been discussed at length is the environment. Our judgment is that this will not be a cutting issue between national candidates in 1972, since the eco issue is almost invariably muted when placed in a *national* setting. Nationally, everyone is for clean air and clean water. Show us the candidate, right, left, or center, who campaigns for pollution. Almost invariably the environment becomes a hot issue only in a *state* or *local* setting when it is drawn as a specific standoff: Keep the factory and the jobs *or* keep the water and air clean.

On a national basis the extremes are: dirty air, dirty water on one side, and the extreme fringes of the ecology movement on the other. The first no one supports. But the rhetoric of the second that demands a stop to growth of the GNP, that calls the GNP the Gross National Pollution, that condemns economic development as an evil polluter, is fashionably chic—and basically reactionary. A freeze in economic growth in the United States means, essentially, freezing the $20,000-a-year college professor into a comfortable tenured upper-middle-class situation where his children go to college tuition-free and he can sail his sailboat in an unpolluted lake. Bearable. Unfortunately, a freeze in economic growth also means freezing the black auto worker at $9,000 a year, with layoffs possible, with no boat, and with no money for a college education for his children. Unbearable. And subject to a brutal backlash at the polls. Anthony Crosland, a British Labour Member of Parliament, has put it succinctly: ". . . those enjoying an above average standard of living should be chary of admonishing those less fortunate on the perils of material riches." The environmental movement in America is too important to permit its injury by identification as an elitist antiworker movement. There are signs this can happen.

It is hoped that it won't. Politics is most often the art of accommodation, and with wise leadership we will be able to have both continued economic growth, with its rising standard of living, and a cleaner environment.

Where, then, does all this leave us in 1972?

It leaves us roughly where we were after the 1968 elections, roughly with the picture of the electoral landscape sketched out in *The Real Majority*. That is, voters torn between voting on the basis of economic concerns on the one hand and social concerns on the other, with the international issue probably playing a smaller role.

SOME CHANGES

But all is not identical to 1968. There have been some changes, and they should be noted here.

To begin, there will be about 11,000,000 voters between the ages of eighteen and twenty-one who will be eligible to vote in the 1972 Presidential election because of the Supreme Court decision of December, 1970. Three immediate questions come to mind. How many will vote? How will they vote? How will these voters differ from those voters over twenty-one?

The answer to the first question, based on recent evidence, is fairly clear. Younger voters go to the polls less frequently than any other age group in America. In 1968, among the eligible population aged thirty to sixty-four, the percentage that voted was 72%. By contrast, of eligible voters aged twenty-one to twenty-four, only *51%* voted. Four states in 1968 permitted persons under twenty-one to vote. Their voting percentage was only *33%*, but mainly in low-turnout states.

If one assumes that about half the newly enfranchised young voters actually make it to the polls in 1972, they will number about 5,000,000 to 6,000,000. There will be about 75,000,000 to 80,000,000 other voters, so the new young voters will represent something like 6% to 7% of the vote. In short, the vast majority of the voters will remain unyoung despite the new voting age. (Also unblack and unpoor, as before.)

How will they vote? The public opinion polls show some contradictory evidence. On the one hand, youth express themselves as more liberal than their elders and more inclined to vote Democratic. On the other hand, both Gallup and Harris polls have shown the strength of George Wallace substantially higher among eighteen-, nineteen- and twenty-year-olds than among their elders. To sample the full flavor of this split, note a Louis Harris Poll that shows that among young Americans, the four most admired Americans are Robert F. Kennedy, Bill Cosby, Neil Armstrong, and John Wayne.

Will their vote differ from the population as a whole? Our guess is that the youth vote will ultimately tally as more liberal and more Democratic than the general population. Indeed, this is almost a rule of American politics: In 1940 young people voted somewhat more for Franklin Roosevelt than did their parents.

Some observers feel that 1972 will see a change in the magnitude of this pattern: a massive outpouring of a heavily Democratic youth vote. If this were the case, it would certainly be a major factor. But our estimate is that the variation of the youth vote from national norms will not be that massive. Moreover, we feel that the percentage of middle-aged voting in 1972 will remain substantially higher than the turnout of those under twenty-five. If these factors hold true, then only a close election could be decided by the young. But of course, in a close election every vote is important. In Detroit a close election can swing on the votes of Maltese-Americans.

One aspect of the youth vote is the most important: No one really knows. There is no track record. So we shall see.

A final thought about the young: At the time of Cambodia/Kent, it was announced that American youth would soon remake the political landscape. But by election day the kids were being called copouts. Twice wrong. The kids didn't remake the world, but they were quietly active in many campaigns and quietly effective, too. On balance, young Americans were more politically active than young Americans used to be, and this will probably continue, a plus for the country as a whole.

Another recent change involves the South. Our judgment prior to the 1970 Congressional elections was that the South was lost to the Presidential Democrats for the foreseeable future. But that climate would seem to be changing somewhat faster than we had indicated. In many areas the old politics of racism is disappearing. In 1970 moderate Democrats such as present Senator Lawton Chiles in Florida and present Governor Dale Bumpers in Arkansas ran strong and successful campaigns. They represented the new center of the Southern electorate, still more conservative than the rest of the nation, but less so than before. And so, what seemed after 1968 as an impossibility now appears only an improbability. For the Democrats in the South that represents progress.

A third change in the American political scene concerns the newly intensified distinction between public policy and electoral politics. Electoral politics deals with the processes of getting elected (and was the subject of *The Real Majority*). Public policy involves issues that range from the location of the town dump to the basic ethics of our society.

There is a great overlap between these two rubrics, but not a total overlap. One can change society by getting elected. And one can change society without getting elected by convincing the public and then elected officials of the merit of specific causes. A case in point was the defeat of the SST in early 1971. It did not come about via change by election. It was based on educating the public and the legislators to what the Stop the SST faction felt was an environmental blunder and an economic monstrosity. Such campaigns are not new in American history (both women's suffrage and prohibition were mainly effected via the public policy route rather than by electoral politics). But in this era of almost total communications coverage, it seems easier than ever before to wage successful public policy campaigns.

This concept of public education is one of the basic themes of *The Real Majority*. Our phrase for it is "moving the Center." If the Center (the power position) can be attitudinally changed, then changes in public policy will flow like a mighty stream.

That is one part of our concept of leadership: *Lead* the Center. The other part says: *Listen* to the Center. *Listen to and lead* the Center. *Both. Not either/or.* Both are what make democracy work. A politician, to serve usefully in a democracy, should be saying two things. First, *"I understand what is bothering you."* And second: *"And here is what we are going to do about it; come with me to the top of the mountain and let me show you a better land."*

In a medical analogy the first statement can be compared to the bedside manner and the second with the prescription of a drug. Every doctor knows that both style and substance are critical. In politics, as in medicine, many complaints are either inconsequential or will heal themselves. And one important role of the political leader is to let his troubled constituents know that somebody up there is listening. That helps the healing process. In fact, by calming the public pulse, it makes changes in public policy easier to effectuate.

It is a central irony of our times that liberals agree readily that social turmoil is a major concern when expressed by intellectuals as "alienation," "anomie," "rootlessness," or, more recently, as "future shock" and a "greening America." But the same general concerns, when expressed by the blue collars as a demand for "law and order" and "values," are regarded by intellectuals as somewhat unclean concerns of use only to demagogues. Liberals must learn to listen so that they can lead better.

The Threat and the Cure

There is a central question that runs through much of the above: *Is it possible that the label of elitism—and the political poison it connotes— will move from the Republicans to the Democratic left?*

To many, the left of the Democratic Party seems to be associated with a new elitism of the upper middle class. It is the left that pooh-poohs the Social Issue after having campaigned in 1970 that they were as tough as any man in the barroom. It is the left that is perceived of as apologizing for the VC flags in the hands of shut-down-the-government demonstrators. It is the left that is so often associated with the extreme "reduced consumption" view of environmental problems.

To many, the leftists (and potentially, the Democrats) appear in smug opposition to so much that so much of America holds dear: social order, social stability, patriotism, a rising standard of living.

If this is so, or if it is becoming so, it portends electoral danger for the Democrats. For many years of liberal Democratic hegemony, it was the Republican Party that was perceived as the party of the elitist: the banker, the broker, the doctor. And it was the Democratic Party that was seen as the party of the little man.

That was the taproot of Democratic power. For the man who chooses the Presidents of this country is the man who bowls on Thursday nights. He is the man in his blue work shirt who is perfectly content to watch the greenies don the beads while he presides over what sociologists Peter and Brigitte Berger describe as the blueing of America. He is a man who is decidedly turned off as he watches the Democrats-of-Despair hand out the campaign buttons of the New Politics, buttons that read MEA CULPA.

If one thinks that the problem we describe has not reached significant proportions, we yield to the remarks of Leonard Woodcock, president of the United Automobile Workers, spiritual heir of Walter Reuther, committed dove, fighting liberal. It is Mr. Woodcock who speaks of the "social snobism of the Democratic Party." Better still, we recommend *Push Comes to Shove,* the work of a Harvard Socialist named Steven Kelman. Young Mr. Kelman describes with bitter accuracy the antiworker bias of the cultural radicals of the left.

For the moment, the actual erosion on the elitist issue has been minimal for a simple reason. George Meany can play golf with Richard Nixon at Burning Tree, but when he goes downtown to his office, he has to look at the unemployment statistics. But the question that ought to throw fear into the heart of every Democrat is this one: What happens if the economy rights itself and Mr. Nixon can chase the radiclibs without cement blocks of unemployment fastened to his ankles?

How does all this affect the Democratic National Convention? For it is the convention where the next major Democratic decision will be made, and so it is to the convention that we ought to look for clues to the direction of the oldest continuous political party in the world.

To begin, one should take note that in a caucus-convention system (which is the system we have in America) militants and party activists will usually wield power disproportionate to their real numbers throughout the electorate. Second, it should be noted that the militants are frequently found at the extremes of the political spectrum. This was so in the 1964 Republican Convention that nominated Goldwater, and it will likely be so at the 1972 Democratic Convention. In 1964 the militants of the conservative right were able to dominate the convention and chose Goldwater. In 1972 the left militants will wield influence disproportionate to their national numbers, but probably not to the point of convention domination.

Militants achieve this power because it is they who are willing to stay at the caucus meeting until 2 A.M., and it is they who are willing to go door to door even when it's raining. That is the source of their strength: rocklike belief and hard, hard work.

That, too, is the source of their potential danger to a national political party—when the militants are also political wingers. Their hard work can win them a state primary when 30% of the voters turn up, their hard work, occasionally, can dominate a national convention; but it can never dominate a national general election when 80,000,000 Americans go to the polls to choose their President. And if the party's candidate is either the handpicked choice of the militants or if he is seen as snug and cozy with the militants, that candidate and his party, by transference, can be severely hurt at the polls.

These abstract political thoughts will have a concrete application at the 1972 Democratic Convention where the big question that both the party and the left faction must answer is whether *the Democratic Party is a movement or a political party?*

If it is a *movement,* convinced that there is but one shining truth that all right-thinking men must accept, then clearly the left must harass, disrupt, and coerce the party and the party's candidate toward its own views. If unsuccessful, they ought to consider acting upon their threat to start a new party—in fact, to institutionalize the movement.

But if it is a *political party*, then what? A political party in the United States operates effectively between the two 35-yard lines of the political football field, wholly aware that there is a major substantive difference between one 35-yard line and the other, aware too that heading starkly for the end zone leads to a political fumble. A political party must keep itself aware that compromise and coalition are the essential tools of political action. It must be aware that it must listen as well as lead and that elite theorizing will only allow Mr. Nixon and Mr. Mitchell to continue to govern the nation.

A political party is dedicated to the proposition that there may be some wisdom in the other fellow's position and, moreover, that a progressive and harmonious nation comes about when the people of that nation—all the people—have a voice in directing the nation. It seems to us this has been the secret of the generation-long success of the FDR coalition.

The professionals in a political party know something else as well: The voters will allow a candidate a regenerative power following a certain amount of indiscretion, but a candidate can change only so much. As in the ancient tales, the beautiful fairy princess may come along and tap the forehead of the ugly frog with her magic wand and say the magic words, "Frog, you're really a handsome prince." To which the frog replies, "Croak, croak." So too in politics. After nomination by an extremist convention, the candidate may turn to the voters and say, "Hah, hah, it was all a joke, I'm really not a frog, I'm a plain old centrist after all, fellow little man." But alas, what the voter hears is something different: "Croak, croak."

Apply this thought to the 1972 Democratic Convention, and if it is victory you seek, stay away from the frogs who croak so beguilingly on the fringes of the pool. Ignore the Rennie Davises and the Lester Maddoxes. And with all respect to the gentlemen involved, do not nominate either of the two Democratic wingers from Texas, Ramsey Clark and John Connally. Listen instead to the progressive voices of the Center.

It was not the purpose of either *The Real Majority* or this Epilogue to concentrate on the personalities of politics. Our concern was not with the who, but with the what, the why, and the how of our political system. Accordingly, we will not say here that Muskie, Humphrey, Jackson, or McGovern will be the Democratic nominee or whether any Democrat will beat Richard Nixon in 1972.

But the nonpersonalistic factors are really more interesting than the personalities, for they shape the personalities. And the factors, we believe, remain much the same for 1972 as they were in 1968. The comingling of the two great issues: Social and Economic. The capture of the attitudinal Center on the basis of these issues. The ability to move the Center. The capture of the allegiance of the masses of the voters, unyoung, unpoor, unblack—middle-aged, middle-class, middle-minded.

American voters want social stability and economic progress—each in the broadest sense. This includes "law and order" as well as "aid to cities." It includes civil rights but not uncivil disruption. The political personality who can best convince the American people that he can deliver on these issues will be known in November, 1972, by the words which we at one time considered for the title of our book: "The Next President."

RICHARD M. SCAMMON
BEN J. WATTENBERG

Washington, D.C.
April, 1971

Appendix

Year	Candidates	Popular Vote	Percent	Electoral Vote
1968	Richard M. Nixon (R)	31,785,480	43.4%	301
	Hubert Humphrey (D)	31,275,166	42.7%	191
	George C. Wallace (AIP)	9,906,473	13.5%	46
	All others	244,756	.3%	—
1964	Lyndon B. Johnson (D)	43,129,566	61.1%	486
	Barry Goldwater (R)	27,178,188	38.5%	52
	All others	336,838	.5%	—
1960	John F. Kennedy (D)	34,226,731	49.7%	303
	Richard M. Nixon (R)	34,108,157	49.5%	219
	All others	503,331	.7%	15
1956	Dwight D. Eisenhower (R)	35,590,472	57.4%	457
	Adlai Stevenson (D)	26,022,752	42.0%	73
	All others	413,684	.7%	1
1952	Dwight D. Eisenhower (R)	33,936,234	55.1%	442
	Adlai Stevenson (D)	27,314,992	44.4%	89
	All others	299,692	.5%	—
1948	Harry S. Truman (D)	24,179,345	49.6%	303
	Thomas E. Dewey (R)	21,991,291	45.1%	189
	Strom Thurmond (SR)	1,176,125	2.4%	39
	Henry A. Wallace (P)	1,157,326	2.4%	—
	All others	289,739	.6%	—
1944	Franklin D. Roosevelt (D)	25,612,610	53.4%	432
	Thomas E. Dewey (R)	22,017,617	45.9%	99
	All others	346,443	.7%	—
1940	Franklin D. Roosevelt (D)	27,313,041	54.7%	449
	Wendell Wilkie (R)	22,348,480	44.8%	82
	All others	238,897	.5%	—
1936	Franklin D. Roosevelt (D)	27,757,333	60.8%	523
	Alfred M. Landon (R)	16,684,231	36.5%	8
	All others	1,213,199	2.7%	—
1932	Franklin D. Roosevelt (D)	22,829,501	57.4%	472
	Herbert Hoover (R)	15,760,684	39.6%	59
	All others	1,168,574	2.9%	—
1928	Herbert Hoover (R)	21,437,277	58.2%	444
	Alfred E. Smith (D)	15,007,698	40.8%	87
	All others	360,976	1.0%	—
1924	Calvin Coolidge (R)	15,719,921	54.0%	382
	John W. Davis (D)	8,386,704	28.8%	136
	Robert M. La Follette (P)	4,832,532	16.6%	13
	All others	155,866	.5%	—

Year	Candidates	Popular Vote	Percent	Electoral Vote
1920	Warren G. Harding (R)	16,153,115	60.3%	404
	James M. Cox (D)	9,133,092	34.1%	127
	All others	1,482,406	5.5%	—
1916	Woodrow Wilson (D)	9,131,511	49.3%	277
	Charles E. Hughes (R)	8,548,935	46.1%	254
	All others	855,786	4.6%	—
1912	Woodrow Wilson (D)	6,301,254	41.9%	435
	Theodore Roosevelt (P)	4,127,788	27.4%	88
	William H. Taft (R)	3,485,831	23.2%	8
	Eugene V. Debs (S)	901,255	6.0%	—
	All others	238,934	1.6%	—
1908	William H. Taft (R)	7,679,114	51.6%	321
	William J. Bryan (D)	6,410,665	43.1%	162
	All others	800,941	5.4%	—
1904	Theodore Roosevelt (R)	7,628,831	56.4%	336
	Alton B. Parker (D)	5,084,533	37.6%	140
	All others	811,234	6.0%	—
1900	William McKinley (R)	7,219,828	51.7%	292
	William J. Bryan (D)	6,358,160	45.5%	155
	All others	396,200	2.8%	—
1896	William McKinley (R)	7,113,734	51.0%	271
	William J. Bryan (D)	6,516,722	46.7%	176
	All others	317,219	2.3%	—
1892	Grover Cleveland (D)	5,556,982	46.0%	277
	Benjamin Harrison (R)	5,191,466	43.0%	145
	James B. Weaver (Peoples)	1,029,960	8.5%	22
	All others	292,672	2.4%	—
1888	Grover Cleveland (D)	5,540,365	48.6%	168
	Benjamin Harrison (R)	5,445,269	47.8%	233
	All others	404,205	3.5%	—
1884	Grover Cleveland (D)	4,875,971	48.5%	219
	James G. Blaine (R)	4,852,234	48.3%	182
	All others	326,023	3.2%	—
1880	James A. Garfield (R)	4,454,433	48.3%	214
	Winfield S. Hancock (D)	4,444,976	48.2%	155
	All others	320,058	3.5%	—
1876	Samuel J. Tilden (D)	4,287,670	50.9%	184
	Rutherford B. Hayes (R)	4,035,924	47.9%	185
	All others	94,935	1.1%	—

UNITED STATES
PRESIDENT 1948

State	Electoral Vote Rep.	Electoral Vote Dem.	Electoral Vote SR	Total Vote	Republican	Democratic	Other	Percentage Total Vote Rep.	Percentage Total Vote Dem.	Percentage Major Vote Rep.	Percentage Major Vote Dem.
Alabama			11	214,980	40,930		174,050	19.0%		100.0%	
Alaska											
Arizona		4		177,065	77,597	95,251	4,217	43.8	53.8%	44.9	55.1%
Arkansas		9		242,475	50,959	149,659	41,857	21.0	61.7	25.4	74.6
California		25		4,021,538	1,895,269	1,913,134	213,135	47.1	47.6	49.8	50.2
Colorado		6		515,237	239,714	267,288	8,235	46.5	51.9	47.3	52.7
Connecticut	8			883,518	437,754	423,297	22,467	49.5	47.9	50.8	49.2
Delaware	3			139,073	69,588	67,813	1,672	50.0	48.8	50.6	49.4
Florida		8		577,643	194,280	281,988	101,375	33.6	48.8	40.8	59.2
Georgia		12		418,844	76,691	254,646	87,507	18.3	60.8	23.1	76.9
Hawaii											
Idaho		4		214,816	101,514	107,370	5,932	47.3	50.0	48.6	51.4
Illinois		28		3,984,046	1,961,103	1,994,715	28,228	49.2	50.1	49.6	50.4
Indiana	13			1,656,212	821,079	807,831	27,302	49.6	48.8	50.4	49.6
Iowa		10		1,038,264	494,018	522,380	21,866	47.6	50.3	48.6	51.4
Kansas	8			788,819	423,039	351,902	13,878	53.6	44.6	54.6	45.4
Kentucky		11		822,658	341,210	466,756	14,692	41.5	56.7	42.2	57.8
Louisiana			10	416,336	72,657	136,344	207,335	17.5	32.7	34.8	65.2
Maine	5			264,787	150,234	111,916	2,637	56.7	42.3	57.3	42.7
Maryland	8			596,748	294,814	286,521	15,413	49.4	48.0	50.7	49.3
Massachusetts		16		2,107,146	909,370	1,151,788	45,988	43.2	54.7	44.1	55.9
Michigan	19			2,109,609	1,038,595	1,003,448	67,566	49.2	47.6	50.9	49.1
Minnesota		11		1,212,226	483,617	692,966	35,643	39.9	57.2	41.1	58.9
Mississippi			9	192,190	5,043	19,384	167,763	2.6	10.1	20.6	79.4
Missouri		15		1,578,628	655,039	917,315	6,274	41.5	58.1	41.7	58.3
Montana		4		224,278	96,770	119,071	8,437	43.1	53.1	44.8	55.2

UNITED STATES
PRESIDENT 1948

State	Electoral Vote Rep.	Electoral Vote Dem.	Electoral Vote SR	Total Vote	Republican	Democratic	Other	Total Vote Rep.	Total Vote Dem.	Major Vote Rep.	Major Vote Dem.
Nebraska	6			488,940	264,774	224,165	1	54.2	45.8	54.2	45.8
Nevada		3		62,117	29,357	31,291	1,469	47.3	50.4	48.4	51.6
New Hampshire	4			231,440	121,299	107,995	2,146	52.4	46.7	52.9	47.1
New Jersey	16			1,949,555	981,124	895,455	72,976	50.3	45.9	52.3	47.7
New Mexico		4		187,063	80,303	105,464	1,296	42.9	56.4	43.2	56.8
New York	47			6,177,337	2,841,163	2,780,204	555,970	46.0	45.0	50.5	49.5
North Carolina		14		791,209	258,572	459,070	73,567	32.7	58.0	36.0	64.0
North Dakota	4			220,716	115,139	95,812	9,765	52.2	43.4	54.6	45.4
Ohio		25		2,936,071	1,445,684	1,452,791	37,596	49.2	49.5	49.9	50.1
Oklahoma		10		721,599	268,817	452,782		37.3	62.7	37.3	62.7
Oregon	6			524,080	260,904	243,147	20,029	49.8	46.4	51.8	48.2
Pennsylvania	35			3,735,348	1,902,197	1,752,426	80,725	50.9	46.9	52.0	48.0
Rhode Island		4		327,702	135,787	188,736	3,179	41.4	57.6	41.8	58.2
South Carolina			8	142,571	5,386	34,423	102,762	3.8	24.1	13.5	86.5
South Dakota	4			250,105	129,651	117,653	2,801	51.8	47.0	52.4	47.6
Tennessee		11	1	550,283	202,914	270,402	76,967	36.9	49.1	42.9	57.1
Texas		23		1,249,577	303,467	824,235	121,875	24.3	66.0	26.9	73.1
Utah		4		276,306	124,402	149,151	2,753	45.0	54.0	45.5	54.5
Vermont	3			123,382	75,926	45,557	1,899	61.5	36.9	62.5	37.5
Virginia		11		419,256	172,070	200,786	46,400	41.0	47.9	46.1	53.9
Washington		8		905,058	386,314	476,165	42,579	42.7	52.6	44.8	55.2
West Virginia		8		748,750	316,251	429,188	3,311	42.2	57.3	42.4	57.6
Wisconsin		12		1,276,800	590,959	647,310	38,531	46.3	50.7	47.7	52.3
Wyoming		3		101,425	47,947	52,354	1,124	47.3	51.6	47.8	52.2
United States	189	303	39	48,793,826	21,991,291	24,179,345	2,623,190	45.1%	49.6%	47.6%	52.4%

UNITED STATES
PRESIDENT 1952

State	Electoral Vote Rep.	Electoral Vote Dem.	Electoral Vote Other	Total Vote	Republican	Democratic	Other	Pct. Total Vote Rep.	Pct. Total Vote Dem.	Pct. Major Vote Rep.	Pct. Major Vote Dem.
Alabama		11		426,120	149,231	275,075	1,814	35.0%	64.6%	35.2%	64.8%
Alaska											
Arizona	4			260,570	152,042	108,528		58.3	41.7	58.3	41.7
Arkansas		8		404,800	177,155	226,300	1,345	43.8	55.9	43.9	56.1
California	32			5,141,849	2,897,310	2,197,548	46,991	56.3	42.7	56.9	43.1
Colorado	6			630,103	379,782	245,504	4,817	60.3	39.0	60.7	39.3
Connecticut	8			1,096,911	611,012	481,649	4,250	55.7	43.9	55.9	44.1
Delaware	3			174,025	90,059	83,315	651	51.8	47.9	51.9	48.1
Florida	10			989,337	544,036	444,950	351	55.0	45.0	55.0	45.0
Georgia		12		655,785	198,961	456,823	1	30.3	69.7	30.3	69.7
Hawaii											
Idaho	4			276,254	180,707	95,081	466	65.4	34.4	65.5	34.5
Illinois	27			4,481,058	2,457,327	2,013,920	9,811	54.8	44.9	55.0	45.0
Indiana	13			1,955,049	1,136,259	801,530	17,260	58.1	41.0	58.6	41.4
Iowa	10			1,268,773	808,906	451,513	8,354	63.8	35.6	64.2	35.8
Kansas	8			896,166	616,302	273,296	6,568	68.8	30.5	69.3	30.7
Kentucky		10		993,148	495,029	495,729	2,390	49.8	49.9	50.0	50.0
Louisiana		10		651,952	306,925	345,027		47.1	52.9	47.1	52.9
Maine	5			351,786	232,353	118,806	627	66.0	33.8	66.2	33.8
Maryland	9			902,074	499,424	395,337	7,313	55.4	43.8	55.8	44.2
Massachusetts	16			2,383,398	1,292,325	1,083,525	7,548	54.2	45.5	54.4	45.6
Michigan	20			2,798,592	1,551,529	1,230,657	16,406	55.4	44.0	55.8	44.2
Minnesota	11			1,379,483	763,211	608,458	7,814	55.3	44.1	55.6	44.4
Mississippi		8		285,532	112,966	172,566		39.6	60.4	39.6	60.4
Missouri	13			1,892,062	959,429	929,830	2,803	50.7	49.1	50.8	49.2
Montana	4			265,037	157,394	106,213	1,430	59.4	40.1	59.7	40.3

UNITED STATES
PRESIDENT 1952

State	Electoral Vote Rep.	Electoral Vote Dem.	Electoral Vote Other	Total Vote	Republican	Democratic	Other	% Total Vote Rep.	% Total Vote Dem.	% Major Vote Rep.	% Major Vote Dem.
Nebraska	6			609,660	421,603	188,057		69.2%	30.8%	69.2%	30.8%
Nevada	3			82,190	50,502	31,688		61.4	38.6	61.4	38.6
New Hampshire	4			272,950	166,287	106,663		60.9	39.1	60.9	39.1
New Jersey	16			2,418,554	1,373,613	1,015,902	29,039	56.8	42.0	57.5	42.5
New Mexico	4			238,608	132,170	105,661	777	55.4	44.3	55.6	44.4
New York	45			7,128,239	3,952,813	3,104,601	70,825	55.5	43.6	56.0	44.0
North Carolina		14		1,210,910	558,107	652,803		46.1	53.9	46.1	53.9
North Dakota	4			270,127	191,712	76,694	1,721	71.0	28.4	71.4	28.6
Ohio	25			3,700,758	2,100,391	1,600,367		56.8	43.2	56.8	43.2
Oklahoma	8			948,984	518,045	430,939		54.6	45.4	54.6	45.4
Oregon	6			695,059	420,815	270,579	3,665	60.5	38.9	60.9	39.1
Pennsylvania	32			4,580,969	2,415,789	2,146,269	18,911	52.7	46.9	53.0	47.0
Rhode Island	4			414,498	210,935	203,293	270	50.9	49.0	50.9	49.1
South Carolina		8		341,087	168,082	173,004	1	49.3	50.7	49.3	50.7
South Dakota	4			294,283	203,857	90,426		69.3	30.7	69.3	30.7
Tennessee	11			892,553	446,147	443,710	2,696	50.0	49.7	50.1	49.9
Texas	24			2,075,946	1,102,878	969,228	3,840	53.1	46.7	53.2	46.8
Utah	4			329,554	194,190	135,364		58.9	41.1	58.9	41.1
Vermont	3			153,557	109,717	43,355	485	71.5	28.2	71.7	28.3
Virginia	12			619,689	349,037	268,677	1,975	56.3	43.4	56.5	43.5
Washington	9			1,102,708	599,107	492,845	10,756	54.3	44.7	54.9	45.1
West Virginia		8		873,548	419,970	453,578		48.1	51.9	48.1	51.9
Wisconsin	12			1,607,370	979,744	622,175	5,451	61.0	38.7	61.2	38.8
Wyoming	3			129,253	81,049	47,934	270	62.7	37.1	62.8	37.2
United States	442	89	—	61,550,918	33,936,234	27,314,992	299,692	55.1	44.4%	55.4	44.6%

UNITED STATES
PRESIDENT 1956

State	Electoral Vote Rep.	Electoral Vote Dem.	Electoral Vote Other	Total Vote	Republican	Democratic	Other	Total Vote Rep.	Total Vote Dem.	Major Vote Rep.	Major Vote Dem.
		10	1	496,861	195,694	280,844	20,323	39.4%	56.5%	41.1%	58.9%
Alabama											
Alaska											
Arizona	4			290,173	176,990	112,880	303	61.0	38.9	61.1	38.9
Arkansas		8		406,572	186,287	213,277	7,008	45.8	52.5	46.6	53.4
California	32			5,466,355	3,027,668	2,420,135	18,552	55.4	44.3	55.6	44.4
Colorado	6			657,074	394,479	257,997	4,598	60.0	39.3	60.5	39.5
Connecticut	8			1,117,121	711,837	405,079	205	63.7	36.3	63.7	36.3
Delaware	3			177,988	98,057	79,421	510	55.1	44.6	55.3	44.7
Florida	10			1,125,762	643,849	480,371	1,542	57.2	42.7	57.3	42.7
Georgia		12		669,655	222,778	444,688	2,189	33.3	66.4	33.4	66.6
Hawaii											
Idaho	4			272,989	166,979	105,868	142	61.2	38.8	61.2	38.8
Illinois	27			4,407,407	2,623,327	1,775,682	8,398	59.5	40.3	59.6	40.4
Indiana	13			1,974,607	1,182,811	783,908	7,888	59.9	39.7	60.1	39.9
Iowa	10			1,234,564	729,187	501,858	3,519	59.1	40.7	59.2	40.8
Kansas	8			866,243	566,878	296,317	3,048	65.4	34.2	65.7	34.3
Kentucky	10			1,053,805	572,192	476,453	5,160	54.3	45.2	54.6	45.4
Louisiana	10			617,544	329,047	243,977	44,520	53.3	39.5	57.4	42.6
Maine	5			351,706	249,238	102,468		70.9	29.1	70.9	29.1
Maryland	9			932,827	559,738	372,613	476	60.0	39.9	60.0	40.0
Massachusetts	16			2,348,506	1,393,197	948,190	7,119	59.3	40.4	59.5	40.5
Michigan	20			3,080,468	1,713,647	1,359,898	6,923	55.6	44.1	55.8	44.2
Minnesota	11			1,340,005	719,302	617,525	3,178	53.7	46.1	53.8	46.2
Mississippi		8		248,104	60,685	144,453	42,966	24.5	58.2	29.6	70.4
Missouri		13		1,832,562	914,289	918,273		49.9	50.1	49.9	50.1
Montana	4			271,171	154,933	116,238		57.1	42.9	57.1	42.9

UNITED STATES
PRESIDENT 1956

State	Electoral Vote Rep.	Electoral Vote Dem.	Electoral Vote Other	Total Vote	Republican	Democratic	Other	Total Vote Rep.	Total Vote Dem.	Major Vote Rep.	Major Vote Dem.
Nebraska	6			577,137	378,108	199,029		65.5%	34.5%	65.5%	34.5%
Nevada	3			96,689	56,049	40,640		58.0	42.0	58.0	42.0
New Hampshire	4			266,994	176,519	90,364	111	66.1	33.8	66.1	33.9
New Jersey	16			2,484,312	1,606,942	850,337	27,033	64.7	34.2	65.4	34.6
New Mexico	4			253,926	146,788	106,098	1,040	57.8	41.8	58.0	42.0
New York	45			7,095,971	4,345,506	2,747,944	2,521	61.2	38.7	61.3	38.7
North Carolina		14		1,165,592	575,062	590,530		49.3	50.7	49.3	50.7
North Dakota	4			253,991	156,766	96,742	483	61.7	38.1	61.8	38.2
Ohio	25			3,702,265	2,262,610	1,439,655		61.1	38.9	61.1	38.9
Oklahoma	8			859,350	473,769	385,581		55.1	44.9	55.1	44.9
Oregon	6			736,182	406,393	329,204	535	55.2	44.7	55.2	44.8
Pennsylvania	32			4,576,503	2,585,252	1,981,769	9,482	56.5	43.3	56.6	43.4
Rhode Island	4			387,609	225,819	161,790		58.3	41.7	58.3	41.7
South Carolina		8		300,583	75,700	136,372	88,511	25.2	45.4	35.7	64.3
South Dakota	4			293,857	171,569	122,288		58.4	41.6	58.4	41.6
Tennessee	11			939,404	462,288	456,507	20,609	49.2	48.6	50.3	49.7
Texas		24		1,955,168	1,080,619	859,958	14,591	55.3	44.0	55.7	44.3
Utah	4			333,995	215,631	118,364		64.6	35.4	64.6	35.4
Vermont	3			152,978	110,390	42,549	39	72.2	27.8	72.2	27.8
Virginia	12			697,978	386,459	267,760	43,759	55.4	38.4	59.1	40.9
Washington	9			1,150,889	620,430	523,002	7,457	53.9	45.4	54.3	45.7
West Virginia	8			830,831	449,297	381,534		54.1	45.9	54.1	45.9
Wisconsin	12			1,550,558	954,844	586,768	8,946	61.6	37.8	61.9	38.1
Wyoming	3			124,127	74,573	49,554		60.1	39.9	60.1	39.9
United States	457	73	1	62,026,908	35,590,472	26,022,752	413,684	57.4%	42.0%	57.8%	42.2%

UNITED STATES
PRESIDENT 1960

State	Electoral Vote Rep.	Electoral Vote Dem.	Electoral Vote Other	Total Vote	Republican	Democratic	Other	Total Vote Rep.	Total Vote Dem.	Major Vote Rep.	Major Vote Dem.
Alabama		5	6	570,225	237,981	324,050	8,194	41.7%	56.8%	42.3%	57.7%
Alaska	3			60,762	30,953	29,809		50.9	49.1	50.9	49.1
Arizona	4			398,491	221,241	176,781	469	55.5	44.4	55.6	44.4
Arkansas		8		428,509	184,508	215,049	28,952	43.1	50.2	46.2	53.8
California	32			6,506,578	3,259,722	3,224,099	22,757	50.1	49.6	50.3	49.7
Colorado	6			736,236	402,242	330,629	3,365	54.6	44.9	54.9	45.1
Connecticut		8		1,222,883	565,813	657,055	15	46.3	53.7	46.3	53.7
Delaware		3		196,683	96,373	99,590	720	49.0	50.6	49.2	50.8
Florida	10			1,544,176	795,476	748,700		51.5	48.5	51.5	48.5
Georgia		12		733,349	274,472	458,638	239	37.4	62.5	37.4	62.6
Hawaii		3		184,705	92,295	92,410		50.0	50.0	50.0	50.0
Idaho	4			300,450	161,597	138,853		53.8	46.2	53.8	46.2
Illinois		27		4,757,409	2,368,988	2,377,846	10,575	49.8	50.0	49.9	50.1
Indiana	13			2,135,360	1,175,120	952,358	7,882	55.0	44.6	55.2	44.8
Iowa	10			1,273,810	722,381	550,565	864	56.7	43.2	56.7	43.3
Kansas	8			928,825	561,474	363,213	4,138	60.4	39.1	60.7	39.3
Kentucky	10			1,124,462	602,607	521,855		53.6	46.4	53.6	46.4
Louisiana		10		807,891	230,980	407,339	169,572	28.6	50.4	36.2	63.8
Maine	5			421,767	240,608	181,159		57.0	43.0	57.0	43.0
Maryland		9		1,055,349	489,538	565,808	3	46.4	53.6	46.4	53.6
Massachusetts		16		2,469,480	976,750	1,487,174	5,556	39.6	60.2	39.6	60.4
Michigan		20		3,318,097	1,620,428	1,687,269	10,400	48.8	50.9	49.0	51.0
Minnesota		11		1,541,887	757,915	779,933	4,039	49.2	50.6	49.3	50.7
Mississippi			8	298,171	73,561	108,362	116,248	24.7	36.3	40.4	59.6
Missouri		13		1,934,422	962,221	972,201		49.7	50.3	49.7	50.3
Montana	4			277,579	141,841	134,891	847	51.1	48.6	51.3	48.7

UNITED STATES
PRESIDENT 1960

State	Electoral Vote Rep.	Electoral Vote Dem.	Electoral Vote Other	Total Vote	Republican	Democratic	Other	Total Vote % Rep.	Total Vote % Dem.	Major Vote % Rep.	Major Vote % Dem.
Nebraska	6			613,095	380,553	232,542		62.1%	37.9%	62.1%	37.9%
Nevada		3		107,267	52,387	54,880		48.8	51.2	48.8	51.2
New Hampshire	4			295,761	157,989	137,772		53.4	46.6	53.4	46.6
New Jersey		16		2,773,111	1,363,324	1,385,415	24,372	49.2	50.0	49.6	50.4
New Mexico		4		311,107	153,733	156,027	1,347	49.4	50.2	49.6	50.4
New York		45		7,291,079	3,446,419	3,830,085	14,575	47.3	52.5	47.4	52.6
North Carolina		14		1,368,556	655,420	713,136		47.9	52.1	47.9	52.1
North Dakota	4			278,431	154,310	123,963	158	55.4	44.5	55.5	44.5
Ohio	25			4,161,859	2,217,611	1,944,248		53.3	46.7	53.3	46.7
Oklahoma	7		1	903,150	533,039	370,111		59.0	41.0	59.0	41.0
Oregon	6			776,421	408,060	367,402	959	52.6	47.3	52.6	47.4
Pennsylvania		32		5,006,541	2,439,956	2,556,282	10,303	48.7	51.1	48.8	51.2
Rhode Island		4		405,535	147,502	258,032	1	36.4	63.6	36.4	63.6
South Carolina		8		386,688	188,558	198,129	1	48.8	51.2	48.8	51.2
South Dakota	4			306,487	178,417	128,070		58.2	41.8	58.2	41.8
Tennessee	11			1,051,792	556,577	481,453	13,762	52.9	45.8	53.6	46.4
Texas		24		2,311,084	1,121,310	1,167,567	22,207	48.5	50.5	49.0	51.0
Utah	4			374,709	205,361	169,248	100	54.8	45.2	54.8	45.2
Vermont	3			167,324	98,131	69,186	7	58.6	41.3	58.6	41.4
Virginia	12			771,449	404,521	362,327	4,601	52.4	47.0	52.8	47.2
Washington	9			1,241,572	629,273	599,298	13,001	50.7	48.3	51.2	48.8
West Virginia		8		837,781	395,995	441,786		47.3	52.7	47.3	52.7
Wisconsin	12			1,729,082	895,175	830,805	3,102	51.8	48.0	51.9	48.1
Wyoming	3			140,782	77,451	63,331		55.0	45.0	55.0	45.0
United States	219	303	15	68,838,219	34,108,157	34,226,731	503,331	49.5%	49.7%	49.9%	50.1%

UNITED STATES
PRESIDENT 1964

State	Electoral Vote Rep.	Electoral Vote Dem.	Electoral Vote Other	Total Vote	Republican	Democratic	Other	Total Vote Rep.	Total Vote Dem.	Major Vote Rep.	Major Vote Dem.
Alabama	10			689,818	479,085		210,733	69.5%		100.0%	65.9%
Alaska		3		67,259	22,930	44,329		34.1	65.9%	34.1	65.9
Arizona	5			480,770	242,535	237,753	482	50.4	49.5	50.5	49.5
Arkansas		6		560,426	243,264	314,197	2,965	43.4	56.1	43.6	56.4
California		40		7,057,586	2,879,108	4,171,877	6,601	40.8	59.1	40.8	59.2
Colorado		6		776,986	296,767	476,024	4,195	38.2	61.3	38.4	61.6
Connecticut		8		1,218,578	390,996	826,269	1,313	32.1	67.8	32.1	67.9
Delaware		3		201,320	78,078	122,704	538	38.8	60.9	38.9	61.1
Florida		14		1,854,481	905,941	948,540		48.9	51.1	48.9	51.1
Georgia	12			1,139,335	616,584	522,556	195	54.1	45.9	54.1	45.9
Hawaii		4		207,271	44,022	163,249		21.2	78.8	21.2	78.8
Idaho		4		292,477	143,557	148,920		49.1	50.9	49.1	50.9
Illinois		26		4,702,841	1,905,946	2,796,833	62	40.5	59.5	40.5	59.5
Indiana		13		2,091,606	911,118	1,170,848	9,640	43.6	56.0	43.8	56.2
Iowa		9		1,184,539	449,148	733,030	2,361	37.9	61.9	38.0	62.0
Kansas		7		857,901	386,579	464,028	7,294	45.1	54.1	45.4	54.6
Kentucky		9		1,046,105	372,977	669,659	3,469	35.7	64.0	35.8	64.2
Louisiana	10			896,293	509,225	387,068		56.8	43.2	56.8	43.2
Maine		4		380,965	118,701	262,264		31.2	68.8	31.2	68.8
Maryland		10		1,116,457	385,495	730,912	50	34.5	65.5	34.5	65.5
Massachusetts		14		2,344,798	549,727	1,786,422	8,649	23.4	76.2	23.5	76.5
Michigan		21		3,203,102	1,060,152	2,136,615	6,335	33.1	66.7	33.2	66.8
Minnesota		10		1,554,462	559,624	991,117	3,721	36.0	63.8	36.1	63.9
Mississippi	7			409,146	356,528	52,618		87.1	12.9	87.1	12.9
Missouri		12		1,817,879	653,535	1,164,344		36.0	64.0	36.0	64.0
Montana		4		278,628	113,032	164,246	1,850	40.6	58.9	40.8	59.2

UNITED STATES
PRESIDENT 1964

State	Electoral Vote Rep.	Electoral Vote Dem.	Electoral Vote Other	Total Vote	Republican	Democratic	Other	Pct. Total Vote Rep.	Pct. Total Vote Dem.	Pct. Major Vote Rep.	Pct. Major Vote Dem.
Nebraska		5		584,154	276,847	307,307		47.4%	52.6%	47.4%	52.6%
Nevada		3		135,433	56,094	79,339		41.4	58.6	41.4	58.6
New Hampshire		4		288,093	104,029	184,064		36.1	63.9	36.1	63.9
New Jersey		17		2,847,663	964,174	1,868,231	15,258	33.9	65.6	34.0	66.0
New Mexico		4		328,645	132,838	194,015	1,792	40.4	59.0	40.6	59.4
New York		43		7,166,275	2,243,559	4,913,102	9,614	31.3	68.6	31.3	68.7
North Carolina		13		1,424,983	624,844	800,139		43.8	56.2	43.8	56.2
North Dakota		4		258,389	108,207	149,784	398	41.9	58.0	41.9	58.1
Ohio		26		3,969,196	1,470,865	2,498,331		37.1	62.9	37.1	62.9
Oklahoma		8		932,499	412,665	519,834		44.3	55.7	44.3	55.7
Oregon		6		786,305	282,779	501,017	2,509	36.0	63.7	36.1	63.9
Pennsylvania		29		4,822,690	1,673,657	3,130,954	18,079	34.7	64.9	34.8	65.2
Rhode Island		4		390,091	74,615	315,463	13	19.1	80.9	19.1	80.9
South Carolina	8			524,779	309,048	215,723	8	58.9	41.1	58.9	41.1
South Dakota		4		293,118	130,108	163,010		44.4	55.6	44.4	55.6
Tennessee		11		1,143,946	508,965	634,947	34	44.5	55.5	44.5	55.5
Texas		25		2,626,811	958,566	1,663,185	5,060	36.5	63.3	36.6	63.4
Utah		4		401,413	181,785	219,628		45.3	54.7	45.3	54.7
Vermont		3		163,089	54,942	108,127	20	33.7	66.3	33.7	66.3
Virginia		12		1,042,267	481,334	558,038	2,895	46.2	53.5	46.3	53.7
Washington		9		1,258,556	470,366	779,881	8,309	37.4	62.0	37.6	62.4
West Virginia		7		792,040	253,953	538,087		32.1	67.9	32.1	67.9
Wisconsin		12		1,691,815	638,495	1,050,424	2,896	37.7	62.1	37.8	62.2
Wyoming		3		142,716	61,998	80,718		43.4	56.6	43.4	56.6
District of Columbia		3		198,597	28,801	169,796		14.5	85.5	14.5	85.5
United States	52	486		70,644,592	27,178,188	43,129,566	336,888	38.5	61.1	38.7	61.3

PRESIDENT 1968

State	Electoral Vote Rep.	Electoral Vote Dem.	Electoral Vote AIP	Total Vote	Republican	Democratic	AIP	Other	% Rep.	% Dem.	% AIP
Alabama			10	1,049,922	146,923	196,579	691,425	14,995	14.0	18.7	65.9
Alaska	3			83,035	37,600	35,411	10,024		45.3	42.6	12.1
Arizona	5			486,936	266,721	170,514	46,573	3,128	54.8	35.0	9.6
Arkansas			6	619,969	190,759	188,228	240,982		30.8	30.4	38.9
California	40			7,251,587	3,467,664	3,244,318	487,270	52,335	47.8	44.7	6.7
Colorado	6			811,199	409,345	335,174	60,813	5,867	50.5	41.3	7.5
Connecticut		8		1,256,232	556,721	621,561	76,650	1,300	44.3	49.5	6.1
Delaware	3			214,367	96,714	89,194	28,459		45.1	41.6	13.3
Florida	14			2,187,805	886,804	676,794	624,207		40.5	30.9	28.5
Georgia			12	1,250,266	380,111	334,440	535,550	165	30.4	26.7	42.8
Hawaii		4		236,218	91,425	141,324	3,469		38.7	59.8	1.5
Idaho	4			291,183	165,369	89,273	36,541		56.8	30.7	12.5
Illinois	26			4,619,749	2,174,774	2,039,814	390,958	14,203	47.1	44.2	8.5
Indiana	13			2,123,597	1,067,885	806,659	243,108	5,945	50.3	38.0	11.4
Iowa	9			1,167,931	619,106	476,699	66,422	5,704	53.0	40.8	5.7
Kansas	7			872,783	478,674	302,996	88,921	2,192	54.8	34.7	10.2
Kentucky	9			1,055,893	462,411	397,541	193,098	2,843	43.8	37.6	18.3
Louisiana			10	1,097,450	257,535	309,615	530,300		23.5	28.2	48.3
Maine		4		392,936	169,254	217,312	6,370		43.1	55.3	1.6
Maryland		10		1,235,039	517,995	538,310	178,734		41.9	43.6	14.5
Massachusetts		14		2,331,752	766,844	1,469,218	87,088	8,602	32.9	63.0	3.7
Michigan		21		3,306,250	1,370,665	1,593,082	331,968	10,535	41.5	48.2	10.0
Minnesota		10		1,588,506	658,643	857,738	68,931	3,194	41.5	54.0	4.3
Mississippi			7	654,509	88,516	150,644	415,349		13.5	23.0	63.5
Missouri	12			1,809,502	811,932	791,444	206,126	1,437	44.9	43.7	11.4
Montana	4			274,404	138,835	114,117	20,015		50.6	41.6	7.3
Nebraska	5			536,851	321,163	170,784	44,904		59.8	31.8	8.4
Nevada	3			154,218	73,188	60,598	20,432		47.5	39.3	13.2
New Hampshire	4			297,298	154,903	130,589	11,173	633	52.1	43.9	3.8
New Jersey	17			2,875,395	1,325,467	1,264,206	262,187	23,535	46.1	44.0	9.1
New Mexico	4			327,350	169,692	130,081	25,737	1,840	51.8	39.7	7.9

UNITED STATES
PRESIDENT 1968

State	Electoral Vote Rep.	Dem.	AIP	Total Vote	Republican	Democratic	AIP	Other	Percentages Rep.	Dem.	AIP
New York		43		6,791,688	3,007,932	3,378,470	358,864	46,422	44.3	49.7	5.3
North Carolina	12		1	1,587,493	627,192	464,113	496,188		39.5	29.2	31.3
North Dakota	4			247,882	138,669	94,769	14,244	200	55.9	38.2	5.7
Ohio	26			3,959,698	1,791,014	1,700,586	467,495	603	45.2	42.9	11.8
Oklahoma	8			943,086	449,697	301,658	191,731		47.7	32.0	20.3
Oregon	6			819,622	408,433	358,866	49,683	2,640	49.8	43.8	6.1
Pennsylvania		29		4,747,928	2,090,017	2,259,405	378,582	19,924	44.0	47.6	8.0
Rhode Island		4		385,000	122,359	246,518	15,678	445	31.8	64.0	4.1
South Carolina	8			666,978	254,062	197,486	215,430		38.1	29.6	32.3
South Dakota	4			281,264	149,841	118,023	13,400		53.3	42.0	4.8
Tennessee	11			1,248,617	472,592	351,233	424,792		37.8	28.1	34.0
Texas		25		3,079,216	1,227,844	1,266,804	584,269	299	39.9	41.1	19.0
Utah	4			422,568	238,728	156,665	26,906	269	56.5	37.1	6.4
Vermont	3			161,404	85,142	70,255	5,104	903	52.8	43.5	3.2
Virginia	12			1,361,491	590,319	442,387	321,833	6,952	43.4	32.5	23.6
Washington		9		1,304,281	588,510	616,037	96,990	2,744	45.1	47.2	7.4
West Virginia		7		754,206	307,555	374,091	72,560		40.8	49.6	9.6
Wisconsin	12			1,691,538	809,997	748,804	127,835	4,902	47.9	44.3	7.6
Wyoming	3			127,205	70,927	45,173	11,105		55.8	35.5	8.7
District of Columbia		3		170,578	31,012	189,566			18.2	81.8	
Totals:	301	191	46	73,211,875	31,785,480	31,275,166	9,906,473	244,756	43.4	42.7	13.5

Data for these tables have been taken from *America at the Polls* (Richard M. Scammon, editor) for the elections back to 1920, and from *A Statistical History of the American Presidential Elections* (Svend Peterson, editor), for the voting from 1916 back to 1876.

Any minor-party candidate polling a minimum of 5% is listed separately; otherwise minor-party, independent, and scattered write-in votes are grouped as "All others." In the elections after 1948 any candidate polling more than 1% is separately listed. The vote by states since 1948 and nationally in the earlier years includes the endorsing votes of other parties (for example, the Liberal Party in New York normally endorses the national Democratic candidates, and the Bryan candidacy in 1896 was actually a Democratic-Populist fusion). In some instances the vote is that cast for several tickets of electors, as for Hubert Humphrey in Alabama in 1968.

Party name abbreviations used are: (R) Republican, (D) Democratic, (P) Progressive, (S) Socialist, (SP) State

BASE DATES FOR 1968

November 14, 1967	Harold Stassen announces his candidacy for the Republican nomination.
November 18, 1967	George Romney announces as a Republican candidate.
November 30, 1967	Eugene McCarthy announces he will enter some of the primaries against Lyndon Johnson's renomination.
February 1, 1968	Richard Nixon announces his Republican candidacy.
February 8, 1968	George Wallace announces as a new, third-party candidate.
February 28, 1968	George Romney withdraws from the Republican race.
March 12, 1968	NEW HAMPSHIRE PRIMARY
March 16, 1968	Robert Kennedy announces for the Democratic nomination.
March 21, 1968	Nelson Rockefeller states he is not a candidate.
March 31, 1968	President Johnson announces he is not a candidate.
April 2, 1968	WISCONSIN PRIMARY
April 27, 1968	Hubert Humphrey announces as a Democratic candidate.
April 30, 1968	Nelson Rockefeller states he will now be a candidate for the Republican nomination.
May 7, 1968	INDIANA PRIMARY
May 14, 1968	NEBRASKA PRIMARY
May 28, 1968	OREGON PRIMARY
June 4, 1968	SOUTH DAKOTA and CALIFORNIA PRIMARIES. Robert Kennedy killed in Los Angeles.
August 5–8, 1968	Nixon and Agnew the Republican nominees at Miami Beach.
August 26–29, 1968	Humphrey and Muskie the Democratic nominees at Chicago.
October 3, 1968	Curtis LeMay becomes Vice Presidential candidate for AIP ticket.
November 5, 1968	General election.

VOTING IN SELECTED 1968 PRESIDENTIAL PREFERENCE PRIMARIES (OFFICIAL RETURNS)

	REPUBLICAN		DEMOCRATIC
NEW HAMPSHIRE	80,666 Nixon		27,520 Johnson write-ins
(March 12)	11,241 Rockefeller write-ins		23,263 McCarthy
	5,511 McCarthy write-ins		2,532 Nixon write-ins
	1,778 Johnson write-ins		1,716 Other write-ins
	1,743 Romney		433 Other ballot candidates
	1,627 Other ballot candidates		
	1,372 Other write-ins		
WISCONSIN	390,368 Nixon		412,160 McCarthy
(April 2)	50,727 Reagan		253,696 Johnson
	28,531 Stassen		46,507 Kennedy write-ins
	7,995 Rockefeller write-ins		11,861 "No Preference"
	6,763 "No Preference"		4,031 Wallace write-ins
	2,087 Romney write-ins		3,605 Humphrey write-ins
	3,382 Other write-ins		1,142 Other write-ins
PENNSYLVANIA	No candidates on the ballot:		428,259 McCarthy
(April 23)	171,815 Nixon write-ins		65,430 Kennedy write-ins
	52,915 Rockefeller write-ins		51,998 Humphrey write-ins
	18,800 McCarthy write-ins		24,147 Wallace write-ins
	13,290 Wallace write-ins		21,265 Johnson write-ins
	10,431 Kennedy write-ins		3,434 Nixon write-ins
	7,934 Reagan write-ins		1,897 Rockefeller write-ins
	4,651 Humphrey write-ins		2,556 Other write-ins
	3,027 Johnson write-ins		
	1,223 Raymond Shafer write-ins		
	3,487 Other write-ins		
MASSACHUSETTS	31,964 Rockefeller write-ins		122,697 McCarthy
(April 30)	31,465 John Volpe		68,604 Kennedy write-ins
	27,447 Nixon write-ins		44,156 Humphrey write-ins
	9,758 McCarthy write-ins		6,890 Johnson write-ins
	1,770 Reagan write-ins		2,275 Rockefeller write-ins
	1,184 Kennedy write-ins		1,688 Wallace write-ins
	2,993 Other write-ins		2,593 Other write-ins

VOTING IN SELECTED 1968 PRESIDENTIAL PREFERENCE PRIMARIES (OFFICIAL RETURNS)

REPUBLICAN

INDIANA

(May 7)

508,362 Nixon

DISTRICT OF COLUMBIA

(May 7)

12,102 Highest delegate vote on organization slate (Nixon-Rockefeller)

1,328 Highest delegate vote on independent slate

NEBRASKA

(May 14)

140,336 Nixon
42,703 Reagan
10,225 Rockefeller write-ins
2,638 Stassen
1,544 McCarthy write-ins
1,302 Americus Liberator
1,728 Other write-ins

FLORIDA

(May 28)

51,509 "No Preference" delegate slate (William F. Murfin, chairman)

OREGON

(May 28)

203,037 Nixon
63,707 Reagan
36,305 Rockefeller write-ins
7,387 McCarthy write-ins
1,723 Kennedy write-ins
No other write-ins reported

DEMOCRATIC

INDIANA

328,118 Kennedy
238,700 Roger Branigan
209,695 McCarthy

DISTRICT OF COLUMBIA

57,555 Highest delegate vote on Kennedy slate
32,309 Highest delegate vote on Humphrey slate
2,250 Highest delegate vote on independent Humphrey slate

NEBRASKA

84,102 Kennedy
50,655 McCarthy
12,087 Humphrey write-ins
9,187 Johnson
2,731 Nixon write-ins
1,905 Reagan write-ins
1,298 Wallace write-ins
646 Other write-ins

FLORIDA

236,242 George Smathers delegate slate
147,216 McCarthy delegate slate
128,899 "No Preference" delegate slate (Scott Kelly, chairman)

OREGON

163,990 McCarthy
141,631 Kennedy
45,174 Johnson
12,421 Humphrey write-ins
3,082 Reagan write-ins
2,974 Nixon write-ins
2,841 Rockefeller write-ins
957 Wallace write-ins
No other write-ins reported

VOTING IN SELECTED 1968 PRESIDENTIAL PREFERENCE PRIMARIES (OFFICIAL RETURNS)

	REPUBLICAN	DEMOCRATIC
CALIFORNIA (June 4)	1,525,091 Reagan delegate slate	1,472,166 Kennedy delegate slate 1,329,301 McCarthy delegate slate 380,286 "No Preference" delegate slate (Thomas Lynch, chairman)
NEW JERSEY (June 4)	No candidates on the ballot: 71,809 Nixon write-ins 11,530 Rockefeller write-ins 2,737 Reagan write-ins 1,358 McCarthy write-ins 1,158 Other write-ins	No candidates on the ballot: 9,906 McCarthy write-ins 8,603 Kennedy write-ins 5,578 Humphrey write-ins 1,399 Wallace write-ins 1,364 Nixon write-ins 596 Other write-ins
SOUTH DAKOTA (June 4)	68,113 Nixon delegate slate	31,826 Kennedy delegate slate 19,316 Johnson delegate slate 13,145 McCarthy delegate slate
ILLINOIS (June 11)	No candidates on the ballot: 17,490 Nixon write-ins 2,165 Rockefeller write-ins 1,601 Reagan write-ins 1,147 Other write-ins	No candidates on the ballot: 4,646 McCarthy write-ins 4,052 Edward Kennedy write-ins 2,059 Humphrey write-ins 1,281 Other write-ins

No candidates were entered in the West Virginia primary and no write-in votes reported. Elections of delegates were also held in Alabama, New York, and Ohio, but in none of these states was there a statewide preference or delegate contest involving national candidates.

TWO AND THREE CANDIDATE NOMINEE PREFERENCES AMONG DEMOCRATIC VOTERS, 1968 (GALLUP)

	McCARTHY	*KENNEDY*	*NO OPINION*
April	36	48	16

	HUMPHREY	*KENNEDY*	*McCARTHY*	*NO OPINION*
May	40	31	19	10

	HUMPHREY	*McCARTHY*	*NO OPINION*
June	56	37	7
July	53	38	9
August	46	42	12

TWO AND THREE CANDIDATE NOMINEE PREFERENCES AMONG DEMOCRATIC VOTERS, 1968 (HARRIS)

	HUMPHREY	*KENNEDY*	*McCARTHY*	*NO OPINION*
May	38	27	25	10

	HUMPHREY	*McCARTHY*	*NOT SURE*
June	48	40	12
July	46	40	14
August	56	38	6

TWO CANDIDATE NOMINEE PREFERENCES AMONG REPUBLICAN VOTERS, 1968 (GALLUP)

	NIXON	*ROCKEFELLER*	*NO OPINION*
January	55	41	4
March	66	30	4
June	65	29	6
July	67	28	5

	NIXON	*ROMNEY*	*NO OPINION*
January	68	26	6

TWO CANDIDATE NOMINEE PREFERENCES AMONG REPUBLICAN VOTERS, 1968 (HARRIS)

	NIXON	*ROCKEFELLER*	*NOT SURE*
February	61	31	8
March	56	32	12
June	61	30	9

	NIXON	*ROMNEY*	*NOT SURE*
February	68	21	11

THREE CANDIDATE PRECONVENTION PRESIDENTIAL PREFERENCES,
ALL VOTERS, 1968 (GALLUP)

	NIXON	*KENNEDY*	*WALLACE*	*NO OPINION*
May 4–8	42	32	15	11

	NIXON	*McCARTHY*	*WALLACE*	*NO OPINION*
May 4–8	39	37	14	10
June 15–16	39	41	14	6
July 19–21	41	36	16	7
August 8–11	42	37	16	5

	ROCKEFELLER	*KENNEDY*	*WALLACE*	*NO OPINION*
May 4–8	42	28	18	12

	ROCKEFELLER	*McCARTHY*	*WALLACE*	*NO OPINION*
May 4–8	40	31	17	12
June 15–16	38	39	16	7
July 19–21	36	35	20	9

	ROCKEFELLER	*HUMPHREY*	*WALLACE*	*NO OPINION*
May 4–8	40	33	16	11
June 15–16	39	38	17	6
July 19–21	36	36	21	7

FOR NIXON-HUMPHREY-WALLACE, SEE LATER TABLE

THREE CANDIDATE PRECONVENTION PRESIDENTIAL PREFERENCES,
ALL VOTERS, 1968 (HARRIS)

	NIXON	*McCARTHY*	*WALLACE*	*NOT SURE*
April 24–May 1	37	40	13	10
May 16–18	40	39	14	7
June 10–17	36	44	12	8
July 8–14	34	42	16	8
July 25–29	35	43	15	7

	ROCKEFELLER	*McCARTHY*	*WALLACE*	*NOT SURE*
April 24–May 1	38	36	15	11
May 16–18	38	35	19	8
June 10–17	35	41	15	9
July 8–14	32	38	20	10
July 25–29	40	34	19	7

	ROCKEFELLER	*HUMPHREY*	*WALLACE*	*NOT SURE*
April 24–May 1	37	39	16	8
May 16–18	37	40	17	6
June 10–17	36	40	15	9
July 8–14	37	34	19	10
July 25–29	40	34	20	6

FOR NIXON-HUMPHREY-WALLACE, SEE LATER TABLE

THE *1968* PRESIDENTIAL CONTEST (GALLUP)

	NIXON	HUMPHREY	WALLACE	NO OPINION
May 4–8	39	36	14	11
May 25–29	36	42	14	8
June 15–16	37	42	14	7
June 29–July 3	35	40	16	9
July 19–21	40	38	16	6
August 8–11	45	29	18	8
September 3–7	43	31	19	7
September 20–22	43	28	21	8
September 27–30	44	29	20	7
October 3–12	43	31	20	6
October 17–21	44	36	15	5
October 31–Nov. 2	42	40	14	4

THE *1968* PRESIDENTIAL CONTEST (HARRIS)

	NIXON	HUMPHREY	WALLACE	NO OPINION
May 16–18	37	41	14	8
June 11–16	36	43	13	8
July 6–11	35	37	17	11
July 25–29	36	41	16	7
August 24	40	34	17	9
September 11–13	39	31	21	9
October 9–11	40	35	18	7
October 27–28	40	37	16	7
November 1–2	42	40	12	6
November 3	40	43	13	4

THE ELECTORATE, 1968

These figures are those developed by the Current Population Survey conducted by the Bureau of the Census. It should be noted that these data include *only* the civilian noninstitutional population. They are for *all persons of voting age,* including aliens, short-term residents, nonliterates in literacy test states, and others who might not be eligible to vote by local law.

All persons of voting age in the civilian
noninstitutional population (in thousands)
Total: 116,535

By Race:	White	104,521	
	Negro	10,935	
	Others	1,079	
By Age:	21–24	11,170	
	25–34	23,198	
	35–44	22,905	
	45–54	22,632	
	55–64	17,730	
	65–74	11,573	
	Over 75	6,895	
By Sex:	Male	54,464	
	Female	62,071	
By Region:	North and West	81,594	
	South	34,941	
By Place:	Metropolitan	75,756	
	In SMSA's of one million or more		41,359
	In SMSA's of under one million		34,397
	Non-metropolitan	40,778	
	Non-farm	35,255	
	Farm	5,524	
By Place:	Metropolitan central cities	35,617	
	Metropolitan suburbs	40,139	
	Non-metropolitan non-farm	35,255	
	Non-metropolitan farm	5,524	
By Education:	(years of school completed)		
	Elementary school, 0–4 years	5,926	
	Elementary school, 5–7 years	9,687	
	Elementary school, 8 years	14,817	
	High school, 1–3 years	20,429	
	High school, 4 years	39,704	
	College, 1–3 years	13,312	
	College, 4 years	7,974	
	College, 5 years	4,685	

By Occupation Group: (for 70,002 employed in the civilian labor force)

White collar workers	*33,709*
Professional, technical, and kindred workers	10,639
Managers, officials, and proprietors	7,826
Clerical, sales, and kindred workers	15,245
Manual Workers	*25,229*
Craftsmen, foremen, and kindred workers	9,904
Operators and kindred workers	12,682
Laborers, except farm and mine	2,643
Service workers	*8,078*
Private household workers	1,463
Other service workers	6,614
Farm workers	*2,987*
Farmers and farm managers	1,857
Farm laborers and foremen	1,130

By Family Income: (for 103,841 in primary families)

Under $3,000	11,293
3,000–4,999	14,557
5,000–7,499	22,870
7,500–9,999	18,920
10,000–14,999	19,744
15,000 and over	9,707
Not reported	6,750

Note: To the age table above should be added 432,000 in the under 21 group eligible to vote in Alaska, Georgia, Hawaii, and Kentucky.

Group Presidential Voting, 1952–1968 (Gallup)

	1952		1956		1960		1964		1968		
	Dem. %	Rep. %	D %	R %	D %	R %	D %	R %	D %	R %	Wallace %
NATIONAL	44.6	55.4	42.2	57.8	50.1	49.9	61.3	38.7	43.0	43.4	13.6
Men	47	53	45	55	52	48	60	40	41	43	16
Women	42	58	39	61	49	51	62	38	45	43	12
White	43	57	41	59	49	51	59	41	38	47	15
Non-white	79	21	61	39	68	32	94	6	85	12	3
College	34	66	31	69	39	61	52	48	37	54	9
High School	45	55	42	58	52	48	62	38	42	43	15
Grade School	52	48	50	50	55	45	66	34	52	33	15
Prof. & Bus.	36	64	32	68	42	58	54	46	34	56	10
White Collar	40	60	37	63	48	52	57	43	41	47	12
Manual	55	45	50	50	60	40	71	29	50	35	15
Farmers	33	67	46	54	48	52	53	47	29	51	20
Under 30	51	49	43	57	54	46	64	36	47	38	15
30–49 years	47	53	45	55	54	46	63	37	44	41	15
50 years & older ...	39	61	39	61	46	54	59	41	41	47	12
Protestant	37	63	37	63	38	62	55	45	35	49	16
Catholic	56	44	51	49	78	22	76	24	59	33	8
Republicans	8	92	4	96	5	95	20	80	9	86	5
Democrats	77	23	85	15	84	16	87	13	74	12	14
Independents	35	65	30	70	43	57	56	44	31	44	25

Index